FALSE PASSAGE

A novel by Harry A. Ezratty

Read Street Publishing
Baltimore Maryland

www.readstreetpublishing.com

False Passage

By Harry A. Ezratty
ISBN: 978-0-942929-45-4
Copyright © 2020

Read Street Publishing
133 West Read Street, Baltimore, MD 21201
www.readstreetpublishing.com
editor@readstreetpublishing.com

Layout/Design: Richard Gottesman, Sutileza Graphics
Cover Photo: Vintage postcard artistically created by Sutileza Graphics

BOOKS BY HARRY EZRATTY

PROLOGUE

MAY, 1968
THE ENGLISH CHANNEL

It was the pain that awakened him. Disoriented, he lurched up in his bunk in the dark and windowless cabin. And then he realized he was at sea, at work. The pain stabbed and then throbbed in his left thigh. He knew that something was very wrong.

Whatever this pain was, its intensity told him he needed immediate attention. In the darkness, Gaspar Fonseca looked at his wrist watch. Its glowing radium dial said 5:10 a.m. *Another two and a half hours before I stand my watch. With this pain, there's no way I can do that.*

Gaspar Fonseca was an Able Seaman aboard the passenger vessel *S.S. American Union* and scheduled to start working the 8 to 12 watch on the ship's bridge. *But what about this pain? I can't work with this pain.* He slid out of his bunk and as he stood balancing himself on the deck in the darkness, the pain worsened, like a knife twisting into his left thigh. He rolled back into his bunk, straightened out his legs and lay still for a while, hoping the pain would disappear. When it didn't, he switched on the lamp by his bed and called out to his roommate.

"Dick. Dick! Wake up. I need a doctor."

Dick Skelley, Fonseca's roommate, turned in his bunk and rubbed the sleep from his eyes. The light from the bed lamp was painful; as if he were looking directly into the sun. Shielding his eyes with a hand he asked, "What's wrong, Gas?"

"I got this pain on my left leg. I can't stand it. Hurts like hell. Like someone's sticking a knife in my thigh on the left side. I got something real bad."

"Can you walk?"

"I don't think so. I tried getting out of my bunk a few minutes ago but it hurt like hell when I put my feet on the deck."

"Sit tight, Gas. I'll get the Doc."

Skelley pulled a tee shirt over his head, stepped into a pair of shorts and tennis shoes, and then scurried into the alleyway outside their cabin. At 5:15 a.m. a cruise ship is quiet; public spaces are empty of passengers and crew, like a hotel in the early hours of the morning. The *S.S. American Union*, the world's fastest, most modern cruise ship and the pride of America's merchant navy, had a ship's hospital on B deck, with an infirmary, operating room and an isolation ward. There was also an X-ray machine and materials necessary for simple and uncomplicated surgery.

Skelley knew its doors would be shut this early in the morning. Using one of the ship's 19 elevators, he proceeded up seven decks to the Navigating Bridge, where he found Chief Mate John Farrow, the officer on duty. He related Gaspar's problem. Farrow picked up the phone and called Malcolm Peters, the ship's doctor, who answered in a husky voice, heavy with sleep.

"Yes, this is Dr. Peters. Who is this? Okay, Mr. Farrow. Yes, you're right, it certainly does sound like an emergency. What's his cabin number? Okay, I'll be right there. Give me a few minutes to get there. And have two seamen meet me in the man's cabin. If he can't walk they'll have to help him to the hospital."

Within five minutes, Dr. Peters, in an ankle-long, navy blue wool bathrobe covering his pajamas, and his feet clad in leather maroon slippers, appeared at Gaspar Fonseca's cabin. It was now completely lit up. The two seamen he had requested were already in the cabin. Peters asked them to wait in the alleyway so that he could conduct an examination. After locating the site of Fonseca's pain and being informed of its intensity, Dr. Peters shoved a thermometer into Gaspar's mouth, took his pulse, checked his heartbeat and peered into his throat and eyes with the concentrated beam of a penlight. Then Peters ran his hand along

Gaspar's left thigh and calf, which drew reactions of pain with each touch. His thigh and feet were not unusually warm. If Doctor Peter's first impressions were correct, that was possibly a good sign. There was no infection yet, so what he thought was troubling this man was in its earliest stages. It could also mean the leg was cool because it was not receiving a flow of blood.

"Hurts real bad doc; like a knife in my side. Hurts worse now than when I woke up," Fonseca complained, pointing to a spot on his left thigh.

Dr. Peters placed a stethoscope at the ankle looking for a pulse and then behind the left knee again looking for a pulse; both sites were weak. Sitting on the edge of Gaspar's bunk, Peters wrote his observations down on a medical chart. After a second check of the calf, he removed the stethoscope from his ears, hooked it around his neck and, following a pause, eyed his patient.

"Can you tell me what's wrong with me, Doc?" Fonseca said, almost pleading.

"If it's what I think it is, and I can't be completely sure without doing more tests which can't be done here because we don't have the equipment, I'm almost certain you have an arterial block. You're going to need treatment immediately."

What Dr. Peters didn't tell Gaspar Fonseca was that there was no time to waste. The treatment was probably surgery and he, Peters, was not a surgeon.

3

1

INTERSTATE I-95
PHILADELPHIA, OCTOBER 2006

Dan Nikolas sat slouched, arms folded across his chest, in the front seat of the passenger's side of a car heading north on I-95. The morning was cool and the air clear, so Dan was able to see for miles around. After a weekend in Washington visiting museums and enjoying the fall weather, Dan, his wife Terry, and their friends Cynthia and Bill Marks were planning a stop in Philadelphia to spend a few hours with some friends before continuing on their way home to New York City. As they neared Philadelphia, just past the airport, Dan sat up and turned to his right with a wistful look.

"It sickens me to see it," he remarked to no one in particular as he brushed back a shock of his graying hair.

"What sickens you, Dan?" Bill Marks asked as he briefly turned his head for a quick look at his friend.

"Here we go again," Terry Nikolas said with a laugh. She was sitting in the back seat with Cynthia Marks. As Dan's wife, she knew what was coming.

"The death knell of a great ship," she explained to her friends in a deep, exaggerated and theatrically dramatic bass voice. "You can always depend upon one of Dan's angry tirades every time we pass along this way."

"What's it all about?" Bill Marks asked.

"All you have to do is look at her," Dan insisted, pointing with his thumb out the window on his right. "See those two ship funnels a mile or so from us? They belong to the *S.S. American*

Union. Once, those stacks were bright red, white, and blue. Look at them now: flaky and peeling. The weather has stripped off most of the paint. Nothing left but dull colors. The rest of the ship is also a mess. I walked through her a few years ago; stuff on the decks laying around loose, stripped of everything of value. She hasn't sailed for over 35 years and no one knows what in hell to do with her. Some guys want to save her as a reminder of America's greatest passenger ship, when she was the fastest one on the ocean. Others want to scrap her. One of my most interesting cases was played out on that ship. That was a long time ago," Dan said with a dreamy look in his eyes.

"No fooling, Dan."

"Be careful, Bill, otherwise Dan will tell you the whole sad story," Terry teased with a broad smile.

"So, after that fascinating introduction, Dan, you have to tell us the story," Cynthia Marks urged as she craned her neck to look past Terry and out the window at the ship's two funnels looming higher than anything around them. Cynthia enjoyed hearing Dan tell of the interesting and dramatic events that went on in the court room and his office. They were more entertaining than her husband's stories. Bill Marks was a partner in an accounting firm.

"That ship has a great history, Cynthia," Dan continued, "She was built on an aircraft carrier's hull and in a national emergency could be converted to carry 15,000 men ready for combat with all the necessary equipment ready for a fight. Or she could even become a fully equipped hospital ship. Her speed was always a military secret when she was in service. Yet everyone in the maritime industry knew she was unusually swift. On her maiden voyage in 1952, the *American Union* broke the speed record for ocean liners and won the Blue Riband, making 36 knots. That's a lot of speed for a big ship; a knot is faster than a mile per hour. It's hard to believe that after more than 50 years that record still stands.

"She could easily have done 40 knots and maybe more. She is almost as long as the Empire State Building is tall, with a crew of over 1,000 and a passenger capacity of more than 2,000. In her day, she was a great ship. Her crew affectionately called her The Big A.

"Other than the piano and the butcher's block, there was no wood on the ship. She was as fireproof as any vessel could possibly be. I had many cases representing seamen who sailed aboard her, who were hurt at work, as well as injured passengers.

"It was very sedate ship. It was a different kind of cruising when you sailed on the *American Union* in those days. Not like today. She had three dining rooms and three classes: First, Tourist and Cabin. It was a maritime caste system. Passengers couldn't go up to a higher class facility unless they were invited. She regularly sailed to England, France, and Germany and, of course, New York, her home port."

Dan Nikolas closed his eyes, folded his arms across his chest once more and traveled back in time to the year 1968 as he continued his story.

2

EMERGENCY ABOARD
S.S. AMERICAN UNION

At 8 p.m. on a warm May evening in 1968, at the German port of Bremerhaven, the *S.S. American Union* let go all her mooring lines. With engines in reverse she worked her way slowly, slipping into the North Sea, then turned south, heading toward the English Channel, which the French call *La Manche* (the sleeve). She travelled about 330 nautical miles at 32 knots until she passed between the ports of Dover, England at her starboard side and the French port of Calais on her port side. She was entering the English Channel. The *American Union* then sailed southwest, heading to her next port of call - New York City.

From her entry into the Channel and until she reached Land's End, the westernmost point of the British Isles, the *American Union* would travel approximately another 330 nautical miles. Forty miles past Land's End lay the Scilly Isles, an archipelago of small, mostly uninhabited islands. It will be the last land passengers will see before entering into the North Atlantic and arriving at New York.

When Gaspar Fonseca awoke with his pain and was later seen by Dr. Peters, the *American Union* was already within the English Channel. As the ship proceeded, Dr. Peters faced two clocks. The first was biological. If there was a block in Fonseca's leg, as the doctor was almost certain there was, it kept blood from circulating down into his left leg. This would soon result in an infection or possibly even gangrene, unless normal blood flow could be restored. To prevent this, Gaspar required an immediate dose of drugs that could dissolve the block or, in the alternative, an operation to remove the obstruction, the dangerous thrombosis impeding the flow of blood to his leg. Since the ship's hospital lacked the appropriate drugs, the only solution was surgery.

The second clock that was ticking was time itself. The *S.S. American Union* was sailing relentlessly forward and the opportunity to deliver Gaspar Fonseca to a hospital where he could receive proper treatment was swiftly running out. The decision to divert the ship, or order a rescue, rested not with Dr. Peters but with Gregory Burn, the captain of the *American Union*.

At 6:12 a.m. Dr. Peters called the sleeping captain in his stateroom.

"We have an emergency, Captain. There's a crewmember, an AB, with what I am certain is an arterial block in his left leg. He needs treatment; either drug therapy or an operation. It should be done immediately. If he doesn't have the proper treatment there may be some very grave consequences for him. Perhaps even life-threatening."

"What kind of block, Doctor?" Burn asked, with remnants of sleep in his voice.

"I can't tell with any degree of certainty. He either has a deep vein thrombosis, or an embolism. Diagnosis is complicated and uncertain for me without proper testing."

"Is it so critical as you say?"

"Oh, yes, Captain. If it's a deep vein thrombosis and not treated soon, only one of the nasty effects can be that the surrounding tissue will begin to die because of lack of blood supply.

"How do you treat this problem?"

"I've already explained. The man either needs medication to dissolve the block, or surgery to remove the blockage. I can think of two drugs that might help: Heparin and Coumadin. They act to dissolve the clot. We don't have those drugs in our dispensary. And then, I can't tell where the block is because we don't have the necessary diagnostic equipment needed to locate it. And Captain, I'm not a surgeon."

"I remember reading somewhere that aspirin was good in these situations."

"The man tells me he can't tolerate aspirin; he gets stomach pains. It's highly probable that with that condition he could have massive stomach bleeding. That's a complication we have to avoid."

"What happens if he doesn't have the operation right away?"

"He'll probably have an infection and if the block continues, he will eventually lose his leg to gangrene because he'll have to go without a reliable blood supply until we get to New York. But we still have time to help him by landing him at a port on the coast.

"Captain, we also have to consider the other possibility: that the clot could break loose and travel to his lungs or his heart. The results could be dire for him. We should be pulling into a port, or call for some sort of rescue so he can get to a hospital quickly to receive proper treatment."

"Can't you treat him on the ship?"

"He needs an operation and I'm not a surgeon. It's a complicated problem. And then I haven't been able to locate the exact site of the block. I would absolutely need some diagnostic tests which I can't perform in our hospital because, again, we don't have those kinds of facilities aboard."

"I thought we had a first class ship's hospital with X-rays and everything."

"Yes, we do. For a cruise ship, it's very good. But not for the kind of testing and surgery this man needs, Captain."

"Well, I can't stop the ship for one crew member. Do we have any doctors aboard as passengers?"

"I wouldn't know. We usually have a doctor or two in First Class, but if we've had any on this trip, I haven't met them. We only sailed from Bremerhaven late last night. I didn't have time to socialize with the passengers."

"Alright, doctor. You go and wake the Purser. I want the two of you to go through the passenger list. Then get back to me and let me know what you were able to find. I won't think of stopping the ship until some other doctors give us their opinions. Hopefully, we have some doctors with us on this trip."

"Yes, sir. I'll get back to you as soon as I can. We need to be acting fast."

Peters hung up the phone and immediately dialed the ship's Purser. After Dr. Peters woke him, Roger Clay rolled out of his bed, rubbed his eyes and stepped into his dress white uniform trousers. He advised Dr. Peters that he was pretty sure that there were five doctors aboard. As he tied his shoe laces, he explained over the phone which he held tightly wedged between his right shoulder and the side of his head, "They aren't all necessarily physicians. Some of these guys are professors with a doctorate degree. They call themselves doctor, too. I'll get the list, we'll split it. At this hour they're probably all asleep, like we should be. Let's see how many physicians we can turn up. Meet me at my office, doctor."

After awakening every doctor on the list, three turned out to be physicians: an anesthetist, a pediatrician and a research physician. Of the three, only the research physician was familiar with any kind of surgery. Once they were told the Captain was reluctant to deviate from his course, all three agreed that Dr. Peters should tell the Captain that as none of the doctors were qualified cardio-vascular surgeons and the necessary diagnostic equipment and drugs were unavailable, the seaman should be landed as soon as possible. Dr. Peters rang up Captain Burn in his cabin, for a second time.

"Captain, I've found some doctors. Since there is no surgeon among them they all agree with me as to how they see this situation and very strongly advise the seaman be sent to a medical facility ashore. They think operating on the ship is futile; a real long shot and dangerous."

"I think you should convince your doctors to try to operate. Get back to me with their decision, Doctor. And keep me posted."

"Captain, the longer we wait the more difficult it will be to get our seaman ashore and attack his blockage on time."

"Doctor, I think that as long as you remain on the phone you're the one delaying this process. Get on with it."

A ship owner's relation to his seamen-employees is not similar to one a worker has with his land-based employer. The work rules and regulations governing those working in offices, shops and factories rarely apply to a seaman. A mariner performs his duties in his special world of a ship at sea. Bank clerks, cashiers or bus drivers labor on land, usually with a day or two of free time during their working week.

By contrast, a seaman works seven days a week. He is away from cities, his home and family. Normally, he enjoys no day off until his ship touches port and he earns a shore leave. The seafarer must, by law, obey every order of his superiors who, through their decisions, control his life and safety together with those of the rest of the crew. Should he disobey a lawful order, a seaman may be guilty of mutiny, a serious charge. For these reasons, a ship owner has a higher duty of care toward his mariner-employee. A land-based employee may leave his or her job at any time he or she wishes.

The rules for a seaman's conduct and the obligations his ship owner owes him are centuries old. Ask most maritime lawyers and they will tell you that theirs is the second oldest profession, the oldest being prostitution. Shipboard work rules pre-date those of land workers by millennia, going back even before the birth of Christ, to a time when men moved passengers and cargo in wooden ships, propelled by oar and sail, across the waters of the known world. The ancient Greeks, Phoenicians, Carthaginians and other seafaring peoples were continuously developing special rules designed to protect their seafarers, their ships and their cargos.

Of necessity, because of the nature of seafaring employment, ship owners had to encourage men to work on ships sailing far from land with liberal working conditions, as they were leaving their loved ones for long periods of time,. Before the 20th century and the advent of the steamship, a seaman's slow-sailing ship was often his home for weeks, months and sometimes even years. He needed guarantees that during his service, he would not be arbitrarily abandoned by a ship owner at a foreign port; nor would he be discharged without funds by the malicious withholding of his justly earned wages.

If a sailor fell ill or was disabled through injury or illness while in the service of his ship, the owner had the legal obligation, called Cure, to procure proper medical treatment for him. The ship owner also had to return an ill or injured mariner to his home port for treatment. And while he was mending, the seaman was entitled to a daily stipend called Maintenance: payments meant to assist a sick or injured seaman to pay rent and purchase food. These benefits pre-date modern labor laws by centuries.

During the early decades of the 20th Century, American seamen benefited from the rise in power of labor unions. Seaman's rights were enhanced by America's Congress, with a series of liberal and social legislation. They were granted a brand new right they had never enjoyed before: the ability to sue their employers for injuries or illnesses suffered as a result of negligently maintained or operated vessels. Seamen could also use the legal doctrine of Seaworthiness, a legal concept in which a ship owner warrants that his ship and its equipment are reasonably fit for service at sea. This is the same law that a car dealer guarantees the purchaser of a new car: that it is reasonably fit for use as he drives it out of the dealer's lot. At law, this doctrine is called the "Warranty of Fitness for Use."

Modern industrial studies revealed that seamen, longshoremen and railroad workers labored in America's most dangerous workplaces. Employment on danger-ridden ships, docksides or railroads had to be encouraged in order to hire men to work in these perilous professions, if America was to become a great industrial power. So, at the beginning of the 20th century, Congress ordered ship owners to clean up their work places or defend personal injury suits brought by their employees, through a new law called the Jones Act for Seamen. The laws concerning Maintenance and Cure and the proper and prompt payment of wages were also enhanced, exposing ship owners to greater penalties and stiff monetary sanctions for failing to provide those benefits as required by law.

The ancient benefit of Cure continued until a seaman could return to work after being found 'fit for duty' by a physician. Fit for duty meant a seaman could return to work with the same ability to perform his tasks as before becoming ill or injured. As an Able Seaman on the *American Union*, Gaspar Fonseca had the right to expect that he would receive the best medical treatment available at the time and place his illness first arose.

It would soon become a contentious legal question as to whether Gaspar Fonseca had received this standard of treatment. Captain Burn did not attempt to land or call for Gaspar Fonseca's rescue. Four doctors, trying as best they could, through surgery, were unable to locate the clot blocking his artery. Three days after their operation, when he arrived at New York, Gaspar Fonseca was rushed to Staten Island's Marine Hospital, run by The United States Public Health Service. There, his gangrenous left leg was cut away.

At 30, the age at which he lost his left leg, Gaspar Fonseca had been constructing some ambitious dreams for his future. He had been studying for an officer's license for the past two and a half years. During his vacations, he attended classes designed to upgrade him to the rank of Third Mate. When he had free time at sea, he lay in his bunk with the books he had received from the course he enrolled in, studying and preparing himself to take the Coast Guard officer's exam to qualify as a Third Officer. Sailing in the ship's deck department, he had accumulated the necessary qualifying experience. Finished with his studying, Gaspar was finally scheduled to sit for the test in July, two months after the block formed in his leg.

With a Third Mate's license and the higher pay that came with it, he and his wife Mira could buy that house in the neighborhood they had been looking at for some time. They could move there within a year or two after Gaspar began earning more money. They could even have another child. He would then study to elevate himself to Second Mate and Chief Mate. Who knows? Maybe he might even become a captain in the future. Others had done it. He knew of a few Puerto Ricans who had become captains. One of them had even graduated from his High School.

Why couldn't he do it too? But all those dreams came crashing down as he sat brooding with his crutches angled alongside his chair in his Bronx apartment.

One day a friend dropped a business card on the table beside him. "Gas, go see this guy. He's a good lawyer. He'll help you. A few years ago he got a lot of money for one of my cousins."

Gaspar Fonseca thanked his friend and said, without any emotion, "Thanks, Ernie, I'll call him when I get a chance." Gaspar slipped the card into his shirt pocket. After his friend left, he pulled it out. It read:

Jack Hoffman, Esq.
BArclay 7-9394

233 Broadway
Woolworth Building
Suite 635
New York, N.Y. 10279

3

TWO LAWYERS MEET
NEW YORK CITY

Dan Nikolas had never met Jack Hoffman, but he knew his name. Every New York trial lawyer, personal injury specialist and anyone aware of the legal profession's brightest stars, either knew or had heard of Jack Hoffman. He was a legend and living right here in New York City.

Years earlier, when it was almost impossible to have a doctor testify against a fellow physician in a malpractice case, Jack Hoffman had somehow managed to string together a collection of talented doctors in the different medical specialties. They helped him win a basketful of medical malpractice cases that other lawyers wouldn't have ever thought of handling. In New York, Jack Hoffman was known as the "Dean of the malpractice lawyers." He also enjoyed a nation-wide reputation and was often called upon to try cases in other states, helping lawyers who wanted the best representation for their clients.

Today, Jack Hoffman called Dan Nikolas' office to arrange for an appointment. He hoped Dan would act as co-counsel in a case in which he had just been retained.

"I have a case I would like to discuss with Mr. Nikolas," he told Betsy Sachs, Dan's secretary, and she made the appointment for him. When Hoffman arrived, he didn't sit in the reception area for long before he was warmly greeted by Nikolas.

"It's a pleasure to finally meet you, Mr. Hoffman. Come on inside. You can tell me what your case is all about."

Dan led the lawyer into his office and on the way, Hoffman insisted Dan call him Jack. Dan offered Hoffman a seat on a comfortable couch, then pulled over a chair and sat opposite him. Jack Hoffman was in his late forties or early fifties, with a soldier's closely cropped hair that was jet black but beginning to show flecks of gray. His face was tan and heavily lined, like that of a man who has fought hard all his life. He was trim, five feet eight, well-dressed and he was full of energy even as he sat, his hands moving compulsively between his briefcase and his knees. Jack Hoffman's eyes were dark brown and he had a smile that said he wasn't as tough as he looked.

"I'd like you to work on a case with me. I plan to handle the medical part and I would like you to work on the part involving ship handling."

"I'd love to work with you. It would be an experience. Tell me about your case."

"I've been retained by a seaman who lost his leg. It wasn't from an accident, but a medical condition that arose while he was working aboard his ship. What I have been able to determine from my research, is that he should have immediately been taken off his ship and sent to a nearby hospital for treatment. Instead, an operation was performed aboard by some passengers who were doctors. None of them were surgeons. As you may imagine, a ship is not the best place to perform a complicated operation."

"It depends on where she was located and the kind of operation you're talking about."

"She was in the English Channel."

"There must have been a good reason the seaman wasn't taken off the ship. What was the operation about?"

"He had an arterial block in his left leg."

"So then he needed immediate attention."

"Exactly. I see you know that. Good. I know nothing about ships. I realized immediately after going over the facts that there was malpractice by the doctors, because they operated and they weren't qualified to do so. And it's contra-indicated to do that: to try to locate a block when a competent cardio-vascular surgeon is not available. To complicate matters for my client, the officers should have taken that unfortunate man off the ship and saved his leg. There is another issue I have to face: even if they had gotten him off the ship, would it have been with enough time to save the leg? So I'll have to work the medical part of this case. It shouldn't worry you, however. That'll be my job."

"That's fine with me. It sounds as if it's something that you're much better at than I am. But let's talk tactics. I wouldn't sue the doctors for malpractice. Here's why: Under maritime law, the ship owner always owes the primary duty to afford your client reasonable medical attention. Let the company sue the doctors, because the company has the obligation to show that they provided the best proper medical attention reasonably available. If the docs screwed up, the ship's recourse for failing to provide proper treatment is to go after the doctors. There's no reason we should be fighting on two fronts. Let the ship sue the doctors.

"We should concentrate on why he wasn't taken off the ship. My best guess is they won't sue the doctors, anyway, for two reasons: first, it's bad publicity to sue passengers and then they would be admitting they did wrong by letting them operate. They would have to defend their doctors and their decision to operate."

"Great. That's why I'm here: for someone to lead me through the maze of maritime law. So I looked around for a maritime lawyer and Abe Katzman, one of the lawyers who rents space in my office, told me about you. He says you sailed for a time."

"Yes, I did. It paid for my tuition at college and law school. I know Abe. We were at law school together. We've bumped into each other from time to time, keeping in touch with how we're getting along."

"That's what he said. I need a maritime lawyer who can prove my guy could and should have been taken off the ship after the Captain learned about his condition. I did some reading about this and I learned from my research that the ship owner, as you've said, has a duty to render reasonable medical treatment to his seamen. I'm convinced that wasn't done here."

"That may be so," Dan said. "What passes for reasonable is always a question, depending on what's available at the time, and other facts. What's not in your client's favor, Jack, is that at sea, the captain has sole responsibility for making decisions about the management of his ship. He must have had some good reasons for not taking your man off the ship. A captain's decision at sea is a difficult doctrine to overcome at law."

"I know that. That's why I'm here and I'm not qualified to tackle that problem on my own. And I'll call you Dan, if I may."

Dan nodded approval with a smile. He took a pen off his desk and began writing on a long yellow pad. "And what's your client's name?"

"Gaspar Fonseca."

"And the ship on which he was working?"

"The *American Union*. He keeps calling it "The Big A.""

"All the seamen call her that." Dan looked up and smiled. Then he asked, "What is his rating?"

"He was an Able Seaman."

"Where exactly was the ship at the time you're saying they should have taken him off?

"I don't know for sure, somewhere in the English Channel. That's why I need a lawyer like you to figure it out for me."

"Well, I'm sure we can determine the precise location. That's going to be crucial in this case, of course. The ship's log should tell us all about that. Did the Captain give any reason why he didn't get him off the ship?"

"At this early stage of the case I don't know, nor does Mr. Fonseca. He tells me only that the Captain could have stopped the ship in order to take him off."

"How does he know that?"

"He claims a friend, who's an officer, told him that. He doesn't want to get him involved unless absolutely necessary. He says it could cause the friend to lose his job."

"He may be right about that. There are other ways to rescue a sick seaman besides stopping a ship. He could have been taken off the ship by a motor launch or maybe even a helicopter. If that was a possibility and the Captain refused to do so and it resulted in the man's injury, you may have a good law suit."

"I'm certain the Captain's failure to get him off the ship resulted in the loss of Mr. Fonseca's left leg.'

Dan remained silent for a few seconds, thinking.

Jack Hoffman continued. "During the time you sailed, Dan, were you ever involved in a rescue from a ship?"

"Never. But I have seen a few. Once I saw a helicopter lift a man off a burning tanker outside Hong Kong harbor. Very dramatic."

"If you can prove that a rescue was possible, then we have another hurdle to jump," Jack Hoffman said with a sour look.

"What's that?"

"Even if he was rescued, we would have to prove there had been enough time to save the leg. That's why I want to work with you. I can get the right doctors and I know the questions to ask to beat the defendant on that score. I'm hoping you can figure out that there was enough time to get Mr. Fonseca off his ship in order to save his leg.

"Are you willing to work with me on that basis? If so, we can settle on a fee arrangement between us," Jack Hoffman said as he extended a hand to seal the pact.

"Absolutely," Dan said as he shook Hoffman's hand. "Have your client here as soon as possible, Jack, and I'll start working on his case."

❧ ❦

Three days later, Gaspar Fonseca swung into Dan Nikolas's office on two shiny aluminum crutches. Three months after the amputation of his left leg, he was still managing the crutches poorly, finding it difficult to accept the reality of his loss. As he sat down, Dan rose from his chair and stretched across his desk with a strong handshake.

Gaspar Fonseca looked around. This was a bright, sun-lit office, which reflected its owner's interest in the sea. On the walls were art works of the oceans and the ships that sailed across them. Gaspar sat next to a table stacked with books about the sea and the charts of many ports. There was a caliper used to measure nautical distances and two old and gleaming-bright brass compasses pointing north. This was a room designed to make seafarers feel at home and make them confident that the lawyer who worked here knew all the intricacies of the law of the sea. He even spoke the special language of the sea and knew all about a seafarer's benefits under the law, which no other American worker enjoyed.

"Mr. Hoffman told me you worked on ships, Mr. Nikolas. I was two months away from getting my Third Mate's license until this." Gaspar patted his stump. His leg had been taken just above the knee.

"He also told me you were working together on my case. I never thought I would have two lawyers working for me. I knew your name before Mr. Hoffman sent me here. Men on the ship talk about you."

"Good things I trust, Mr. Fonseca?"

"Mostly, yes," he grinned.

"Well, now that you do have two lawyers, let's talk about your case. There are some basic questions for us to go through. I need to understand some things about you."

Dan looked at his new client: he was a handsome man with an olive cast to his skin. His hair was straight and black and shiny, as were his eyes. He had the look of someone who had not been sleeping well for a long time and was carrying a great psychological burden. Gaspar Fonseca spoke with a slight Spanish accent, as he was born in the Puerto Rican mountain community of Comerio. Brought to New York as a child, he had attended New York City's Maritime Trades High School. His schoolhouse was a World War II Liberty Ship docked at a pier at the end of East Twenty-Third Street at Manhattan's East River. The ship, the *S.S. John W. Brown,* was on loan to the New York City Board of Education from its owner, the Federal Maritime Commission. It was the same government department that owned the *S.S. American Union.*

Gaspar Fonseca examined his new lawyer; a man a few years, maybe six or seven, older than himself with green eyes, brown hair and a friendly smile. He was taller than Gaspar and trim too, with an air of confidence about him that allowed Gaspar to trust and confide in him, just as Jack Hoffman had told him he could.

On a form he had specially prepared, Dan entered detailed information about his new client: name, address, age, education and work and medical histories, the date of the incident, the name of the ship and a history of the events that brought him to Jack Hoffman's office. After collecting all this important information and more, Dan sat back and said:

"In your own words, I want to hear what happened to you."

Gaspar Fonseca set his crutches on the floor, rubbed the stump of his lost leg, took a deep breath and began his narrative. It was the tale of how he had lost his leg, the same tale he had been telling himself dozens of times a day, every day since its amputation.

4

SURGERY ON THE HIGH SEAS
THE ENGLISH CHANNEL

As the *S.S. American Union* steamed through the English Channel, Dr. Malcolm Peters met with the three passenger-physicians in the ship's coffee shop. They sat in a quiet corner at a square table while the galley crew was busy working over the clatter of dishes, silverware and coffee cups they were setting out for the morning breakfast buffet. Only a few passengers, those who had risen early, were gathered at the buffet counter, placing breakfast on their trays. The four doctors went over Gaspar Fonseca's medical situation. Dr. Peters, now dressed in his uniform, requested service from a busboy, who quickly set down four cups and two carafes - one of tea and one of coffee- in addition to a large plate piled high with pastries, warm croissants and butter.

It was now 6:49 a.m. and Peters was nervously looking out a window while twirling a butter knife. He watched the first bright layers of dawn begin to light up the sky, knowing that as the ship sailed forward there was very little time left to help Gaspar Fonseca. If he was right in his diagnosis, and he was certain he was, time was critical with respect to treating the problem, assuming it could even be treated. The three doctors sitting at the table in front of him were a medically diverse group:

Samuel Diggs, an anesthetist, was a Harvard-educated Bostonian who taught anesthesiology at Harvard Medical School. Michael Grinstein was a New York pediatrician in private practice and Howard Ross, the oldest of the group, worked at a research laboratory at the National Institutes of Health at Bethesda,

Maryland. Of the three, only Dr. Ross had some minor experience with surgery, working on animal dissections. Dr. Peters filled his colleagues in with his diagnosis.

All three were unanimous in advising that Gaspar should immediately be landed and sent to a hospital facility ashore, since none of them was a surgeon nor a vascular specialist, and testing would be needed to locate the block. After their consultation, Dr. Peters picked up a phone at the Maitre D's desk located a few feet away. He dialed Captain Burn. It was now 6:57 and the Captain had gone from his cabin to the bridge.

On the back of Gaspar's medical chart, Dr. Peters had been making a separate record of his conversations with Captain Burn and the other doctors. This record carefully detailed the times of day he had spoken with the three doctors and Captain Burn. Whenever possible, he included what he considered to be the familiar landmarks he saw along the Devonshire coast as the ship proceeded forward from the Channel into the Atlantic Ocean. Somehow he felt this information was going to be needed in the future. He wanted to make sure that neither he nor his three colleagues were going to be the ones taking the blame for anything that went wrong.

While waiting for the Captain to come to the phone, Peters made a new entry, noting that he had called the Captain for the third time. Then he entered in his memorandum the time, 6:58 a.m.; that he had spoken with the doctors, and set down their opinion as to what should be done. He underlined the word 'unanimous' three times. When the Captain finally came to the phone, Peters spoke loud enough, so all the doctors could at least hear his side of the conversation. Their table was less than thirty feet away and Dr. Peters looked at his colleagues, shaking his head with a pessimistic look from time to time.

"Dr. Peters here again, Captain. I've consulted with the three doctors. None of them is a qualified surgeon. They all agree with me. The seaman should immediately be sent to a medical facility ashore. I noted that since the last time I spoke with you, his leg is getting a little warmer. That's not a good sign."

"What does that mean, doctor, that his leg is getting a little warmer?'

"He's not getting a blood supply to his leg so it's probably susceptible to becoming infected in that area, besides being exposed to some other life-threatening problems."

"How do you treat this problem?"

"Captain," Dr. Peters said in an exasperated and frustrated tone, "I've already explained the nature of this emergency to you. We could give him Heparin or Coumadin, they are clot dissolving drugs. But unfortunately, we don't have them stocked in our drug inventory. I've told the doctors that. So they are strongly advising you to get the man off the ship. It is necessary for him to get competent medical treatment immediately, which they don't believe they could give him"

"What's the alternative?"

"To getting him off the ship?" the doctor asked incredulously. "There isn't any. He needs treatment immediately. He needs to get off the ship so that he can be operated on or get the necessary drug therapy I just told you about."

"These other doctors, can they operate?"

"In an emergency, I don't know. But it's not realistically possible. None of them are qualified surgeons. They might operate only if they are convinced it is impossible to get the seaman ashore to a proper facility. You know we physicians take an oath to do no harm. We might not be doing the best thing for this man by operating on the ship, instead of making every effort to get him ashore."

"Trying to get him ashore endangers the ship, doctor," Captain Burn said as if he were scolding a petulant child. "It also means we get to New York late, which means big overtime for the longshoremen, tugs and ship handlers who are waiting for us. See what you can do here, I mean on the ship. We always get to New York on schedule. I don't want that record, or mine, spoiled on this trip."

"Are you telling me you want me to convince the doctors to operate?"

"Yes."

"Well, sir, then I'll do my best, even if I and the doctors are really against it. And remember, Captain, I can't force them to do anything if they consider it dangerous. After all, they are passengers and not crew members."

Peters hung up the phone. Looking dejected as he turned toward the doctors, he paused to enter the last words of his conversation with the Captain on his chart.

"The Captain won't land the seaman," he said apologetically. As he finished his entry in his chart, he underlined the following words twice: I asked the Captain if he wanted me to convince the doctors to operate and he said 'yes'.

Dr. Grinstein said: "We heard the conversation, Dr. Peters. I suppose we have little choice but to operate on this man."

"Let's get ready," Dr. Ross said. "We don't have the luxury of time." Dr. Diggs nodded in agreement.

While the doctors were consulting, Gaspar Fonseca lay in the hospital's infirmary, awaiting some decision about what would be done with him.

"Dick, where the hell are the docs? They better hurry up. This pain is murder,"

"Didn't the doc give you a shot to kill the pain?" Skelley asked.

"He said he couldn't because it was important for the other doctors to know where my pain was."

"Here they come."

A young, tall and smiling doctor approached Gaspar.

"Hi, I'm Dr. Grinstein. I'm going to examine you. Just relax and let me know where you feel the pain."

"Okay, doc. I got a sharp one right here."

Gaspar pointed to a spot on his left thigh. Grinstein's hands moved expertly across Gaspar's thigh and calf. Then he felt the toes, the pulses at his ankle and behind his left knee. While Dr. Grinstein was performing a physical exam, Dr. Ross was searching through hospital drawers and closets for scalpels, surgical gowns, head covers and rubber surgical gloves. Dr. Diggs was rounding up all the pain-killing material for anesthesia he could find. After Dr. Grinstein's examination, both he and Dr. Peters lifted Gaspar onto a gurney and wheeled him to the X-ray machine. Gaspar could hear them talking about his condition and the preparations they were making. Dr. Peters had alerted the ship's nurses to get to the ship's hospital to assist the doctors.

"I don't expect we will get much information from X-rays without the necessary dye to locate the block, but we have to try anyway," Dr. Grinstein explained as he swung the X-ray machine to place it over Gaspar's left leg. After reviewing the X-rays, all four doctors were in accord. The X-rays failed to reveal anything helpful.

"It's no surprise," Dr. Ross remarked. "It was a long shot anyway. But we've lost precious time so we have to get working fast, to try to locate the block. What we'll be doing is more like exploratory surgery, because we don't know where that damn block is."

Dr. Peters came over to Gaspar as he lay on the gurney. He stood over Gaspar, whose eyes were closed. He opened them and looked at Dr. Peters, who said, "You need an operation, and right away, Mr. Fonseca. We can't get you ashore so I and these three doctors will be operating. You'll be in good hands. If we don't operate right away you will probably have some bad consequences. You have blockage which is keeping the blood from flowing down into your lower leg. Do you understand that unless we act you are almost certain to lose your leg? Do we have your permission to operate?"

"Is an operation absolutely necessary, doctor?"

"Yes, Mr. Fonseca. Absolutely."

"You have no choice, Mr. Fonseca," interrupted Dr. Grinstein.

"Then do what you have to do, doc," Gaspar responded half-heartedly and with a choking fear in his throat.

Dr. Peters called the bridge a fourth time and spoke to Captain Burn.

"Captain, we are going to operate on seaman Fonseca. Is the sea calm, sir? We don't want any sudden movements while we are working down here."

"They are telling me that radar shows a calm sea. I'll make sure the ship rides steady, doctor. If necessary, I'll put out the stabilizers."

Ship's stabilizers were developed during the 1930s. They were invented to minimize the ship's rolling motion and help make passengers feel more comfortable in rough seas. While the use of stabilizers creates a drag on the ship's forward motion, slowing her down, Captain Burn knew it would only be for a short while and he would be able to make up the time. After all, the ship would still be moving. It wasn't as if he had to stop her altogether to perform the rescue he didn't want to make. Captain Burn hung up the phone and returned to his chair to look out at the sea in front of him. He told one of the officers on the bridge to keep a steady eye on the radar.

Two of Gaspar's shipmates, who shared his blood type, answered the call to donate blood if needed. They sat in the hospital's waiting room. At 7:27 a.m., the doctors prepared for surgery. They scrubbed, dressed into surgical gowns, sanitized the operating area and anesthetized their patient. Finally, at 7:48 Dr. Howard Ross made the first cut into the flesh of Gaspar Fonseca's left thigh along the site where the doctors suspected the block would be located. At 7:55 a.m. the *American Union* was now sailing into the Celtic Sea, proceeding into the open expanse that was the Atlantic Ocean

"The last thing I remembered before the operation," Gaspar Fonseca told Dan Nikolas, "was a bright light above my head and the faces of the four doctors looking down at me. Maybe it was in my mind, Mr. Nikolas, but I thought even though they were wearing masks I could see looks of concern in their eyes. I awoke with my left leg numb and wrapped in bandages. Dr. Ross was standing beside me with a grave look on his face.

"'I'm sorry, Mr. Fonseca,' he told me. 'We couldn't locate the block. We'll have to see what happens when we get to New York'

"That's three days away, doctor,' I told him. And then he said, 'I know.' After that conversation I heard Dr. Peters call Captain Burn."

"Hello, Captain? The operation was not a success. What do I think will happen? He'll probably lose his leg because it can't go for three days without an adequate blood supply. We should call New York to have an ambulance ready at the pier to take him to the Marine Hospital at Staten Island as soon as the ship lands."

The United States Public Health Service maintained seamen's hospitals throughout the major seaports of the United States. Their main mission was to render necessary medical services to the seamen of all nations.

Slowly, Gaspar's pain returned as the anesthesia wore off. Added to that familiar stabbing pain was a new one to torment him: it was where Dr. Ross had made the incision. He tried not to look at his leg because it was turning ugly colors. Every time a doctor came to inspect his leg, he hoped the pink color of health would be restored. But when the blanket over the leg was lifted, he saw its color turning a darker purple and his heart raced with fear, feeling the thumping of his heart. Although no one any longer said he would be losing his leg, Gaspar knew what would happen.

"When the ship arrived at Pier 86 in New York, an ambulance was waiting for me. It took me to Bowling Green in Lower Manhattan and then it rolled me on to the Staten Island Ferry. We continued on to the Marine Hospital where my worst fears came true. My left leg was removed above the knee. I lost my leg forever."

Dan Nikolas set back in his swivel chair after noting the last facts of Gaspar's narrative. "That's quite a story, Mr. Fonseca. Are they fitting you with an artificial limb?"

"Yes, they are trying but it seems that my stump hasn't completely healed yet and it's still very painful. That has to get better before they can fit me. You know, Mr. Nikolas, all the while I was in the hospital I knew I lost my leg yet I felt my leg just as if it was still there, as if I could still touch it. But I knew it's wasn't there."

"That's an interesting phenomenon, Mr. Fonseca. The doctors call it a phantom leg."

5

PIER 86
NEW YORK CITY

Manhattan's Pier 86 lies between the Hudson River and 12th Avenue, New York City's westernmost street. On a frigid and windy January morning framed by a cobalt blue and cloudless sky, Dan Nikolas waited for the men and women of Customs and Immigration to clear passengers and crew off the *American Union* before he could ascend the ship's gangway. While he waited, he sat in the comfortable warmth of a coffee shop across the way, directly facing the ship's bow. He watched progress on the ship through a steamy window, the inside dripping plump beads of water that skated down to its bottom ledge.

Whenever possible, Dan liked doing his own investigations. It gave him the opportunity to keep up with the feel of life and work aboard a ship. It also allowed him to learn more about all the new technology that had developed since he stopped sailing more than a decade ago.

When he interviewed young attorneys for a job in his office, he insisted they understood first-hand what mariners had to do to earn their living sailing aboard a ship at sea. He wanted them to personally go down into the engine room. He wanted them to understand how a winch or a gravity davit worked on deck and to know the proper way to moor or release a ship at a pier. He insisted they understand the work performed in a ship's galley to feed a crew three meals a day, seven days a week. It meant dressing in work clothes and wearing running shoes when they went aboard a ship to do an investigation and sometimes coming away from a ship with greasy hands and trousers. He also warned prospective candidates they might have to work holidays or even at the midnight hour.

"A ship works on a tight schedule," he would explain, "but she can be erratic too – she gets delayed because of heavy weather or a breakdown of an engine at sea, or maybe a berth's not available for her and she has to wait hours before she can dock and all of a sudden she's late. And so we have to meet her at midnight instead of noon or ten in the morning. It can be frustrating and can sometimes make a shambles your personal life."

Then, he would issue his final warning: "If you have a problem with that, let me know now, before we have conflicts about these things later on." Most of the young lawyers, wanting to become maritime specialists, accepted Dan's rules.

Watching passengers descending the gangway, followed by uniformed Customs and Immigration officers, Dan drained his coffee cup and wiped his mouth with a paper napkin. He then placed the leather strap of his 35 millimeter camera over his right shoulder, buttoned up his winter coat, tucked his scarf over his throat and neck, folded his copy of the New York Times into his brief case and left the restaurant, walking into the knife-like wind. As he ascended the gangway, he saw Lucille Moore talking with the seaman at the gangway watch.

"Good morning, Dan. What are you doing here this freezing day?"

"Hello, Lu. I came up to see one of my clients at Times Square. He has to sign some affidavits for his case so he can answer the interrogatories you served on me."

Times Square was the area on the ship located deep in the bowels of the *American Union*. It was a place in one of the lowest decks of the ship, which was unknown to passengers. Times Square was formed by two long passageways; one running from the ship's bow to the stern; the other an intersecting passageway at mid ships that ran across the width, or beam, of the ship. It was also known as 'thwart ships'. At this busy intersection lots of social activity and commerce, legal and otherwise, was carried on by the crew. There was also a store here. Seamen called it the "slop chest." Here a seaman could buy cigarettes, underwear, work clothes and other personal items.

"While I'm here I thought I might also take some photos of the Promenade Deck, fore and aft, for the Fonseca case." Dan explained.

"You know you should be making a formal request to take photos in any area on one of my ships. You shouldn't be coming up here without permission." Lucille Moore said weakly and with a friendly smile.

"Yeah, but Lu, we both know you're going to have to let me do it, anyway. This way we save time. I don't have to come here twice and you don't have to watch me twice, and do all the unnecessary paper work to get the Court to give me permission to take photos, which I'm entitled to take, anyway."

"Alright, just wait here until I get a man to accompany you. I don't want you roaming around my ship like a lone wolf, especially in Times Square. When you're finished with what you're doing, I'll be in the First Class Dining Room. Catch up with me there. I want to talk to you about Fonseca. We need to know where we are going in that case."

First, Dan went down to Times Square. It was busy; some crew members were getting ready to leave the ship for a short time at home. Others were in the slop chest buying personal items. Money was passing hands for some men who were playing numbers; friends were meeting there so that they could arrange to get a lift to their destinations ashore. Other attorneys were there, waiting for their clients. They were colleagues who Dan knew and they often spoke with each other about their cases.

After attending to his client, Dan took the elevator to the Promenade Deck to shoot a roll of 30 frames of film, fighting the wind and cold. Then he entered the ship once again, welcoming the friendly warmth and walked down the grand, carpeted staircase to the *American Union'* posh First Class Dining Room. He always smiled when he saw the art work along the staircase: Aluminum seagulls with their wings extended! This ship was the most fire-proof of any that had ever sailed. There were only two pieces of wood aboard: the piano and the butcher's block in the galley. All the fabrics, draperies, curtains and upholstery were made of fireproofed material. Chairs and bed frames were constructed of aluminum.

The First Class dining room was busy with busboys setting up for the company's executives, who always ate lunch here when the ship docked in town. Dan saw Lu Moore sitting across the dining room at a circular glass coffee table. She was in conversation with a crew member who was standing alongside her next to a square, weight-bearing post.

Brown, Sykes and Bellham, the law firm representing the *American Union,* always sent a lawyer to the ship when she docked in New York at the end of every voyage. Most trips had injuries and illnesses among passengers and crew. There might be other legal issues, too. It was good strategy to have one or more company lawyers present to handle these problems and try to resolve them before people left the ship and litigious lawyers were retained. Lu saw Dan entering the dining room and she ordered coffee and pastry after she waved him over to her table. After passing through the busy dining room, Dan greeted her:

"Hi. How's Ray?" Ray was Lu's mother, Rachel Moore.

"She's fine. I expect you to give me copies of the pictures you just took."

"You know you don't have to ask me for them. I'll give you a complete set as soon they are available." Dan said as he pointed to his 35 millimeter camera

"Who did you see in Times Square?"

"Conrad Fornalski, one of the wipers in the engine room."

"Oh, yes. We should be settling that case."

"Any time you offer me enough money."

"I'll look at it when I get back to the office and call you about it. I'm sure we can come to an agreement on that case. It's not too complicated"

Dan Nikolas and Lu Moore were "friendly enemies." They had been classmates at law school. Later on in their practices, they were thrown together as adverse counsel, Dan representing seamen and passengers and Lu defending her company-client against their claims.

Lucille Moore was an outstanding student and lawyer. She was Law Review, and graduated third in her class. After graduation she clerked in the United States Federal Court in the Eastern District of New York, in Brooklyn, for Federal Judge Amos Coombs. When she decided to enter the world of the large prestigious law firm, she had difficulty finding a position. Any man with her credentials would have had little trouble getting into a top Wall Street law firm, but not a woman. One day a friend told her a large firm was looking for a young lawyer. Maybe she should give it a try.

"They might hire a woman," her friend said. "You never know. I heard they've had trouble finding a suitable lawyer: seems like the hiring partner is looking for the perfect lawyer and having a hard time finding one."

Bradley Rogers, the partner in charge of the maritime department at Brown, Sykes and Bellham, interviewed Lu. He told her about his problem hiring someone who could work with him. He was more than pleased with Lu's qualifications.

"If I hire you, it will be to work in the maritime section. I don't know what you have planned for your career specialty, but this is the only opening in this firm. You'll have to work with me and settle personal injury claims and try cases, too. I do all the commercial and corporate work for our shipping clients. Is that a problem?"

"No sir. I was hoping to be doing corporate work and writing legal opinions. But I'm ready to work here in any capacity and learn how to become a trial lawyer."

Lu Moore would have agreed to anything in order to get into a Wall Street firm.

Bradley Rogers called Judge Coombs, whom he knew, and got a first-rate recommendation about Lu. She was pleased to be hired, even though she certainly wouldn't do corporate work and might never be asked to prepare a legal opinion. She would, however, be earning more money than a judge's law clerk, she told her mother.

Now that she finally had her foot in the door of a Wall Street firm, mother and daughter could move into a larger apartment in a better neighborhood. Lu would no longer sleep on a pull-out couch in the living room. She already had her eye on a new apartment that was small but each of them would have a bedroom. And the neighborhood, on University Place in Greenwich Village, was much more desirable.

In her third year at Brown, Sykes and Bellham, Dan and Lu met again. Dan was working with one of the firm's attorneys, when Lu passed by. She recognized her old classmate through the opened door and stopped to say hello.

"Hi, Dan. What are you doing here?"

"Lu! Hi, there. I'm trying to negotiate a settlement with one of your colleagues and he's giving me a rough time," Dan said with a laugh.

"Dan and I were in law school together, Ken. Be gentle with him," Lu told her colleague with that broad smile Dan remembered from years ago.

"Have you some time for coffee, Lu? I haven't seen you since we graduated. I have to catch up with you."

"There's a dining room for staff down the hall. When you're finished with Ken, my office is two doors down. Come in and we'll have some coffee. You're invited too, Ken."

"It's okay, Lu, I've got a brief to finish. I'll leave you two to go over old times."

As they sat in the dining room, Dan realized how lovely Lu was. At school he was too busy working and studying to really notice her, other than that she was one of only six women in a class of 97 men, and that she sat nearby. She still had that wide smile and a head of reddish, curly hair that she cut close. She had the same trim shape. Now she was obviously trying to downplay it by wearing a two-piece suit she felt was more relevant for a serious lawyer than an attractive young lady. They each filled in the gaps of their lives since they graduated law school. After they finished their coffee, Dan asked Lu to dinner and she said yes.

They became friendly. Dan and Lu would go out together as two accomplished lawyers who enjoyed each other's company. Each had similar ideas about life; each had worked hard to earn a law degree, as they came from lower middle-class families. Lu had little time for romance and Dan didn't seem to treat her as anything but a good friend. As Lu began trying cases, they enjoyed the clashes they experienced on opposite sides of a law suit.

Lu Moore confided to Dan that her goal was to become a full partner in her firm. She knew it would be difficult for a woman to break into the "Men's Club," yet she never doubted that one day she would be invited in. But Dan saw Lu differently. He saw her as someone he could be working with. She really understood the law of the sea and she was acquiring a good reputation among attorneys and judges as a trial lawyer. Even the U.S. Marshals, who patrolled the hallways of U.S. District Court Houses, respected her. Dan wanted to see her in his office. Her presence would certainly be an asset for both of them. She would probably be happier with Dan, not having to concern herself with how her image came off to some of the partners in a large, male-oriented office. At first, he never told Lu what he was thinking and it was why he saw her so often and kept up on her activities in the court room. Sometime soon, he thought, he would have to ask her to leave her firm, come into his office and eventually become his partner. And maybe even more, he thought.

After a few years, Lu's hard work was becoming rewarded. It was no secret that the partners at BSB would soon be asking her to join them. She was the best and most accomplished trial lawyer in the firm and she was good at corporate work, too. In the past year and a half, Rogers had been giving her the opportunity to write legal opinions and handle other commercial matters for the firm's steamship clients. Often, partners in other specialties asked Lu to do research or write an opinion for them. Dan, too, had attained a level of proficiency to where he was recognized as one of the better maritime lawyers in New York. Both lawyers were close to the top of their profession.

Dan walked over to Lu's table and sat down. He waited for her to sign some documents which she handed to someone who looked like a young lawyer and who immediately left them alone.

Lu pushed a rattling coffee cup over to Dan, which she then filled to the top. She knew Dan drank coffee black, without sugar.

"So, what are you looking for in the Fonseca case?" Lu asked as she stirred small amounts of milk and a package of lo-cal sugar into her coffee. "I don't see it as a big case. I did an analysis for my client the other day. Unfortunately for you, the Captain had to make decisions based on time, location, the safety of the ship and the passengers aboard. He's the one that makes the decisions. I don't know how you're going to overcome that. It's a basic problem for you."

The people at A.U. Lines were looking at the Fonseca case much more closely than any other in claim. Their Captain's decision was open to question by the plaintiff's accomplished lawyers, but their lawyers were telling them not to worry; the law favored them. Nevertheless, it was not good public relations for a prominent shipping company running "the world's most famous ship," as the executives always liked to call the *American Union*. They would have liked to see that case out of the way, resolved amicably and without a public fuss. It was annoying them. It was like the buzzing fly that persists on landing on your nose. They informed Bradley Rogers and Lu Moore that, while they felt no responsibility for the unfortunate Gaspar Fonseca, they would like this case resolved quickly and quietly, even if a relatively small amount of money had to be paid. Nuisance value, they insisted on calling it.

"Perhaps a small amount relative to the loss might settle the case. After all, Nikolas and Hoffman are pros and they certainly know and understand that at sea the captain's authority is supreme. And even if the seaman got off the ship, could he have been helped? It might have been too late to do anything for him," Jerry Keller, the head of claims at A.U. Lines, had often told Lu and Bradley Rogers.

"Did you know that my client was two months away from sitting for his Third Mate's license, Lu?" Dan said, after he blew into his cup to cool the coffee.

"No. I didn't. How awful for him. That complicates matters. But I have to be objective. It still doesn't change my thinking about the case. Captain Burn says it would have been dangerous to try to get into one of those ports on the Southern Coast of England: shallow drafts, piers that can't accommodate a ship the size of the *American Union*."

"I don't know about that. At this point, I'm not sure the Captain was so correct."

Lu ignored Dan's remark. "I don't have any authority now. I would recommend Lloyd's pay $50,000, if you would agree to take it. I might recommend that much only because your client lost a leg. And this case would be very expensive to try. You'll probably have to discuss it with your co-counsel, Jack Hoffman. What's he like? I have never met him. I'm looking forward to it."

"In my opinion, he's one of the best trial lawyers around. He's got a good mind."

"You do have a heavy gun with Hoffman, but that doesn't help your case. Even if you get past the Captain's decision, you still have some solid medical issues to overcome. What I just said was not an offer. It's only a recommendation, if you're inclined to accept. The claims people feel this case only has nuisance value."

"No. I can't even think about that number. I know that Jack won't, either. What's your personal opinion of its worth?"

"My opinion has no bearing here. It's what the claims guys think its worth. They're backing the Captain's handling of the situation, as do I. I'll tell them you're looking at it as if it were a major case to be tried."

Lu sipped her coffee then smiled the wide smile that always captivated Dan. "Call me at home tonight. There's a great movie on the West Side I want to take you to. It's one of those French *film noire*; I know you'll like it."

After returning to her office, Lu Moore called Jerry Keller at A.U. Lines. Keller was a non-practicing lawyer who had had abandoned the profession to become a claims manager. Lu filled him in on the matters she had covered that morning aboard the *American Union*. When she finished she said, "Dan Nikolas was on the ship this morning."

"What in hell was that son-of-a-bitch doing on the ship?"

"He wanted to see a client who had to sign some legal papers in one of the cases he has with us: that Fornalski case that happened in the engine room. We should close that one out. It's an easy one and we owe the money. The accident was our fault. He also took some pictures of the deck for the Fonseca case. I spoke to him about the case."

"Hell, I don't remember you telling me he asked us for any Court permission to make discovery of the deck area."

"He didn't, but I let him take them anyway. You know he'll get the right to do it. So why waste time and spend your money fighting him when you know any court will order us to let him have the discovery he needs?"

"Well, screw that bastard and that son-of-a-bitch Hoffman he's working with. Let them sweat for everything they get. That prick Nikolas has a lot of cases with us and I have been noticing that you and he are very cozy."

Keller liked treating Lu as if she were a man. He enjoyed using foul language whenever they spoke over the phone. He thought it made her uneasy. And he erroneously felt he could intimidate her that way. Lu ignored his language, which often angered Keller, since no matter how he tried he was unable to manipulate her.

"I hope you aren't insinuating what I'm thinking," Lu said icily into the receiver. "He is an old friend. We both represent our clients and that is where our friendship ends. He wouldn't give me an inch on a case. And I certainly wouldn't give him one, either."

"Okay, okay. Cool down. So what did you discuss about Fonseca?"

"I was prodding him to see if he would settle the case. I wanted to understand what he was thinking."

"How did you do that?"

"I asked him what he thought about $50,000 for the case if I could convince you to give it to me."

"See what I mean? You don't have any authority to offer that prick or anyone else any money at all on that case."

"Slow down. I didn't offer him a dime. I told him I would recommend $50,000 if he would accept it. He turned me down anyway. At least we know he's looking at this one as a biggie. It's almost certain we'll have to prepare it for trial. I've tried to get rid of this case because you've been telling me and Rogers that you really want to see it closed. So I have been trying my best to do that for you."

"Well, watch your step with that son-of-a-bitch, Nikolas. He's a slippery bastard. As far as I'm concerned, and I include some of the people in your office with the same thinking, Nikolas is not someone you should be friendly with."

6

TETERBORO AIRPORT
NEW JERSEY

As Dan Nikolas was setting enlargements of the photos he had taken of the promenade deck of the *American Union*, atop a large oak table in his conference room, two young lawyers who worked for him walked in. Charley Becker and Drew Sloan slowly strolled around the table, as if they were inspecting the merchandise offered on a table at a flea market. They both looked carefully at the shots for several minutes, lifting them for better views and then setting them down. They made no comments.

"Did you each have a good look?" Dan asked his colleagues. They each nodded affirmatively.

"Good, then let's talk about Fonseca. We have some important issues to investigate in this case. First, we have to figure out how they might have gotten Fonseca safely off the ship. Then we have to concern ourselves about our experts. There's Dr. Sean Welles, a neuro-surgeon who will work with Jack Hoffman. Charley, you'll accompany Jack. You need to learn all you can about arterial blocks and learn what Dr. Wells will testify to at trial on that subject. Jack tells me the doctor served in the Korean War with a combat unit, and will testify to the speed that is necessary when there is a cut-off of the blood supply to a limb.

"Second, we have Professor Martin Stein, who'll testify about the economic loss our man suffered and will suffer in the future. Drew, you and I will work with him."

Drew Sloan coughed to get Dan's attention.

"Excuse the interruption, Dan. About those photographs," he pointed to the top of the table. "Are you thinking that Fonseca could have gotten off the ship with a helicopter? If so, how do we go about proving that?"

"Yes, I am. And I was getting to the proof. You will follow it up. Find out all you can to see if it was possible to make a helicopter airlift. Go and find us a helicopter pilot. Take a set of these pictures with you. Here is a list of questions I prepared for a helicopter pilot. See what you can get from him and if he'll come to court and act as our expert," Dan said as he pushed a folder filled with photographs and questions across the table in Sloan's direction.

"I want each of us to start reading the latest cases on a captain's legal obligation to deviate from his course in the case of a medical emergency. Then we all will write succinct memos and put our heads together to figure out how the company failed to act properly. The idea, of course, is to hit them with liability. When we're finished preparing this case, I want each of us to be ready to try it on the maritime issues alone, if it should come to that in an emergency. Jack Hoffman will be responsible for the medical part of the case. You two will be sitting at trial with Jack and me, taking notes that may be used on cross examination."

৯০ ৵

Drew Sloan drove his yellow Plymouth convertible to Teterboro Airport, 12 miles west of Manhattan, along the flat tableland of the marshy New Jersey Meadowlands. He was familiar with the small airport and knew it was not used for large commercial aviation. Sloan often passed Teterboro when he sought alternative driving routes on his way between Manhattan and his home in New Jersey. He did some research and learned that Teterboro's runways were not constructed to accommodate the heavy jets that landed at La Guardia, Kennedy or Newark airports. Teterboro was home base for private planes, smaller corporate jets, local charters and Air Taxis. And he learned it was also home to Whirlybird Aviation, a helicopter company that flew executives to and from Newark, La Guardia, Kennedy and to local factories and businesses in the area. Sloan left the office before noon to get to the airport.

As he drove onto the grounds, Sloan noted a Twin Beech, its two propellers roaring as it sat on the runway, its wings vibrating, awaiting permission for takeoff. Across the body of the fuselage was inscribed a company name and logo. He parked his car and walked to the wooden control tower located at the northwest corner of a hangar with ALL AVIATION painted across it. He saw a janitor by the door and asked for directions to Whirlybird Aviation.

"You go out the way you came in, then make the first right. You go about two or three hundred yards. On your right, that's where you'll find Whirlybird," the man explained, pointing the handle of his broom in the direction he was sending Sloan.

Sloan had seen Whirlybird listed in the Yellow Pages and decided Teterboro, a low-key airport, would be a good place to start on his mission to find a helpful helicopter pilot. He planned to arrive unannounced for an informal chat with one of Whirlybird's pilots. Maybe even retain him as an expert for the plaintiff.

Sloan followed the janitor's instructions until he saw a bright red hangar, looking like a barn, with its name painted on it in black letters: WHIRLYBIRD AVIATION INC. Next to the hangar in an open field, three helicopters were parked neatly alongside one another, their rotor blades looking like the ribs of naked umbrellas. A fourth helicopter was rising, like an elevator, into a bright blue and cloudless sky.

After requesting to see the manager, stating that he might want to hire a helicopter, he was ushered into a utilitarian office, its walls filled with glossy black and white photos of various models of helicopters. He introduced himself to Jim Garrett, the company's manager, who looked more like a cow-poke than a pilot. He had a weather-lined face and curly blonde hair tumbling down to his shoulders. Garrett wore a cowboy's shirt with pearl colored snap buttons and two slits for pockets on either side of his chest. The pants of his jeans were stuffed neatly into a pair of dark brown alligator boots that rose to just below his calves.

"What can I do for you?" Garrett asked with a friendly smile.

Sloan explained Fonseca's case and that he was trying to determine if a helicopter could have taken Gaspar Fonseca off the *American Union*. He also advised Garrett that he was looking for an expert witness for the case.

"Wish you would'a called me before you came here, fella," Garrett explained in a deep and pleasant Southwestern accent. "I regularly testify for a passel of insurance companies on helicopter accident cases. They certainly wouldn't take kindly to me testifying for a plaintiff."

Garrett paused, pulling on his right ear lobe. He looked directly into Sloan's eyes and said, "Tell you what. You say this fella of yours lost a leg?"

"Yes, and he's a young guy, around 30. He lost his leg two months before he was going to take a test to qualify as a ship's officer. If you can't help me, maybe you can refer me elsewhere."

"Shame. I know a lot about that stuff. It's the lack of blood supply, you know. I was a Warrant Officer flying 'copters in Nam. I know how important it is to get wounded soldiers to a hospital as fast as possible. We were a specially trained crew. I flew the 'copter. One of the men went down to pick up a wounded fella and we had a medic to help out once we got the fella into the ship. If we didn't get the wounded guys to a medical unit real fast, some of them would lose arms and legs, maybe even their lives. A very important job we had.

"Once in a while I took some real risks in order to get to a hospital on time to save some G.I. Yeah. Time, she's a real son-of-a-bitch. You're always fighting her, and you don't always win the damned race. I know what your sailor boy was facing. It's a danged rotten thing. Tell you what, I'm gonna give you some hints. I can't let a fella who lost his leg go without some help. Whatever I tell you, it ain't stuff you learned from me. Agreed?"

"Of course."

"What'cha got in that envelope you're holding? Pictures of the ship?"

"Yes, I do. Here's the lot for you to look at. They were taken about a month ago. I think it's a good representation of what the deck was like at the time our man needed to get off the ship."

Garrett looked at the photographs of the promenade deck. After a few minutes he glanced at his wrist watch.

"Tell you what counselor; let's go get us a hamburger, some fries and a Coke. It's lunch time and I'm taking you to the best hamburger joint for miles around."

Garrett rose from his desk, standing six-feet two inches, and shouted into his waiting room. "Emma, me and the counselor here, we're going to Clancy's for some grub. I'll be back in a couple of hours or so."

Sam Garrett put on a pearl grey Stetson, a pilot's dark and stylish sunglasses, and a worn leather jacket. He ushered Drew Sloan out the door.

Garrett was right about Clancy's. It seemed to Sloan as if everyone from the airport ate here. The dining room was filled with customers. A couple of dozen airplane models hung from the ceiling on invisible wires. There were World War I bi-planes and propeller-powered passenger planes, World War II fighters and bombers and a host of sleek modern jets, all of them swinging in the wind whenever a door opened. Clancy's catered to Teterboro's working men and women. Sloan saw mechanics with the names of their companies sewn on the backs of their greasy coveralls; pilots in crisp sky-blue shirts, black ties and military-style insignia bars on their shoulders; secretaries, some in slacks; and airline executives in suits and ties who filled out the busy and noisy crowd.

"Let me see them pictures, again," Garrett said after they were seated and gave their order to the waitress, who greeted Garrett as a regular diner. Garrett pored over the copies once more, spending more time with some than with others. He put a finger on the foredeck and swept his hand across others. On one photo, he tried getting a top-down view but that was impossible.

"Looks to me like there are at least two spots where you could use a helicopter to get your guy off that ship. That's on the stern and then this here other one on the bow. You see where those deck chairs are located on the bow? That's a good spot."

Garrett placed a finger on the area, then set that photo on his lap. He moved to another photograph, looked at it silently for a while, as Sloan waited for some information he hoped would be useful in the Fonseca case.

"That there is another area here on the stern which also seems to be available. But there are two problems I see that should easily be resolved."

"What's that?" Sloan asked as he bit into a juicy hamburger that had just been brought to the table.

"As I said, it looks as if I could hover with a 'copter over there, either on the bow or the stern. But these here photographs are side views, so I really don't know what my exact space is. Aside from that, I see a whole slew of wires, radio, radar, guide wires and such. And some other stuff there I'm not familiar with. Never seen 'em before. They would have to come down before I could put a 'copter above the deck. You have to find out what could come down and how long it takes to remove the lot.

"I gotta' make it clear to you. I ain't setting my 'copter on the deck. That's too dangerous. I'm gonna' hover over the deck, like a humming bird, low enough to lift a sick man up into the 'copter. You get me, counselor?"

"Yes, I do. So what else needs to be done?"

"You definitely need a deck plan for the ship. You need to have the exact dimensions of the area where you propose a pick-up. You know, you'll need the ship's beam and the length, fore and aft, of this particular area. Can I mark up this photo?"

"Go ahead, Jim. I have more of them."

Garrett drew a pen from his shirt pocket and made a large circle on the picture.

"As I said, you have to determine if those wires and such could be removed. Then, and this is very important, you'll need to find out from the Brit Air-Sea Rescue unit if a helicopter could get to your ship from their base and then back to a hospital. That's a matter of distances and helicopter fuel capacity. I can't tell you that without examining ship's speed and location and the kind'a copter the Brits were using. You're gonna' need those things. Obviously, I can't do that for you.

"I remember there is a helicopter base on the Channel at Culdrose, near Plymouth. I used to keep up on those things when I flew in Nam, because I wanted to know what other rescue pilots were up to, mebee even learn a few things I could use in my rescue missions, you know."

Garrett picked up the photo sitting on his lap and drew a large circle on that one as well, simultaneously swigging his Coke directly from the can.

"We know about that base and we're trying to get that stuff," Sloan advised Garrett.

"That's good. But I wouldn't use an American helicopter pilot as my expert. You should get one of them Limey guys. The company's lawyers would have a difficult time on cross examination overturning his opinions. The Limeys do that recue work all the time. They know what can and can't be done."

"I really appreciate your ideas and your help, Jim. I have to thank you for the orientation. We hadn't thought about an English helicopter pilot. I'll certainly look into it."

"Will you be able to get a deck plan?"

"Sure. I already have the ship's log. The deck plan shouldn't be a problem. When I get back to my office, I'll do the necessary paper work to ask for them."

"I can't emphasize how important them dimensions are. You'll need that ship's log you say you already got, because it lets you know where the ship was in relation to the rescue base and how fast she was moving. Maybe, you'll discover that an Air-Sea rescue couldn't be made."

"Why is that?"

"The ship might have been past the 'copter's range. They might only have a 250 to 300 mile range. And then there's the issue of fuel capacity. That's about all I can do for you, young fella. I hope it helps your client win his case and gets him back into society. I seen a lot of GI's feeling sorry for themselves after they lose a limb. It's like the end of the world for some of them. It takes time to get out of their depression and accept their loss.

"And don't try paying for the grub or sending me a fee," Jim Garrett said with a broad grin as he shoved his hand into his pocket to pay the bill, "because it will look as if you tried to bribe me and I was stupid enough to accept."

7

OFFICES OF BROWN, SYKES AND BELLHAM
WALL STREET

Bradley Rogers' secretary called Lu Moore over the office intercom, requesting that she come to Rogers' office. It was actually more in the nature of an order than a request. The prestigious law firm of Brown, Sykes and Bellham occupied the top three floors of a 42-story Wall Street office building. Lu left her office and took the special elevator, which ran only three floors directly to the penthouse, where all the senior partners were based.

There were many more and larger windows on this floor than on the two below. Each penthouse office window offered splendid views of New York City. The elevator itself opened on to a circular lobby and a large window looking south to New York harbor, where Lu could see the Statue of Liberty and Staten Island. From the west side of this floor she could see the Hudson River and New Jersey. The eastern view captured the Brooklyn Bridge, the East River and Long Island. There was the north view to Upper Manhattan, the George Washington Bridge and the New Jersey Palisades, a natural stone wall that plunged vertically into the Hudson River. The view was a not-too-subtle expression of the power and importance this law firm enjoyed, and of its partners who had attained the good fortune in their professional lives to reach this floor.

This was what Lu had been working for; the pinnacle of her ambitions. Although being a woman had been a handicap, she knew she was now close to breaking into the exclusive Men's

Club. It was what women activists, who were clamoring for more equality, were calling "breaking the glass ceiling." Recently, hints had been dropped around the office that the men on this floor liked Lu's work. They were thinking that at some time in the very near future she might have her own office with her own vista and get to sit up here with them at this position of influence and power.

Lu walked into Bradley Rogers' office accompanied by his secretary. Rogers owned a Brooklyn Bridge view. He rose from his desk and greeted Lu with a broad smile and a friendly handshake. It helped remove the taste of the order Rogers' secretary had made earlier over the phone.

"Good morning, Lucille. Thank you for coming up. Take a seat. Want some coffee? Mrs. Stacey, bring us some coffee please." Rogers returned to his desk and there was a moment of awkward silence until Mrs. Stacey left the room and closed the office door to maintain privacy.

"Keeping busy are you, Lucille?" Rogers was circling around the purpose of this meeting.

"Yes, sir, there's always work to do."

"I know. And you must know I appreciate your dedication and loyalty to the firm and, of course, your talents as a lawyer. You have exceeded my expectations of what you would accomplish in this firm when I hired you"

What's this leading to? Lu thought.

Rogers coughed when he needn't have.

"I received a call last night from Jerry Keller of A.U. Lines. He's a bit disturbed. Mind you, I don't give too much credence to his insinuations, but I can't afford to ignore them. That's what I'm trying to resolve here. After all, A.U. Lines is one of our most important shipping clients. They have 18 cargo ships and, of course, the *S.S. American Union.*"

"Excuse me sir, it's 21."

"Twenty-one what?"

"Twenty-one cargo ships." Lu hated to correct her boss but she had this nagging feeling that somehow she was being tested.

"Ah," Rogers said with a smile. "I hadn't realized they had so many; all the more reason to keep them happy, don't you agree Lucille? And I appreciate having someone working with me who is aware of everything that goes on around the office. It's especially good to know that under me, you are our leading maritime associate working on that account."

Bradley Rogers didn't wait for an answer.

"Keller seems concerned about your relationship with Dan Nikolas. He has a lot of cases with us, this Nikolas, isn't that so?"

Rogers knew Dan had many cases with the firm. He was the senior partner on all the maritime cases and had dealt with Dan directly on many occasions especially when Lu was out of the office on a trial or on vacation.

Maybe he's trying to emphasize the relationship, Lu thought.

"What about Nikolas? He does have a lot of cases with us."

"You tell me. I understand that he's a friend."

"Yes, he is. I've known him since law school. And he has many cases against all the shipping companies, including A.U. Lines which we represent, and he also has cases against many companies we don't represent."

Rogers shuffled in his seat, coughed once more. His face turned red.

"I'm sorry to be asking this and please don't misunderstand me; I have to ask you. Is your friendship romantic? If so, might your friendship be a conflict of interest?" Rogers asked with an uncharacteristic tone and speed, almost as if he was asking Lu a question regarding a bodily function.

Lu wanted to scream. Rogers had no right to ask these questions. But she remained silent for a moment. After all, she was only an associate in this law firm and on her way to becoming a partner. She didn't want to muck that up. So she answered calmly and in a soft voice.

"No sir, I wouldn't say we're romantic. We go out together from time to time: dinner, sometimes a movie or a Broadway show. Mr. Rogers. I believe you are entering into my private life, which has nothing to do with my position in this office.

Respectfully, I don't believe you have the right to ask me these questions. And I view this as a possible form of harassment."

"Don't misunderstand me, Lucille. I don't wish to invade your privacy or harass you. I want you to understand that I am the last person in this office who would intrude into your private life. I'm just trying to figure out if there's a conflict arising from your relationship with this man. As the head of this section, this nasty job has fallen on my shoulders. I have to resolve this situation which has been put squarely before me so that I can go back to my partners and satisfy them that we have no fears of a conflict of interest."

"I don't see that there's a conflict, if that's what you are implying. I have never allowed him any advantages on any cases we have together based on our friendship and I never will. Nor has he ever asked me to do something out of the ordinary because we are friends. Actually, because we are friends, we trust each other to tell the truth and accept what we tell each other when we are discussing settlements. So far, I have never been disappointed with that arrangement. It has worked out quite well, as far as I am concerned. That saves both of us a lot of time and money and I move cases with him on this basis. Yesterday, I told him I might recommend a certain figure on a case, if he were willing to settle it now. He told me he wasn't interested. I didn't banter with him any further because I knew he was telling me the truth. As a result, I'm getting that case ready for trial."

"Which case is that?"

"Gaspar Fonseca, an AB on the *American Union*."

"Yes, yes, I remember, the seaman who lost a leg. What was your suggestion to Nikolas?"

"Fifty-thousand."

"That's a good number. I might have also suggested it. We are being pressured to settle it, you know. What was the reaction to your suggestion?"

"He wasn't interested."

"Did he try to negotiate for more money?"

"No. And you are surely aware, sir, that some lawyers think they are buying rugs at a bazaar when negotiating with us. They tirelessly bargain back and forth. It's wasteful and for me, frankly degrading. Often makes us do more work than is necessary. With Dan, there's no haggling, no wasting of my important time. I never offer him money I don't have. If he rejects my suggestion, as he did yesterday, unless he tells me what would positively settle the claim, I don't spend any more time on settlement talks. If he does give a number and I feel what he wants is fair, I try to get it for him. If not, I tell him I can't. I won't pursue it any further and I tell him that we should get ready to try the case. I find these negotiations the most efficient and pleasant I deal with. "

Lu took a deep breath before she continued. "I'd like to work with all lawyers in the same way but, unfortunately, it's not so. No one at A.U. Lines or any insurance carrier we deal with has ever complained to me that I'm giving Dan Nikolas too much money on any case."

"No. You're right about that. I have had no complaints about your settlements in the time you've been here. How long have you been here with us, Lucille? Five years?"

"Six years, sir."

"Six. I can't believe it. In those years you have behaved in an exemplary manner. In my opinion, you are the best associate in the office and undoubtedly our best trial lawyer. It seems to me as if Jerry Keller is complaining about nothing. Yet he is a client. We can't afford to forget that."

"I've had this same conversation with him on several occasions. In fact, we had one just yesterday. He seems to feel I'm treating Nikolas differently than other plaintiff's lawyers."

"Yes, he complained that you let Nikolas aboard the *American Union* yesterday to see a client and take photographs without a discovery request from him."

"He's not the only lawyer that comes aboard our ships. Almost any lawyer that has a case with us comes on our ships to get their clients to sign documents or conduct other business like signing settlement releases or affidavits needed during a case. Nikolas was going to see a client who probably didn't have time to get to his office because the man wanted to spend the short time he had in port to be with his family. That's true of other plaintiff's lawyers who also come aboard for the same reasons. We recognize that and allow it. When I'm on duty, I always make sure the lawyers are accompanied by one of our officers, as I did yesterday with Nikolas. I've told every lawyer who works in our section to do the same when I'm not there."

"Maybe we should stop that."

"That's company policy. It has nothing to do with me. A lawyer who represents a seaman should have access to his client. Otherwise it delays the movement of the cases. I can't see the company preventing that. If you cut them off, it's almost certain you'll hear from the Seaman's Union about it. Big Sam Cassidy will be all over you in a minute. You're inviting trouble."

Big Sam Cassidy was the president of the American Seaman's Union. Cassidy was always ready to take on the shipping companies, to the delight of his union members.

"I know that most courts will make sure seamen's lawyers have reasonable access to their clients. Some judges favor seamen and their rights over other plaintiffs who sue in the courts."

"I understand. Yes, and sometimes it puts those of us defending the shipping companies at a disadvantage."

"It's supposed to do that. It's part of the social legislation Congress enacted to protect seamen. We who represent the companies may not like it, but it's something we all have to live with."

"What about the pictures? Keller tells me that he took pictures and that he had no permission to take them."

"I could have prevented him from taking them. But as I told Keller, ultimately he has the right. All he had to do was make a demand on us to allow it. You certainly wouldn't consider fighting him. The Court would order us to let him on. It's just a matter of saving time, money and eliminating needless paperwork."

"Lucille, we are not in the business of making life easy for adverse counsel. By making him work for everything he is entitled to, we increase our billing hours."

Lu was silent. She would not comment on Rogers' last remark.

At that moment, Mrs. Stacey knocked on the door and was admitted by her boss' command to enter. She carried a highly polished and bright silver tray with a gleaming silver coffee pot surrounded by two china coffee cups on saucers. They were fashioned by Spode. It was another of this law firm's careful attempts to create an image of elegance in everything it did. She poured coffee into two cups, remained silent, waiting for an order. She saw Rogers nodding for her to leave and quickly left the room, closing the door behind her.

"How many cases do we have with this Nikolas fellow? Rogers asked.

"I don't know exactly."

"I would like you to get me an exact number, the names of the cases and their current status. I want to know if they are in the court, if we have trial dates. You know, a full status report. Does he have cases with other companies that we represent?"

"Well, sure. He's a well-known maritime lawyer. He's popular with the seamen. He sailed with many of them while he was at school. So he knows ships, and they remember he was once one of them.

"I can't say for sure how many cases he has. I wouldn't be surprised if he has between 250 to 300. Not all of them with us, certainly. He has a few lawyers working for him, so those numbers are probable, maybe even more. I never thought to ask him how many active cases he has."

"All right, Lu. Get me that list of what he has with this office. That should include all the companies we represent. And I think perhaps you should be considering your future relationship with Nikolas."

"Are you suggesting that I end our friendship?"

"That's up to you. Only you know what's best for you and your career."

Rogers swept his hand across his room, stopping at his window. The Brooklyn Bridge was below and a tug towing an oil barge was cutting a triangular path with its wake of creamy white waves across a shimmering East River. In this law firm only the privileged could aspire to that scene. Lu was beginning to feel, and it was not for the first time, that Bradley Rogers was protecting her. She asked herself: "Why?"

8

THE BRONX

Sitting in Dan's office, Drew Sloan explained what he had learned during his meeting with Sam Garrett at Teterboro's Whirlybird Aviation.

"This guy, Garrett, told me it's very important for us to get the dimensions of the area a helicopter pilot has to fly over with his craft. He also says we need the ship's log, which we already have, and a deck plan, which we don't have as yet. He emphasized that it would be best to use an English helicopter pilot who does Air-Sea Rescues in the Channel to testify at trial, instead of an American pilot. Garrett felt that a British pilot would be more authoritative."

Dan said, "That sounds logical. Prepare a Request for Discovery to make A.U. Lines produce the deck plans for the *American Union*. I want to see them as soon as they come in. Then get on the phone with the British Embassy in Washington. Talk to the military attaché and find out what we have to do to interview one of their English Navy helicopter pilots and maybe even bring him here to testify. Find out everything about the process, costs, everything."

"I'll do it right away."

᧔ ᧙

Law firms that regularly litigate cases begin preparing them for trial as soon as a retainer is signed. They locate witnesses, take pre-trial testimony and perform all necessary Discovery as if every case is destined for the trial court. In fact, less than five-per-cent of all law suits filed in American courts ever go to trial. But no meaningful settlement can ever be arrived at without amassing all the necessary facts that eventually must be revealed at a trial. The give and take in settlement discussions always recognizes that, in court, each side has its pluses and minuses. During negotiations, attorneys may feel they do not care to leave a particular case for a jury to decide. By settling a claim, lawyers can control its outcome. Leaving a jury to determine a verdict and the amount of damages is always chancy. At the end of an exhausting trial, it is the jury who tells the lawyers which side has to pay damages or has to walk away without any recovery at all.

Every trial lawyer weighs the risks of a trial, because at some time during his career he has probably lost cases he should have won and prevailed when he should have lost. Sometimes it's better to talk it out and walk away with money - as in that trite expression, "A bird in the hand is worth two in the bush." But sometimes, even after all the long, hard sessions and good faith negotiations, the parties have no choice but to resolve their issues in court.

Dan Nikolas and Jack Hoffman know Gaspar Fonseca's case is one of the five percent, because A.U. Lines has aggressively expounded two excellent defenses. Dan is faced with the first and timeless defense: the Captain always has control of his ship. This is why he is known by his other name on commercial vessels: Master. He not only controls the movement of his vessel but he decides the fate of everyone aboard her. Opposing the second defense is in the competent hands of Jack Hoffman. The defendant will ask the jury: Would there have been enough time to save Gaspar Fonseca's leg, even if he had been brought to a medical facility in Devonshire?

In order to win his part of the case, Dan Nikolas must prove to the jury one of three things: that Captain Burn's decision not to land Gaspar Fonseca was based on misinformation as to his ship's physical position, or that he was wrong as to what he understood he could or could not do to help Gaspar or, finally, that Captain

Burn meant, in a callous and improper manner, to continue his ship onward, even though he knew he could have safely and timely landed a seriously ill seaman ashore. Proving any of these would cast Captain Burn guilty of failing to provide Gaspar Fonseca with the necessary medical treatment a ship owner owes his seamen.

Jack Hoffman, on the other hand, has the job of determining the stage of Gaspar's embolism, and then proving it was early enough that it could have been properly treated if he was taken off the ship in a timely fashion. That would be a tough task, one that Jack did not seem to be too concerned about. Jack Hoffman was all confidence, as he always was when assuming the responsibility of taking on a client and fighting to win his case.

The ship owner, of course, takes opposite positions: the Captain's decision was correct. And, even if the Captain had gotten Gaspar to a facility, it would have been too late to save his leg. Thus, diverting the ship would have been a useless and even a potentially dangerous act on Captain Burn's part. This is why the ship's log becomes a crucial piece of evidence for each side. Dan will use it to track the vessel and try to show a rescue would have been safe and timely. The company will use its log to show Captain Burn was helpless to assist Gaspar Fonseca because of the ship's location at the time of his distress.

Fortunately for Gaspar Fonseca, civil cases differ greatly from criminal cases, with respect to the burden of proof necessary to present a case to a jury and win at trial. Criminal cases require that a jury may only convict a defendant if it determines guilt beyond a reasonable doubt, a very high burden of proof. In civil trials, however, as Dan always tells jurors in his opening remarks, "You need only find the weight of evidence is just slightly greater for one party against the other."

As he explains this important legal principal to the panel, he extends two cupped hands before him, pretending they are the scales of justice. He thrusts them out to the jury. He holds one hand just a slightly bit higher above the other as he tells them:

"There you are, ladies and gentlemen, just a slight amount of proof is all you are going to need to find for my client when you go into the jury room to deliberate the issues in this case."

Aside from all the necessary legal work to insure that this case gets into court and before a jury, Dan and Jack must paint a sympathetic picture of their injured client. The jurors do not know Gaspar Fonseca or the members of his family; he is someone they have never met, an unknown quantity who is asking them to dispense justice in his favor. In his case, Dan will tell the jurors, justice means an award of a large sum of money to compensate Gaspar Fonseca for the terrible loss he has suffered. So Dan and Jack must present sympathetic snapshots of their client to the jurors as a flesh and blood supplicant; a helpless victim who has suffered grave loss at the hands of his employer. Through his attorneys, Gaspar Fonseca requests the jury to render a favorable judgment to make up for the loss he must live with for the rest of his life.

In this case, a jury may only dispense justice with money. No jury can restore a lost limb or a lost life. Money alone is what will compensate Gaspar Fonseca, not only for his lost leg but for his loss of past earnings and those he cannot earn in the future. Jurors must also consider in their verdict, should they find for Gaspar, an abstract amount called in legal terms, Pain and Suffering. They will award this amount only if they find the company guilty of negligence. If they believe, in their good judgment based upon the facts presented to them during trial, that Gaspar has suffered this physical pain and suffering, then they may determine its sum and include it in their award.

To help the jury translate Pain and Suffering into dollars and cents, Gaspar must appear as a sympathetic human being whose life has been substantially altered and dramatically shattered because of the defendant's negligence. It is this loss of his quality of life that the jury must be made to understand. In his closing argument, Dan will tell the men and woman who are deciding this case that, "Unfortunately, you as jurors cannot restore my client's leg. You can only compensate him for this loss with money. And only you, not the lawyers, not even the Court, can determine what that amount should be."

In the courtroom, neither Dan nor Jack will call their client 'Mr. Fonseca.' They will address him always as 'Gaspar'. But his lawyers will take special care to address him this way with dignity and not in a condescending manner.

Dan learned early in his career that if he could not understand a client's personal pain and reactions to a serious injury, it would be impossible for him to convey them to a jury. So, on an unusually warm Sunday morning in November, Dan Nikolas drove north of Manhattan, up the East River Drive to the East Bronx, where he would meet with Gaspar Fonseca, his wife Mira, their five year old son Ronny, and Gaspar's widowed mother and two younger brothers. It was more than six months after the loss of Gaspar's leg and Dan was hoping to be able to get a firm idea as to how he was adjusting to the loss.

The Fonseca family lived in the North East Bronx, south of Pelham Parkway, a wide, grass-lined avenue with well maintained, middle-class apartment houses and private homes. The Fonsecas rented one of two apartments on the bottom floor of a neat, brick-constructed two-story garden apartment house near Morris Park Avenue. A sturdy wooden ramp had been constructed covering one half of the wide three-step stairway leading from the sidewalk to the Fonseca apartment's entrance. Gaspar was still having difficulty with the healing of his wound, so he continued to need crutches and a wheel chair until an artificial leg could be permanently fitted for him.

Today, Dan would accompany Gaspar, Mira and Ronny to church. Mira Fonseca is an attractive woman, three years younger than Gaspar. She is a slim, petite woman with dusky colored skin, raven-colored hair and large ebony eyes. After a quick cup of strong, inky black Puerto Rican coffee laced with hot milk and a sweetener, accompanied with some buttered toast in the apartment's cheerful kitchen, everyone piled into the family car. Mira drove the six streets to church for an early mass. Once, before his loss, Gaspar and his family would have walked leisurely to their church on a warm and pleasant day such as this one. Dan observed Gaspar closely and noted he was managing his crutches only somewhat better than on his first visit to his office several months earlier.

"He makes every effort to do things without help," Mira said softly with a half-hearted smile. She looked around, making sure her husband was out of earshot. "When he goes out into the street he has problems. I have to wheel him down the ramp and he tries not to recognize his friends. He doesn't want them to see him on the street like this. Sometimes he tells me he's only half a man. I die when I hear that from him, Mr. Nikolas."

After Mass, Dan spoke with the parish priest in his office. "Gaspar is a loss to us," lamented Father Marino. "When he used to come home on vacations, I always counted on him to help coach the boys on the baseball and football teams. They love him and enjoyed the stories he told them about what it's like to be a sailor. He did a handyman's work for me, like painting the office or replacing a window pane. Stuff like that, you know. Then, after he would finish he would always smile and say, 'I'm pleased to do this for you and the church, Father.' Now when he comes to church he just sits and sulks. I try to understand how he feels. We must do something for this good man."

When they returned to the Fonseca home, Gaspar told Dan, "My mother and brothers will be here for lunch. They want to meet you."

"And I want to meet your family, Gaspar. That's one of the reasons I'm here today. Tell me as much as you can about yourself and your family before and after your accident, while we wait for them to arrive."

"Well, Mr. Nikolas, I always wanted to go to sea, you know. I graduated from Maritime Trades High School, in Manhattan."

Gaspar pointed proudly to his diploma. It was framed under glass, hanging outside the living room in the narrow hallway leading to his bedroom in the rear of the apartment. "I am the oldest of my brothers. I had to help out after our father died, so, I enlisted in the Navy and served on deck. After three years I knew I could never become an officer, so I decided to sail in the merchant navy. In my last year in the U.S. Navy, Mira and I got married. We knew each other from church. Five years ago, we had Ronny. Now all I think about is what will never happen; I mean becoming an officer, having another child or getting our own home."

"How long had you been studying for your Third Mate's license?"

"Almost three years. You sailed, you know how hard it is to work at sea; you drop into your bunk tired after a long day. But then I studied. And I was finally there. Just two months away from sitting for my Third Mate's exam. Then this shit." Gaspar's voice trailed off as he looked to the side of his body with the missing limb.

"I try not to feel sorry for myself, but it's hard. I guess it'll be better when I get a new leg and I get used to this situation. But I'll tell you, it is very hard sitting around all day having people wheel you around and doing things for you that you used to be able to do for yourself." He slammed an open palm across one of his crutches.

"It's only temporary, Gaspar, you'll be up and around soon with a new leg. Others have lost their legs and they have made a new life for themselves." Dan observed with encouragement.

"I don't know, Mr. Nikolas. I can't do anything but be a seaman. How can I do that without a leg?"

"You'll go back to school and learn a new profession. Maybe you'll work for a steamship company in the office, or like a Port Captain. I expect to get you enough money so that you can go back to school to learn some new things without worrying about how you'll support yourself."

After a while the doorbell rang and Dan heard voices; a woman and some men. Mira escorted them into the living room.

"Momma, this is one of our lawyers, Mr. Nikolas. Momma doesn't speak English too well," Mira explained apologetically.

"That's okay. I speak Spanish. *Con mucho gusto, senora Fonseca,*" Dan greeted Mrs. Fonseca, taking her hand. She was obviously delighted with this courteous Spanish-speaking Anglo.

"And these are Gaspar's younger brothers," Mira continued: "Miguel, we call him Mike. And Roberto, he's Bobby."

The men shook hands and everyone found seats in the living room. For a few moments there was an uncomfortable silence. Then Mike said, "I'm a carpenter. I put that ramp up, the one on the steps, for Gas. As soon as he gets a new leg, I'm gonna' rip that mother out. Then he'll walk down them steps like nothing ever happened. Right, Gas?"

Mike patted his oldest brother on the back of the neck. Gaspar didn't react; not a laugh, not a smile. Bobby made a fist which he shook above his head.

"Yesiree, right on," Bobby shouted enthusiastically. Finally, Gaspar smiled, but mostly because he thought that he was expected to.

Senora Fonseca went into the kitchen to prepare the lunch she had brought with her. She had cooked the food at home and brought it in large ceramic pots, which her sons carried. After reheating and adding some extra touches like spices and more sauce, she doled out the Latino favorites of steaming rice, gleaming yellow from an infusion of saffron, and small, pearly black beans peeking up throughout the plates. They leaned against baked chicken breasts and legs. At the corner of each plate were fried plantains, called *tostones*, round and firm and sizzling hot and there were shiny-yellow *amarillos*, sweet and tasty. Savory garlic enhanced the food. For dessert there was the favorite, *flan de coco* - coconut flan. They ate on a table that Mira opened up in the living room to accommodate all of them. Little was said as they ate the meal, except to compliment momma Fonseca on her cooking.

Dan spent the whole day with the family, learning what life with the Fonsecas was like before Gaspar's leg was taken from him. Dan discovered that Gaspar was a generous man who, with his brothers, made sure his widowed mother was comfortable in her own apartment.

The brothers had played touch football and softball with the men of the neighborhood. They loved to go fishing at City Island, a nautical community only a few miles drive from this apartment. The three brothers would bring home fish they caught, to be crisply fried, whole, with plenty of garlic in olive oil, with the head and eyes looking up at the diners. Creole style.

Bobby, the youngest, was in his third year at college. Gaspar had been helping with tuition and books. Now Bobby told Dan in a whisper he was wondering if he could continue. He had already transferred to night school in order to work during the day. The loss of Gaspar Fonseca's leg was a heavy stone thrown into a pond; its ripples widening much past the center.

Dan kept careful records of everything he learned; they would be transcribed into a folder and used by Gaspar's expert witnesses. Dan would be meeting again with Gaspar's family. On his second visit he would come with Jack Hoffman, who would focus on the psychological comparisons between Gaspar's personality before and after the incident. Jack would inspect the family closely to determine which among them were the most articulate, as he would be using one or all of them as witnesses during the trial. Jack Hoffman would make sure he got detailed comparisons of Gaspar's personality before and after the loss of his leg.

"Maybe we'll use all that information and maybe not," Jack explained to Dan, "You never know in this business. But we've certainly got plenty to give to our expert."

9

JUDGE'S CHAMBERS
FOLEY SQUARE

At the office, Drew Sloan prepared a memo for Dan and Charlie Becker, detailing a phone conversation he had with the military attaché at the British Embassy concerning the use of a British military officer. Sloan had been informed that the Devon coastal cities of Plymouth, Exeter and Tourquay, all on the English Channel, had up-to-date cardio-vascular facilities. The Royal Navy maintained a Helicopter Air-Sea Rescue service at Culdrose, south of Plymouth. It was the 771 Naval Air Squadron led by a Commander Robert Masterson.

"Should we want to use Commander Masterson as an expert," Sloan said, "we would have to pay the equivalent of his salary and all perks to Her Majesty's Government. He has to agree to act as a witness. We fly Masterson to New York and back to England, First Class. Put him up in no less than a three-star hotel. Of course, we would be responsible for all his food and local transportation. It probably would be best for someone to go to England and interview Commander Masterson to be sure that he would make a good witness for us, and then sign the agreements necessary to employ him. I guess you and Jack would have to think about the great expense involved."

"I don't think we have a choice, Drew. Have we received the dimensions and layouts we need from the deck plans and the ship's log? And Jack Hoffman also needs all the ship's hospital records for Fonseca's treatment and surgery."

Gaspar's complaint had recently been filed in the federal court and it was now in the early pre-trial stage, each side collecting the documents it sought from the other.

"I already served A.U. Lines with another extensive Request for Production of Documents." Sloan advised Dan.

That afternoon Dan got a call from Lu Moore. "Dan, I received your request for the *American Union'* deck plan. I have to oppose it."

"On what grounds?"

"You can't have them because of national security. Judge Costello's clerk asked us to appear at his chambers to work this out. He asked me to call you and get a date we can agree on. How is tomorrow at 11 am?"

"I can do it, but I don't understand your opposition. See you then."

Located in Lower Manhattan, Foley Square is where New York City's legal heart is located. It is what urban planners like to call a pocket park. Foley Square is only several blocks long, and just a few streets wide, with grass plots and trees. Its size is deceptive in relation to its power. The New York State Supreme Court for the County of New York (Manhattan), the state's highest court of original jurisdiction, is located at 60 Centre Street, fronting on to the Square. The building reflects the law's majesty. Built in 1927, its ten large, white Greek columns guarding the wide entrance are both massive and impressive, reminding the public of the law's attachment to classic Greek and Roman principles.

Next door, The United States District Court for the Southern District of New York hears cases filed in the federal legal system. It, too, has ten imposing Greek columns on its frontage. It rises higher than New York State's Supreme Court building and also houses the United States Court of Appeals for the Second Judicial Circuit, a jurisdiction just one level below the U.S. Supreme Court. Just off the Square, the City's Criminal and Civil Courts of lesser jurisdiction do their business.

The Square was named for Thomas "Big Tom" Foley, an early 20th Century Tammany Hall politician, ward healer, district leader and popular tavern owner; a reminder that in New York, the courts and their power are often born in the backrooms of club houses belonging to political parties.

In order to be conveniently situated to its courthouses, lawyers have located their offices in the area surrounding Foley Square.

Gaspar's case was to be tried in the U.S. District Court, because federal law governs a seaman's life from the moment he steps aboard his ship to all the necessary legal protocols required to terminate his employment. Federal law mandates the seaman's employer as to how he must feed his crews while at sea. It legislates the hours a mariner works, which are very different from those of a worker on land. Federal law dictates when and how a seaman receives his pay; it also obliges the ship owner to make his workplace reasonably safe. The laws for the management of seamen-employees are available for everyone to read. They are a series of liberal labor statutes found at *United States Code Annotated, Volume 46.*

When a seaman joins his ship, he signs an agreement called Ship's Articles. It is the contract of employment between the seaman and the ship owner. Articles are signed for every voyage on every American ship bound for the high seas and foreign ports. It binds the seaman and his vessel to each other. A ship at law is an entity with legal capacities, responsibilities and rights, much as a corporation has. Ship's Articles are a seaman's pledge to work for a stated time: a month or six weeks, or for a specific voyage such as from the port of New Orleans, Louisiana to the Port of Cherbourg, France and return. The ship, on its behalf, pledges to employ him for those times as long as he is healthy and does not violate the terms of the Articles he has signed.

A seaman's diet is also mandated by the Articles. During the 17th, 18th and 19th centuries seamen suffered from the dread disease scurvy, because they lacked vitamin C in their diet. Congress has insured American seamen would receive adequate amounts of the vitamin. Besides an adequate supply of Vitamin C, seamen receive daily portions of meat, eggs and green vegetables, as set forth in the Articles. Today, many of these rights are enforced by Seaman's Unions, who have incorporated basic federal regulations into their Collective Bargaining Agreements.

Part of a ship owner's legal duty to his seamen is the obligation to afford him reasonable medical attention should he fall ill or become injured while in service aboard his ship. Gaspar and his lawyers claim he was never afforded that right.

The case of *Fonseca Vs A.U. Lines* concerns itself with whether or not the owners of the *S.S. American Union* fulfilled their duty to render proper medical care. Filed in the United States District Court for the Southern District of New York, Gaspar Fonseca's case has been assigned to Federal Judge Warren Costello and is scheduled for trial.

Judge Costello's chambers are large and comfortable: its décor is set off with dark wood paneling, wall-to-wall royal blue carpeting, oak desks, comfortable leather chairs surrounding a large conference table. The walls behind the Judge's desk are lined with many diplomas from his college, law school and certificates for the many courts in which he has been admitted to practice before his elevation to the bench, together with his Presidential appointments to various federal positions.

After graduating from law school, the Judge spent three years in the Army as an officer in a Judge Advocate's unit. After that, he clerked for a Federal Judge and then received an appointment as an Assistant U. S. Attorney. He was appointed by the President to be the U.S. Attorney for the Southern District of New York and finally, a judge of the U. S. District Court. Most of Judge Costello's legal career has been spent within the tight, powerful world of Foley Square. A judge for the past seven years, he has yet to succumb to boredom at his work.

Warren Costello is a tall, burly man who wears dark, horn rimmed glasses. More than three decades earlier, he was an All-American half-back for Colgate University's "Raiders." He parts his dark brown hair down the middle and is friendly to those who appear before him. When necessary, however, he can be tough on lawyers. Judge Costello's job is that of an umpire. He stands squarely between the attorneys for the litigants, interpreting and applying the law as it is set forth in The Federal Code of Civil Procedure. He may rule on motions with written decisions and interpret the legal principles of evidence as they arise during a trial in his courtroom.

At times, he also acts as if he were a referee in the boxing ring. He separates hotly contesting attorneys, reminding them where they are and how they must act, should it happen that they lose control in his courtroom. Judge Costello likes decorum in his courtroom. Presiding over a bench trial, that is, a trial conducted without a jury, he acts as both judge and jury. Judge Costello has only one client: the Constitution of the United States.

Aside from the Judge and his law clerk, who is a recent graduate of a prestigious law school, six persons sit around the room. Lu Moore and a young lawyer from her office sit to one side of the Judge's desk. Dan and Drew Sloan sit at the other. There's also a man whom Dan doesn't know. He's not a lawyer because he isn't at ease in this room and instead of the lawyer's ubiquitous briefcase, he is guarding a large, shiny black leather portfolio pressed tightly against his chest by two folded arms.

That's the ship's deck plan. I wonder what's up? Next to this man sits one who looks like a lawyer, although Dan has never met him before, either. Judge Costello, who knows both Dan and Lu, addresses them by their first names.

"So, Lu, why are you opposing Dan's request for the ship's deck plan?"

"The plans are a military secret, Judge. I brought one of the naval architects from Cox and Gibbs to court to explain it to you." Lu pointed to the man with the black portfolio. "They designed the *American Union* which, while it is a cruise ship, has many military secrets involved in its structure, power plant and purpose. We can't allow them to become public in a law suit."

Judge Costello looked at the man holding the portfolio. "You're the architect?"

"Yes sir, Judge. I'm one of them. There are many of us."

The man rose from his seat and bowed as if addressing royalty. He continued to hold on tightly to his portfolio.

"This is Mr. Alfred Collins from Cox and Gibbs, sir; he'll fill you in on the situation, with your permission of course," Lu offered.

Judge Costello waved a hand with a nod. "In just a minute Lu, first I have some of my own questions."

"And who are you?" The judge asked the man in a dark suit sitting next to Mr. Collins.

"Perry Simms, Your Honor. I'm counsel for the United States Maritime Administration in Washington. We are the owners of the *S.S. American Union.*"

"And why are you here today, all the way from Washington, Mr. Simms?"

"I'm basically an observer, Judge. We are letting Miss Moore argue our position. We are convinced she will properly explain the situation to the Court."

"Okay, Lu, so now let's hear what you have to say."

"Well, Judge, if I may, this vessel was built in 1952 for the Federal Maritime Commission under special circumstances. A.U. Lines operates the ship under a long-term agreement. The vital information concerning her construction, speed and power plants have all been military secrets since her launching, because this ship was built to be converted into a military transport in time of war, or a hospital ship, should such a need occur. To reveal the deck plans and other vital ship's information would be publishing military secrets."

"What have you got say about all of this, Dan?"

"I need the deck plan to prepare my case, Judge." Dan was not ready to explain his helicopter idea, although he assumed Lu was on to why he wanted them, anyway.

"I don't know what the fuss is about. I have already taken photos of some of the decks. I would guess thousands of vacationing passengers on the ship have done the same over the years. And there must have been hundreds of newspaper and magazine articles about her, with pictures of her decks. The travel agents have brochures with renditions of the ship with deck plans for all the decks. A.U. Lines has no rules that I am aware of, forbidding photographs of the ship or travel agents revealing deck plans. And there have been dozens upon dozens of newspaper and magazine articles about the ship, also with photographs. What I need are dimensions, which the brochures don't reveal."

Collins coughed; his way of calling attention to himself. "Your Honor, there are wires and other lines on the deck which receive, transmit and perform vital and secret information. We can't have them made public."

Collins unfolded a three-feet long artist's rendition of the *S.S. American Union.* It had a cutaway view of the vessel as seen from the port side, revealing 17 decks, from below the waterline to topside, showing cabins, staterooms, dining rooms, lounges, passageways, theaters, libraries, the ship's hospital, elevators, and on the lower part of the ship, the huge and powerful turbines manufactured by General Electric that power the ship through the seas.

Collins pointed to the two smoke stacks on the topmost deck and said in an unsure voice, "These wires running fore and aft alongside the stacks are there for reasons of national security. They cannot be removed. Then there are wires on the lower decks that serve the same purpose. If the defendant is thinking about bringing a helicopter to the ship these wires would be a definite hazard. A great risk, sir. The Captain cannot remove them to accommodate a helicopter."

So they are anticipating that I will be arguing for a helicopter rescue and want to close the door on that, Dan thought.

"What have you got to say about all of this, Mr. Simms?" Judge Costello queried.

"The Maritime Administration agrees with Mr. Collins and Miss Moore and strongly opposes Mr. Nikolas's request. To allow him to have the plans would be opening to the public all of the ship's military potential. In time of war it could be the cause of her destruction. To date we have kept these matters secret. We would not like to reveal them now."

"Well, Dan, it looks as if we have a problem. What's your position?"

"Judge, I'm not asking for speed, hull configurations or power plant construction. We all know the ship has two speeds. One we read about in the newspapers and magazines; it's the one for which the *American Union* has won prizes. She's the fastest cruise ship afloat. Everyone knows that. She also has another speed that's a military secret. I'm not interested in that one for my case, nor am I interested in the power plant."

"Can you tell me why you want the deck plans?"

"You know I have to do a complete investigation, Your Honor. Perhaps there is something I will discover that I can use in the prosecution of my case. As I said, I already have photos of the deck. Why would the deck's dimensions or a deck plan be a secret?"

"That sounds reasonable," Judge Costello agreed, as he pulled on an ear lobe.

"The Maritime Commission also opposes the use of any photographs taken by Mr. Nikolas, Your Honor." Lu argued, cutting in. "There are wires and other material which relate to the use of secret equipment on the ship and we can't have them made public since they are connected with deck dimensions. The wires and other materials don't appear in any travel brochures. And they are not mentioned in any of the newspaper or magazine articles, since the Maritime Commission made sure they weren't."

Lu took a deep breath before she continued. "A.U. Lines operates the ship for the Maritime Commission as a commercial venture. In our agreement, we are specifically forbidden from revealing any facts which have been designated by the Maritime Commission as military secrets."

Simms rose from his seat, interrupting Lu and handed Judge Costello several sheets of paper. "The secrecy clauses are here, Judge." He handed Judge Costello several pages which were underscored with yellow highlight.

Judge Costello read the clauses then said, "If you people are so damned fussy about secrecy, why don't you prevent passengers from taking pictures on deck?"

Simms coughed but remained silent for a moment. Then he said, "The Maritime Commission was not aware that was the case." But it was obvious to Judge Costello and everyone in the room that Simms was lying.

"It's hard to believe that, Mr. Simms. Are you really going to argue before this Court that the Maritime Commission was unaware of passengers taking photographs on a cruise? Or even that newspapers and magazines ran articles about its ship?" Judge Costello did not pursue the point but gave Simms a sour look and made a dismissive sign with the back of his hand. Then he looked at Collins and said with a beckoning of his right hand, "Let me see the cutaway view and the deck plans, Mr. Collins."

Collins shot a glance at Simms as if he needed his permission to give the deck plans to the Judge. Simms nodded an OK.

Judge Costello said impatiently, "Come on, come on, you don't need Mr. Simms' permission to give me the deck plans, Mr. Collins."

The Judge opened the portfolio and examined the plans. He studied them carefully, looking at the blue prints and turning the pages until he had gone through many of the long sheets. He shoved the deck plans and the cutaway rendition back into the portfolio and said, "Frankly, I can't make much sense of this."

Lu repeated her argument. "Judge, we strongly object to the deck plans being given to Mr. Nikolas, on the basis that it's a military secret."

"I understand your point. The Court certainly doesn't want to put the vessel, its crew and passengers in jeopardy in time of war. I have no choice but to deny you the use of the deck plans, Dan. But I will allow you to use the photographs you took."

"May I consult with Mr. Simms for a moment, Judge?' Lu asked.

"Go ahead."

After a few minutes, Lu addressed Judge Costello.

"Your Honor, I speak both for my client and the Maritime Commission, when I ask you to reconsider your decision with respect to the photographs."

"How did the plaintiff come to have these photographs?"

"Mr. Nikolas came aboard ship and personally took them."

"Were you aware he was doing that? And if you were, why didn't you stop him from taking the pictures?"

"Yes, I was there and allowed him to do it. We all know that if I prevented him from taking pictures, he would have asked you to issue an order. I was saving everyone's, including the Court's, valuable time."

"If you would have forced him ask me for an order, you could have raised the security issue then. Instead, you allowed him take them. Why should I prevent him from using them at trial? Everyone here today acknowledges that thousands of passengers have taken photos over the years. Besides being in heaven-only-knows how many family albums, they have appeared in newspaper and magazine articles, not to mention publicity and travel brochures. How many years has the ship been sailing?"

Simms answered, "Sixteen, Your Honor."

"For heaven's sake Counselors, in that case I feel that preventing use of the photographs would be unfair. Can you give me a good reason why should I prevent the Plaintiff from using them when everyone else has been taking photos for almost two decades without having them taken from them? Dan, are the photos you took here with you? If so, I want to see them."

Dan opened his file, took out a packet of photos in an envelope secured with a thick rubber band. "Here you are, Judge. These are the photos I took about a month or so ago".

Judge Costello asked, "Are there any signs aboard that say passengers are prohibited from taking photos? I note that when I walk across the Brooklyn Bridge there is a sign that warns pedestrians not to take photographs. When I asked someone about it, they said it was a holdover from World War II."

Judge Costello sifted through all 30 photographs. Before he could comment, Lu Moore said, "To answer your last question Judge, I don't believe there any such signs. But a party may possess some evidence which the Court decides it cannot use in litigation for many reasons. This is certainly one of them. We believe we have given you very good reasons: the ship being involved with national security."

"That may be so Lu, but I'm not inclined to change my mind in this matter. Thousands of people have taken photos of the ship. Neither your client nor the Maritime Commission has ever done a damned thing to stop it. The pictures may be used in evidence by the Plaintiff. That's my ruling. But as I said, the Plaintiff may not have the deck plans."

For Dan, it was not a victory. Without the deck plans and their dimensions, the photographs were useless. But he was not yet ready to let his adversary know that. They left the courthouse; Lu, her young associate, and Simms and Collins in one group and Dan and Sloan in another. Lu broke away and spoke to Dan. She invited him to lunch to discuss the case alone. Dan sent Sloan back to the office.

Kreager's Restaurant is a short and pleasant walk south of nearby Foley Square. It is across from City Hall. Located on Park Row, it is one of the city's culinary landmarks. Kreager's has been feeding New Yorkers for over a century. During the 19th Century, Park Row was home to dozens of New York City's newspapers, magazines and other publications. Reporters, editors and copywriters working on Joseph Pulitzer's fabled *New York World*, Julius Ochs' influential *New York Times*, William Randolph Hearst's *Journal* and Horace Greely's *Tribune*, regularly patronized Kreager's, which was a working man's restaurant. After their papers were 'put to bed,' newspaper men would step up to the foot rail at Kreager's 'Men Only' bar, capping off a hard workday with a restorative whiskey or a bracing nightcap before heading home. By the early decades of the 20th century, most all of New York's newspapers had left Park Row, moving uptown to Midtown Manhattan.

The newspapers' time on Park Row is now part of New York's colorful and racy history. Only the bronze statue of Benjamin Franklin, patron saint of America's printers and newspapermen, remains on Printing House Square. Once a workingman's restaurant, today in the middle of the 20th century, Kraeger's has been taken over by New York's lawyers and politicians. Park Row is close to New York's City Hall, its Municipal Building, the City's Courts and Lower Broadway. That's where many influential law firms do their business. At any lunch or dinner, the Mayor of New York City or his cabinet members may be seen dining at Kreager's.

Kreager's is a venerable and admired restaurant, a venue that always captivates its first-time diners. Its current owners have carefully insured that not only is dining here a fine culinary experience, but that observing the dining room's surroundings is a trip back in time. Original 19th century gaslights line the street entrance and the dining room walls as well. Time-worn theater posters advertise the stars of the era of the 1800s. Newspapers in their original editions, mounted in highly polished cherry wood and ebony picture frames, shout out headlines in large, bold-black letters. They recall the great events of a time past: Lee's surrender at Appomattox in 1865; the Great Blizzard of 1888; the sinking of the U.S.S. *Maine* in 1898, the cause of the Spanish American War; the Titanic disaster of 1912; and the assassination of an Arch-Duke at Sarajevo in 1914, which signaled the First World War.

Kreager's is no longer a place where rough and tumble workers order a hearty stuffed cabbage or a snowy-white bratwurst sausage surrounded by mashed potatoes covered in a thick, dark gravy, all chased down with a golden, foamy beer drawn from an ivory handled tap at the bar. The "Men Only" bar is now open to women and is part of an elegant restaurant serving dishes described in French and German with English translations printed between brackets. Kreager's beers are imported, as is the wine, which is favored above all other spirits at lunch.

After being seated, Lu said, "Dan, I had a disturbing conference with Bradley Rogers the other day."

"What was it about?"

"You."

"Me? Why?"

"Jerry Keller at A.U. Lines believes our relationship jeopardizes my ability to be objective in any of the cases we are working on together."

"What crap! You know I have never taken advantage of our friendship. Keller's a dope and everyone who deals with him knows it."

"Yes. But he seems to feel there is something sinister going on between us. They could audit every case we have together and find nothing wrong in any of them. Yet Rogers had the nerve to ask me if we were romantic. I told him there's nothing romantic between us, that we go out from time to time, but there's nothing serious."

"He asked you if we were romantic?"

"Yep."

"What balls. Knowing you, you must have been steaming."

"I was. But I kept it to myself, although I did complain a little."

A tall waiter interrupted the conversation. He did his best to give the impression that he was waiting on a table a hundred years earlier, dressed as he was in a black jacket, black string tie, a sparkling white shirt and inky black trousers. His shoes were also black and mirror-bright. Surrounding his waist and tightened with a long bow string, hung a long white butcher's apron that ran down to just below his knees. He stowed a stubby yellow pencil behind his right ear. A spotless and starched white napkin was draped over his left forearm. The waiter pushed two oversized menus in front of his diners. The menus had Kreager's name and logo written in gold and were jacketed in brown leather covers. Waiting for them to peruse the menu, the waiter stood poised, his pencil at the ready. Dan ordered a chef's salad with an iced tea and Lu ordered a shrimp salad and a diet Coke. The waiter nodded with an approving smile, then disappeared to leave Lu and Dan to resume their conversation.

Dan asked, "What do you plan to do about all this? Everyone on the street knows you're next in line to get a partnership. It's a great coup for you: a female partner there. It's a first and you deserve it; you've worked hard to get it. Will this be a roadblock? "

"I don't know. Sometimes I think they are testing me to see if I have some steel up my ass. Then again, knowing who the partners are, I'm sure they aren't happy about what they hear. They look at you and all plaintiffs' lawyers as interlopers. It's very short-sighted, I think. Without you, we would have less work and less income. Much of the maritime department spends its time defending seamen and passenger lawsuits."

"Well, Lu I'll go along with whatever you want to do. I certainly don't want to stand in your way," Dan said as he sipped his iced tea. "Especially where your future partners are concerned. But again, I don't like to see them taking advantage of you. You work very hard. Maybe you should step out of every case we have together. But they certainly can't tell you not to invite me to your house for dinner."

"No, Dan, I can't do that. If I do, I think they'll lose respect for me. Let's try this and see if it works. I'm going to make you jump over every hoop for me. Everything we do, from here on in, has to be in writing, including all settlement negotiations."

"That sounds okay, if you think it will work. I have another solution. I hope you will give it serious thought"

"What's that?"

"Quit these bastards. They aren't looking out for you. They only care about themselves. Come into my office. Within a year you'll be a partner; that's how good I know you are."

Dan was beginning to have more than friendly feelings for Lu. It would be good for the two of them to be together professionally. And then, who knows? Anything might happen. He had been looking at her as more than a colleague. She was a lovely and exciting woman and he enjoyed spending time with her.

"Thanks for the offer, but I can't do that. I have a goal – to become a partner in a large and important law firm. That's what I have to do. It's what I've been working for ever since I entered law school. I can't give it up now, when I'm so close."

I guess she doesn't feel the same, Dan thought.

The salads arrived and they spoke of a classmate who had just become a judge.

10

LONDON

Heathrow, the world's busiest airport, was bustling with thousands of people moving in every direction. As Dan stepped off his plane and into the international terminal, he saw the usual groups of passengers burdened with baggage carried by hand or strapped to their backs, scurrying to get to their final destinations in London or to make a connecting flight elsewhere. English and Commonwealth citizens were shunted to special waiting lines, while all other passengers were directed over there, to that line. Dan always marveled at the super-long reach of the old British Empire, once one of the world's largest. When he was a youngster they used to say, "The sun never sets on the British Empire." He could see the truth of it on these lines for processing British and Commonwealth citizens.

Humanity is there in all its colors; Asians, Africans and Caucasians. There are Sikhs, with their distinctive head dresses, beards and flowing moustaches from India; West African women in their gorgeously colored Dashikis; Levantines in robes, headdresses and sandals; Indians and Pakistanis, Asians from Hong Kong, Malaysia and Singapore and the black men and women of the Britain's Western Hemisphere Empire in the New World - the Jamaicans, Barbadians, Antiguans and the rest - all of them belonging to the recently independent island cultures of English-speakers once known as the British West Indies. England's vast colonial past disappears slowly.

After passing through Customs and Immigration, Dan taxied to his hotel on Half Moon Street. Around the corner were the crooked streets of the old and once bawdy neighborhood, Shepherds' Market. It is just off Park Lane in London's Mayfair district. He always liked these undisciplined streets, which reminded him of New York's Greenwich Village. After unpacking in his room, he changed clothes and went down to the hotel's bar for a Bourbon and water.

When he finished his drink, Dan strolled through Shepherds' Market. It was a cool evening and he stopped to look into the familiar windows of the shops that always attracted his attention. The military shop that had the array of toy soldiers was closed at this hour but the window was lit and Dan knew that the owner regularly changed his display of miniature, lead foot-soldiers and cavalrymen. They were always set out in their colorful and meticulously accurate uniforms, complete with medals. Today, there was a regiment of two-inch-high soldiers in 19th century uniforms in accurate Regimental colors. There were also cavalrymen with lances astride their steeds, lined up to execute a charge against an army of Napoleonic foes, each side eager to have a go at the other. In the far corner of the window stood three, two-foot-high British Grenadiers, each detail of their uniforms including medals and armaments marvelously discernable.

As Dan stood by looking into the window, a father, his young son in tow, also enjoyed the imaginative displays. The father pointed out the medals and uniforms to the lad, who was receiving the information with obvious delight.

Dan continued on past a Turkish restaurant that had opened since his last visit six months earlier. He scanned the menu housed on the outside wall within a glass cover and made a mental note to try dining here before leaving London. He went up Curzon Street, as he always did when in Mayfair, reading the blue and white oval plaques nailed into buildings, advising pedestrians about the homes where historic personages had once lived. He walked on toward the house near Berkley Square where he would meet with his friends, the Barrister Randolph Dumont and his wife, Freda.

When Dan needed an attorney to represent his clients for arbitration in England under a Lloyd's insurance policy, he called on Randy Dumont, a trial lawyer, or Barrister as the English call them. The two men had met years earlier in Panama City when each represented different crewmembers of a tug boat in a salvage claim off Panama's west coast. Travelling together to and from the Panamanian oil port city of David, Dan got to know Randy and to respect him.

At Dan's request, Randy had spoken with Commander Robert Masterson, the Commander of a helicopter base in the English Channel, with an eye toward determining if he would make a good witness. Randy was prepared to give Dan his opinion. It was now eight in the evening and Randy was home with his wife. Freda was a Dutch lady who taught political science at the London School of Economics. The Dumonts were expecting Dan and they had set a place for him at their dinner table. Their flat was one of several located in what had once been a Victorian mansion. The conversion of the old building permitted them to live elegantly on the second floor, in a high-ceilinged apartment with a large fireplace topped by an ornate gilded mirror in every room. The windows in their apartment still had their original 19th century blown glass, which distorted the street view almost like the mirror in a fun house.

Dan had always admired the English system of legal advocacy, which divided the responsibility for clients between Solicitor and Barrister. The Solicitor works in his office and refers clients to the Barrister. He also prepares wills, deeds and other legal documents. If a matter requires a trial, it is the Solicitor who "instructs" his client to the Barrister. The Solicitor is also responsible for much of the trial preparation. When the matter is ready for trial the Barrister, whose workplace is almost exclusively in the courtroom, gets the Solicitor's file (usually a day or two before trial) in a package neatly bound by a red ribbon. The Barrister's role begins when he pulls at the bow that opens the package. Once, long ago, Barristers were almost always from the upper class, and they pretended to be aloof as to the payment of their legal fees. They received it in pouches hanging from their back, where the client unobtrusively placed the agreed upon amount of Guineas, each one valued at a pound and a shilling, coin of the realm.

Dan enjoyed accompanying Randy to court and watching him at work in one of the world's most dramatic and accomplished legal settings. The British Barrister, in wig and long black gown, faces an adversary and a judge who is also bewigged and gowned. Many a Barrister's wig, which is made of horse hair, has an interesting history. Randy's, he once told Dan, formerly belonged to a Chief Prosecutor in the one-time colony of Rhodesia.

In the English court system, even the most prosaic trials are filled with centuries of tradition. Opposing counsel are always civil and deferential to one other, often cynical or slyly witty, but always civil. And judges will comment on the testimony, much to Dan's surprise. It is the stuff of dramatic theater, especially in criminal cases. Barristers, since they appear regularly in court are, in Dan's opinion, among the world's great trial lawyers. So accomplished are they that the system grants the title QC or KC (Queen's or King's Counsel). Those favored with such a coveted title, and only about ten-percent receive the honor, are retained by the Crown to prosecute or defend cases on its behalf. It is a most impressive system.

While there are American lawyers who try cases exclusively, they are very few and, of necessity, they are very active in the pre-trial process. Dan is neither Solicitor nor Barrister. He is, like most American lawyers, a combination of both.

After an excellent dinner prepared by Freda, Randy volunteered to call a colleague at Admiralty House to smooth the way for obtaining permission to release Commander Masterson to act as a witness in America. Ten years older than Dan, Randy Dumont was slender, of medium height with ginger colored hair and sea-blue eyes. He spoke with the accent many Americans were accustomed to hearing in movies or on television, that of the upper-class and privileged Englishman. Even though he was a QC, Randy Dumont liked trying cases where he defended those who were down on their luck.

Freda was Dan's age, dark haired with bright brown eyes and a light complexion. She stood at five feet four inches, but had an aura about her that made her appear taller. She is accomplished at her profession of teacher. She had come from her native city of

Rotterdam to study at Cambridge, where she met Randy, who was lecturing at law.

As they sat in the Dumont's large living room after dinner, sipping brandy with a pleasant fire going to cut the late-hour London chill, Dan outlined how he was going to present his case. Randy volunteered some ideas. He had previously called Dan in New York to advise him to come to London to meet personally with Commander Masterson.

"I sat for an hour or so with your Commander fellow, as I told you on the phone last week. We met at my club. I think he'll make a fine witness for your side. But you have to decide for yourself. He also has some very good ideas as to how a rescue could have been made. He told me he would be doing some research for you, which he hoped would be completed by the time you got to London. That's why I suggested you come to England. I also made some notes, Dan. They may be of some assistance for you at trial. I have to remember you Yanks are not always civil to each other in the courtroom."

Randy smiled, then went into his study and returned with a large envelope that he handed to Dan. "These notes should be of some value to you."

"Thanks, Randy, I'll look them over when I get back to the hotel. I'm sure they'll be useful."

"When will you be seeing Masterson?"

"Tomorrow afternoon. I'm taking a flight to Halston"

"Yes, that's right next to Culdrose."

Freda said, "Wear something warm, Dan. It gets chilly there. The wind blows strong." Then she asked some questions about Gaspar's physical condition and his future. Later, Randy nodded in approval or sometimes gently suggested another approach, when Dan detailed how he and Jack planned to present their case to the jury.

11

CONFERENCE ABOARD
S.S. *AMERICAN UNION*
MANHATTAN

Captain Gregory Burn sat in his office aboard the *S.S. American Union,* which had docked at its usual pier in New York earlier that morning. His other title – Commodore - recognized that not only was he the leading officer aboard his ship, but that of all the captains who were working for A.U. Lines, he was the most important in rank. He commanded the *American Union,* the company's largest, most prestigious and important ship.

Tall and broadly built, Burn had a large chest that stretched his shirt and pulled at its buttons. He had a florid face and a full head of dyed black hair. Six feet tall, Burn was a formidable presence. He was an even more imposing figure in his dark blue uniform with metallic gold braiding circling his jacket's cuffs and the stiff shoulder boards, signifying his rank.

Captain Gregory Burn was not fond of lawyers and now he had two of them on their way to his ship, one of them a woman. He huffed at that. The third person, the company's claims manager, Jerry Keller, was also someone he was not too fond of. While he knew Keller was a lawyer, at least he didn't practice his profession. These people were interfering with the important business he had as captain of the "World's Greatest Ship," as he always liked to call the *American Union.* He had been warned by company executives to cooperate with his visitors. That he would do, even if he considered it a waste of his precious time.

He created an informal surrounding by not sitting behind his desk, as he usually did when addressing underlings. Instead, he chose to sit at a couch in front of a low coffee table in his large office. The couch could comfortably accommodate four people, but Captain Burn would sit there alone today, the table creating a barrier between him and these interlopers. His orderly placed three plain aluminum office chairs with arm rests, on the other side of the table, facing him. It was a setting designed to emphasize who wielded power in his room and on his ship.

When the *American Union* docked in New York, Captain Burn wished to be with his family, just as the lowest ranking seamen aboard his ship wanted to be with theirs. After cleaning up routine paper work, a limousine would drive him to his home in Westchester County's village of Scarsdale, where his wife awaited him. Today's intrusion delayed his homecoming, yet he was determined to be civil despite this unwanted inconvenience to his personal life.

As the visitors walked into Burn's office, if it was not immediately evident to them how power had been arranged, then they failed to deserve the positions their clients had entrusted to them. Jerry Keller shook Burn's hand, reminding him that he had previously met Bradley Rogers and Lucille Moore, company attorneys. Burn nodded with a grunt.

"Sit down, please. May I get you something, coffee, tea or anything else you may desire? I know Miss Moore. She's been on my ship often after we dock and I've had the opportunity to speak with her a few times about problems arising during some of our crossings. Welcome aboard to you all." Captain Burn was going to be as pleasant as possible.

Keller took the lead. Having often dealt with this difficult man he knew what he was thinking. Keller had heard Burn's litany dozens of times: "Don't waste my time with lawyers. They don't sail my ship." The *American Union* belonged to the Federal Maritime Commission and was operated under charter by his employer, yet to Burn it was always his ship.

"Thank you, Captain," Keller said. "We don't want any coffee right now. We know you are a busy man and we would like to get you on your way home as soon as possible. We're here to speak with you because we are preparing the case of Gaspar Fonseca and must have some facts from you."

"Which case is that, Mr. Keller?" Burn asked sitting back on his couch with his arms folded across his chest in "show me" fashion. His beefy legs were also crossed.

"He's the seaman who lost his leg almost a year ago. The case is going to have to be tried." Keller paused and swallowed. "We can't settle it and you are one of the leading witnesses for the defense."

"Me? Why me? I already wrote a report that you folks pestered me for on that situation months ago."

"Perhaps we should let Miss Moore, who is preparing our defense in the case, explain it to you," Keller said, happy to be relieved of making any further explanations. "Lucille, you have the floor."

Lu leaned forward in her chair. "Captain Burn, you were in command of the ship, so the other side is going to make you explain every knot of speed and every nautical mile you travelled. And we know that by law you'll have an advantage, since as the ship's captain your decisions are always considered to be in the best interests of the passengers and crew and, of course, the ship."

"Certainly, Miss Moore, my decisions are always carefully considered and correct," Burn said with a smugness Lu did not appreciate. "Now suppose, young lady, I refuse to testify at this trial?"

"Speaking as defense counsel on behalf of your company, it could be seen as an admission to the jury that we are hiding something. In any event, the attorney representing Fonseca is very accomplished. He's no fool; he'll certainly subpoena you. Then you'll be forced to testify."

"What kind of law is this that takes me away from my ship - from my helm, where I belong?" Burn replied testily, unfolding his legs. He leaned forward, looking directly into Lu's eyes.

"The law applies to everyone, Captain Burn." Lu was beginning to understand Keller's warning that they were dealing with a difficult client. "If you fail to appear you could be facing a monetary fine and maybe even jail for continued refusals. I'm not saying you're going to jail, but it is a possibility. The company will certainly take the position that it cannot be responsible for paying your fine as it results from your refusal to comply with a court order, which you are legally responsible to comply with."

Burn realized Lu was talking about a recommendation she definitely would be making to the company. *She's a tough bitch*, he thought. "So what am I supposed to do, Miss Moore? Let me in on my role."

"For now, we need to know two things. Later on we will get more detailed with respect to your testimony. First, why didn't you deviate from your course to bring Fonseca to a hospital or allow an Air-Sea rescue?"

Burn answered, with a surprised look on his face, thinking, *How can she ask me such a question?* "I'm not changing course and delaying a trip when I have working gangs in New York waiting for us. The overtime would be murderous for the company. You are all fully aware our company is losing lots of money as it is."

Burn could immediately see that his visitors didn't like his answer. He backtracked, sat back on his couch, folding his arms and crossing his legs again. He thought for a while then said, "I have to check my ship's log. I can't remember where I was when I was first notified of the man's illness. It was so long ago. A year, you say. If memory serves me, we were probably out into the open sea. Too late to help anyone. To late to get anyone off the ship."

Lu shot Bradley Rogers a frustrating look. She had seen the ship's log and knew the ship was inside the Channel when Burn was first notified of Gaspar Fonseca's condition by Dr. Peters. The issue would be: where exactly was the *American Union*, so that a rescue attempt could be considered futile?

"Captain, let's leave it there for now. But we will certainly have to address that problem later. I would like you to be prepared to answer it for me. We have reason to believe that Fonseca's lawyer is going to try proving that a British Navy rescue helicopter could have gotten the seaman off the ship. I am sure we'll be hearing more details on that theory later. For now, he hasn't given us any details on that. What's your position on that?"

"A helicopter! What kind of crap are you handing me, young lady? You lawyers are always figuring out ways to make trouble and more money for yourselves. A helicopter! Hah, I don't think so. No! Never! I'm not risking my passengers and crew and maybe even my ship. No! No helicopters! Don't you realize that if a helicopter falls on my ship it could jeopardize my passengers and crew and cause severe damage to my ship? That's my position. It's too damned dangerous, too damned risky. You have to consider lots of things: wind, sudden gusts and maybe even the helicopter's engine failing while it's over my ship. If it comes to it, I'll let the jury know it's dangerous. They'll understand. They can't be so stupid as to not understand."

Lu was considering the volatility of the Captain's response as he grew more heated with each sentence. How would jurors react to him? Was his passion misplaced? She knew there would be more trouble with her next statement.

"You'll probably be required to get off the ship and miss a trip because the other side will want to take your deposition."

"There you go. I lose crew members every time there's an accident or one of them gets sick. According to the union agreement, when a man gets off my ship for whatever reason, he can't come back for thirty days. We have to sign a relief man on in his place, even if my regular man is only out for a day or two. It fouls everything up. It's hard to run a ship like that, especially where an officer is concerned. Neither I nor my officers belong to the seaman's union. We belong to the officer's union. Under that agreement, the company will also have to find another captain while I'm gone. And I'm sure they'll have to guarantee him a month too, maybe even more."

"We'll let you get back to your affairs for now," Keller said in soothing tones, designed to quiet an angry man and end this session.

Burn calmed down, rose from his couch and said, "When do you expect that I will be needed?"

Rogers said, "Soon, probably twice, once for your deposition and again for your testimony at trial, if it comes to that."

Lu felt Rogers was right in letting Burn know right away about the full extent of his role in this trial. There was no sense withholding the fact that Burn would be inconvenienced at least twice.

"Twice? Not once, but twice!" Burn shouted, his belligerence returning. "Good day, gentlemen and lady." He did not follow them out to the main deck, nor did he shake their hands.

As they descended the gangway to the pier, Keller asked, "So what are you thinking? He's always been difficult, no question about it. He's the Captain of the world's greatest cruise ship. He's not used to people telling him what to do. He's the one who gives the orders."

"He has to cooperate with us. Our whole defense is based on why he didn't get the seaman off the ship. After all, he's the Captain. He's the one who makes all the decisions. But he has to explain that to the jury in a humble way." Rogers emphasized.

"I'm also concerned with how he's going to come off to a jury," Lu added with concern. "He deals with us as if we're Ordinary Seamen on his ship and he's the Admiral. The jury isn't going to like that. I'll say this in his favor; he is the Captain. He is the man in charge and he is the one that has to make all the critical decisions that have to do with the ship's safety. Nikolas will have an almost impossible task to show Burn's decisions in this case were wrong. We have a really good defense as long as Burn can convince the jury he wouldn't deviate from his course because of safety considerations, and not tell them he tried to save the company some bucks.

"That bit about the helicopter was perfect. I can make a jury understand the safety factor and probable peril there. And I can emphasize the Captain's responsibility to everyone on the ship and the ship itself, not to mention the helicopter crew, which you may have noticed he left out of his danger scenario. I can work up some good testimony on those points. But we have to tone him down. He has to come off like a humanitarian concerned with safety and lives, not like the impatient autocrat he is."

Jerry Keller said with a laugh, "I don't envy you, Lucille. You have to make the jury see a pussy cat instead of an angry tiger.

Burn is the classic case of the man with too much power, who abuses it."

"That's why I would like to see this case settled. But I can't convince Nikolas that he has a difficult one. I tried feeling him out for $50,000. That's less than a third of what it could cost us just to defend it."

Keller's eyes were slits accompanied by a scowl. "You shouldn't have offered him anything without consulting me."

"I offered him nothing. I asked him if that would settle the claim. If he had said 'yes,' I would have tried to get it from you."

"I don't have a problem with that number, Lucille. I might even go to $60,000. After all, there is always a possibility of exposure here, as there is in any case going before a jury. You never know what jurors will do. It's that you went ahead and discussed a settlement without consulting me or getting my approval. Would you be doing that with any other lawyer besides Nikolas?"

"No; since most other lawyers would have considered it an offer of settlement, just as you did. Nikolas understood what I was doing. If he considered that number, then he knew I would try hard to get it for him. It was not a commitment on my part to settle, but a commitment to try to get what he would settle for."

"Lucille," Bradley Rogers interrupted. He was anxious to separate Lu and Keller and end the bitter banter going on between them. "You and I have an important appointment with the president of the seamen's union. Let's see how that comes off. Then we'll concern ourselves with our Captain Burn. Jerry, we'll get back to you with respect to our difficult Captain."

Bradley Rogers wanted to add "and Mr. Dan Nikolas" but he held his tongue.

৯৺ ৵৻

"Big Sam" Cassidy was known to the seamen on America's ships and the workers on America's docks and piers. The two-fisted, ex-seaman had traveled a long way from toiling on the decks of rusted and badly-managed freighters to become President of one of America's most powerful maritime unions. He may have been dressed in an expensive, tailor-made suit, but he still looked like a brawling deckhand, even to his broken nose. Cassidy's long political reach extended from legislators in those states with important seaports, to America's Congress, dispensing generous campaign contributions to those sympathetic with his union's agenda.

Lu and Rogers were meeting with him and the union's attorney, Hillel Kornbluth, at the Union's Headquarters. The purpose was to discuss a serious problem facing A.U. Lines. The *S.S. American Union* was losing money fast and the company had to do something to stop the free-fall. In 1968 travelers no longer had to sail across the Atlantic on a three- or four-day trip to attend to business or to enjoy a European vacation. New, swift jet planes could now cover the same distance in eight hours. For the past three years, the *American Union* had been leaving New York with her passenger lists showing only 600 to 800 passengers, sometimes even less. This was less than half her capacity. Yet even though passenger traffic dropped, the crew's compliment remained the same – more than 1,000. At times, the *American Union* sailed with almost two crew members for every passenger, a financially impossible ratio. As Labor and Management sat opposite each other in the union's clubby boardroom, Cassidy, his outsized hands with their scarred knuckles folded before him, came bluntly to the point.

"So what's troubling you, Bradley?" Cassidy always enjoyed being familiar with ship's executives, their lawyers and especially ship's captains. It let them know that he was as powerful as they and that they had to treat him as an equal. He was now one of them, even if he wasn't born into power or privilege, as had many of the lawyers and ship's executives. Even if he wasn't a graduate of an Ivy League law school or college, or any college for that matter, and didn't belong to the right clubs, Big Sam was proud that he had earned his power with those two large, scarred fists poised before him across the conference table.

"Have you looked at the passenger lists on the *American Union* lately, Sam?" Rogers said as he pulled a dozen sheets of paper from his brief case. "Here are the lists for the past ten trips." Rogers shoved the sheets across the table in Cassidy's direction, his gold cuff links made a noise as they struck the conference table. "You can keep those copies. I made them for you to keep."

Sam looked at Rogers' cuff links. He had several in his jewelry box and made a mental note to buy another pair for himself - a pair like Rogers had: gold and heavy, a real sign of affluence. He swiped at the papers with a wave of his hand, creating a wind that moved them into a flutter.

"Yeah, you know that I'm always aware of what's happening on my ships," Cassidy admitted, as he picked up the papers. He looked at each one of them perfunctorily, nodded in agreement and handed them to his lawyer, who also cast a quick glance at them.

To Cassidy, any ship on which his union members sailed was "his." When Cassidy and Captain Burn met, a sore point between the two was which of them was the boss of the Big A. Burn knew Big Sam could shut his ship down with a strike. And Cassidy was aware that when at sea, his members were under the tight and rigid discipline of their Captain.

Hillel Kornbluth dug into his briefcase and pulled out a collection of sheets, put on his reading glasses and compared them to Bradley Rogers' lists. He nodded affirmatively to Cassidy. "These are correct, Sam,"

Rogers continued, "Then if you agree with these lists, you have to understand we can't keep running the ship at a loss forever, even with a government subsidy. We have two serious problems. The first is that the entire American cruise fleet is facing some big competition from foreign-flagged ships. They pay their crews less than we do. They pay their governments less taxes than we do and they don't have to follow all the safety regulations we do."

"That's what they call competition, Bradley," Cassidy said, with a broad smile. But even he understood this was a serious meeting and his smile quickly vanished. Rogers ignored Sam's comment.

"Part of the problem with competition is that when you consider wage levels, pension plans, overtime and other benefits, we pay your members more than four to five times what a foreign flag cruise ship pays their seamen."

"That's what unions are supposed to do. They're supposed to get the best benefits available for their members."

Rogers acted as if he didn't hear Cassidy's answer.

"We have another problem, Sam. Passengers don't want to wait three or four days to get to Europe when they can fly there on jet planes cheaper and get to their European destinations in eight hours."

"These foreign flag ships are doing Caribbean cruises. How come you don't?"

"The *American Union* is too big for most island docking facilities. And the ship's draft is too deep to sail into some of those ports, even if they had the proper docks."

"So what are you trying to say, Bradley?"

"That if you want the *American Union* to continue sailing and providing jobs for your members, we all have to be realistic, management and labor, and we need to come to an agreement to cut out some of the crew. We're willing to work out a formula of a ratio of so much crew for so many passengers for each trip based upon the amount of passengers sailing."

"Impossible," Hillel Kornbluth interrupted. "There's nothing we can do about it. We have a Collective Bargaining Agreement with you and the rest of the American shipping community. We can't go back to our members and tell them they are going to lose jobs on only one ship. We'll have a riot in the union hall."

"You're right, Hilly," Cassidy said, addressing his lawyer while unfolding those huge hands, which were now pointing at Rogers and Lu. "Your people have to understand that I can't do that. As the union's President, I would be committing suicide." He ran his pointing finger across his throat, emphasizing his statement.

"And as the union's attorney," Kornbluth added, "I wouldn't even discuss it with our board members. Some of them would like to have Sam's job as President. They're already preparing themselves for the next election, which is only a few months away. Cutting down on jobs would be a big issue, which could probably lose Sam his job. We can't have that."

"You shouldn't be so hasty, Mr. Kornbluth. Think about this dispassionately." Rogers suggested. "In the long run, if you don't cut out a few jobs, there's a real possibility that there will be no jobs at all for anyone, ever. And that your union and all your members will be facing a financial crisis."

"No. I can't put myself and Sam in a position where Sam tells his members they will lose jobs and that we are the ones who agreed to do it." Kornbluth responded.

"If you won't try to resolve this with us, I can't be responsible for what may happen." Rogers said.

"Is that a threat, Bradley?" Cassidy asked, his eyes narrowing into slits.

"It isn't a threat, Sam. It's an economic realty which will result in a financial disaster, not only for my clients but for your union as well."

Rogers stood up slowly. "I'm leaving now, Sam. Think hard about what I just said and proposed. It's a good solution for you and my client."

As Rogers left union headquarters with Lu, he said, "This ship is coming to the end of its days. As you know, Lucille, ships have a 25-year life span, according to the way most of their mortgage loans are made up. Ships last much longer than that. It's a pity, because I doubt that the *American Union*, which is now only 16 years old, will make it to her 18th birthday."

12

RESCUE FACILITIES AT CULDROSE, U.K.
THE DEVONSHIRE COAST

Dan arrived at Halston's civil airport before noon. The flight from London was somewhat bumpy, as heavy clouds shrouded the whole Channel coast. At times, although he sat at a window seat on the small, 16-passenger De Havilland Heron powered by two propellers, he was unable to make out any landscape whatsoever. Once, when he looked at the clouds below, he could see the shadow of the Heron set in the center of a rainbow.

After a smooth landing, he made his way to the helicopter base at Culdrose, inquiring at the security gate for the location of 771 Air Squadron. He was permitted entry after he showed the guard an Admiralty pass and asked how he could locate Commander Robert Masterson.

"That's the Commander there, sir," said the guard, motioning to a tall man who had just walked away from a helicopter as its rotor blades began starting up with a high pitched, ear-blasting, mechanical whine. "That's Commander Robert Masterson, sir, walking away from the helicopter," the guard said in a loud voice meant to rise over the engine's noise.

Dust rose up and around Masterson as the craft lifted off its landing pad. He was crossing the field and when he saw Dan, he pointed, with great emphasis, to a building about 250 feet away. Dan ran, crouching, toward the hangar, shielding his eyes from the dust blowing up from the ground. Once inside, the two men settled in Masterson's office, both of them shaking dust from their clothes. They introduced themselves to one another.

"I've been expecting you. When I saw a civilian, I figured it to be you. Admiralty advised me you want me to come to New York to give testimony in a seaman's case," Masterson said, as he rubbed the chill from his hands. "Your Barrister friend, Dumont, spent some time with me. Was he satisfied that I would do well in the witness box?"

"He said you would do quite well."

"Good! Never been to America. I look forward to it."

Masterson stood over six feet tall. He advised Dan that he was a career military officer and a graduate of the Royal Naval Academy. He sat ramrod straight in his chair. Masterson was 44 years old with wavy black hair that showed no strands of grey. He had hazel eyes which were friendly and he spoke, as did Randy Dumont, with what the English call a "U" accent; that of the country's well-educated upper class.

"Have you arranged with Admiralty yet to retain my services?" Masterson asked, as he moved his swivel chair in order to reach some papers sitting on a small table behind his desk.

"Yes, that's all been arranged Commander, and quickly, I may add, thanks to Randy Dumont. You have to sign this paper they gave me. It's your agreement to the arrangement."

"Make it Robby, everyone calls me that. Now tell us something about your problem. Dumont said you had lots more to tell me than he had"

Dan explained the facts of the case and how a helicopter rescue fit in. Masterson was quiet as he listened to Dan's exposition.

When Dan was finished Masterson said, "Well, as Dumont and you have explained, you're trying to show a Captain's decision was flawed. That's a bit sticky, I must say. We all know that at sea, a Captain is the final authority. But let's see if I can be of some help. We do Air-Sea rescue all the time in the Channel. Most times, ship captains co-operate with us. Understandably, they are anxious to get sick and injured persons off their ships as soon as possible, as they should be.

"This is what you'll need to collect for me in order for me to help you make some sense of my testimony: a deck plan with the ship's overall dimensions; photos of the deck fore and aft; and the ship's log, so I can track her speed and movements in the Channel and locate her by the minute from Dover where she enters the Channel until she leaves at Land's End and enters into the open sea. I've already checked our log for the day in question and also the local weather, to see what conditions prevailed, which is very important in our rescue equation. Are you familiar with ships and maritime terms?"

"Yes, I am, Commander. I can provide you with everything you asked for except for the deck dimensions. The company claims it is a military secret that can't be publicly revealed. The Court has already ruled at a Hearing with respect to that issue, in the company's favor. That's why I can't get them for you."

"What's so bloody secret about an ocean liner? I've seen your ship going back and forth in the channel regularly. She doesn't seem too hush-hush to me. She is quite speedy, I do admit."

After Nikolas explained the facts, Masterson said: "Pity. I can never fathom you legal chaps. When you have some information or testimony that can clarify an issue, the other side puts up obstacles in the way. Even when you really need them in evidence so the jury can consider them. It doesn't make any sense. At any rate, this is why the dimensions are so important: when we make a rescue, as we are approaching the ship, the Captain gives us those statistics. My lads have to know how wide and long their field of rescue is. They never touch down on a ship, except in extreme emergencies. But my lads do have to know what's available in case they need to do so in an emergency, such as the engine stalling. They also have to know what the deck looks like. My chaps are usually seeing a particular deck for the first time, so they have to know what areas are safely available for pickup.

"I'll have to think hard on that problem and work around it. But if a Captain tells me he can't give me the numbers I need, I'm afraid I shan't send one of my helicopters over the ship. I won't risk my crews or the helicopter. I must say it's damned callous of a Captain to refuse to rescue a sick crewman. Let's go to the tower. You can watch a helicopter making a rescue and get a sense of what we do, before you return to London.

"I would have liked to have you along on one of the rescue missions, so you can see first-hand how we work. But we are forbidden to carry civilians on a mission unless it's a medical emergency. In that case, we can transport a medic to drop him on a ship. I could bring you along if I had special permission, which mostly takes close to a century or so to get. So what I have done is arranged for you to go out in one of our tenders so you can watch rescues up close. I have a set of coveralls for you to put over your clothes so you don't get them messy with grease."

Once in the Channel, Masterson pointed to a helicopter which became smaller as it made its way over the water. When it was nothing more than a large fly to the naked eye, it paused in mid-air then began its slow descent.

Through field glasses, Dan could see a line playing out from the helicopter to a tanker below that, although it was not moving, bobbed on the waves of a grey, choppy sea filled with whitecaps. He could also see that the Channel was busy with freighters, tankers and even a passenger liner. It was easy to understand how maritime traffic could possibly complicate an air-sea rescue.

"Where are the nearby medical facilities, Robby?" Dan asked as he resumed tracking the rescue through his field glasses.

"Depending upon where we would have picked up your chap and how much petrol remained in our tank, we'd have three options. The best hospital would have been Plymouth. Two other alternatives are Tourquay and Exeter. They are smaller cities, but they do have good emergency medical facilities. After I read the ship's log and check with the hospitals to see what facilities were available that day, I will be able to tell you where we could have deposited him.

"It's certain that if we would have made that rescue, the doctors would have been sure to inform us via radio, that time was important. They always do in these cases where there's a blockage of the arteries or any severe hemorrhaging. That fact also has to enter into where we would have brought your sick chap. In my time here, I have never had a ship's Captain refuse to assist us with revealing his ship's dimensions. So as I said, I have to work this out with my pilots. Don't worry. We'll figure it out. Get me all the ship's statistics available to the public; you know: length, beam, draft, how many decks there are, etc. Those statistics are not taboo, I trust?"

"No, they're not. Knowing you would need them, I brought all of them with me," Dan said as he handed Robby Masterson a large envelope from his brief case. It was filled with all the vital statistics for the *S.S. American Union.*

"Let's get you back to land," Masterson said, as he rifled through the papers Dan had just given him.

இ ஷ

Charley Becker and Jack Hoffman sat on a green leather couch, waiting in Dr. Sean Welles's office as he attended a patient in an examining room. Charley took the time to survey the doctor's academic credentials which hung neatly on the walls behind his desk: Bachelor of Science, University of Indiana; Doctor of Medicine, Johns Hopkins University; Internship in Cardio-Vascular Medicine, New York University; Board Certification for Cardio-Vascular surgery; certificates from the Medical Corps, U.S. Army; a Commendation from the U.S. Rangers; Board Certifications for cardiology and surgery.

Sitting on Dr. Sean Welles' desk was a colored plastic model of the human heart that came apart to reveal its four chambers. Charley Becker didn't look too hard. He was always squeamish when it came to peering into the body's organs and at the sight of blood, too. He could never make it as a physician. At one time, he had thought of becoming a psychiatrist, but it meant attending medical school, slicing into cadavers and administering needles. Yet he did note that the arteries leading into the model heart stuck out like dry spaghetti strands. One poster on the office wall showed healthy arteries and arterial flow while another portrayed those with disease blocking smooth transit.

The door opened and Sean Welles entered. Jack Hoffman had told Charley that Welles had been deployed with the Rangers in battle and that he had treated wounded men in the field during the Korean War. Fifteen years later he still looked like an elite

Ranger. Six feet four and lean, with a close crew haircut showing grey at his temples, Welles extended a strong hand to Charley and a warm bear hug to Jack, a longtime friend.

"Where's Mr. Nikolas?" he asked Jack Hoffman.

"In London. He's arranging for a helicopter pilot to testify at the trial."

"He's going to need one. I've gone over your client's medical records. In order to help you with my testimony I'm going to have to know how long the block existed, which is difficult at best. Probably we'll have to make an educated guess. And then, of course, I need to know how much time was available to get him to the nearest operating room once he was taken off the ship."

"I don't think at this time we can tell you how long the blockage existed. We can tell you when our client first felt pain. And I have to tell you that, at least for now, we can't make a helicopter rescue from the ship itself." Jack informed Welles.

"No? How come?"

"We can't get the ship's dimensions because they are a military secret. Our helicopter expert says they wouldn't have made a deck pickup unless they had those dimensions. Dan called me from London so I could let you know at our meeting today, that that was the case. Then there are a bunch of wires that cover the deck that are used for secret stuff. They can't be removed or touched. So they are in the way of any helicopter rescue we might consider that could be made directly from above the ship." Charley explained. "It's a big problem, but Dan tells me that the Brits will work it out."

"Well, I don't know too much about sailing. I leave it up to you guys to figure out how to get him off the ship." Welles paused with a look of frustration. "You know I can't give an opinion that makes any kind of sense in this case and which I can defend on cross examination, without knowing when he's off the ship and from that time, how long it takes to get him to a hospital. There is another alternative. I wonder...could they have gotten a qualified surgeon aboard? That's something you might consider. If it is an alternative, then you have to figure out how to get one on the ship and then we have to determine if he would have been of any help.

"In the meantime, I can tell you that the cut-off of blood flow for a long period of time will almost certainly result at least in an infection. Since your client eventually went over three days without an adequate flow, I would have expected gangrene to eventually result, as it did in this case."

The lawyers and the doctor spoke for half an hour. Welles explained, for Charley Becker's benefit, how a thrombosis forms and how its location is determined in preparation for surgery by injecting dye into the affected area or using an ultra sound device so that a surgeon can see where to make the proper incision.

"Jack, get back to me when you know how much time you had to get your guy to the hospital. Then we can talk again." Welles shook Charley's hand and in a goodbye gesture gave Jack Hoffman another strong hug and led them to his office door.

13

PREPARING FOR TRIAL
MANHATTAN

The Maritime and Aviation section at Brown, Sykes and Bellham has, in addition to Lucille Moore, six young lawyers under Bradley Rogers' tutelage. No one in this section ever calls him Bradley, not even Lu Moore who has been his head associate for three years and had worked with him almost daily for three years before that. Lu supervises these attorneys and prepares and personally tries the firm's most significant and important maritime cases. She assigns trials of less importance to those beneath her.

One of them,, Steven Jessup, was not, in her opinion, ready to handle the more important trials. But despite her reports that he lacked the necessary experience and maturity, someone, Lu could not determine who, had moved him up to become Lu's assistant. Tradition at Brown, Sykes and Bellham requires a lead associate who is becoming a partner to nurture and then recommend a successor to take over his position. Lu was thus forced to prepare Steven Jessup for two jobs: to assist her in the trial of *Fonseca* vs. *American Union Lines*, and to prepare Jessup to take over as her successor when she would be called to a partnership.

Preparing for trial, lawyers gather as much information as possible from their adversaries. This is the pre-trial phase of a law suit called Discovery. Parties request and adversaries must deliver reports, letters, documents, photographs and the opinions of experts, as well as those refuting expert's positions on the other side. If the case involves a personal injury, then a plaintiff must provide pertinent medical reports and submit to an examination by a physician retained by the defendant. In this way, each side learns everything it can about conditions arising from alleged negligence. Both sides of a dispute may also take the oral testimony of witnesses or all parties to an action. Reports concerning an injured party's earnings lost in the past and those the plaintiff will claim to be lost in the future, are prepared by qualified economics experts and are vigorously attacked by opposing experts. Attorneys may also request an inspection of the location where an accident occurred and take photographs of the site for use at trial.

Some law firms file motions to harass or make an opponent work on needless matters. It is a strategy used to draw an attorney's attention away from the important work of the case and is called "papering your opponent." The pre-trial phase of a law suit may take months and sometimes even years, depending upon the availability of witnesses, access to the workplace, documents and other factors such as motions addressed to the Court requesting delays for illness or inability to comply with requests, more time thus being needed to gather the information requested. More serious pleas may be made to the Court claiming that the material requested is not susceptible to discovery for a variety of reasons to be battled out in court.

During this process, Lu Moore has carefully assessed Steven Jessup. She knows that at this stage of his career he still lacks the drive, intellectual ability and ambition to oversee six lawyers. He will have to manage litigation, prepare documents necessary to charter vessels, and negotiate insurance claims for lost cargo and damaged vessels. These claims often run into many millions of dollars. When and if Lu moves upstairs, Jessup must also exhibit a solid work ethic and an unflagging loyalty to Brown Sykes and Bellham.

The Fonseca case will be Jessup's first time sitting in an important and complex trial and Lu was concerned that he was not all what she wanted him to be. If she was asked, however, she would not have revealed her doubts. Steve Jessup was not her first choice; he was the choice of some unknown and powerful partner sitting in the penthouse and she could not complain about Jessup's upward movement impelled by an anonymous partner.

When a civil case proceeds to trial, it is the plaintiffs who have the burden to prove their case. They must show, by a preponderance of the evidence, that it is more likely that the facts of the matter before the jury favor their position than not. It is called making a *prima facie* case. If unable to meet this basic burden, plaintiffs risk having a judge dismiss their case before it can even get to a jury for their consideration. Thus, where cases are legally slim, lawyers strive to somehow get the case to the jury any way they can, in hopes that sympathy or a good trial presentation may result in a favorable verdict.

When a case is ready for trial, all parties to the litigation should have exhausted every opportunity to discover reports, documents and the names of all witnesses and the opinions of all experts. Each side then has a fair idea of what their opponents will present to the jury, as well as the strengths and weaknesses of each case. At this stage of a case's development the trial lawyer carefully threads his discovery together like Christmas popcorn on a string. Because of all this intense activity, Dan Nikolas, Lu Moore and, to a lesser extent, Jack Hoffman have been thrown together on the phone, at depositions, or in court in legal combat, on almost a daily basis for the past three weeks.

Dan and Jack know that very few, if any, cases are perfect. Sometimes a case lacks an essential piece of evidence needed to convince a jury in a way a trial lawyer would like. Sometimes a witness blurts out an unanticipated surprise fact or an unwelcomed comment made during testimony that changes the tone of the case. Dan is faithful to the old adage among trial lawyers: "A case is not won in the courtroom; it is won in the office."

Good homework and preparation allows the attorney to enter the courtroom with a degree of confidence that he has done all the work necessary to make a solid case. And, most important, that his witnesses won't surprise him.

During the many weeks Dan and Lu are thrown closely together as adversaries, this case with all its facts is now revealing itself. With each deposition and delivery of documents, it soon became evident to Lu, Bradley Rogers and the people at A.U. Lines that if, by a very slim chance, the company lost this case, a money verdict would not be the only bad result. If A.U. Lines and its Captain could be shown to be insensitive to a crew member, how might the company treat a passenger? How would a loss at trial affect the company's public image?

Yet Lu and Rogers are sure of their legal position. They have persistently assured A.U. Lines that, based upon the law, evidence at hand and his testimony given during his deposition, that Captain Gregory Burn had made good, legally proper, and sound decisions to protect the lives of those aboard his ship. This included the lives of the helicopter rescuers and the safety of the vessel itself. They advised the company that it had an excellent chance of winning this case. At the offices of Brown, Sykes and Bellham, the maritime section worked long, hard hours to insure a jury verdict favoring their client.

Bradley Rogers had not tried an important case in two years; not since he became confidant of Lu Moore's ability as a trial lawyer. Since then, he acted mostly in a supervisory capacity and as a negotiator of claims. All the company's hopes in this case rested with Lu Moore, the firm's best trial lawyer. For Lu, it would be her last significant trial before she moved up to the partners' floor and she worked hard to insure its success. A win would insure her invitation to become a partner.

"Perhaps," Jerry Keller told Bradley Rogers during one of their telephone conversations, "Nikolas might be approached with a larger and sweeter offer in the Fonseca case."

"Sure." Rogers responded. "However, it depends on the offer. The other day I was going over our work log. We've put in a lot of hours getting this one ready. So, I can imagine, have Nikolas and Hoffman. They have been working with Lucille Moore almost daily for the past few weeks, taking depositions and exchanging exhibits. We may be at a point where they would just as soon try it as settle, because no settlement will compensate them for their work or even make their client happy."

"I have authority for $125,000. If the other side shows any interest, I might be able to squeeze out another $25,000. "

"I honestly don't think that settles it, Jerry."

"Let's try. We have nothing to lose. After all, the law is with us and Nikolas and Hoffman must know that, too. They're pros. They have to know when to walk away from a losing case."

"All right, we'll give a try. I'll tell Lucille to get on it right away."

"No, no, no, I want you to do the negotiations directly with Nikolas. Keep Lucille out of it. I don't trust her."

At seven p.m., Lu and Dan were having dinner at Kreager's after finishing another long day of depositions. Testimony had been taken of Professor Martin Stein, the economics expert. It was a day full of numbers, salary projections, life expectancy and work life expectancy, interest applications and their applicability and how to establish their rates based on the history of interest rates. The two lawyers were trying to relax but they were also going over the necessary plans to take testimony on Thursday of Dr. Ross, the research physician who was employed at the National Institutes of Health in Bethesda, Maryland, who had operated on Gaspar Fonseca.

"We should take the 8 a.m. Eastern Airline Shuttle from La Guardia to National at D. C. I'll rent a car at the airport,"

"Thursday is going to be Jack's show."

"I look forward to seeing him at work."

Lu was cut off suddenly as Bradley Rogers stood over their table.

"Good evening, Lucille; good evening, Mr. Nikolas. Enjoying your dinners?"

"Lu and I were making arrangements for our deposition in Washington the day after tomorrow. Sit down, Mr. Rogers, have dinner with us." Dan offered Rogers a seat.

"You call our young lady Lu. I never thought to call her that." Rogers seemed to be emphasizing the fact. "No, you two make whatever arrangements you need to make, I don't want to interrupt; besides, I'm here with a client," Rogers said as he motioned to a table across the busy dining room with his chin.

"She's been Lu ever since we sat in the same row in law school. M is for Moore and N is for Nikolas. When we sat alphabetically we were two seats away from each other," Dan explained, trying to defuse Rogers' from thinking that it was a pet name used between a romantic couple.

"Ah, yes. By the way, Mr. Nikolas, will you be in your office tomorrow morning?"

"Yes, I will."

"What time might be best to call you?"

"Any time before noon. I have an appointment outside the office after that."

"Good, you'll hear from me tomorrow morning."

Bradley Rogers left Dan and Lu puzzled. Lu wanted to go to Rogers to ask what this call was about but held back. She would wait until tomorrow morning to find out.

"Lu," Dan said, "we've spent a lot of time together these past few weeks. I'm beginning to see you in a different way."

"What does that mean?"

"I think you know. You're more than a good friend."

"Yes, I've thought about it too. We have been moving into a closer relationship and I like it."

"So do I, Lu."

"Maybe Rogers was not so wrong to ask if we have a romantic attachment," Lu said with a wide smile.

On her desk next morning, there was a note for Lu from Rogers. He wanted to see her, first thing. Today, as she entered Rogers' office there was no offer of coffee. He shot out a question as if it had been seething in his mind for a time and he could not wait to relieve himself of it. "What were you doing having dinner with Nikolas last night?"

"After a full day of depositions filled with numbers and statistics by an economics expert, we needed to get rid of all that stuff in our heads and try to relax. You have no idea how listening to testimony about interest rates and future projections can numb your brain. Then we had to make arrangements for our deposition of Dr. Ross in Washington tomorrow. That's on for tomorrow. Nikolas explained that to you last night."

"The two of you looked close."

"I have made no secret that he and I are friends and that the friendship would have no bearing in any way on cases we work on together."

"In the last month and a half I have at least eight reports of the two of you having lunch and dinner together."

"For God's sakes, Bradley! Are you having me tailed?"

It was the first time Lu addressed Rogers by his first name and spoke to him in a loud voice. He seemed not to mind.

"Of course not, Lucille. You know I wouldn't do that." Rogers said, adopting a paternal tone even as his face turned red.

Lu was discovering that Rogers had a mentor's affection for her.

"Jerry Keller has been after you. I don't know why. Did you two ever have words?"

"No. I don't particularly like him. He's crude. We have had our differences but we've never had a fight or anything like that."

"He went over my head to our managing partner Dudley Hayes, complaining about you and Nikolas. Hayes dropped it in my lap," Rogers said almost as an apology for what was he was going to say.

"I don't understand. What was dropped in your lap?"

Rogers coughed. "You understand Lucille, this is not my decision but one made by the partners as a group. I've always been quite satisfied with your performance and loyalty to myself and to this office. I have always boosted you to the partners. I have been convinced from the first time you came to this firm that you would be an asset to us. I have been pushing you for partner since the beginning of last year. There was a lot of opposition because of your sex, but I think I overcame that prejudice. However, you will not get to be a partner unless and until you satisfy the others that you are not too cozy with Dan Nikolas. Because they think you favor him to the detriment of our clients."

"I thought we settled this nonsense. How am I supposed to defend myself about having contact with a man who has a significant amount of cases with this law firm?"

"You know what Dudley Hayes told me? The owner of the New York Yankees tells his players that he doesn't want to see any of them talking or getting friendly with anyone on the opposing team."

"That's dumb; doesn't Hayes realize I have to talk to my opponent? It's at the heart of the adversarial system. We're taught in law school how to address our opponents at Moot Court and debates. Where did those men go to law school? Is that what they teach them at Harvard and Yale? Don't talk to your adversaries?"

"I know, I know. It's the friendship the partners don't like. I thought I warned you about this several months ago. Now what are you going to do about it?"

'I'm not sure I can do anything about it. This is childish. I'm not sure I understand how to deal with it."

"Lucille, I don't know how to say this. Keller called me yesterday. He wants us to offer Nikolas $125,000."

"At this point, he will never take it."

"I know. I told Keller both sides have put in a lot of work. It may not be enough. I'm sure Nikolas and Hoffman have already spent many thousands of dollars in expenses. I understand Nikolas went to England to get a helicopter expert."

"Yes, he did. I'll do my best with this offer. I'll discuss it with him tomorrow on the way to Washington. Now maybe you can tell me what this business of you calling him today is all about."

"Umm, well, Keller wants me to do the settlement negotiating. I guess it's part of the nasty problem of how he sees your close friendship with Nikolas. He wants you out of the negotiations."

"Dan won't settle with you, even if he wanted to. He's no fool. He's going to sense something is wrong: suddenly you're doing the negotiating. That alone should keep him from even thinking of a settlement. Because whatever you offer him, he'll think you are holding back from your real authority."

"I might have another $25,000 to put on the table."

"I'm sure that won't do it either."

"You're going to Washington tomorrow. Finish what you need to do today, then disappear from the office and don't come back until Monday. That should give you enough time to make up your mind as to what you will do about your relationship with Nikolas. This coming Monday is the first Monday of the month. That's when we partners have our monthly lunch meeting to discuss matters in the office. I'll have to tell them what you have decided to do. Meanwhile, I'll feel Nikolas out on the offer.

"Lucille, I have been with this firm for 30 years, 23 of them as a partner. Life has been good to me. I've sent three children to college. One of them graduates from law school next year. He can't join us because we have a policy against family working in the office. I have made enough powerful friends to place him well. He'll never have to worry about earning a good living in our profession.

"When the time comes for me to retire, I'll have a pension with no financial worries. It's all there for you, too, if you make the right decisions. I can't make them for you. But I would like to see you enjoy all that. I know you don't come from a privileged background as many of us partners do. You worked hard to get to this level. You are a brilliant lawyer, one of the best I've ever had the pleasure of working with. You would be an asset to this firm. I would hate to see you throw all that away. If I can help, I'm here to do that for you as I always have been."

"I can't believe this is happening. When we last discussed this, I honestly thought you were testing my mettle. I was wrong. Now what do you suggest I do?"

"What is it you want out of life, Lucille? What is the path you wish to follow? If you can truly answer those questions, that is what will help you decide what to do."

After Lu left, Rogers slumped in his chair. He sat quietly for several minutes, thinking about how carefully he had nurtured Lucille these past years. *Of all the young associates marked for advancement in this firm, I touted Lucille highest above all the others. She is the best qualified, the most representative of what a partner in our firm should be. Now it's up to her. She's the one to decide what to do. I hope she will not throw it all away, for her sake and for my own as well. After all, I might be considered a poor judge of talent.* He straightened up, reached for the intercom and buzzed his secretary.

"Mrs. Stacey, please put in a call for me to Mr. Dan Nikolas."
He put the receiver back into the cradle and rubbed the bridge of
his nose with his fingers. This was not a call he wished to make.
Instead of having the upper hand, because he had the money to
settle a case, he would be the one on the defensive, having to
explain why Lucille was not calling to offer a settlement. At times
one has to do some distasteful things to keep a client.

14

DEPOSITION
BETHESDA, MARYLAND

On a gloomy Thursday morning, Dan and Jack Hoffman arrived at La Guardia Airport's Eastern Airlines Shuttle Terminal with just a few minutes to spare before their flight was scheduled to leave. An anxious Lu Moore was waiting for them. As they mounted the plane Jack, who was astute enough to understand something was going on between his two young colleagues, took a separate seat across the aisle, allowing Lu and Dan to sit alongside each other, sipping orange juice offered by a flight attendant. It would be a short flight; less than 250 miles in the air. Lu said nothing to Dan about her meeting with Bradley Rogers. Dan opened the conversation.

"Your boss called me yesterday, the way he said he would, in the morning, before lunch. I thought it best not to call you to discuss it until you were away from the office. By the way, he liked how I call you Lu. He said he would be trying it. I think he knew I would be telling you that, so that you wouldn't be surprised when you heard it."

"How much did Rogers offer you?"

"A hundred thousand. I told him he was insulting me." Lu made no comment about the offer or the amount and Dan didn't ask her if she knew how much the company was willing to offer. Then he said, "Then Rogers said if a little more would settle it he would try his best to get it. I told him not to bother. What's going on in your office? When I asked him why he was calling and not you, he said you were busy."

"Jerry Keller's been keeping a log on all the times we've been seen together outside the office. He's telling Rogers and the partners that I can't be trusted, that something sinister is going on between us."

"What does your boss say?"

"I'm surprised. He's backing me all the way, but Keller has the ear of the managing partner and he's pressing Rogers to force me to make a decision about our relationship."

"Lu, I know I love you and you know where I stand. You're in line for a big boost in your career. Think hard about it, though. I don't want to be in the way of something you've dreamed of attaining all your life. However, you do have some good alternatives. We can work something out. We can work together. We'll do well. I'm positive of that."

Lu was silent. She took Dan's hand, squeezed it hard, her eyes blurred with tears. She spent the rest of the flight reviewing the questions she had prepared for Dr. Ross. Her firm had arranged to use the conference room of the law firm in Bethesda they teamed with whenever they required Washington counsel. When the lawyers entered the office, Dr. Ross was sitting in the waiting room. He seemed peeved at having to give up a day's work.

"How long will this deposition take?" Ross asked. "You're taking me away from some important work I need to be doing in my laboratory. This whole matter is distressing. We, all of us, acted out of a professional duty and a necessity to help a human being who was suffering from a serious medical condition. Now we are bothered with having to take time out from our work to give testimony. Will I have to appear at trial?"

The lawyers looked at each other and gave the answer they usually advanced. Dan said, "We hope not and we'll do whatever we can to spare you that inconvenience."

Ross mumbled an unintelligible word. In truth, Ross could never be forced to come to New York if he didn't wish to. He lives in Maryland, and Judge Costello's subpoena powers do not extend outside his federal district of New York.

They walked to the conference room, the doctor settling into a comfortable leather chair to which he had been directed, opposite the lawyers. The court reporter sat alongside Dr. Ross. He would record the day's testimony on narrow ribbons of paper running through a black dictating machine. Dr. Ross raised his right hand, faced the court reporter and swore to faithfully tell the truth about the matters in this case. The wall clock in the conference room read 10:30 a.m. when Jack Hoffman began his questioning.

Jack's questions showed a depth and knowledge of medicine equal to a physician's. He referred to no notes. His fluency with medical terms was impressive. He did not hesitate in his approach. Jack Hoffman asked incisive questions: What size and type of clamps were used? Where were they placed? How was the line of incision made? What type of scalpel was used? What did Dr. Ross see once he made the incision? The questioning went on and on, each question rapier-like. It seemed to Dan that this was not a deposition but two physicians in dialogue. Jack Hoffman surely deserved the admiration he received from his colleagues.

Lu's turn with Dr. Ross would have to wait until after a short lunch break. As brilliant as she was, her questions lacked the clarity and urgency Jack had displayed. Dan knew that when Lu returned to her office she would work hard to reach Jack's level of knowledge. If anyone could do it, it would be Lu. She would have to be ready for Jack at trial.

By 4 p.m. in the afternoon both sides were satisfied they had elicited all the facts they needed from Dr. Ross. What was certain was that Dr. Ross was not a Board Certified surgeon. Yet of all the doctors aboard the *American Union*, he was the only one familiar with surgical procedures. His work as a research physician regularly involved dissecting and removing glands, organs and other parts from the bodies of research animals.

Dr. Ross could not say where the ship was when they decided to operate, except that he and all the doctors had been told a rescue could not be made from where they were. That fact pressured the doctors to proceed with surgery despite a consensus among them that Gaspar would be better served if he were taken off the ship quickly, to a facility with proper equipment.

"Yes," Dr. Ross had responded to one of Lu's questions, "possibly non-surgical intervention, such as certain medicines, could have been used in this case. It would have depended on the type of block and how long it had been in place before it could have been effective. But the hospital facilities aboard ship were not stocked with those drugs."

Dr. Ross made it clear that neither he nor his colleagues held out much success for the operation, but that it needed to be done even if there was only a small chance the block could be located. To have left it alone would have certainly doomed Gaspar to more pain and no chance at all of saving his leg. So, even though the odds were against them, the doctors reluctantly agreed to try.

At the end of the session, Dr. Ross was told he would receive a copy of his deposition to read and make corrections if needed, then sign it. Once signed, Dr. Ross's testimony could be used in a variety of ways by the lawyers before and during trial.

On the way out of the office Dan approached Lu. "Jack wants to hang out before we go back. You're invited to stay with us. We're going to have a drink."

"Thanks. But I have to get right back. I won't be in the office tomorrow. I have some personal business to attend to. I'll send Steve Jessup to work with you on the exhibits, unless you want to wait until I come back on Monday."

"It can wait a day. I would like a break, too. We've been so busy getting this case together for trial that I've let a few things go that needed attention in the office. Can we talk over the weekend?"

Lu grabbed Dan's hand, held it to her face and kissed him. "No, I don't think so. I need to be thinking," she paused, then said: "I know I love you, Dan. I hope it's not a problem for either of us."

"Lu, don't forget what I said. There are alternatives."

After Lu left for the airport, Dan and Jack Hoffman sat in a booth at a quiet corner of a bar in a nearby hotel. Dan was sipping a Bourbon and water while Jack had already finished two Scotches.

"I drink, you know." Jack said as he twirled his glass over a soggy paper napkin. He had loosened his tie and opened his shirt collar. Dan knew this was going to be a very informal session.

"I don't apologize. They say it's the trial lawyer's curse. I don't get drunk. It's rare that I do. How about you Dan, do you drink a lot?"

"No, I never got hit with the curse, as you call it. I do like to relax after a trial with a shot or two. That's about as far as it goes. I'm impressed with your knowledge of medicine. How is it you became a lawyer? You should have been a doctor."

Jack took a long, last sip from his Scotch and soda, called the waiter over to order another. He asked Dan if he wanted another, but Dan put the palm of his hand over his glass and said he was fine with the one he had.

"Well, I'll tell you, young man. In the year before World War II began, when I graduated from Columbia University, there was no room in America's medical schools for a Jewish boy whose parents were immigrants from a shtetl in Poland and who could barely speak English. The first name on my birth certificate reads 'Jacob.' They had these quotas, you know: just so many Jews, Italians and Negroes a year, in those schools. I was never lucky enough to be able to get on the right line with the right school at the right time. The doors were always shutting in my face. So I became a lawyer. Even today, that law firm your Miss Moore works for wouldn't have a Jew working there, let alone for a partner. Maybe someday."

"She's up for a partnership in that firm."

"Is that so? Well, maybe there's some hope in this world if they're seriously thinking about making a woman a partner. She's very bright. Anyone can see that."

"Yes, she is. So finish your story."

"Ah, yes. After the War, when I got out of the army and became a lawyer, I made some money and saw to it that my younger brother, David, became the doctor in the family. Ten years after me, when he applied to a medical school, we had already beaten the fascists and, supposedly, anti-Semitism, too. It was a little easier to get accepted into a medical school. And David, God bless him, made it."

The waiter brought Jack's fresh drink, sliding across a large round serving tray, together with a bill which Jack promptly paid

125

before Dan could. He took a sip and continued, "Whenever I needed help understanding something I had to explain to a jury, my brother Dave helped me. He's an orthopedic surgeon and a fine one, too. Board Certified, graduated from Emory University Medical School. I'm proud of him. After he began practicing here in New York, if I had a case involving neurology, he'd send me to one of his friends for help. After a while, between studying the medical books and being assisted by a cadre of friendly and highly competent physicians, all of them willing to help Dave's older brother, I became an amateur physician. Those doctors also helped me because secretly, and they never told me, but I came to understand that they wanted to shine a bright light on the incompetents in their profession."

"Jack, you are more than an amateur."

"Save your praise for the trial. That little cookie opposing us today was out of her element. But I can see she's bright. I expect her to give me some real trouble after she does some studying and we get into the court room."

ॐ ॐ

A taxi chauffeured Lu Moore from LaGuardia Airport to her University Place apartment in Greenwich Village. As she opened the door she called out, "Mom, are you home?"

"Back here in my room, honey."

Lu and her mother, Rachel Moore, lived in a large one-bedroom apartment. A sitting room was converted into a bedroom for Ray, as Rachel was always known. They knew things would get better once Lu moved up in her firm: a bigger apartment or maybe even their own house in Westchester, where they would have lots of room and outside, the flower garden they both wanted. Ray would give up her job at the protest magazine where she worked, editing poorly written manuscripts and marking them up as best she could so they became reasonably readable.

Blonde, with broad streaks of grey in her short cropped hair, Ray Moore was a slim Vassar graduate with a Master's degree in English Literature from Columbia University and not too pleased with her job. Once Lu moved up she could quit and look for a better one at her leisure. Ray had been raising Lu alone since her daughter was six, after Ray's husband had abandoned them. They were more than mother and daughter: they were good friends.

"What's wrong, honey?" Ray asked as she came from her bedroom to greet her daughter. She could see the slump across Lu's shoulders, the frown and the color drained from her face. *This isn't my Lu*, she thought.

Lu dropped into a chair and without removing her jacket began narrating the events of the past few days. Ray poured a cold glass of white wine for her daughter. When it came to liquor, Lu hardly drank anything stronger than wine.

After Lu finished her drink, Ray asked, "What are you going to do?"

"I don't know, Mom. I hoped we could talk about it."

"It's your decision to make. But if you want to, we can talk about it, of course."

"We have been planning to enjoy the benefits of what a partnership would bring to us. Give me some input. You are going to be as much affected as I am. I want you out of that magazine as soon as I can manage it. Then maybe you can do some work that you can be proud of."

"Hell, sweetheart, don't be concerned about me. I don't like the way you've been looking lately. You've lost weight and you look pale."

"I've been working hard on this case that's coming up for trial. It will probably be the last one before I become a partner. I have to win it. It needs to be the last case I have as an associate, before I become a partner."

"What does Dan have to say about all of this?"

"He's like you. He says it's up to me. And Mom, he told me he loves me."

"That's great, Lu. I like him. It's about time you met someone who wants you to be his wife and take care of you. How do you feel about it?

"I told him I love him"

"So where's the problem?"

"He doesn't want to block my way. It seems as if being a partner in this firm is like becoming a judge. You have to be careful who you associate with. My association with him is greatly suspect."

"Ridiculous. You're not a judge. What sort of people work at your office that they can't take your word on an issue of friendship? What about Rogers? Has he noticed you don't look too well?"

"He doesn't pay much attention to the talk, but he's being finessed by the managing partner, who pressures him about me. All along, Rogers has been the one pushing for me upstairs. I never really knew it until these last few days. He painted a beautiful picture of how good life has been for him since he became a partner and that he's looking forward to a great retirement. He assured me that all of that is mine, if I want it.

"That's what I've worked for since I entered law school; a partnership in an important firm, something a woman can't count on no matter how talented she is. And for me it's only finger-tips away, but I'm beginning to have doubts that I can attain it."

"You haven't answered my question. How do you feel about the kind of men you may have to spend the rest of your working life with, draining you as they do?"

෨ ෴

Dan stepped out of a cab at Broadway and 80th Street. A pleasantly cool March evening called people out to the street. Broadway vehicular traffic, broken up by a concrete divider, was competing with crowds of strollers waiting for a green light to cross safely. He stopped at Zabar's Delicatessen, had the counterman put together the makings of a sandwich, selected a long and crusty French bread in which to stuff the food, and then walked to his apartment on Riverside Drive and 81st street. He was pleased there would be no work on Gaspar's case tomorrow. He had files on his desk that needed his attention. Tomorrow would be Friday. Maybe he could take off early and go to a movie, then maybe even have a Chinese meal. Even if he was alone, it would be relaxing.

As he walked home he thought of how he and Lu could be together, now that they knew they felt the same way about each other. His mind was filled with how they would spend the coming weeks and months together: how he would bring her flowers; how they would enjoy a weekend or two together away from the city. He would check out some of those country inns he'd seen in the Travel Section of the *Sunday Times*. He would help her get some more color in her face. But first, they had to finish with Gaspar Fonseca's case. Maybe he could convince her to leave that law firm that was sapping her strength, wilting that special smile she had and causing her to become so tired.

Once in his apartment house, he took the elevator to the sixth floor, still thinking of Lu. It was hard to think of anything else since he left Jack Hoffman at La Guardia Airport over an hour ago. It was dark in his apartment. He paused for a moment before he switched on the lights, as he always did at night because he enjoyed looking through his windows at the Hudson River in the dark and the lights of the New Jersey shore across the way. He checked his telephone for messages. *Good*, he thought to himself, *No messages. I'm in no mood to return calls either tonight or tomorrow.*

After preparing his sandwich, he poured a glass of iced tea and settled down on his couch in front of his television set to watch the Mets play the St. Louis Cardinals in a spring training game in Florida. It had been a long week and he told himself that he earned this little bit of quiet relaxation. He had finished the last of his second glass of iced tea when the phone rang.

15

CONVERSATION WITH GASPAR FONSECA

"Mr. Nikolas it's Mira Fonseca." Her voice was raspy. She was gasping for air.

"Something wrong, Mira?"

"It's Gaspar," she paused and then said in a whisper, "he tried to commit suicide."

"Oh, no! Is he okay? When did this happen?"

"He didn't hurt himself. I took the knife away from him. But he's crying and shouting and banging on the walls. I'm worried that he'll hurt himself. It happened about a half hour ago."

"Get your son out of the house, immediately."

"I already called Mike and Bobby. Mike is on his way to take Ronny to his house and Bobby is here with me now. Gaspar's shut up in the bedroom, shouting and banging on the walls. He tries to hit anyone who comes into the room. I'm afraid someone will be calling the police with all that noise."

Dan could hear sharp rapping sounds over the phone "I'll be right there."

Residents of Manhattan's Upper West Side who garage their cars, know it may take as long as half-an-hour for a car hop to fetch it. They patiently wait at the valet's booth, watching other cars negotiate steep and narrow ramps from some unknown space several levels above. When they hear a car screeching, its horn blowing to prevent a collision at each tight and narrow turn, they expect it to be their car. Tonight's retrieval took only 15 minutes.

It was after 11:00 p.m. when Dan pulled up to a spot in front of the Fonseca home. As he left his car, Mira pulled a window curtain aside, saw him coming up the steps and opened the front door for him.

"Where is he?" Dan asked.

Bobby Fonseca answered, pointing to the back of the apartment.

"He's in the bedroom, Mr. Nikolas. Be careful. He uses his crutches to try and hit whoever opens the door."

"Okay. Bring me a tall glass of water with lots of ice in it." Dan knocked on the bedroom door.

"Hi, Gaspar, it's Dan Nikolas. Can I come in so we can talk?" There was no answer.

"I have a glass of water for you. It's cold, with ice. Come on, we can have a private chat. Just the two of us. You and your lawyer. No one's here but you and me."

Still no answer.

"I need to talk with you about your case." Dan knocked louder on the door.

"Alright, wait a minute. Then come in. Just you, Mr. Nikolas, come alone, with nobody else. Just you alone."

The room was dark. Gaspar turned on a lamp that was set on a table beside his bed where he had retreated. He was on his back, dressed in a pair of sky blue pajamas, his eyes red from crying. Dan settled into a small metal folding chair beside the bed, handing the glass of water to Gaspar, who took two long swallows. There were scratches and dents on the wall where Gaspar had struck it with his crutches.

"Mira shouldn't have called you and bothered you at your home so late at night. It's not a problem for you."

"But it is, Gaspar. Every aspect of your life and your condition arising from your loss, physical or mental, is my concern. It's part of what Jack Hoffman and I have to present to the jury. If you are distressed, I have to know that and I have to let the jury know that, too. So now you have to tell me what's eating you."

After a long pause Gaspar said: "I can't live with this." He grabbed the stump of his left leg. "Every time I look at it I think I can't stand to be a cripple forever."

"Take it easy. You won't be like this for the rest of your life. You'll get a new leg and then you'll get around without a crutch or a wheel chair, just a cane. You won't be depending on anyone any more. Your economic condition is only temporary. You'll go back to school and learn a new profession and begin earning a good living.

"If we're successful in court you should have no money worries for the rest of your life. Then you'll look back at this night and wonder why you made such a fuss about taking me away from my Mets-Cardinals game." Dan made an unsuccessful attempt at some humor.

"No, I can't live with this. Look, my stump isn't healing. Every time they fit me and they put the stump into the socket it gets like raw hamburger. I can't stand to look at it and the pain isn't so pleasant either."

"You have to hang on, Gaspar. You have a wife and a son. It can't be easy for them, I mean seeing you like this. You have a long life before you. Are you ready to abandon your family? They'll have a hard time carrying on if you harm yourself. What about your mother and brothers? Think about the sorrow they will feel if you hurt yourself. Think about all the young soldiers that come back from war without an arm or a leg. They all made new lives for themselves."

"It's easy for you, Mr. Nikolas. You aren't missing a leg."

"That's true. I'm not missing a leg. But it's not easy for me to see you like this and to have this conversation with you. I'm trying to give you the benefit of what I have seen of men like you. They overcome their misfortune; they go forward and they make new lives for themselves and their families. They have children, they have work; they go on to become important contributors to their community."

Gaspar took another swallow of water. He stuck his hand into the glass and pulled out a cube of ice which he ran across his forehead and then over his eyelids. The two men remained quiet for several moments then Gaspar said,

"I'm okay now, Mr. Nikolas."

"Are you sure?"

"Yes."

"Good. Then I suggest you get some sleep and stop frightening all of us."

Gaspar shot a weak smile at Dan, who rose from his chair and went into the living room where Mira and Bobby were talking in whispers.

"He's all right for now. But someone has to stay with him during the night. He may get excited again. I wasn't happy with what I saw. He needs help as soon as we can arrange it."

"I already told Mira I would stay here tonight," Bobby said.

"Do you drink, Mr. Nikolas?" Mira asked.

"For now, soda, or maybe juice if you have it."

"How about some orange juice?"

"Fine."

Mira put a glass and a carton of orange juice in front of Dan. He poured some juice and downed it in one gulp. He looked at Mira and Bobby

"Tomorrow morning, first thing, I'll call the Marine Hospital for a psychiatrist. Don't worry about the cost. The Marine Hospital will pick it up. Why is he having such trouble with the fitting of the leg? This is the first I hear about it after he complained months ago when I was here. I thought that problem was over."

"He's always been complaining that it never fits properly. I told him to call you but he's stubborn. He says the stump has to heal, then it will be okay,"

"Let's find another company. There's no reason for him to be in such pain so long after his amputation. I'll arrange for a new company tomorrow. If this one can't help him, we'll have to find one that will."

Mira smiled. "Thank you, Mr. Nikolas."

"Call the office after one o'clock. My secretary, Mrs. Sachs, will have the name of a new company to fit Gaspar. If he acts up again, call the office. We'll call the Marine Hospital again if we have to.

He's a veteran. If you need help right away, like immediately in an emergency, you should call the VA hospital at Kingsbridge Road, they'll send an ambulance right away. They are only 20 minutes from here."

When Dan left it was after midnight. If he could, he would sleep late tomorrow. As he turned the key in his ignition and put his car in reverse, he thought to himself: *Tomorrow, after I tell Jack about this, I'll call Steve Jessup and tell him that we're adding another expert witness. It may delay the trial but it can't be helped.*

The next day, in the afternoon, Lu called Dan at his office.

"Steve Jessup called me at home to tell me you're adding another expert, a psychiatrist to the case. Is that true?"

"Yes. Fonseca tried killing himself last night. How are you feeling, Lu? "

She passed over Dan's question. "You know we are past the time in which we were ordered by the Court to notify each other with the experts we were going to use."

"I'm aware of that. Unfortunately, Fonseca's psychological health doesn't seem to be on schedule to coincide with Judge Costello's court orders. I notified your office this morning, as soon as I was aware of the condition, which only surfaced late last night after we got back from Washington." Dan did not like this conversation. Lu's voice was cold, like the touch of steel.

"I'm moving the Court to prevent you from adding a psychiatric expert on the grounds that it is too late and that there's been no previous allegation on your part about any mental or psychological injury."

"Do what you need to do. The Court has to be convinced this is a result of the loss of Fonseca's leg and that there was no sign of the condition until now. Judge Costello is no dope. He'll figure it out. And by the way Lu, read my complaint carefully. You'll find a clause for mental pain and suffering. It's boiler plate. I put it into all my personal injury complaints. If you had any problems with it, you should have asked me to produce proof to substantiate the claim, which you never did. If you had done so a couple of months ago, I might have had to dismiss the claim for lack of proof."

This conversation was getting out of hand. Dan wished he hadn't been so confrontational. But Lu is opposing counsel and this is developing into an important aspect of Gaspar Fonseca's case. He couldn't treat Lu with kid gloves. No, he was going to be as icy as she. But, in an effort to calm their conversation he asked once more how she was and if she had made a decision.

After a long pause Lu answered. "I'm very tired and I haven't decided what to do. Don't get me off the track, Dan. Let's see what Judge Costello has to say. You'll get my motion early next week. This is an unfair surprise you've dropped at my doorstep. I can't allow it." She hung up abruptly.

Dan looked at the receiver and said, "Damn, what the hell was that all about?"

16

A.U. LINES
BOWLING GREEN, MANHATTAN

Saturday morning, Ray Moore called Dan to tell him of the conversations Lu had with Rogers and that she was told to make up her mind about what she was going to do by Monday morning.

"So that explains yesterday's conversation," Dan said.

"What conversation was that?"

"It's nothing important Ray, except that she wanted to be left alone this weekend. Where is she now?"

"She went out for a long walk. She's been gone for two hours. I told her all this had little to do with her relationship with you. What these men are demanding of her violates her privacy. The way I see it, if they bully her on this issue, what else might they think of pressuring her to do in the future? What passed between you two these last few days does complicate things. She told me about it. I'm happy for her, Dan. She needs someone to care for her besides a mother. I'm very worried about her. She's tired and looks like a ghost. She's so pale and tired."

"I noticed that too. She's been counting on this partnership for a while, Ray. Now she sees it slipping through her hands. That's why she works so hard. Your daughter has a strong personality. Eventually she'll do what she thinks is best for her."

"Should you talk to her?"

"I already have. She knows my position. She now has to decide for herself."

❧ ❦

Saturday morning is not the usual time for the top executives of A.U. Lines to meet with their lawyers. However, the reason for today's conference is unusual. They are in an office discussing the future of the *S.S. American Union.* They are meeting at the company's executive offices in a building near the U.S. Customs House at Bowling Green. It's at the southernmost tip of Manhattan. New York City was born here with the founding, in 1625, of the Dutch trading colony of *Nieuw Amsterdam.*

The company's plush waiting room is filled with bright prints portraying Dutch windmills and the wooden sailing ships of 17th Century Holland's merchant navy. The boardroom itself is filled with aerial photographs of the company's many freighters and two large oil paintings, one of the *S.S. American Union* and the other of her predecessor, the *S.S. Columbia.* The room's large windows frame a score of freighters and tankers plump with cargo sitting heavy in on the waters of New York Harbor, waiting to be unloaded. There is also the smaller traffic: tugs and work boats moving across the waters of one of the world's major sea ports.

Present at this extraordinary meeting are Frank Moss, CEO of A.U. Lines; Lawrence Foyle, Vice President; Simon Flint, the company's Chief Financial Officer and attorneys Bradley Rogers and Dudley Hayes, of Brown, Sykes and Bellham. After Simon Flint reads a discouraging two page financial report about the *American Union'* economic health, he sums up the situation in his own words: "Here it is, Gentleman. The *American Union* is hemorrhaging financially. Regardless of what we do, we can't stop it. We are losing the cruise passenger traffic to airplanes. It is affecting the company's health and overall profit picture. Our cargo ships, which are profitable, are picking up the losses of the *American Union.* Frankly, I don't know how much longer we can sustain it.

"Also, the Maritime Commission is hinting that the *American Union* may no longer be serving the military mission it was originally designed to carry out. That should almost surely end the operating subsidy we get from the government. They are talking about planning to lift the military secrets aspect of her capacities. To me, that means her days are numbered. Once that happens, I'm sure they no longer have any reason to keep her sailing with a government subsidy. If that's so, we'll have to lay the ship up because we can't make up the difference."

"That's certainly a bleak picture," Frank Moss interjected.

"Bradley, give us a run down on your meeting with Sam Cassidy."

"He won't move to resolve our problem."

"Might he be negotiating? Looking for some sort of advantage?"

"I don't think so. He has a union election coming up. He says the solution I posed, which you all previously approved, puts him in peril of losing his job at the next election. If he loses, he goes back to work at sea or retires. I don't see him hanging up his gloves. And I don't see him back working on ships anymore. He's lived the good life and has been on the beach for 20 years. He really wants to continue as president."

"I have to go along with Bradley," Dudley Hayes added. "Cassidy is difficult to deal with because he has some real personal interests to keep things as they are."

"What about the union's lawyer? What did he have to say about your proposal, Bradley?"

"Kornbluth? He's in tight with Cassidy. He's on his coat tails. If Cassidy goes down, so goes the lawyer."

"Doesn't Cassidy understand that he'll lose over 1,000 jobs? Losing only 400 or 500 seamen instead, is a viable solution."

"Frank, you're right but you don't understand his strategy. Right now, he's at the Union Hall telling his membership that the big, bad company is trying to throw their brother union members out of work and on to the beach, and that he's fighting the good fight to keep those jobs for them. If we close the ship down then it's the fault of the company, not the union leadership. He points the finger at us and he's as clean as can be. He loses the cruise ship, but he still has the cargo ships to represent."

"Simon," Moss turned to his financial officer, "Can you see any profits by cutting back on service in other areas?"

"I'm afraid not, Frank."

"What have you got to say, Larry?"

"We are not alone in facing this problem. The people at Moore-McCormack Lines, which run the *Brasil* and the *Argentina,* and American Export Isbrandtsen Lines, running the *Atlantic, Constitution* and *Independence,* tell me they are having the same headaches with regard to fewer passengers booking passage on their ships and their loss of profits.

"The way things are, I don't think the *Brasil* and the *Argentina* will reach sweet-16 flying an American flag. As far as the other ships I've just mentioned, it is almost certain they will also be laid up very soon. The days of cruise ships flying American flags are over. We must realize it and act accordingly. And we all face the same problems of trying to compete with the cheaper-run foreign flag ships and, of course, the jet plane.

"It wouldn't surprise me if those other companies are having a meeting like this one. If not, it is certain they will, and sooner rather than later. I don't know if they have spoken with Cassidy. If they have, then they probably got the same answers we did.

"I'm sure we can all agree that Cassidy is short-sighted. But my personal opinion is that even if he worked out an agreement with us, America's supremacy as a commercial maritime power is over. We are quickly arriving at the point when we will not be able to compete economically with foreign flag vessels. In cargo service we are already seeing some strong competition, which I expect will get tougher in the future."

"You paint a dark picture, Larry." Dudley Hayes observed.

"I have been investigating this problem for a while. Frank asked me to look closely into this situation last year. My strong recommendation is that we get out of the passenger business as soon as we can and concentrate on cargo. As I said, our cargo ships will eventually surrender to those of the runaway flags of convenience. When will that happen? I can't say exactly, but we have to be prepared for it."

Frank Moss leaned forward and said: "Then, gentlemen, I believe we can all agree that unless someone can come up with a viable solution, we all know what needs to be done. Bradley and Dudley, get in touch with the Maritime Commission and start the necessary procedures. Reluctantly, we will have to think about shutting down the world's greatest cruise ship… and as soon as possible."

"Bradley? It's Lucille. I apologize for calling you at home on a Sunday afternoon. I have to talk to you."

"Don't be concerned, you're not interrupting anything here. I'm alone and watching a tennis match on television. What's up?"

"Can you get some more time for me to make up my mind with respect to the Nikolas issue?"

(Pause) "And what do I tell my partners tomorrow about why you want more time?"

"On Friday, when I wasn't in the office, Nikolas called and told Steve Jessup that he was going to be adding an extra expert--a psychiatrist, because his client tried to commit suicide. I need some time to file a strong brief opposing this move. I can't be thinking about anything else for the present. It is another thrust of injury we need to defend. Personality changes can lead to a runaway jury, because there is usually a lot of sympathy involved, which we must avoid.

"I'm going to oppose Nikolas's motion as a surprise and that it's past the time the court ordered us to name all experts. Judge Costello may take a few weeks to decide this issue. I want to get the opposition in his hands as soon as possible so we don't delay the trial, which is a little over three months away."

"Doesn't he have to file an amended complaint?"

Lu sighed, letting out a puff of air. "I'm afraid not. The original complaint had a boiler plate cause of action for mental damages. We denied the allegations, of course, but we never put him to the proof. It's my fault. I take the blame."

That's just like Lucille. She doesn't pass the buck. But if I check around I'm sure I'll find someone else who's responsible. "Do you think the Court will go along with your motion?"

"I don't know. You never know how Judge Costello will rule. But we can't let Nikolas waltz in unopposed. This attack is a major concern for us."

"Yes, you're right. It is a major concern. How long will it take for Judge Costello to decide?"

"I can't say. I will ask the Court to expedite the issue, since we are some three months to the trial."

"You finish whatever work needs to be done. I'll get you another week. The partners will understand the emergency and your reaction to it. But you definitely have to resolve the issue by whatever extra time I can get you."

"I know. I know. Thanks, Bradley. I won't cause you any more problems. I'll resolve it, I promise."

"By the way Lucille, who prepared the answers to the complaint?"

Lucille waited several seconds then said, "Steve Jessup."

17

NEW DEVELOPMENTS

The phone in the conference room rang. It was Betsy Sachs, interrupting a conference Dan was having with a client. Betsy said quietly and in a troubled voice, "It's Mira Fonseca. Her husband just killed himself."

Dan picked up the phone. "Mira, what happened?"

"Gaspar killed himself about two hours ago, Mr. Nikolas." Dan could feel her anguish and he imagined the tears rolling from her eyes.

"How, Mira, how? How did it happen?""

"We were at the new rehab unit you arranged for us. They were fitting his artificial leg. He said he had to go to the bathroom. He left on crutches, found an open window in the hallway and jumped out. Five stories, Mr. Nikolas. Five stories down."

"Where are you now?"

"At the police station. I even had to identify him for the police. I almost fainted when I saw him."

"Can you get home okay from there?"

"Yes. Bobby came and he will drive me home. I can't even think of driving a car."

"Then have someone call me when you get home. I will be at your house tonight." Dan buzzed Charley Becker on the intercom, "Charley, we need to amend our complaint."

"Why? What's happening?"

"Gaspar's committed suicide. Make a wrongful death allegation for me to look at. I'll call Jack right away."

Jack Hoffman was silent when he heard the news. Then he said, "I'll have to call our psychiatrist, Dr. Feinberg, and ask him to work up an opinion on this matter. It's a good thing he had the opportunity to examine Gaspar twice in the last six weeks. I'll get on it right away, Dan."

"Jack, do me a favor. You call Lu Moore and tell her the news. But do it right away. Tell her we are amending the complaint to add a wrongful death action. Hang up before she starts shrieking."

Since Gaspar Fonseca's trial was now eight weeks away and her motion regarding the expert list had not yet been decided, Lu asked the Judge for an expedited meeting to determine this latest event. The call she had received from Jack Hoffman was a blow she could never have anticipated. Her motion addressing the attempted suicide was now moot. Gaspar had finally succeeded in doing away with himself. Now she would need to redo much of her brief to cover the suicide itself. After that was done she filed it with the Court. Then she stopped in at Judge Costello's office and spoke with his law clerk to arrange for an expedited emergency hearing as soon as the Court could hear the parties. She explained to the Judge's clerk the new complications arising from Gaspar's death and that the trial was now only eight weeks away.

Judge Costello scheduled a meeting in his office within two days. The parties were to appear for an early morning conference at 8:15 am.

Lu and Dan had not met since their deposition in Washington. Lu had left all the discovery work to Jessup. Now they were in the Judge's anteroom sitting silently after nodding "hello." Dan felt that quiet greeting was best, since a junior lawyer accompanied Lu and was sitting next to her. He was certain that whatever conversation passed between them would be reported to the partners.

At 8:20, the attorneys were rushed into Judge Costello's chambers by his law clerk who said, "The Judge scheduled this early meeting with you as he starts charging a jury in a criminal case at 8:30, so try to finish up as soon as you can,"

Dan looked at his watch and thought: *Only ten minutes to decide an important issue of an amended complaint adding an action for damages due to a death. It's obvious the Judge has already made up his mind.*

Judge Costello was already buttoned up in his judicial robes and leaning on the door that led to his courtroom. One hand was clutching the door knob. It was a certain sign that he had already made up his mind but nevertheless still wanted to hear what the lawyers had to say on the subject.

"Dan, you had no indication that your client was going to show emotional problems until he tried committing suicide over a month ago?"

"Right, Judge. He was depressed, as you might expect after losing a leg, but no major mental problems surfaced at first. Jack Hoffman and I had to rely on the treating physicians to give us a complete picture of his mental condition. Other than some medication for depression early in his treatment, which is surely understandable and was quickly suspended, there was no indication of an attempt to commit suicide or of any significant mental or personality problems. I calmed him down after his first attempt. When I left him, my impression was that I never thought he would carry it out. I've seen suicide attempts before. You know, they say a suicide attempt is a call for attention. I felt this was a call for attention. It wasn't. I was wrong, it was the real thing. It turned out to be the real thing."

"Why isn't Jack Hoffman here today? I really would like to hear what he has to say."

"He's trying a case in Brooklyn, Judge. After Fonseca's first attempt, Mr. Hoffman immediately alerted our psychiatrist so that we would get to know exactly the state of our client's mental condition. We were careful to make sure Mr. Fonseca was available for the Defendant for examination. They chose not to examine him."

"I would have liked to have seen Hoffman here today," the Judge said in a testy mood. "Why didn't you examine the plaintiff, Lu?"

"I felt I had to wait for your decision before we went to the expense. We never thought he would commit suicide, either."

"And you say, Dan," the Judge inquired, "that your original complaint includes a clause for mental pain and suffering?"

"It does, Judge. Now we want to amend it to add a count for wrongful death."

"Yes, I can see that. Lu, why didn't you put him to the proof on the point of mental pain and suffering?"

"Because he wasn't pursuing it. This is unfair. Dan was supposed to list all experts months ago, according to your pre-trial order and he didn't list any psychiatrist. Aside from being an unfair surprise, it will delay the trial."

"Are you arguing that I should deny these two new damages altogether?"

"I am, Judge."

"That's a pretty rough decision you want me to make."

"I know Judge. I cited some law on that point for you."

"I read those cases, Lu. I'm afraid they don't help you too much. They relate to instances where the plaintiff's attorney was aware of the damage and either concealed it or failed to go forward within a reasonable time with proper proof to determine the extent of the damages. You're not suggesting that Dan purposely waited until now to reveal his client's mental condition?

"No. But we'll be prejudiced with a delay in the trial."

"Why?"

"We have all our witnesses ready and have paid them part of their witness fees to insure their presence. That's an extra expense if we have a new date. We'll be charged for the trial date whether we go to trial or not. Then the witnesses may not be available on any new date that may be set."

"I'm sure Dan has the same headache."

"I do, Your Honor. And I have a witness coming here from England. To change the trial date would cause a lot of bureaucratic red tape to re-schedule him. He's English military."

'Well, you two, the trial is eight weeks away. Can you complete whatever discovery is needed on this point so that I can begin trying this case?" Judge Costello leaned heavier on the door knob twirling it, anxious to get into his courtroom.

"I suppose so. But I'm unable to guarantee it." Lu advised.

"Then finish it up as best you can. Dan, you cooperate, however you must, with Lu. If she tells me you have failed to do so, then I'll strongly consider denying you the right to bring this cause of action through your motion. If I'm convinced that you tried your best in the next few weeks, but Lu can't complete her discovery, I'll very reluctantly put the case over for a new trial date. Keep my clerk informed. I need to know about your progress so that I can manage my calendar."

Judge Costello leaned his body across the door, turned the doorknob and disappeared into his courtroom. Before the door closed Dan and Lu could hear the court attendant call out "All rise!"

As they walked out of Judge Costello's office Dan asked Lu, "Are you okay?"

"No. I'm very tired and confused. And I need a lot of sleep."

"Have you made up your mind about what you're going to do?"

"Yes, I have. That's why I'm so screwed up. I'm watching everything I worked for going down the drain."

"Why haven't you told me what you decided? It's been weeks since we've seen each other."

"Because where you're concerned I'm a coward and I couldn't tell you."

"Let's have some coffee and talk about this before go you back to your desk. Let's go to my office."

"No. There's a restaurant over there." She pointed up the street in the opposite direction from Dan's office.

"I think it'll better if we go there. Only the FBI knows who's trailing us," she said with a smile. "I'll send my junior back."

Understanding her reluctance, Dan gently led her by the elbow toward a luncheonette that was almost empty. The early breakfast crowd had thinned out.

"Lu, I don't want to be in your way. We can put ourselves on hold. I can't think of being with anyone but you. But I've told you before. There is another way. You don't need to be running yourself ragged and ruining your health. There's a place for you in my office, even a partnership. What do you say, Lu?"

"This is so hard. If it was two men who were friends they wouldn't be kicking up so much dust. I can't think of anything but making that partnership, which I'm so close to getting."

"I understand how you feel. But I'm not happy about it, about what it is doing to you. I'll keep pushing you to get away from that office. Do they know how we feel about each other?"

"Not yet. I suppose they'll find out very soon. They know everything about me. It's eerie. It's like the Gestapo is on my tail. Maybe the junior I just sent back will be asked to make a report about us when he goes to the office."

"Then tell them you won't work on any cases in which I act as counsel."

"I doubt that would work anymore. I know how these guys are thinking: they think that I can always read files to help you out with information, even if I'm not working on them; that I can clue you in secretly on what's going on."

"Don't you see how foolish it is to carry on with those ghouls? It doesn't make sense to think about associating with them."

"Dan, I'm so close, I have to go on. I have already told them that I will no longer work on any cases, other than Fonseca, in which you are counsel. That should satisfy them. Maybe after I become a partner I can resign, when I know I've reached my goal."

They sipped the last of their coffees. Lu put a hand over her eyes as if she was shading them from the sun and lowered her head so Dan could not see her face. She stood up from her seat and said, "I have to go, darling. I'll call you."

Dan noted her tears. It was only the second time in all the years he had known her that he had seen Lu with tears. He watched her as she walked away from him and into the street.

When she returned to her office, Lu called her secretary. "Please have Mr. Jessup come to my office." When Steve Jessup arrived Lu directed him to a seat. Her face was dark and stern. Jessup could hardly have failed to notice her mood.

"Steve," Lu began, "when you prepared the answers to the Fonseca complaint, why didn't you pursue the issue of mental pain and suffering? I put you in charge of all the pleadings. I was led to believe that you were highly capable, ready to take over my position. I suppose I should have been supervising you more closely, but I relied on your ability to handle everything. Now, not only are we facing psychiatric charges, we also have a death action to defend."

"Lucille, you know what Nikolas filed was boilerplate. It's in all the complaints filed by every plaintiff's law suit against us. Unless they pursue it, I don't pay much attention to it. No one does."

"Then why didn't you move to dismiss for failure to present proof? Didn't you think that it was a potential damage to be pursued?"

"After I read all the medical records, there was nothing in them to alert me that there might be any mental condition involved in this case. Aside from some depression at the outset, for which there was minimum treatment, there was nothing to alert me to psychological damages. Even Nikolas and Hoffman didn't pursue this area. They didn't even list any psychological experts."

"That's the same argument Dan Nikolas used to get a psychiatrist in as an expert witness at the last minute and to amend the complaint to include a wrongful death. We should have moved to dismiss that part of the damages alluding to mental damages. Now we are faced with having to defend psychological damages and a death action. And we only have eight weeks to do it. Make an appointment immediately to have a psychiatrist get us up to date on Fonseca's mental condition. We don't have much time. You should have heard Judge Costello; he was adamant about wanting everything finished before the trial date."

"Yes, I'll get on it right away."

"And Steve, from now on I want to see everything you do, every sentence, every dot, every comma. You put it on my desk before it gets sent out to opposing counsel or the court. You do realize that this is not your problem alone, but *our* problem. I'm responsible for your work. I relied on you to handle this correctly. Your lapse here reflects directly upon me. My confidence in you was misplaced. I don't know how to deal with this. If I go down, I'm afraid you'll be going with me."

೪ ೫

Jerry Keller's secretary passed a call through to his office. The caller and his voice were familiar to her, but today he seemed unusually nervous. She could feel that he was out of breath and very edgy.

"Hello, Uncle Jerry. Hi, it's Steve. I'm facing a big problem here at the office. It's that Fonseca case. First the guy tried to commit suicide. Then he really did it. It's causing some real problems at the office."

"Yeah, I know all about it. We were supposed to be in Court today. Do you know what happened with Lucille today? She was in court and I haven't gotten her report yet."

"She just got back and we immediately had a conference. I wanted to get to you before she did. She told me Judge Costello is letting psychological damages and wrongful death in. We have less than two months to prepare a defense. The judge isn't too interested in giving us a delay. We have to be ready for trial."

"That's not good news."

"I know, but that's not why I called, Uncle Jerry. She's blaming all this shit on me. She really let me have it"

"How could that be?"

"I was the one who prepared the answers to the complaint and didn't follow up on the psychological damages. They were boilerplate in the complaint. You know, happens all the time. Neither Nikolas nor Hoffman ever followed up on it either. So I didn't pay any attention to it. You know everyone files complaints like that. They try to cover everything like a bed sheet whether they have a case or not."

"So you screwed up, nephew. Why didn't you push them to provide proof of the claim? Never mind, I don't need an answer from you. It's already done. The execs at A.U. Lines won't be happy to hear this latest news. But Lucille Moore's the head associate in the maritime section. She's responsible for you and the others under her. She has to swallow what you do or don't do."

"She knows that. She said if she goes down, I go with her. I promised to be more careful the next time."

"That bitch! Don't you worry, Steve. I'll fix that bitch's ass real good. I didn't get you into that firm to have you chopped down like a tree. Does anyone know I'm your uncle?"

"No. You told me never to mention it to anyone it and I haven't."

"Sit tight and don't worry. I'll fix everything."

"And Uncle Jerry? The junior that went to court with her this morning told me when he came back, that she had coffee with Nikolas after they left the courthouse."

"Did he go with them? She told the partners she was breaking contact with him."

"No. He didn't go along. She sent him back to the office and the two of them went off alone to some nearby coffee shop."

18

APPROVAL CLAUSE

"Was Gaspar's psychological condition chronic?" Dan asked Jack Hoffman.

"Maybe. It could be an iffy situation. I don't know yet. I haven't got a final report from our psychiatrist."

"How about being able to understand the situation in eight weeks when we go to trial? I have to know, so that we can tell the jury what we want them to consider as damages. We have two separate arrows. First, the mental pain and suffering he experienced before he died and then, of course, his death."

"I'm waiting for Dr. Feinberg to give me a final report. We should divide closing remarks to the jury. I'll do the medical part and you the negligence."

"A good idea, Jack. I've spent little time on the medicals since I know they're in your good hands."

'That reminds me, Dan. I've been meaning to ask you. On separate pages at the back of the medical records prepared by Doctor Peters, there are entries that read something like the ship's log you've been showing me. It has a time next to every conversation and everything that was done with respect to Fonseca. Some of them even have the ship's physical locations. Is that usual for a ship's doctor?"

"No, it's not. I haven't seen those reports since I've been leaving the medicals for you. Make a copy for me and I'll examine them when I get a chance. There may be something here we can use."

Jack took Dr. Peters' report and shoved into a folder. "I already made an extra copy for you," he said as he passed the folder over to Dan.

"I'm getting Dr. Welles ready for trial. As soon as I have my psychiatrist's report I'll get him ready for trial. When does your helicopter man get here from England?"

"Two days before trial. I suppose you want him to get together with Dr. Welles to determine time lines and helicopter speeds?"

"Yes. It's very important that the two of them meet."

"I'll make sure he's available for you."

Lu knew there was a problem when Bradley Rogers dropped into her office unannounced. He was dressed in a tan cashmere sweater over a blue shirt and dark trousers. He wore no jacket. His tie was loosened and the top button on his shirt was opened. As he sank into a chair he let out a blast of air from closely parted lips, looked at Lu and said in an urgent tone, "Lu, since you made up your mind about Nikolas, I notice you have lost some weight and look pale. Do you want to take a few days off before trial to take the pressure off?"

"No. I don't need a rest. I've been working overtime, getting all the files I've been working on up to date before I turn them over to you for reassignment. As soon as all that is done, in about two or three more days, I won't be so tired."

"The men upstairs may want you to cut off all relations with Nikolas entirely, even outside the office. Are you ready to do that?"

"How can they ask me to do that?"

"If you want to be a partner in this law firm, your future partners can ask many things of you. In any event, it may be moot. Jerry Keller is looking to take your scalp. He doesn't want you to become a partner. He's raising hell for your failure to follow up on the psychological damages. Now, he says A.U. Lines is facing a big exposure. He's not too happy about that."

"I'm already preparing a set of questions for the jury which will require them to detail how much, if anything, they are awarding for that particular problem. If it's out of line, I'll ask the

Judge to set it aside. If he won't, we have an appeal. Even a good judge like Costello can make mistakes."

"That's good strategy, but you may not be trying the case."

"What!"

"You are aware that A.U. Line's insurance policy has a clause allowing it to approve any defense counsel the company selects. In the 30 years I have been dealing with Lloyd's, that has never been a problem. But Keller has been in touch with London, complaining about you. If he can convince them you are not to A.U. Line's liking, they will ask us to release you as head counsel in the Fonseca case."

Lu sat back in her chair, in shock. Her throat was dry. All her plans were disappearing like a wave erasing footprints on a beach.

"What does it mean, upstairs?"

"I can't say for sure. First, before anything dramatic happens, Lloyd's has to dismiss you. They haven't done that yet. They know how good you are since they get regular reports about you that I have to send them. Then, the men upstairs will probably be very reluctant to pass over you for partner for just one *faux pas*. After all, we are not losing the client. All the partners know all about your abilities. That should allow them to overlook this incident. Everyone makes mistakes, including the guys upstairs. They're not angels sent from heaven and they know it. As long as we are not in danger of losing the client, I believe you're safe."

"Bradley, I let them know how far I was willing to go to become a partner."

"I know Lucille." He stood up from his chair looked at her and said, "Get some sleep, damn it. You can't appear in front of a jury the way you look". Then he added, "Lucille, were you aware that Steve Jessup is Jerry Keller's nephew? I just found out this morning. Jessup also told Keller you had coffee with Nikolas the other day, after your court session."

Lu looked at Bradley Rogers and muttered to herself, *this is getting out of hand.*

19

PREPARING FOR TRIAL

Lu Moore called Dan at home. "Dan, even though I've made my decision, the partners want more blood. But I really want to move upstairs. Except for Fonseca, since there is no time to get a new lawyer who's capable of taking over, I'm turning all the files that you and I are working on, over for reassignment."

"What will you do if they ask you to stop having any contact with me outside the office?"

"They already have warned me about that. I'm prepared to agree to that, too. I know it sounds cold. This is what I have worked for all my life. If I were a man I wouldn't have to make these decisions. I hate them for forcing me to make them. But there it is."

"I've told you before. Forget about the partnership. Join me in my practice. I can guarantee you that we'll do well together." Hearing no reaction from Lu, Dan said sadly, "I used to say I understood this aspect of you. But I don't anymore. I'm warning you that I am going to do everything I can to get you away from that office. It's not healthy for you. Anyway, I don't wish you success in the case, but I wish you good health and success away from that office. I mean it."

Lu did not respond. Instead she said "Good night, darling," and quickly hung up.

Dan, Jack Hoffman, Drew Sloan and Charley Becker sat around the table in Dan's conference room. Before them there were neatly stacked towers of papers. One stack contained all the Pleadings in the case: the complaint, answers, motions, court orders and Judge Costello's decisions, Interrogatories filed on behalf of both parties and their Answers, Requests for Admissions and their Responses. All these documents were marked up with notes made by Gaspar's attorneys after they had carefully read each document and re-read them to link them up with verifications or denials of statements made by deponents or other witnesses in other contexts.

It is a long and tedious procedure, but a necessary task.

A second stack contained several booklets bound with blue or white plastic spiral spines. They represent every deposition taken of witnesses and experts. Colored stickers jut out from them - a hundred bookmarks and more- reminding this syndicate of legal talents where, they had all agreed, certain important testimony had to be brought out to the jury for their consideration during trial. These depositions require long hours of careful reading and cross-referencing with other testimony, looking for inconsistencies or verifications of a particular fact.

Along the far edge of the table lay the exhibits gathered during pre-trial discovery: they include the ship's logs, the charts of the English Channel, photographs of the *S.S. American Union* and photographs of the ship's operating room. There were photos of the helicopters that Commander Masterson's 771 Squadron would have used on a rescue mission, had it been asked to do so. A few weeks earlier, Masterson sent on a movie he had taken of an actual Air-Sea rescue.

When Lu Moore reviewed it, she quickly filed a motion to exclude that piece of evidence from use at trial on the grounds that it was irrelevant and not a true representation of any recovery that could have been made on the *American Union*. The film, she argued, would confuse and prejudice the jury. Judge Costello had yet to rule on this motion which, of course, Dan had opposed.

Then there were the medical records. According to the Federal Rules of Civil Procedure, a defendant is allowed to investigate a claimant's physical condition during the years prior to his or her accident. All American steamship companies require their crews to have physical exams before they sign Articles. Seaman's unions perform this task. Gaspar's sign-on physicals for the past ten years were stuffed into a large manila envelope. Copies of any other medical treatment he received during the decade prior to the loss of his leg, whether aboard ship or on land, whether pertinent to the injuries in this law suit or not, were placed into another envelope. Copies of all of these records had previously been delivered to Lu Moore at her formal request.

Dr. Peters' written record of Gaspar's operation and treatment noted aboard the ship, were placed in see-through plastic envelopes, as were the voluminous records of the Marine Hospital, which also contained the efforts of the rehabilitation company hired to fit a prosthesis, or false leg, for Gaspar Fonseca. Altogether, during the months before trial the discovery yielded thousands of pages which had accumulated before going to trial. Each of these pages also required close inspection by lawyers and their experts, to be weeded out as either irrelevant or important in the preparation of a *prima facie* case. Both sides, working hard, had completed all the extra work necessary within the time Judge Costello had ordered them to complete their discovery on the new issues that had arisen late in the pre-trial. Now, both sides were ready for trial.

Dan sees the preparation for a trial as similar to presenting a play for a theater audience. He is both producer and director. He determines which witnesses best play the roles in his law suit-performance. Which of his witnesses will he allow to testify, for best effect? Which witness is not one Dan thinks will help his case. He plans which facts will get into testimony and then into the record. He determines what fact or evidence he must leave out because it is repetitive or will detract the jury's attention and is of little value, anyway. He decides how long a witness-actor can testify before becoming a bore. He decides the order of the evidence as it unfolds, for the greatest impact on the jury. It is, after all, a story he is telling the jury. It must have a logical start, a coherent middle and a good final act that will remain in the minds of the jurors when they begin their deliberations.

Dan reviews the questions he will ask. They are always carefully prepared in advance, as if they were lines in a script to be used by a role player. He rarely reads directly from the notes. He memorizes them and then delivers his lines as if he, too, were an actor in his own play. In truth, he is so familiar with this case that he can tell you most anything about it without having to refer to the documents. That is, almost anything.

For the first time in all the years he has been trying cases, he does not concern himself with the medical part of his presentation. It's Jack Hoffman's concern. While they are each focused on their part of the trial, both men are somewhat aware of what the other is doing.

Dan knows that lawyers use long complicated words to describe their professional activities. So for his opening remarks and the presentation of questions during trial, he pares down his words wherever possible; four syllable words are cut down to three; three syllable words to two. Two syllables to one. Which words won't the jury understand or have problems with? He will eliminate them, if possible, substituting a word or words more familiar. If he has to use big words, then he must be sure to explain their meaning to his jury. He makes sure jurors learn that a bulkhead is a ship's wall and that a ship's ladder is her staircase with handrails, just like the jurors have in their homes. A ship's ladder is not something you prop against a wall to do a paint job. It's important, because during this trial some witnesses will be regularly using maritime terms with which the jurors are probably unfamiliar.

"Starboard is the right side of a ship, ladies and gentlemen of the jury, and port, the left side. A mariner measures speed in knots and distances in nautical miles. It is important in this case that you, the jury, understand that these measurements differ from everyday land measurements and these differences are intimately involved with the reasons Gaspar Fonseca became a man without his left leg, Pay attention, please, because I will be explaining these differences to you during the trial, together with their application."

All this Dan will tell the jury.

In a large law firm such as Lu Moore's, there are many more lawyers to assist in this process of preparation. She has paralegals to sort out the documents and do the work of matching up and cross-indexing testimony. Her work will be similar to Dan's, except that she must concentrate on a strong cross-examination of his witnesses, to either soften their testimony or destroy it altogether. Unlike Dan, she is also going to be handling the medical portion of the case in her client's defense.

If Dan and Jack can't make out their *prima facie* case, Lu needn't go any further. She will ask the court to dismiss it, which, if granted, ends any chance the estate of Gaspar Fonseca has of recovering damages, unless it is appealed to the Second Circuit Court of Appeals.

When Congress gave a seaman the right to sue his employer for negligence, that right was not extended to his wife and family or any other person to also sue for any damages they may have suffered as a result of the seaman's loss. Gaspar Fonseca's death means that his estate is the sole beneficiary of any award the jury may be disposed to give him. Thus, since Gaspar Fonseca had never executed a will, only those entitled to share in his estate pursuant to New York State law would be able to recover any money as his legitimate heirs. For the moment, under New York law, if Gaspar wins his case the beneficiaries will be Mira and Ronny Fonseca.

20

DOWNGRADING LUCILLE MOORE BROWN, SYKES AND BELLHAM

With three days left before the trial, four of the senior partners at Brown, Sykes and Bellham ordered the firm's dining room closed to everyone from 10 a.m. until lunch time. Some important decisions were going to be made and the partners wished to meet privately to consult about them. It was the only place available, as all six conference rooms were in use. Only four of the eight senior partners were in attendance: Bradley Rogers, Dudley Hayes, Robert Carney and Grady Roul sat before Lu Moore and Steve Jessup, who had been summoned first thing this morning. Dudley Hayes, the firm's managing partner spoke first.

"Lucille, although both you and Bradley have been positive in your assessment of our chances for a defendant's verdict in *Fonseca vs A.U. Lines,* we can't lose sight of the fact that a loss would be very distasteful. A.U. Lines fears that if that happened, it would appear to the public as a callous and uncaring company. Especially in view of the latest development of the seaman's suicide, you certainly understand that we can't allow that to happen," Hayes went on.

"So we have come to the following solution which we feel will avoid any problems with respect to your relationship with plaintiff's counsel." Hayes paused, cleared his throat with an unnecessary cough, and continued. "You will be relieved as lead counsel in the case, Lucille, and you will assist Steve Jessup in every way you can. He will assume the role of chief trial counsel."

"What's the reason for this?" It was the blow Lu was expecting.

"Lucille, be assured that we have not changed our view of your importance to our firm or your fine talents as a lawyer. It's just that we are being pressured by A.U. Lines. We also feel it is best to avoid any appearance of your partiality to Fonseca's attorney. Jerry Keller, acting for both the company and the insurer, insists you be taken off the case as lead counsel. The partners asked me to select a suitable replacement for you. I suggested Steve Jessup, without consulting with you. I hope you agree. He is, after all, directly beneath you in the Maritime Department."

"I suppose so," Lu answered, almost in a trance. She wasn't really hearing Hayes' words as they were coming slowly and in a deep growly drawl, as if in a dream where everything was happening in slow motion. They came to her muffled and difficult to comprehend. *They've got me in a corner. I have to agree. Somehow I have to get out of this. They're dismissing me like an old shoe. They have drained everything they can from me and are now casting me aside.*

"You should get someone else to work with Steve," Lu suggested. "I'm sure he may be self-conscious with me sitting at his side. After all, I am his supervisor."

"Nonsense," Robert Carney interrupted. "No one knows the case as well as you, Lucille."

Then why remove me, knucklehead?, she thought.

"Absolutely, sir, I want her beside me. We'll be working like a team as we have been all along preparing this case," Steve Jessup added, both giddy with his new role and jittery with its acquired responsibility.

"Seems to me that I'm to be the sacrificial lamb, Gentlemen? No matter how this case turns out, I'm the fall guy. If we win, young Steve here gets all the laurels. If we lose, we have Lucille Moore to blame. You're not even giving me the opportunity to fall on my face as lead counsel."

There was a silence in the room. All the partners looked down at the table tops in front of them and away from Lu except Bradley Rogers, who made an attempt at saving Lu's position, dignity and future in the firm.

"Lucille," he suggested, "perhaps you could make a set of questions for Jessup to use at trial. Steve could use them in direct and cross examinations."

Lu ignored Rogers' suggestion. Then she said: "Is all this because you don't trust me to be professional in my dealings with Mr. Nikolas? If it is, then I take exception to everything that's going on here today. And I wonder how you would even want me in the same court room with him."

"No, Miss Moore. We are being pressured by a client to do this. It's not something we dreamed up." Grady Roul stepped in. He still wasn't looking directly at Lu. "We're all aware of your abilities and would not do this unless we were asked to do so by a client who is a significant contributor to our firm's income. We do this in the best interests of the firm."

"We only have three days before trial. I suggest we let Steve and Lucille get to work on the trial preparation," Hayes, the managing attorney, ordered.

After the two lawyers left the dining room, Grady Roul asked his partners to remain. "Gentlemen, we may be facing some very real difficulties with Miss Moore." He smiled with all teeth bared.

"How is that, Grady?" Rogers asked.

"Are you aware of a recent act Congress passed called the Equal Employment Opportunity Act? It's only a couple of years old, came down in 1966, I believe. It allows employees, such as Miss Moore, to bring suits against their employers for religious, color, racial, age, or sexual discrimination. We could be facing a law suit if she tries to prove she was discriminated by us because of her sex."

"Where's the discrimination if a client pressures us to do this?" Robert Carney asked. "I don't see it at all. It isn't our decision to put her down. After all, we have been thinking of making her a partner."

"We are her employers. And how many women partners are in the firm? We are the ones who are acting as the potential discriminators. We could always tell the client 'no.' This law is so new I can't say whether what you are suggesting, Bob, is a good defense. There are very few cases reported as of now. But even if we were sued and Miss Moore couldn't prove her case, the publicity for us is not what I would care to have brought out in the newspapers or within our legal community. We could have a difficult time hiring a secretary."

"Where do we stand on making her a partner?" Robert Carney asked.

"That's not for us to decide here today. There are four other absent partners. They also have to be consulted." Rogers insisted.

"Maybe yes, maybe no. Among the four of us, how do we stand?" Roul pressed. "As for me, I don't believe I can trust her."

"I go along with Grady." Carney agreed.

"You can't be serious," Bradley Rogers said. "She's the best and brightest associate in this firm. She's done everything we asked her to do with respect to her relationship with this Nikolas fellow. To lose her would be like throwing away a gem. As far as I am concerned, she continues to be best in line for the next partnership opening."

"I agree with Brad," Hayes added. "She has acted to accommodate us in everything we asked of her. No doubt, she is the best candidate for partner regardless of her sex. I want to see her move upstairs."

"Have you told her she was being considered for a partnership?" Carney asked.

"Not formally. But everyone in the office knows we have been discussing it and so does she. We've asked her to train a successor and re-assign all her cases. That could only mean we are moving her upstairs or firing her. She knows she's moving upstairs. You can't keep something like that secret for very long. It's even on the street," Rogers responded.

"Do you think she knows about this discrimination law, Bradley?" Carney asked.

"This is a very bright lady who reads up on all the new laws, not just Maritime. Of course she knows."

"Then I suggest we still keep her in line for a partnership. This way we keep benefitting from her talent. It will also avoid strife and our firm becoming the object of public rebuke. We can always dig up something in the future that will disqualify her. Then we can ask her to leave politely and with a good excuse."

"We'll have to see what our other four brothers have to say about that," Rogers said, raising his voice in anger. "We should meet as soon as possible to discuss this. It's underhanded and not worthy of us. If we are not going to advance her, she has a right to know now. In the meantime, let's give those two young people all our support. We want to win this case," Rogers emphasized as the partners rose from the table and returned to their offices.

"And, Gentlemen," Roul added as an afterthought, "If it comes to it, I am sure that we, all of us partners, could testify that she was never seriously considered for a partnership."

"Not I," said Bradley Rogers.

"Nor I," echoed Dudley Hayes.

21

GREENWICH VILLAGE

Jack Hoffman's spacious apartment is on the 15th floor of a recently constructed 16-story condominium on East Eighth Street, just a few blocks from Lu Moore's University Place apartment. Yet the two lawyers might have been living miles apart. Jack's building rises near Cooper Union College, an institution with an historic pedigree. Abraham Lincoln debated Stephen Douglas in the school's Grand Hall, delivering his famous campaign speech of February, 1860. That speech was credited with giving Lincoln the boost he needed for his presidential ambitions. Since then, Manhattan has grown up around the area of the school. Nearby businesses bustle with commercial activity. Jack is conscious that over the last century, three nearby bridges visible from his apartment, the Brooklyn, Manhattan and Williamsburg, have spanned the East River connecting Long Island to Manhattan and the rest of the American continent.

Lu Moore's apartment is not as spacious as Jack's. While she lives on a respectable street, her apartment house is 40 years old and does not have the amenities that Jack's building affords him. Lu has no air conditioner, no dishwasher and the view from her windows look out onto other apartments, which necessitates that her shades must often be lowered.

Jack, who is a recent widower, greets Dan at his apartment door with a glass of Bourbon and water, filled with ice, remembering what Dan was drinking when they were in Bethesda. The two men had agreed that this work session should be outside the office and informal, during the evening and only between the two of them. The purpose was to set final strategy and the presentation of the case in an orderly manner, so that there would be no confusion in the jury's minds. They also had to deal with Gaspar's dramatic last-minute suicide. How was Jack going to handle that issue in his medical presentation? And how should they dovetail their parts of the case to take advantage of each other's witnesses?

Jack told Dan that it was important for the Fonseca family to testify about Gaspar's pain, his loss of ambition and other symptoms, all of which pointed to severe depression. The rules of evidence provide for the right to read into the record any part of or all testimony taken during a deposition of a witness who is unavailable at trial. That certainly applied to Gaspar Fonseca. The rules also permitted any party to read any selected portions of the opposing party's deposition taken as cross examination, into the record. Dan had been thinking about that one for a long while.

The two lawyers went over Gaspar's testimony carefully and highlighted only those portions Jack planned to read into the record. Since Dan also planned to read Gaspar's testimony, it was agreed to first read his entire testimony into the record.

"I'll make copies of these pages related to his mental condition," Jack said. "I'll give them to our psychiatrist so that he can get a good picture of Gaspar's state of mind before his suicide. If you read Gaspar's entire deposition and I read selected portions later, we have two shots at his mental condition. Then give me a copy of the family's testimony that you'll be using on trial, which our psychiatrist will also need in order to form his final opinion about Gaspar's mental state before and after the loss of his leg. Fortunately, our psychiatrist accommodated us by examining Fonseca right after his suicide attempt. If he hadn't, we would have a difficult time showing what our client was like before that."

After two hours, they finished their work. Jack went into his kitchen and came out with two trays of food neatly wrapped in plastic covers and obviously catered. As they ate, Dan said, "Lu Moore lives nearby, on University Place."

"It's none of my business, Dan, but the two of you seem close."

"We went to law school together. Later we became adversaries and now a little more than close, as you put it," Dan said as he plunged a fork into a layer of buffalo mozzarella. "That's causing her some problems."

"How is that, if I'm not intruding on your privacy?"

"No, it's okay. I've been pushing her to leave her office and work with me. She told me before I came here that they've taken her off the case as lead counsel. She's reduced to assisting. The partners say the client insists on that because she and I are friendly."

"Seems a foolish thing to do to a bright young lady they're considering for a partnership. Who will be trying the case?"

"Steve Jessup. I've met him a few times. I don't know too much about him except that Lu has never been impressed with him." Dan took a long sip of ice water. "He is one of the lawyers Lu regularly supervises. He's been groomed personally by Lu for quite a while, to take over her place when and if she ever gets to become a partner and move upstairs."

"Maybe we can make him look stupid. Is she really certain she wants to work with a bunch of jerks who would sacrifice her like that? Your offer to take her into your office sounds like a good solution to this problem."

"Yes, but she wants to be a partner there. It is an obsession with her. You have a great idea. I'd like to make Jessup look like a dope. Then maybe we can break her free from the partners."

"Well. I hope your young lady will learn something from this situation."

After they finished eating Jack said, "Have you looked at those extra entries I gave you the other day which come from the ship doctor's notes?"

"Haven't had a chance, Jack. I'll get to them. I'll give them to Masterson to look at when he gets to New York."

"Something bothers me about them. I never saw notes separated like that and I can't make too much of speed and landmarks. It's odd to me. I haven't ever seen doctors make separate notes like that."

171

Dan said good night to Jack. As he rode the elevator down to the street, he thought he might drop in on Lu. It wasn't yet 10 o'clock, so it would be early enough. What would she say? Would she be happy to see him? Or would she seem awkward in light of what she had told him during the last few days? No. His presence would only irritate the situation so close to the trial. He walked west along Eighth Street, then turned right on to University Place and passed by Lu's apartment house. There were the familiar street level buttons for ringing up an apartment to gain entry into the building. Should he ring Lu's apartment?

He looked up. There on the third floor he could see that lights in her windows were burning. He walked toward the door then stopped at the threshold. *To hell with it,* he muttered to himself. *It's the way she wants it, I have to respect it.* The night was pleasant, so he decided to take a short stroll through Union Square. He walked north across the Square to Seventeenth Street and Broadway, where he hailed a cab and directed the driver to Eighty-First Street and Riverside Drive.

22

THE TRIAL BEGINS

Those close to Dan Nikolas know he regularly opens his office around seven a.m., as it gives him a few undisturbed working hours. The next morning, two days before the Fonseca trial, his phone rings at seven-fifteen.

He knew who it was. "Good morning, Lu. How are you?"

"I'm not too good. I didn't want to call you yesterday because I knew you would be busy. And I didn't want to call you at home last night because I was afraid our conversation would get too maudlin. I couldn't have that."

"You wouldn't have found me at home. I was at Jack Hoffman's last night. He lives near you. I almost dropped in on you. But then I thought I shouldn't"

"You would have been welcomed. Ray would have loved to have seen you. I've been reduced to assisting Steve Jessup, who is lead counsel now."

"Did you forget that you already told me that? Don't you get all muddled, now. Even though you're only assisting, you still have some professional obligations to keep your head on straight. I didn't like the way you looked the last time I saw you. You looked drained, pale and unhappy. Give all this up, Lu. Come into my office. Jack and I are going to do everything we can to make your Mr. Jessup look stupid. When the case is over, we're hoping you'll look like a queen and tell those guys, who are going to be your partners, to go to hell. I mean it. They need to be told off."

Lu just wanted to talk. "They don't trust me. The official position is that A.U. Lines doesn't want any smell of a conflict of interest. Even though I've assured the company that they have a good chance of winning this case, they are disregarding my evaluation."

Dan ignored Lu's last remark.

"What does it mean for your partnership hopes?"

"I really don't know. I'm dealing with a bunch of scared men who are looking at the fees they might be losing. Instead of kneeling to the client, they should be more assertive and make them understand they have a good case. I have the nasty feeling that they are carrying me for now and that after this case I'm on my own."

"You're allowing them to jerk you around. Fight back. I've told you that more than once."

"I can't help it. They hold the keys to my becoming a partner."

"You do have some legal redress. If it comes to that, I can find you a first class lawyer to represent you in a discrimination action."

"I know. I know. I pray I don't have to resort to that."

"Lu, during the trial will you be expected to assist with questions and suggestions?"

"That's the idea."

"Write down every question and suggestion you make to Jessup and hang on to them. Don't lose them. You may need them in a show-down with those asses who are your bosses."

"I will. Thanks for the advice. I appreciate it. I should have thought of it myself but maybe, as you can tell, I'm not thinking straight these days. Good luck to you on trial." She wanted to say "I love you," but didn't. It would have created an emotional problem for her.

"I love you, Lu. I won't wish you good luck. You know why."

"Yes, I do. Have a good day. I'll see you at trial." She laughed in the way Dan loved, a childish giggle, then said, "Don't make eyes at me in the court room." Dan could imagine the smile on her lips.

From the first moment Commander Robert Masterson walked into Dan Nikolas' office two days before trial, he captured everyone's eye. Dressed in his dark blue Royal Navy uniform, with his military bearing and precise British accent, he was an instant object of curiosity and delight. Dan ushered him into the conference room, where Masterson had his first look at the piles of evidence on the table.

"It's a bloody piece of business you're putting together here, Dan," he said as he swept his hand over the table. "I have the ship's route and the helicopter I would have used to make a proper pickup. My lads would have been flying Wasps. The Wasp would have been best with its longer range than the Scout. For now, that's only a guess until I put all the facts together. It can take over four passengers. But I have to be certain as to when the Captain says he was first aware of the need to call for assistance."

"By the way, Robby, did you take a look at these notes, made by the ship's doctor? I haven't had time to examine them, I've been so busy. Perhaps they can help you."

"I received them just before I left the UK. I haven't had time to go over them, either. Leave me alone. I'll first have to make projections for using my Wasps. It'll take a while. Then I'll figure out if your doctor's notes help us any way. Please get me some calipers, a sharp pencil and a ruler. After I'm all finished with these calculations, I'll knock you up." He looked up to see Dan's big smile.

"Ah," Dan said, laughing. "I was forewarned about that expression. I know it means I'll call you on the phone. When you are finished, Robby, you will have to be prepared for your testimony at trial. How long will you take to finish your projections?"

"Not too long, I only have to verify petrol capacity with regard to exact distances to Plymouth, Exeter and Tourquay and, of course, look at your doctor's notes."

In the days and hours before appearing at Court to begin a trial, there is a frenzy of last minute work. Jack Hoffman is at Dr. Welles' office preparing his testimony. While he's there, he hands the doctor a sheaf of paper.

"What's this, Jack?"

"I asked Dan Nikolas for them and he got them for me, Sean. These sheets are the menus the company prepares to feed their crew. Read them carefully. I have a feeling you could use them to your advantage when you're on the witness stand under cross examination."

When Jack is finished with Sean Welles, he goes on to Dr. Marcus Feinberg, the psychiatrist, for last minute preparations. He gives Dr. Feinberg the marked up copies of Gaspar's deposition testimony. Then he hands him the proposed testimony the family will give at trial. He asks Dr. Feinberg to also study them carefully.

Charley Becker is in his office with Professor Stein going over the financial losses that will be presented at trial. Dan and Drew Sloan are working with Mira, Gaspar's mother and Bobby, his brother. Dan had already determined that brother Mike's testimony would be repetitive and could be done away with.

The testimony of every witness has been typed into script form with questions and answers, and then placed into a booklet for each of them. While neither Dan nor Jack will ever directly read questions from these booklets during trial, they make sure each question is asked, marking them off with a red pencil as they go along.

At the Court House, Dan and Jack arrive with Sloan behind them, towing two large cartons secured to a small hand cart. The contents will be spread out neatly and evenly on counsel's table in four piles, each about six to eight inches high. Over his years as a trial lawyer, Dan has learned that the jury is always curious about what those piles contain.

"What's in them?" they ask themselves. When they first appear, stacked out on the counsel table, Dan has instantly captured their interest, whetted their curiosity. As the trial progresses, Dan makes sure the jury watches the piles dwindle, satisfying them about each fact and event contained within the wordy booklets and papers. He picks up documents listed as exhibits from the table with a flourish and a reverence. He shows them to each witness as they take the stand and asks them to testify as to the relevance of each important fact or piece of evidence. Extra copies of certain significant exhibits have been made, one for each juror and one for the Court to examine personally.

Dan knows the jury will be impressed with the neatness of his stacked piles. They will feel a certain satisfaction when the last of the exhibits has been picked up, used and then set away after their relevance has been explained and they have been docketed into the voluminous court record. At trial's end, all those exhibits will go back into the cartons and, hopefully, the jury will be convinced that the plaintiff has apprised them of every necessary and pertinent fact of the case; and perhaps more importantly, that both he and Jack have satisfied the Jury that every promise of facts they have been told the plaintiff intends to prove, have indeed been proven. Now they are ready for the defendant's assault. But as psychiatrists say, "First impressions are the ones that last."

The first impressions of this case were the ones Dan and Jack Hoffman will be making. Hopefully they will be strong because there is another psychological adage, "Last impressions are lasting impressions."

Dan wants to have a lock on the jury's full attention because after the defendant presents its case, which is designed to destroy and debunk all the careful work he and Jack have carefully presented, it will, hopefully, still stand, strong and true. After the lawyers have presented their case and rested, neither side may go back to correct an error or change testimony. At that point, Judge Costello will take over. He will charge the jury, explaining the law and how they are obliged to faithfully apply it in this case. The jury leaves the court room to discuss what they have seen and heard during the trial and try to translate all that into a fair and just verdict.

Before jury selection begins and as Dan sets up his documents in the almost empty courtroom, he sees Captain Burn sitting in the last row. Burn is wearing a U.S. Navy uniform with rows of colorful medals across his chest. For those who know and could read them, his shoulder boards and the gold stripes circling his cuffs read "Rear Admiral, United States Navy". Lu and Jessup, who had arrived before Dan and Jack, are setting up their table. Dan and Jack come over to shake hands with opposing counsel.

"I expect the Judge is in his chambers, I'm asking for a conference immediately." Dan advised.

"What's the problem?" Jessup asked.

"There's the problem." Dan pointed to Captain Burn, who was looking straight at the judge's bench and ignoring the four lawyers in conversation.

"I don't understand."

"Don't you think that a witness dressed in a U. S. Naval officer's uniform with all that fruit salad on his chest is designed to prejudice the jury?"

"No, I don't," Jessup said in a loud and belligerent voice. "He is a Rear Admiral in the Naval Reserves." Lu stood silent, showing no emotion.

"Let's leave it to the Judge. I'll ask the clerk to tell the Judge we want to speak with him."

Judge Costello stood up from his desk and greeted the lawyers as they entered his chambers.

"Good morning. Whatever problems you two have, have you tried working them out?" The Judge looked at Lu and Dan.

"I'm not lead counsel anymore, Judge," Lu informed Judge Costello. "This is my associate, Steve Jessup. He's running the case. I'm assisting."

"Are you okay, Lu? Why the change?"

"Strategy, Your Honor, strategy."

"Welcome to you, Mr. Jessup," Judge Costello said with a puzzled look on his face. "Is this your first time before me?"

"It is, Your Honor."

Judge Costello sat back in his chair. "I won't waste time telling you how I expect you to behave in my courtroom. Lu will fill you in on that. Now tell me, what's the problem here?"

Dan stretched at the corner of his seat and said, "There's a witness sitting in the courtroom right now wearing an Admiral's uniform. He's only a reserve officer, according to Mr. Jessup. I believe his uniform is designed to prejudice the jury in the defendant's favor. I don't want the jury to see him in that uniform."

"Which one of you thought that one up?" Judge Costello asked pointing to Lu and then Jessup, who turned red and said,

"I did, sir."

"Is he an Admiral?"

"In the reserves, Judge."

"Well, Mr. Jessup, that's stretching it a bit, don't you think? Mary," Judge Costello called to his secretary, "there's a gentleman in the courtroom in a Navy uniform. Ask him to come to my chambers."

Judge Costello pointed a finger at Jessup.

"Young man, as Miss Moore will tell you, I don't like end runs in my courtroom. I'm an old football player. I didn't appreciate them when I played football and I don't like them in my courtroom."

Burn entered the chambers, looking confused. Judge Costello greeted him cordially, asked him to be seated and began asking questions. After eliciting his name and the fact that he was the Captain of the *American Union*, the Judge asked, "Why do you come to my court room dressed in an Admiral's uniform?"

"I discussed it with Mr. Jessup. We both felt it would be a good idea for the jury to know who I am and my importance."

"Those facts will have to be brought out by your lawyer during trial, with the proper direct examination. Do you wear this uniform all the time?"

"No, sir."

"How often do you wear it?"

"Once a year. I wear it while I'm on reserve duty, for about two weeks. Sometimes I might wear it as long as a month."

"Then I can't allow you to wear that uniform in my courtroom. It's deceiving."

"How about the uniform he wears aboard ship, Your Honor?" Jessup said as he looked at a note Lu had just passed to him.

"How often do you wear that uniform, Captain?"

"Every day while I am at sea, Judge."

"You may wear that uniform to my court. And Mr. Jessup, you will be careful to advise the jury that it is not a military uniform but a company uniform that he wears, as Captain of his ship. If you fail to properly do so, there will be hell to pay. I will then have to advise the jury and it won't be pretty for you. And, by the way, get him out of the courtroom. He's a fact witness. He's not supposed to be there."

Dan smiled. The case was starting out just right for the plaintiff and for making Jessup look stupid. Lu looked straight ahead, stony-faced. Dan noticed she was folding the note she had passed to Jessup and placing it into her jacket pocket.

Great sweetheart, keep it up.

Picking juries in a civil case in a United States District Court hardly ever evokes the drama of picking a jury in a criminal trial. In criminal cases, lawyers spend time digging deep into the psychic and personal lives of prospective jurors to learn if they can be fair, how they feel about crime, punishment, the death penalty if relevant, and the criminal who is on trial.

In civil trials the Judge addresses jurors, asks the basic questions such as "are the jurors acquainted with any of the attorneys in this court?" or "do any of the jurors or their immediate family work in a law office or a steamship company?" If an attorney has some doubts about a juror, he may not express them directly but only through the Judge by written request.

Each side may dismiss four jurors without any explanation. It's called a peremptory challenge. An attorney looks at a juror. He or she may not like how a juror looks or perhaps the juror is a civil servant or an accountant, notorious among plaintiff's attorneys for their conservative outlook and disinclination to hand out large money awards.

Unfortunately for all trial lawyers, it is a two-way street. A trial lawyer may remind a juror of a teacher who failed him in math; or the way a lawyer dresses may create a negative attitude.

An unlimited amount of jury dismissals are permitted for cause, such as prejudice in favor of a litigant, expressing distaste for persons trying to recover damages or, personal knowledge of a litigant or one of the attorneys.

Aside from outright prejudice, Dan has always felt that any 12 disinterested persons could arrive at a fair verdict. A veteran lawyer whom he knew at the beginning of his career had often told him: "I believe in God, the U.S. Constitution and the American jury system."

Some law firms in significant cases have been known to hire persons, picking them at random from pedestrians on the street, to act as jurors. A mock trial is then held before them. After their verdict, they are asked questions about the presentation and why they found for or against a particular party. But Dan feels the jury is a collective mind; a unified consciousness and that they most often arrive at the correct decision after a proper trial presentation.

A jury has finally been picked together with two alternates, in case any juror falls ill or becomes disqualified. Dan began his opening remarks. He narrated the facts of his case, making some important promises about what he intended to prove during trial. After each promise he pointed to the pile of booklets on his table. He told the jury that Jack Hoffman would be presenting the medical part of this case; that Jack would show them that there was adequate time to help Gaspar Fonseca and that they could expect Jack to make closing remarks about the medical case at the end of the trial.

Dan was purposely piquing the jury's curiosity. He knew he could keep every promise he and Jack made, because the answers were already there, buried deep inside those documents, depositions and exhibits. He knew from speaking with jurors, after a trial was over, and a jury verdict rendered, what happens if a promise is not kept. It is a negative for the lawyers. There is a strong focus on unfulfilled promises during jury deliberations, often going badly for the lawyer who made them.

After Dan concluded his opening remarks, Steve Jessup addressed the jury, attacking the plaintiff's position, making promises of his own. Jessup emphasized two strong facts: The captain of a ship makes all the decisions while at sea, and Captain Burn's decisions in this case were made after much consideration and always thinking of the safety of the lives of his passengers and crew and his ship and cargo. Then Jessup told them to listen carefully to all the testimony about the location of the ship. He told them that he was going to show them that it was too late to make any effective rescue. Finally, Jessup told the jury that when both sides have rested their cases, he was confident they will find for his client, since all the law and the facts were on his side.

Not a bad opening, Dan mused. He hears and senses Lu's hand in it, but the delivery is flat. It reminded him of a high school recitation: memorized with pre-arranged emphasis and pre-choreographed hand movements during certain parts of the presentation. There is no juice here, no passion expressing this lawyer's belief that his client is really free of all the malfeasance the plaintiff has accused it of. Dan knew not to get too cocky, however. Lu sits beside this lawyer. She won't allow this case to get out of hand. If Jessup has half a brain, he'll do everything she suggests.

To open his case, Dan presents Gaspar's widow Mira, his mother Philomena, speaking through an interpreter, and his brother Bobby as the first three witnesses in the case.

Mira tells the jury of her life at home before Gaspar lost his leg. She details their dreams; the plans they had made for after Gaspar would become an officer and began earning more money. They would have found a new home, one they would own, instead of renting. It would have been in a new neighborhood, where there were good schools for their son Ronny to attend. They dreamed of having another child, which they would have been able to afford. Mira then goes on to tell the jury how the couple loved each other; how when Gaspar came home from a trip he often brought gifts for her and Ronny and his mother and brothers. How she would look forward to the few days they would be together between trips. They would go dancing. Gaspar loved to dance. He was always laughing and making jokes. The couple would visit family and friends. When he was on a month's vacation, the family would go to the beach or even to the country for a weekend. He would fish with his brothers and play ball with his friends in the neighborhood. Mira would show Gaspar the little repairs that needed to be done in the house, and he would fix them.

Now Dan asked Mira how it was after Gaspar's leg had been removed.

"He was not the same, Mr. Nikolas."

"In what way, Mrs. Fonseca?"

"In many ways. They were trying to fit him with an artificial leg, but they were not successful. His leg would get full of pain every time they tried putting on that new leg. He would complain of the pain. Sometimes when he was alone and he didn't know I saw him, he would cry. There were other things, too."

"We'll get to those. Tell us what did he do about his leg?"

"We went to the people who were fitting him for an artificial leg. We complained to them about the pain, but it was always the same. He suffered so much because every time they tried a new leg he would be in pain. We complained again and again. Finally, Mr. Nikolas, you found a new company to work with him. His artificial leg was never any good. Gaspar complained of pain with every step he took. Many times he refused to put the leg on because he was in so much pain. So then we used a wheelchair. His brother Mike, who is a carpenter, built a ramp on the steps into our house so I could wheel him up and down."

"Was he ever able to use his leg without pain?"

"No. Never."

"Mrs. Fonseca, what was your family and social life like after Gaspar lost his leg?"

"You can imagine. He was home all day, sitting in the corner of the bedroom, looking at the walls, no more laughs, no more jokes, no more dancing. He told me he didn't want to spend time with our son because he didn't want to him to see his father without a leg. And he would ignore me for most of the day. We spoke mostly at meal time or when I had to help him with his leg or he needed me to help him to do something.

"The only time he saw his friends was when they came to the house. He hardly ever went out. Sometimes when I went shopping or it was a beautiful day, I would insist that he get into a wheel chair and take him out. But he was not happy to go and he would tell me so.

"He would get very angry at little things. When he wasn't sitting alone, he would sleep for hours during the day. He was always angry. When we would speak, I asked him if he would think seriously about going back to school so that he could learn something, like how do you call it? A skill. Yes, a skill. Then he would shout at me and say 'don't bother me, I can't think of that now.'"

"What, if anything, did he tell you about himself or any plans he had for the future?"

"Nothing. He wasn't thinking about the future anymore or any other plans either, like he used to do before he lost his leg. He even tried committing suicide one night. And you remember, Mr. Nikolas, you came over to the house after I called you. You were able to calm him down."

"What happened after that?"

"He went to a psychiatrist. But that didn't help either. He finally killed himself." Mira's last words were barely audible. Dan filled a glass with water from a carafe which sat on his table. He handed it to Mira, who had drawn a handkerchief from her handbag and was drying her tears. Then Dan asked the court reporter to read back Mira's last answer.

"I don't believe the jury or the court heard it, my client was speaking in such a low voice."

"Mrs. Fonseca, do you want a short recess?" Judge Costello asked.

"No sir, I can go on."

"Are you sure, Mrs. Fonseca? I can call a recess if you wish," Judge Costello was insisting.

"Thank you, Judge, I want to finish this now. I don't want to wait any longer."

"Then go on with your direct, Mr. Nikolas," Judge Costello ordered, waving at Dan to continue.

"Please tell us where you were on the day your husband committed suicide."

"We went to the new people who were fitting him for an artificial leg. He had suffered so much because every time they gave him a new leg he would cry in pain. Finally, Mr. Nikolas, you found a new company for him. We went to their office in a building. It was on the fifth floor. While we were waiting Gaspar complained of the pain.

"I told him to take a pain killer that his doctor had prescribed. Then he said he needed to go to the bathroom. That was the last time I saw him alive. I was waiting for him to return when I heard people yelling and shouting. They said someone had jumped from a window. I knew immediately it was Gaspar. He went down five stories. I looked down from the window and there he was. I saw him lying there on the floor of the alley. He left his crutches by the window. It was horrible. I didn't want to, but the police made me identify him. It was terrible to see him like that. Dead, I mean..." She stopped to regain her composure.

Dan looked up at Judge Costello and said, "With your permission Your Honor, I would like to approach the witness."

"All right counselor, go ahead."

During an examination an attorney may not go near a witness unless the Court permits it. Dan held Gaspar Fonseca's artificial leg in his hand. He held it chest high and showed it to the jury and then to Mira. It was made of leather and metal, with straps hanging down. It was in the shape of a leg and it was hollow.

"Mrs. Fonseca, do you recognize what I am holding and which has been marked as plaintiff's Exhibit Four in Evidence?"

"Yes, I do."

"Please tell us what it is."

"The last artificial leg Gaspar was using before he died."

Dan stood beside Mira. With two hands he gently placed the leg in Mira's lap.

"Can you please show the judge and jury where Gaspar's stump was placed in this artificial leg?"

"Yes." Mira said as she picked up the leg gingerly as if it had some negative quality to it. She turned first to show the jury, then she turned in the other direction so the judge could also see the leg, just as Dan had instructed her to do when he was preparing her for her testimony that she would give in Court.

"Here in the part they call the socket," she said as she held it high, pointing to the socket at the top of the leg.

"How do you know this?"

"I would help Gaspar put on the leg every time he used it. When he took it off, I would help him again with it."

"There are some dark spots on the lining in the socket. Do you know what they are?"

"Yes, I do. These are blood spots

"If you know, please tell us how they got there."

"Gaspar would have a cloth that covered his stump. When I would help him remove the leg, the cloth on his stump, it would often be bloody and spots went from that cloth into the socket." Again Mira raised the socket to show the Court and the jury the blood spot, by pointing to it with a slender finger.

"Mrs. Fonseca, you have told us about how your husband's life changed with your son, his family and friends. Can you tell us what the relationship between the two of you was like after the loss of his leg?"

"Yes. Gaspar lost interest in life. He had no ambition. He never spoke about his future or how it would be when he would be able to use his artificial leg. We stopped being together as husband and wife."

She paused, her cheeks turning hot, her face red with the last words she had uttered. *That the world should know that Gaspar did not want to be with me,* she thought. *How embarrassed I am.* "I had hoped that when he received his artificial leg things would change. But that did not happen." She put her handkerchief to her face again and dabbed the corner of her eyes, which were red with tears.

"Thank you, Mrs. Fonseca. No further questions."

Jessup rose from his chair. He had no choice but to be civil. Mira was still sobbing and drying her eyes. She still held the leg, which lay lifeless across her lap.

186

Lou passed a note to Jessup. *Get that leg out of her hands. NOW!* Jessup nodded and signaled the Bailiff to take the leg from Mira, who gladly surrendered it. Lu looked at Dan with admiration. *He milked that leg and the widow's tears to perfection. Now let's see what my Mr. Jessup can do.*

"Do you need some time or a break, Mrs. Fonseca?" Jessup opened his cross examination as a humanitarian, and in a low and soothing tone.

A good start, Lu thought

"No, thank you. I want to finish this now."

"How about some more water?"

"Yes. Please." The Bailiff brought Mira some water which she gulped down.

"Did your husband ever get angry at home before he lost his leg?"

"Sure. Doesn't everyone?"

"Well, I mean did he fly off the handle, as we say, or lose his temper easily?"

"When Gaspar came home from a trip he would sometimes get angry because some things hadn't got fixed by the landlord while he was at sea."

"And did he like sitting in a corner by himself when he came home from a trip?"

"Yes. After a time at sea, he liked to be alone. But not for hours like after he lost his leg. I understood that he wanted to be alone then."

"What about your intimate life? What was that like before the loss of his leg?"

Mira's face turned a dark crimson. "I don't know what you mean."

"I think you do, Mrs. Fonseca. How was your sex life?"

"For me it was good." Mira stumbled with her words, angry at having to go through this private part of her life again. "I had…I had nothing to compare it to. Gaspar was the only man I ever knew. It was good. I was happy with Gaspar…life was good. After he lost his leg, we didn't have an intimate life, as you call it."

Lu felt a stir in the jury box and a quiet murmur in the spectator area. Mira turned her face away from the jury so they could not see her displeasure and shame at having to discuss this matter.

Jessup stood immobile and disoriented, searching his notes for the next question. "What were his eating habits like, Mrs. Fonseca?"

"I don't understand the question."

"What I mean is, what did you feed him when he was home?"

"When he came home he was only at the house for a day or two, maybe three. I would give him salads, soups. He liked Creole food: you know fried fish, fried plantains, rice and beans. Often we would go to a restaurant where he would have a steak. When he was on vacation, for a month or so, I would feed him that way too."

"Did he eat cheese and ice cream?"

"Yes, he liked them both."

"How about cake?"

"He liked all types of desserts."

"After he lost his leg, did he read newspapers or books?"

"Once in a while he would read a newspaper. That was about it."

"And his friends, when they came to the house, how did he act?"

"I think he didn't want to see them. But when they came to the house he was happy they came."

"So he wasn't unhappy all the time, as you testified?"

"I suppose so."

"He talked with his friends, isn't that so?"

"Yes."

"How about laughing? He laughed with them when they came to your house to visit him didn't he?"

"Yes, but not like before."

"When you say not like before, you mean before he lost his leg?"

"Yes."

"And his mother and his brothers, he was always happy to see them wasn't he?'

"Yes."

"And he talked with them and laughed with them, right?"

"But as I said, not like before."

"So he wasn't always shut off from everyone as you previously testified. I'm right, am I not?"

"I guess so, but it definitely was never like before he lost his leg."

"Thank you, Mrs. Fonseca. I have no further questions."

Gaspar's mother took the stand. She was dressed in black, a thin woman with wiry black hair turning grey and bony hands that never remained still during her interrogation. She was assisted in her testimony with a translator.

"Good morning, Mrs. Fonseca," Dan began his questioning in a friendly voice.

"Good morning to you, sir."

"Would you please tell us what your relationship with your son was like."

"Gaspar was a good son. Before he lost his leg he helped me every month with my rent and food." She responded to the first question Jessup fired at her.

"How often did you see your son?"

"You know he was a sailor, a merchant marine. So I couldn't see him all the time. We lived close to each other. So I would see him when he came home from working on the ships. On his vacation, I saw him all the time. We lived near each other."

"How would he act when he was with you?"

"You know Gaspar, always laughing, joking. My youngest son Roberto, who lives with me, plays the guitar. So Gaspar and Roberto would sing songs in Spanish that I remembered from Puerto Rico and that I taught them."

"Did he sing with Roberto after he lost his leg?"

"No, never. He never even came to my house. I had to go to his house when I wanted to see him."

'How was he with Roberto and Miguel, your other son, after he lost his leg?"

189

"Quiet and moody. Sometimes he would laugh and joke, but not often."

"When you went to his house what was he like?"

"Quiet and moody." Mrs. Fonseca said as her eyes were glistening. She was fighting back her tears. "He would get very angry and shout at Mira for no good reason and my grandson, little Ronny, too. Then I would take his hand and whisper to him to stop. I would kiss him and he would quiet down."

"Did Gaspar help you with the rent and food after he lost his leg?"

"No. They had no money, Gaspar and Mira. He only had a disability check and their savings. He was trying to get a disability pension from his union. That hadn't come yet. He told me he had to file a lot of papers and that it took time. Sometimes, if she had it, Mira would give me some money. But that didn't happen too often."

"Thank you, Mrs. Fonseca."

Jessup was next with cross examination.

"Good morning, Mrs. Fonseca."

"Good morning, sir."

"So, from your own testimony your son laughed and joked sometimes after he lost his leg."

"Yes, mister, but never like before. My son was never the same as before. He was never the same until the day he killed himself. "

"Did he enjoy your cooking?"

"Oh, yes, he always did," she smiled, recalling fond memories.

"What did you make for him?"

"I cooked how I learned on the island. I made rice and beans, fried *plantains*, *amarillos*, fried fish, whole with the head on it. Sometimes I would go the store and get *bacalao*, that's a fried codfish. He would eat that for breakfast."

"Did you make French fries for him?"

"Sometimes. And Mira would make that for him too."

"Did he eat fried chicken?"

"Yes, Mira and I both made that for him until he lost his leg. Then he was on a different diet. He didn't eat fried foods anymore."

"You mean he didn't because the doctors told him to stop, isn't that so?"

"Yes, I believe you are right about that."

"Thank you for your testimony, Mrs. Fonseca. I have no more questions."

Bobby Fonseca bolstered the testimony of Mira and his mother. He added individual incidents which the psychiatrist would put to good use in his assessment of Gaspar's mental state. On cross examination, Jessup elicited good testimony for the defendant about Gaspar's short temper and desire to be alone at times even before his loss.

Now it was time for Dan to read the deposition of Gaspar Fonseca that he and Lu had taken more than a year earlier, during the pre-trial process. The jury was aware that Gaspar was no longer able to testify. But here he was; Gaspar Fonseca was not speaking in person but from words memorialized through his deposition, telling his story, in his own words and with clarity.

He recalled how he awoke with the frightening pain on his left side, how his life had changed after doctors operated on him on the ship. The dead man told the jurors, answering Dan's questions through the mouth of a third party who had never met Gaspar Fonseca. This third party spoke dispassionately, reading the words recorded so many months earlier, before Gaspar committed suicide and lay in a heap in a dark alley like a bundle of clothes waiting to be taken to the laundry.

Gaspar remembered how he had been in the ship's hospital for three frightening days, in pain all the time; watching his leg turn ugly colors; and he told the jury how they took his leg away from him in a hospital on Staten Island. It was not, of course, the voice of Gaspar Fonseca, but that of a Court clerk substituting for him, reading from the printed page, reading of his despair and frustration. But the clerk was obliged to read with disinterest, without the passion and grief Gaspar would have displayed for the jury had he still been alive to tell them his story in person. The jury heard Gaspar tell of his lost hope of becoming an officer, of earning more money, of buying the home he and Mira had always wanted, of having another child. The jurors learn how life had changed for him, physically, emotionally and financially. They heard of his anguish, that led to his decision to end his life.

"The pain follows me day and night. I have a prosthetic leg today, but even after months of nagging pain in my stump, I still cannot be properly fitted and I struggle to walk with it. I feel as if I will never be able to work and earn a living."

The Court Clerk must read this deposition colorlessly, without emotion. Yet, as he went on, he paused to control his emotions, to maintain the necessary neutrality he is required to assume before the jury.

During the taking of this deposition, at Dan's request, Gaspar had rolled back his pants leg to show Lu his artificial leg. At that point in the reading, the jury's attention is again drawn to the leg which the bailiff had taken from Mira and placed on a table with the other exhibits. Dan does not fail to give the jury a second opportunity to see leg up close again, by picking it up and holding it high above his head for the jury to see. Repeat, repeat, repeat until it sinks into the minds of the jurors and stays there, the memory of the hollow false leg made of leather, straps and metal. The artificial leg meant to substitute for the real one made of bone, flesh, nerves, tissues and muscles and with the warm blood of life flowing through it.

Jessup had his turn at reading Lu's cross-examination at the deposition. He read Lu's questions to Judge Costello's clerk. After covering his change of life style and other matters, this question had been asked by Lu: "Mr. Fonseca, did your doctors explain the reason for the block in your leg?"

"Yes, they did."

"What were you told?"

"That some deposits collected in my blood and blocked an artery as they moved through my body."

"Did they change your diet?"

"Yes."

"They told you to stop eating fatty foods, fried foods and sweets didn't they?"

"That's true."

"Mr. Fonseca, you got angry at home, didn't you, before you lost your leg?"

"Yes."

"Can you explain why?"

"I don't know exactly. Sometimes it's because things weren't the way I wanted them to be. Sometimes when I came home from a trip I expected to see something fixed that was broken the last time I was home and it's wasn't. Stuff like that."

"How about on the ship? You got angry there too, didn't you?"

"Yes. If things aren't done right, then someone can get hurt badly or even get killed, so we all have to make sure everything is done the right way. The way it is supposed to be. If it isn't, I get angry."

"Are you familiar with that expression 'flying off the handle'?"

"Yes, I am."

"Would you define it as someone who gets out of control with his temper?"

"That's as good a definition as any."

"You've found yourself flying off the handle at work or at home, isn't that so?"

"I have to say yes, but only rarely."

"How about sitting alone? You do that often, don't you?"

"On the ship I would like to be alone after a day's hard work. Because I had to study for my officer's license."

"You did that often didn't you?"

"Yes."

"How about at home?"

"I liked it better at home because things are more comfortable and familiar than on the ship. I didn't go off alone too often.

"How about after your accident?"

"After the accident, yes."

"Do you ever feel things won't get better?"

"Yes, I do. But that happens only after the accident. When I'm like that, I try to get out of that mood. I look at my leg and it is very hard to think things will ever get better."

After the first four witnesses had completed their testimony, the jury had a solid picture of a broken man. Lu and Jessup's cross examinations of Gaspar, Mira, Mrs. Fonseca and Bobby Fonseca raised some real issues about Gaspar's moods and mental state before he lost his leg. They all admitted that Gaspar could be moody and often liked to be alone. On cross examination, Bobby Fonseca admitted that his brother "would fly off the handle from time to time. But nowhere near as often as he did after he lost his leg." At the close of the reading of Gaspar Fonseca's testimony, Judge Costello adjourned for the day.

"We'll resume tomorrow at 8:30 a.m. I remind the jury that they are not to discuss this case with anyone. Even at home with your family."

23

THE TRIAL CONTINUES: GASPAR'S HEALTH

"I've been thinking about calling Captain Burn to testify in our Direct case," Dan informed Jack Hoffman, Charley Becker and Drew Sloan when they returned to the Nikolas office at the end of the first day of trial.

"What's the point?" Charley asked. "We know the defendant is going to call him."

"It might make sense to tie him down right away, so that when Commander Masterson testifies we have Burn boxed in. I can have Burn treated as a hostile witness and I don't have to worry about asking him leading questions. And maybe, after he testifies, we won't have him hanging around the Court House looking like a damned movie star in his fancy uniform. Could be the other side sends him home or maybe he leaves on his own. I hear he can't stand lawyers. If we call him first, Jessup will have to deal with Burn's testimony early.

"Another reason might work in our favor. It puts the issue of whether or not Gaspar could have been evacuated from the ship early on with the Captain's explanation, instead of us guessing what he was thinking. We can spend the rest of the case tearing his explanations apart. It's unorthodox, but if we call Burn as our witness, he is locked in with his testimony. Hopefully, Masterson can give us some arrows we can use against him."

"Good idea," Jack Hoffman agreed. "I like it. Let's do it."

"They'll probably have to call him back if Masterson makes him look foolish," Drew Sloan offered.

"So then we have a second shot at the bastard," Jack Hoffman said, rubbing his hands together happily.

"We have time for deciding what we will do with Burn, anyway. Jack is on next with the medicals. He plans to be busy for at least four days with all the cross-examinations. If anyone has objections to using Burn as our witness, we'll discuss it again. Now let's review today's testimony. I'm concerned that all that testimony about Gaspar's personality before the loss of his leg had elements of anger and introspection."

"They're setting us up for pre-conditions of depression and anger. They're hoping the jury will find that Gaspar was already loaded with personality disorders and that his suicide was a result of a condition that existed long before he lost his leg."

Dan shuffled through his notes and stopped at a page. "Jack, what's this crap about what Gaspar was eating?"

Jack said "I know where the bastards are going. They are trying to show our man was the cause of his own problem. But that's irrelevant to our case. They are trying to draw the jury away from the real issue which is: why wasn't he taken off the ship? And if he was, would they have been in time? Let's never lose sight of that. Otherwise, we let ourselves fall into their trap, which is that perhaps Gaspar's eating habits were the cause of his problem. It may be, I don't know. But by law, as you explained to me, he had a right to get the best medical attention available to him at the time."

"Jack is right. We mustn't lose focus," Dan said, slapping his hand on the table for emphasis. It's irrelevant what he contributed to his physical condition, if he contributed at all."

"I made notes to go over the aspect of his personality regarding anger, with the psychiatrist on direct examination." Jack said. "Don't worry; I'll be plugging every hole."

❧ ❧

The next days belonged to Jack Hoffman. Since Doctors Diggs and Ross lived in Boston and Maryland, respectively, the New York Court had no subpoena power or jurisdiction over them. They could not be forced to come to the trial and none of them would consider attending voluntarily. Jack had expected that and was prepared to read carefully-selected sections from their depositions, which had been taken during discovery.

Jack opened by reading the depositions of the absent doctors. It set the scene aboard the ship and the consultations among the four doctors, all of whom were in agreement to get Gaspar off the ship as soon as possible. After Jack was finished, Jessup read portions of cross-examinations of the two doctors which had been taken by Lu. The readings took all morning and another three hours in the afternoon, after a lunch break.

On the following day, Dr. Grinstein, who resides in New York, testified in person after being subpoenaed. He told of the reluctance of all the doctors to operate, since they lacked proper facilities and a qualified surgeon. He testified as to his physical examination of Gaspar and that in his opinion, infection had not yet set in. On cross-examination, Dr. Grinstein, echoing the other doctors who had testified, was unable to tell the jury where the vessel was during their consultations or where they were when they began operating.

"Once we were committed to operating on the man, I don't think that any of us was concerned about where the ship was. At least I wasn't," Grinstein explained.

Dr. Grinstein did confirm that Dr. Peters had told the three doctor-passengers that the ship was rapidly leaving the area where a rescue could be had and that as more time passed, it would be difficult, if not impossible, to get Gaspar Fonseca off the ship. Grinstein, who examined Gaspar after Dr. Peters, testified that, "In my opinion, after personally doing an examination of Mr. Fonseca, I had to agree with Dr. Peters that we were dealing with a thrombosis and that we had better do something to help this man and do it quickly."

"What was your decision as to treatment?"

"We, all of us, had to rely on the information Dr. Peters told us, that the Captain wanted us to go ahead. He didn't want to stop or re-route the ship. And, in fact, we all heard Dr. Peters talking to the Captain on the phone and we knew there would be no stopping the ship or making any kind of rescue attempt. And so we operated out of a humanitarian necessity."

Dr. Grinstein admitted he knew nothing about ship handling and had to rely on the Captain's assessment of the situation.

"At any time that morning, before the operation, did you know where the ship was located?" Jessup asked.

"I would have to say no, except that I had the impression that we were still somewhere in the English Channel because I could see a coast line."

"But you weren't certain of that either, isn't that so?"

"Yes, that is so."

When Dr. Peters took the stand, he related to Jack Hoffman his first impressions of Gaspar Fonseca's medical condition and his conversations with Captain Burn concerning getting Gaspar proper medical care. Jack showed Dr. Peters his medical report, an exhibit in evidence, and asked him to read it and verify that it was he who had prepared it and that it was correct as to all the medical details he had entered. Dr. Peters verified the report as his and as being correct.

Then Jack added an off-hand question. "Does your answer to my last question also include the reverse side of the last two pages of your report?"

Dr. Peters picked up his medical report and went to the last two pages. He turned them over, then looked at them and said, "Yes, that is correct. I prepared those last pages. "

"You're sure, doctor?"

"Yes, I am. That's my handwriting."

"Can you explain to the Court and jury why they are on the backside of the last two pages of your medical report?"

"Yes. Those pages do not relate to medical information. I wished to keep them apart."

At the end of Dr. Peters' direct testimony, Jack addressed the Court.

"Your Honor, we would ask the Court to make this witness available for further testimony, if needed by the plaintiff."

"For what purpose, Mr. Hoffman?"

"The plaintiff may wish to call the doctor on a matter not involving his treatment of the deceased. To question him now would be out of context and create some confusion."

"Very well. Dr. Peters, you are to make yourself available for further examination. Counselor, can you tell the Court when you will call the doctor?"

"Probably tomorrow. No later than the day after."

Lu sat up. She was troubled by the last questions Jack had asked Dr. Peters and his request to call the doctor back for further questioning. It seemed strange, out of the normal array of medical questions she would have expected. It seemed as if Jack was headed in another direction, away from the field of medicine. But she shook it off. Jack Hoffman was the medical expert. He wasn't going to go into anything else such as ship handling.

She pulled the exhibit from its place and looked at it. She gasped, putting her hand over her mouth to stifle the sound. She hoped no one had seen or heard her. On the backside of the last two pages, written in great detail, were the locations of the ship and the times when Peters examined Gaspar, and had conversations with the Captain, or the other doctors.

How had she missed that? She was so busy with her own personal problems at the office, that it slipped by her. And Jessup missed it, too. It passed him by. She would have to match Dr. Peters' memo up with the ship's log. She couldn't do it now because she needed to listen, to pay attention to what was happening during the trial. She closed the exhibit, with the gnawing feeling that things were not going too well. Yet she knew Dan would still have a difficult time overturning the basic rule: The Captain is the last word on his ship. So far, Captain Burn had convinced Lu that his decisions were correct. *Let Dan get out of that,* she thought. *The law is with me.*

The direct and cross-examinations of Doctors Peters and Grinstein took up the rest of the second day and half of the third day. On the afternoon of the third day of trial, Jack was going to introduce the jury the elements of Gaspar Fonseca's mental state. He now called the psychiatrist, Dr. Marcus Feinberg.

As Dr. Feinberg stood by the witness chair, he raised his right hand affirming his oath to tell the truth. According to the Rules of Evidence, the retired psychiatrist had to satisfy the defendant and the Court that he was an expert in his field of psychiatry, in order to render his medical opinion for the jury to consider. He began with a long review of his professional career. Dr. Feinberg told the jury he had earned his BS in psychology at Stanford University, then studied for a medical degree at New York's Weill-Cornell Medical School. He performed his psychiatric internship at the Long Island College of Medicine with Professor Alfred Adler, for the short time Adler taught at the school before his death. This was the same Dr. Adler who, with Carl Jung, were Sigmund Freud's earliest pupils.

Dr. Feinberg began his psychiatric career on staff at New York City's Bellevue Hospital. Less than a decade later, he left Bellevue for the Department of Psychiatry at the medical school at the University of Chicago, where he eventually became its Dean. Board certified, with a long and distinguished international career, Feinberg had received many awards and honors for his work in the field of psychiatry and mental trauma. He wrote 21 books on psychiatry, 14 of which were texts for students and the rest for laymen. During his career, he wrote over 160 articles which appeared in medical journals in the United States and throughout the world. Dr. Feinberg retired from academia in 1962, becoming available for private consultations.

Seventy-four years old, the doctor was stocky and bald with a wispy fringe of grey hair. He wore a suit that was obviously not selected for style but for its utilitarian qualities. When he spoke, it was with the air of a recognized authority, yet he was also a kindly and patient teacher, obviously pleased to be sitting before the jury, instructing them and passing along what he knew about the field of psychiatry, to which he had devoted his professional life. Professor Feinberg knew he was dealing with lay persons, so he was careful to use words they would understand.

Under Jack Hoffman's guiding hand, Dr. Feinberg presented a sad picture of a depressed Gaspar Fonseca, whose condition, taking into consideration his first attempt at suicide, would have required psychiatric care in excess of three years, perhaps even more, depending upon Gaspar's reaction to the treatment and his will to get better.

From his observations about Gaspar's first suicide attempt, Dr. Feinberg explained that his depression was initially hidden. The first attempt at suicide was the result of a full blown depressive state that grew with the frustrating mismanagement of his artificial leg. The doctor's opinion was that Gaspar suffered from a chronic depression which began a few months after the traumatic event of the loss of his leg.

"He might have benefitted from group therapy in addition to private sessions, which he would have needed," he explained.

"Dr. Feinberg, did you examine the statements I gave you of Gaspar Fonseca's wife, mother and two brothers?" Jack Hoffman asked.

"Yes, I did."

"And did you personally examine Mr. Fonseca?"

"At your request, I examined him two days after his suicide attempt and then again a week and a half before his unfortunate suicide," Dr. Feinberg said after putting on his reading glasses and checking his notes to insure the dates.

"Based upon your examination of Gaspar Fonseca, his medical records and reading the narrative reports of Gaspar's family concerning Gaspar's behavior before and after the loss of his leg, can you tell us what mental, if any, symptoms he exhibited?"

"I can." Dr. Feinberg rummaged through a manila folder he had brought with him to the witness stand. "Yes, here it is. I was able to determine that he experienced a serious trauma, which was the loss of his left leg just above the knee. As a result of that, he exhibited a loss of hope. That showed up because he could no longer plan on becoming an officer, and had no alternative plans for his life when I spoke with him.

"Then there was the loss of his regular job. He was also experiencing chronic pain, which was magnified because his artificial leg could not be fitted properly. I made the following note after his first visit: 'He has a strong feeling that things will not get better and exhibits moods of depression.'

"In my experience over the years, I have noted that if a patient suffers only some of these symptoms which I have just detailed, or even just one of them, which might be so pronounced and significant that it overwhelms him or her, it is a probable signpost of suicidal tendencies. Mr. Fonseca showed me that he had all of these symptoms, some more pronounced than others. If these symptoms do not disappear, that is a red flag that we may be dealing with a possible suicide.

"I can point out an example that might be relevant to you. I refer to the suicides during the Great Depression, when the Stock Market crashed. Many persons were faced with loss of hope, or perhaps loss of all their money, which I could equate with the loss of a job. Their loss was so great that they didn't need a host of extra problems. In Mr. Fonseca's case, he showed all these problems, a certain gateway to suicide."

"Dr. Feinberg, based on your examination of all of the records and interviews with Mr. Fonseca, do you have an opinion as to what caused these symptoms?"

"Yes, I do."

"Would you please explain your opinion to the court and jury?"

"With the loss of his leg, Mr. Fonseca's whole life, which was based upon his physical ability to perform his job, and other things, collapsed. For example, he was a seaman. From the very detailed description of his work aboard ship that he gave me, I learned that he was required to do heavy labor and move from place to place on his ship. Even as an officer, which he told me he had hoped to become, he would have been required to assist in heavy tasks from time to time; he would certainly have had to ambulate around the ship as before. He lost his job and knew he could never regain it, because of the permanent loss of his leg.

"So he has lost his life's work, because he can no longer perform those duties as a seaman. Then he shows me a loss of hope for things getting better for him in the future. Even more, he has lost the hope that they can ever get better. Now he can no longer become an officer, something he studied hard for years to accomplish, and was only two months away from attaining.

"His wife has told us that their matrimonial intimacy disappeared, something he was reluctant to admit to me. This would affect him as a husband and cause him an indignity with respect to his wife. It became something neither of them cared to freely discuss with me. I have observed this phenomenon over the years amongst Hispanics. It is a very private matter and it was a significant event for the both of them. I had to pull this information from Mrs. Fonseca, as I suspected that they had no intimate relations. It was something I have often seen in my career. So I was not surprised when it came out.

"He cannot go fishing with his brothers or play sports with the men of his neighborhood. His priest says he no longer does handyman jobs. He experiences and complains of chronic pain. All of these matters arise after, and as a result of, the loss of his leg. These symptoms I have previously described are among the most common cause of suicide. So my opinion is that it is the loss of the leg which caused these symptoms and was also the direct cause of his suicide."

"Thank you, doctor.

Jessup immediately attacked Dr. Feinberg.

"Doctor, you never treated Mr. Fonseca, isn't that true."

"Yes, that's so."

"And from a reading of your report, you state that your opinion is based upon just two visits of one hour or so for each. Isn't that so?"

"No. I read medical reports of the psychiatrists at the United States Marine Hospital and the transcripts of the narratives made by his family of his mental and social condition before and after the loss of his leg. The latter reports are important, since they gave me a good picture of his state of mind at different times in his life."

"Wouldn't your opinion have been more definitive or even different if you had treated him for, let's say, three months or more?"

"Not necessarily. The signs of depression were definitely there during my examinations and they continued. I read the reports from the psychiatrist at Marine Hospital up until a week before his suicide. The doctor noted that he continued to exhibit lack of ambition and enthusiasm, sexual dysfunction, sleeping long hours, among other symptoms that I would say are road signs for a potential suicide. These symptoms lasted for almost a year, which would qualify his depression as a chronic condition. I also took into consideration the statements of his family as to what this man was like before he lost his leg.

"He was ambitious, looking to elevate himself in his profession, planning to add another child to the family, moving to a better neighborhood. I don't see any major depression before he lost his leg. You have to understand that most people during their lives undergo some periods or forms of depression, no matter how minor they may be. It doesn't mean that person has a depressive personality. Such a personality that is chronic arises from long and frequent bouts of depression."

"And you say three or more years would have been needed in treatment?"

"At least. Since I was not the treating physician, it could be possible that he might need more than three years. Then, of course, group therapy."

"Wouldn't flying off the handle, anger and the introspection his family testified to during this trial, under oath, about periods before he lost his leg, be a sign of latent depression?"

"Perhaps, but they are not significant in my opinion. He was a functioning human being with an important job on his ship and his eye firmly on the future, as I have already told you. At best, to answer your question, his condition after he lost his leg could be an exacerbation of a pre-existing and non-disabling condition. That means that Mr. Fonseca, as do most of us, perhaps, and I emphasize perhaps, had a facet of his personality as you or I may have, such as a fear of heights, crowds or animals. It doesn't disable us or make us dysfunctional. I don't think it made Mr. Fonseca dysfunctional before he lost his leg.

"Such a person with these phobias works around them. They compensate by keeping away from heights, crowds or animals. But I want to make it very clear, Counselor, my opinion is that I strongly doubt that he was in any way dysfunctional or even troubled or disabled by any pre-existing condition, if, indeed, one ever existed at all, as you have intimated."

"So you can't tell this Court and jury if he had a pre-existing condition, isn't that so?"

"With any degree of certainty? No one can, at this point in time. But from my examination of Mr. Fonseca and based on all the records and his family history, I would have to say no, there was no pre-existing condition."

"Assuming three years was needed to finish treatment, as you have testified, might we say that he would have been cured at that time?" Jessup continued.

"We do not speak of curing a mental condition, because we cannot cure it in the sense that it goes away or disappears. We speak of treating it. It is more likely than not, that after his treatment was concluded he would have had to require sessions in the faraway future to help him along. It is my opinion, based upon my experience, that if after three years he was discharged, he still would have been a candidate for some treatment or treatments in the future. A mental injury is like an injury to the body. You break a leg. Some folks mend with no after-effects; others go through life with a limp. The break is always there and even the man with no after-effects today, may suffer from a traumatic arthritis, years later. Perhaps ten or 20 years in the future, maybe more. Certainly Mr. Fonseca would have benefited from group therapy sessions."

"When you examined him, did you alert Mr. Fonseca to the possibility that he was a suicide candidate?"

"No, I did not."

"Why not?"

"He was already receiving, after his first suicide attempt, competent psychiatric care at the Marine Hospital. I was only retained to give an opinion on his mental condition, not to treat him. To do anything else would have been to interfere with another doctor's course of treatment. That would have been an improper violation and breach of ethical conduct on my behalf. Certainly, telling him he was a suicide candidate would have been presumptuous of me. That would have been up to his treating physician. According to the records I have examined, the doctors at Staten Island also did not so advise him."

"So you were convinced that he was receiving good psychiatric care?"

"Yes, I was."

"Could you have been wrong?'

"I am familiar with the reputation of his treating psychiatrist at the Marine Hospital. He is competent, as I said earlier."

"But you have said that his medical chart at the Marine Hospital does not indicate that he is a suicide candidate?"

"Yes. But it is obvious to me and surely to any other competent psychiatrist, that from the type of treatment he was receiving, Mr. Fonseca's doctor was concerned with these symptoms and was vigorously working on them, just as if he was an avowed and possible suicide candidate."

"Doctor, you were paid to render your opinions here today, were you not?"

"Yes, Mr. Hoffman already covered that. I will receive a fee for my time in Court, the examination of Mr. Fonseca and for preparing my report."

"You have testified in Court before on other cases isn't that so?"

"Only since my retirement, yes. During my career, I did not have the time to make Court appearances."

"No further questions."

Jack Hoffman rose from his chair. "Your Honor, I would like some re-direct."

"Go ahead, Counselor."

"Dr. Feinberg, how many times have you appeared in Court as an expert witness?"

"In the six years since my retirement, maybe seven times. No more than eight, including this case."

"What criteria, if any, do you employ for consenting to testify on behalf of a litigant?"

"I must be thoroughly convinced, after examining a claimant, that I can help the Court and jury to understand the mental conditions at issue in a case."

"Did you follow that rule in this case?"

"Of course, Mr. Hoffman."

"Finally doctor, do you make a distinction between being retained by a plaintiff or a defendant when you testify?"

"No. I help any plaintiff that may have a legitimate reason to present a condition to the Court and jury or any good reason on the part of the defense to show a condition is not true as alleged by a claimant."

"That's probably the reason you haven't been in court as an expert many more times than you have been."

Jack saw Jessup rise from his chair to object and before he could do so, Jack said, "Withdrawn."

Direct and cross examination of Dr. Feinberg took all day.

The next day Jack Hoffman called as his next witness Dr. Sean Welles, who took the stand, looking more like a military commander than a physician. Standing six feet three inches and lean, his hair was cut short in a close crew-cut, G. I. style, and giving way to a mix of salt and pepper coloring. After covering his academic and professional qualifications, including the many articles he wrote for medical journals, Jack led Dr. Welles into his experience with insufficient blood flow to limbs.

"Dr. Welles, would you please tell this Court and jury when, during your medical career, you first personally encountered problems of blood flow to limbs."

"During medical school, when we made rounds I would see such conditions. The first time I was obliged to treat them was when I was out of medical school as an intern. After I finished my internship I went into the Army. I volunteered for combat and was assigned to a Ranger infantry team in Korea. I was with them for seven months in combat and saw many wounds connected with severed arteries causing cut-off of blood flow to limbs."

"How many cases of thromboses have you treated during your medical career?"

"I can't exactly say, but in over 20 years of practice, which includes my time in the Army and then my cardio-vascular residency, I would say over two hundred, maybe more."

"Aside from operating, what has been your experience through your training and observation, as to any other procedures which might have been available to remove a clot such as the one the plaintiff in this case experienced?"

"There are the drugs Heparin and Coumadin, which are routinely used to dissolve the clots that form, such as the one Gaspar Fonseca had."

"And could you explain the procedure used in operating?"

"Using a dye which we inject into a patient's arteries, we could locate the block and proceed to operate in that area because we know where we are looking for the block."

"Was that done in this case?"

"No. I was advised that they had no proper dye available in the ship's hospital."

"What about drugs that might be used to dissolve the obstruction?"

"I have been advised that they were also not available in the ship's inventory."

"Returning to your time in the Army, could you please explain what you saw of combat wounds that you could equate to what Mr. Fonseca suffered?"

"I saw all types of wounds: bullet, shrapnel, bayoneting and bludgeoning."

"Keeping in mind the medical condition Gaspar Fonseca suffered, can you tell us which of these wounds were similar in effect to those on the battlefield?'

"All of the ones I mentioned, except perhaps bludgeoning."

"Please explain how they were similar."

"A bullet, shrapnel or knife wound slicing into an artery on the upper part of a limb, cuts off the blood supply to the lower part of that limb. While it's not a block such as Mr. Fonseca experienced, the effect is exactly the same. No blood flows into the lower part of the limb. It then becomes starved for blood. In an embolism or clot situation, the blood supply is cut off is like a dam that holds back water from a river. It, too, creates a situation where the limb is starved for blood nourishment."

"How did you treat such a situation in combat?"

"On the battlefield, we tied off the area above the wound with a tourniquet to prevent further loss of blood. We also sanitized and dressed the wound."

"Then what do you do?"

"As a battlefield medic, I was attached to a fighting unit that would treat men who had suffered all types of injuries from life-threatening to superficial wounds. We were, in effect, a Triage Unit."

"Please explain what a Triage Unit does."

"We had to make some quick and important decisions and sort out the wounded on a priority basis. We identified those that needed immediate attention because their injuries were life threatening and separated them from other soldiers who may have also had serious wounds, such as fractures, but which could, nevertheless, wait. On the bottom of the list were the superficially wounded. Those injuries often allowed soldiers to return to combat after simple treatment such as cleaning a wound, removing shrapnel that was not deeply embedded, or cleaning and bandaging a scrape."

"Taking into consideration those injuries to the arterial system to which you have previously testified, where did those soldiers stand with respect to priority levels?"

"They were always top priority. We had to get them out immediately. We had to get them to a field hospital right away. If we were not in time, either a severe infection or gangrene would have resulted. It's the same problem that Mr. Fonseca's blockage presented. We mustn't forget loss of blood, too. Although on the battlefield, we stopped the flow from a damaged artery, you can't tie it off forever. If you do, then you are creating another area with starvation of blood."

"How did you get these wounded soldiers to a hospital?"

"If the hospital unit was distant from the battlefield we called for helicopters. If they weren't available or if we were close to the

209

hospital unit, an ambulance would evacuate the wounded soldiers."

"Later in your civilian career as a cardio-vascular surgeon, how did you treat a block such as the one Mr. Fonseca had?

"Depending upon how long the block was in place, there are the drugs I already mentioned that may dissolve a block. Otherwise, you have to treat patients the same as those battle wounds I described. Get them to a hospital as soon as possible. Because delay brings on the same bad results as in a battle wound, if it's not treated immediately."

"Please describe the bad results."

"There are several. In the case of a blood clot, it could break free from its position in the artery. Once dislodged, it travels in the blood stream running from the leg, let's say, to either the lungs, in which case the patient suffers a pulmonary thrombosis, or it could travel to the heart, causing a coronary thrombosis. Either of those conditions are serious and life threatening. Of course, that's not a concern with a battlefield wound. But if we are dealing with a clot that remains in place, as did the one in Mr. Fonseca's case, it cuts off the blood supply to the extremity, in which case an infection or gangrene could result if not treated immediately."

"Taking into consideration that the medical facilities and drugs that were not available on the day that Mr. Fonseca was operated on the *American Union* and assuming you were not a qualified cardio-vascular surgeon as you have shown us to be, would you have operated on Mr. Fonseca?"

"That's a difficult question for me to answer. I was not present aboard the ship. I can't testify as to what was going on the minds of these physicians. An operation of that type is highly complicated. Yet we know from the facts that occurred on that day that the patient was not going to get off that ship. To have left him to suffer for the three days it was going to take to get to New York, knowing that almost certainly he would contract gangrene and lose his leg, that's tough. I would also have to consider the additional possibilities: that the clot could break loose and travel to his lungs or his heart, causing death. Since I was not on the spot and actually faced with these realities, I don't really feel I am competent to answer your question.

"I can say this however: assuming, as you have asked me to do, that I was not a qualified surgeon, I doubt strongly that I would have been the person to do the actual surgery. That's based upon my personal knowledge of what is required to do this type of procedure. We have an expression in our profession: 'the operation would have been contra- indicated.' It's a tough choice either way, since the Captain refused to get him off the ship. Because of that, the patient will most likely suffer... whatever you do under those conditions you have asked me to consider."

"Doctor, would you, for the record, please detail the medical reports and other documents you were given in order for you to understand what happened to Mr. Fonseca?"

"Yes, I was provided with the medical report of the ship's doctor, which included diagnosis, treatment and a description of the operation that was performed on the ship. I was provided the operative report from the Marine Hospital, that's where his gangrenous leg was finally removed. There were also reports for treatment after the amputation and the efforts made to fit him with an artificial limb.

"I also had the medicals for pre-sign on physicals performed by his Union physicians for the past five years before his block. In my opinion, they were unremarkable with respect to his cardio-vascular condition. I also read the depositions of the four doctors who were involved in the shipboard operation. Then there were psychiatric entries which I read but did not feel were pertinent to the opinion you asked me to prepare. I also read the testimonies of the seaman's wife, mother and brothers."

"Did you have the opportunity to examine Mr. Fonseca before he died?"

"Yes, I did."

"Based upon your reading of the records and your examination, have you come to an opinion as to what caused the gangrene in Mr. Fonseca's left leg?"

"I do. Of course, it was a block of an artery which caused the failure of adequate blood supply to his lower left limb. It can cause infection or the death of the cells, what we call an infarction. In extreme cases, such as the one experienced by Mr. Fonseca, gangrene occurs. So the cause of the gangrene was a failure to receive proper immediate treatment to either surgically remove or dissolve the block."

"Are there different types of blocks?"

"Yes."

"Please explain."

"You have two types. One is the deep vein thrombosis and the other occurs closer to the surface."

"Do you have an opinion as to the kind Gaspar Fonseca suffered?"

"Yes. My opinion is that in this case we are dealing with a deep vein thrombosis. Because when the doctors operated on the ship, they didn't go deep enough into the limb. That may be why they didn't find the block. The other reason may be that they weren't looking in the right place."

"Can you tell how long the condition lasted before the operation?"

"No, I can't with any certainty."

"Can you tell us why not?"

"With deep vein thrombosis, pain does not often manifest itself immediately or even at all. This was an unusual case where the patient did suffer pain. I have no way of knowing what the case was in relation to time. What I mean by that is, I don't know if the pain manifested itself immediately or after minutes or perhaps even hours. The only thing that I was able to determine for certain was the actual time Mr. Fonseca first complained of pain. The first indication we have was about 5:30 in the morning. And significantly, his leg was still cool which means, to me, and to the doctors who examined him, one of two things. That no infection had yet set in. That was a good sign. It could also be cool because the limb was receiving no nourishment from the flow of blood. In any event, it means to me that they had little choice but to treat the man immediately, because they did not have a good history about the onset of this problem. When I am faced which such a case myself, I always act with speed."

"So, I ask you to assume that you would have seen Mr. Fonseca on the morning that he made his first complaint. What, in your opinion, would have been the proper medical treatment that you would have rendered?"

"Taking into consideration that the proper medication was not available, I would have had him taken off the ship immediately and gotten him to a proper facility for treatment which, if done quickly, may have consisted of drugs to break up the block, or a sound wave or dye procedure to locate the block and or surgery to remove the block. You want to make sure that the clot doesn't break free; that you get to it before it could break loose. There is another procedure. The leg could have been encased in ice to stabilize the situation. That's a procedure that has been used successfully with an infected or ruptured appendix if the patient can't be operated on immediately."

"Do you have an opinion as to the quality of treatment he received aboard ship?"

"Yes. First, it's clear that the doctors who operated did the best they could. However, they were hampered because they lacked the proper drugs and diagnostic tests to determine where the block was located and what type of block they were dealing with. There is also the issue that there was really no physician qualified to perform this operation. To use an analogy, I would say these doctors were flying blind. I wouldn't expect there to be such a specialist or even a qualified surgeon, for that matter, on a passenger ship. And, of course, they were told that the Captain would not evacuate Mr. Fonseca. From what I read of the doctor's depositions, they were hoping they could find the block, but they were also aware that they didn't have much hope for success."

"Do you have an opinion, within a reasonable degree of medical certainty, as to what caused the loss of Mr. Fonseca's left leg?"

"Yes, I do. It occurred because he lacked blood supply to his left leg, which was a result of the fact that he was not treated immediately. The delay caused the patient to wait three days until the ship reached New York. That delay was definitely the cause of the gangrene that resulted. By the time he reached New York, the doctors at the Marine Hospital had no recourse other than to amputate."

"Thank you, doctor."

Jessup began his cross examination looking at his notes.

"Doctor Welles, you don't know with certainty what kind of block Mr. Fonseca had?"

"No, because I didn't see it. But my opinion, based upon my many years of experience, tells me that it was a deep thrombosis."

"From reading the medical reports of the Marine Hospital where his leg was removed, were you able to determine what kind of block was involved?"

"No, and that's because the report only covers the amputation of the leg and the state of the arteries in his body and does not describe the type of block Mr. Fonseca experienced. We will never know what kind of block he had. But I am certain it was a deep vein thrombosis. But the type of block is moot because all blocks require immediate attention."

"Your Honor, I move to strike all of Dr. Welles testimony concerning his opinion."

"I'm afraid not, Mr. Jessup, you asked him to determine the kind of block that was involved. You called for his opinion."

Jessup continued after clearing his throat "And do you also agree that you can't say at what stage the block was at when the doctors saw him on the ship?"

"That is so. But I must only add to a degree."

Lu hurriedly scribbled a note to Jessup. *Don't pursue this line of questioning any further!!* Jessup read the note and crumpled it up into a ball which he dropped on the table. He was going to ignore Lu's note. She picked it up, smoothed it out and stuck it into her jacket pocket.

"So then Dr. Welles, how can you say, based upon your opinion that you don't know how long the condition existed, that if Mr. Fonseca was immediately sent to a hospital, it would have saved his leg?"

"That's easy, Counselor. I read Dr. Peters' report of his diagnosis and Dr. Grinstein's observation just before the operation. At that time, according to both doctors, Mr. Fonseca's upper leg was still somewhat cool. That meant to me, and to the doctors as well, that there was possibly no infection as yet. If it gets hot, it's a danger sign for infection. It was not warm enough to be at the stage where nothing could be done except amputation.

"But again, as I have already testified, it could also mean that the leg is cold because there is no blood flow. It's a fifty-fifty situation. So, in my opinion, even under those conditions there may have still been time. Swift action was still required nevertheless, because you don't know at what stage of the condition we are dealing with or even why it's definitely cool. Doctor Peters recognized that fact by advising the Captain of the condition. It was obviously significant to Dr. Peters, but not to the Captain who, after all, is not a physician."

Lu tried hard not to show her frustration. She placed her left hand across her forehead as if she was shading her face and looked down on the table, shuffling papers with her free hand. Jessup rebounded from Dr. Welles's last answer; he straightened his tie and, fussing with his jacket, went on.

"Doctor," he said, in a voice barely audible, "Did you have the opportunity to read the medical reports with respect to the health of Mr. Fonseca's arteries? I specifically refer to the examinations he underwent at the Marine Hospital after his leg was removed."

"Yes, I did."

"What were you able to determine from your reading?"

"He was in good general health but there were some small calcium deposits in his arteries and he had a moderately high cholesterol count."

"And the cholesterol you speak of is what physicians call bad cholesterol, correct?"

"Bad cholesterol. Yes."

"And they were in such an amount that was not normal for a man of Mr. Fonseca's age, isn't that so?"

"I would have to agree to that. Yet it was not of a nature that was an emergency."

"Assuming you are correct about deep vein thrombosis, aren't such blocks usually caused by persons who are sedentary, like office workers, people who don't walk or do exercising often?"

"Yes. Mostly, they are the ones who are targets of thromboses."

"Then how do you explain Mr. Fonseca's condition? There has been testimony during this trial that Mr. Fonseca worked hard, was active and moved around a lot."

"He doesn't fit the standard definition. However, it is not that unusual. There are always exceptions to every rule."

"And might his arterial and cholesterol conditions be attributed to his eating habits?"

"That might be one of the factors. We are beginning to understand that genes, heredity and other factors should also be considered in such conditions."

"Did you read the depositions of Mr. Fonseca's wife and mother concerning his diet when he was home on leave from his ship? That he liked cheese and ice cream and fried foods and fish fried in butter and steaks?"

"I did."

"In your examination, were you able to determine Mr. Fonseca's weight with respect to his age and size?"

"Yes."

"And would you admit that he was overweight?"

"He was overweight by about less than ten pounds. He was not obese. If he was, it could have been a complicating factor. In his case, I would say it was not."

"And you would agree with me, that weight and diet have a great deal to do with the conditions you saw of his arteries in the hospital reports?"

"It is a factor, yes. But I would have to do a study of his family history to determine if heredity factors were also involved. For instance, I knew his father was dead, but nowhere do I see why or how he died. In light of your questioning, it could be important to know that now. It was not of any consequence to me in my opinion earlier. I was asked to determine what standard of treatment was the correct one at the time the emergency arose."

"The conditions we have just been discussing would have been a factor to consider in any operation, isn't that so?"

"Of course, Counselor. We always take a patient's physical condition into account when we go into surgery. Based upon the condition of his arteries, which was in its early stages, I don't think that it would have been a major problem. He didn't have high blood pressure, which is another concern."

"Assuming he was taken to a facility based on the necessity for immediate attention, the surgeons wouldn't have had the time to determine the state of his arteries, isn't that so?"

"I suspect that's so because of the time constraints. But any surgeon would be on notice if the arteries were susceptible to a block. He would act accordingly. But I doubt that in this case there was any time to do anything other than to locate the problem and immediately attack it. He wouldn't have had time to do much else."

"Do you have an opinion as to whether the doctors on the ship engaged in malpractice by operating, since they had no expertise in surgery or of the cardio-vascular makeup of the body?"

"I've already said that if I was on the ship I would not have operated, lacking the knowledge I have in cardio-vascular surgery. On the other hand, I was not there, so I don't know what went on in the minds of the doctors. How they saw this emergency unfolding. So I couldn't give an opinion on that question."

"Getting back to a person's diet, would you agree with me that it is a significant factor for clogging up a person's arteries?"

Lu scribbled another note. *Where are you going? You covered this. Leave it alone.* Jessup read the note and handed it back to Lu with a contemptuous gesture.

"It could be one of them, as I have already testified."

"Based upon your reading of the testimony of Mr. Fonseca's wife and his mother concerning his eating habits, might his diet have been a factor?"

"Yes. That's a possibility."

"So would you agree with me that Mr. Fonseca was a contributor to his own condition with the foods he ate?"

"Not necessarily."

Something's wrong here. Jack Hoffman is not objecting. This line of questioning is irrelevant to the issues. Something is wrong, Lu thought.

"I don't understand, Dr. Welles. You just testified his eating habits contributed to his condition."

"Just a moment, Counselor; I said possibly."

Sean Welles dug into his portfolio and came up with a handful of papers.

"These are menus that show the food served to the crew aboard his ship. There are eggs, ham, sausages and bacon served almost every morning for breakfast. There are fried potatoes, fried fish, fried chicken and other fried foods. There are cheeses of all descriptions and ice cream and creamy desserts. There are cakes and other sugary foods. If a man chose not to eat eggs and bacon for breakfast, he could have a sugary cereal with cream or milk, both loaded with fat and unnecessary calories.

"All these could have possibly contributed to a condition in Mr. Fonseca's arteries. You have to take into consideration that, while at sea, he couldn't select the foods he could eat, or go to any restaurant of his choice. He might reject the food offered but then he might find himself going hungry. I would say his employer was more of a significant contributing factor to his condition. Much more so than the diet he had at home, since he ate more meals aboard ship than at his home."

They dropped a bomb and Jessup deserves it. I warned him to cut off this line of testimony, Lu thought with anger. Jessup stood immobile and stunned. He could hear laughter, not only from those sitting in the courtroom, but from the jury as well. Jack rose quickly and said, "Your honor, I would like to put these menus as Exhibits in Evidence for the plaintiff."

Jessup was still recovering from Dr. Welles' answer. Lu hated to do it because the jury would know that she considered Jessup's questioning ineffectual and Welles' answers significant. But it had to be done. She stood up and said in a loud voice.

"Objection, Your Honor. First, they are not listed as evidence in the pre-trial order. Then, we have no grounds to determine the authenticity of the menus, so I would respectfully ask you to strike the doctor's testimony with respect to the menus and not allow them in evidence."

Judge Costello, the umpire, went to work. "First Miss Moore, Mr. Jessup opened the door to this line of questioning, so I'll only subject Dr. Welles' answers to proof that the menus or the food provided by the defendant is genuine as described. Dr. Welles, where did you get these menus?"

"Mr. Hoffman gave them to me.'

"For what purpose?"

"He wanted to give me an idea of what Mr. Fonseca was eating aboard ship. That was after we reviewed the medical reports and saw some buildup in the arteries."

"Mr. Hoffman, where did you get the menus?"

Jack rose, buttoned his jacket and had a smile on his face. He was obviously enjoying the trap he had set for the defense.

"From a crew member, Judge. I would decline to name him for fear of retaliation. If the Court requires, we could subpoena the menus from the defendants."

"Hmm. Miss Moore, would you look at those menus, please? And would you tell me if they appear to be genuine to you?"

"They seem to be genuine; they have the company's logo. But honestly, Judge, I can't vouch for them."

"I'm going to do the following. I'm having them marked as Exhibits for Identification only, as they are not yet in evidence. I'm going to take a short 30 minute break. You can use the phone in my office, Miss Moore. You call your client and have a messenger bring the same menus to Court for the dates Dr. Welles produced. In the meantime, I'll explain what's going on to the jury.

"We have to verify or declare these menus as false. If they are false, I will instruct you not to accept Dr. Welles' testimony only as to what appears on the menus. If they are true copies, you are free to accept his testimony as to the menus. Should that be the case, I will have them marked in evidence and you may review them when you deliberate, if you wish to do so. In the meantime, you may not look at the menus, as they are not yet in evidence, but marked for identification only, because Dr. Welles referred to them. My ruling does not preclude the plaintiff from bringing another qualified witness to testify as to the food served aboard the *American Union*. We'll recess and be back in 30 minutes."

Judge Costello wasn't happy about this delay and the way the surprise arose. As a one-time trial lawyer himself, the Judge had a grudging admiration for Jack Hoffman, and what he had just done.

. Lu came back in 15 minutes. She took Dan aside and said, "There's no need to bring the menus down here. They were compared over the phone. They are genuine. You must have given the menus to Jack."

"For heaven's sake, of course I did, Lu. Jack doesn't know anyone on the Big A."

"You must have some good friends on that ship. You know I can't let you aboard any more without a fight."

"Let's see what Big Sam Cassidy and the courts have to say about that, Lu."

Judge Costello returned to the courtroom. After everyone was seated, Lu advised him the menus were genuine. The Judge had them marked into evidence, advising the jury they could now read them and they could consider Dr. Welles testimony in its entirety.

"Do you have any more questions of the doctor, Mr. Jessup?"

"Yes, sir."

"Doctor, take the stand so Mr. Jessup can finish his cross-examination. You are still under oath, doctor," Judge Costello advised.

"Dr. Welles, how soon after a blood supply is cut off would you say a person needs to be treated to prevent infection or gangrene?"

"That's hard to say. Sometimes the cut off isn't complete, so the limb isn't totally starved. Of course, the location of the block is also important. To be on the safe side, I would say immediately."

"Based upon your reading of the records and all the facts, isn't it true you can't say with any degree of certainty when it was too late to help Mr. Fonseca?"

"I can say that when he first complained at 5:30 in the morning he should have been immediately removed. Not only did Dr. Peters recognize that, but so did all the three doctors. My opinion is that at that time, if he received the proper treatment, his leg would have been saved."

"No more questions of this witness."

"I'm finishing early today as I have other court business to attend to in another case," said Judge Costello. "So we will reconvene tomorrow at 8:30. Good day to you all."

On the start of the fifth day, Dan led Professor Martin Stein through important testimony. With charts large enough for the jury to see from their seats, the professor, who taught Economics at Columbia University, detailed Gaspar's loss of past earnings and the projections of his future losses.

 Stein presumed Gaspar would have received his officer's license and, with it, an increase in salary, pension benefits and vacation pay. Then Professor Stein projected hikes in pay for the future, based upon past increases in wages negotiated by the officer's union over the past 15 years. At 30 years of age, it was projected that Gaspar would have had another 32 more productive working years left. Although American workers generally retire at 65, Professor Stein explained, it was determined by the U.S. Department of Labor and Statistics that, unlike a worker on land, the average seamen retired at 62 because of the taxing nature of his work and higher exposure to injury,

Jessup began a vigorous attack by implying the interest rates the professor used were too high and that his projections for future losses were inaccurate. After an hour and a half of cross-examination along these lines he asked, "Professor Stein, you agree that Mr. Fonseca did not have an officer's license at the time he lost his leg."

"That is so."

"So you took it for granted that he would have passed his exam and that he would have achieved his officer's license?"

"Yes."

"On what did you base this premise?"

"Mr. Fonseca told me so when I interviewed him. He was very confident that he would have passed the examination."

"You had no other verification?"

"No, sir."

"Did you make any financial projections based upon his never making officer?"

"No."

"Your Honor, may we approach the bench?"

"Yes," said Judge Costello with a beckoning motion of his hand.

Jessup said in a whisper out of the jury's earshot, "I move to strike all of Professor Stein's testimony relative to future projections. It is based on Mr. Gaspar's attaining officer status, which he never did and could not prove he ever would. Since there were no projections with respect to his earnings as an able seaman, I ask the court to limit damages to past losses only and deny any consideration of future losses for lack of proof."

"What about it, Mr. Nikolas? What's your position?" Judge Costello was very formal since all the remarks at the bench were being recorded by the court reporter.

Failure to prove future damages for 32 years would be an economic blow. Those losses could run into more than a million dollars over three decades. Dan said, "If the Court permits, I would like the opportunity to present evidence to that effect in the next few days."

"Alright, I'll hold the motion in abeyance till you present your proof, Mr. Nikolas."

Dan then asked the Judge, "If Professor Stein could make a projection for future losses based upon the deceased's status as an Able Seaman, which he was at the time he lost his leg, would the Court permit it?" At this point, Dan did not know how he was going to overcome this problem.

"How long would it take him to do it?"

"An hour, perhaps two at the most."

"Alright, let him make one. I may permit him to testify as to those projections. Have him here first thing tomorrow morning with the projections, because we're leaving early today again. I'll decide, based upon his testimony, if I will allow it. You may continue with your cross examination, Mr. Jessup."

"In that case, Judge, I have no further questions of this witness and reserve the right to cross-examine further, should the need arise."

"Noted, Mr. Jessup. Let's take a break until tomorrow morning at 8:30. I have some motions to resolve this afternoon. Until then," Judge Costello rapped his gavel.

"So unless someone comes up with a good reason not to, I'm calling Captain Burn after we finish with Professor Stein, when we return tomorrow," Dan advised his three colleagues.

24

THE TRIAL CONTINUES
THE LOGBOOK

Lu Moore was slumped at her desk, her chin inside two cupped hands extended from her forearms on her desk. After a short rap at her door, Bradley Rogers walked in without an invitation, and sat down in the chair facing his colleague.

"Are you alright, Lu?" he asked. "What are you doing here at one o'clock?" You should be at the trial."

"Yes Bradley, I'm fine. The Judge recessed early for the day." she said as she raised her head up from her hands. Her eyes were red, not from tears but because she had been working long hours without sleep. Her face was ashen.

"Go home, Lu. Get some sleep. You need it. I've never seen you like this."

"I just prepared a memo which I don't want anyone but you to see until the trial is over. Please keep it quiet until then."

"I presume it's about the trial. How's it going?"

"I've seen much better. I don't want to bad-mouth Jessup, but he's been taking some real chances. I think he's anxious to prove he's top notch and doesn't need me. In the process, he's screwing up."

Lu passed a three-page, hand-written evaluation of the trial to-date, over to Rogers. Stapled to it were the crumpled memos she had passed on to Jessup and which she had retrieved after he had refused to follow her suggestions. Rogers read Lu's memo and then read the notes. He sat back in his chair and slapped the papers with the back of his hand.

"Lu, you have to fix this up."

"As far as what's gone into the trial record up to now, you know as well as I do, it's too late. We will win anyway because they still haven't proven Captain Burn was wrong in his decision not to evacuate Fonseca. The log definitely shows the ship too far from help and a helicopter couldn't make a rescue under those conditions. That leaves a motor launch, which would have taken much longer than a helicopter to reach the ship. And then, they can't prove how far gone he was in order to treat him. Although Dr. Welles said he was not past help, when our doctors testify they'll strongly dispute that opinion. So I think we are in a good position to come up with a verdict in our favor."

"What's to be done with Jessup? He could screw up what's left of the trial."

"I suspect he will. But it isn't my call to make. Your partners made their decision. Now they have to stand by it. I have given this law firm everything I could give, emotionally, physically and intellectually. I wrote this evaluation for obvious reasons. I hate to have had to do it. I wrote it to protect myself, so that all of you would know the truth. I'm trying to save my position in this law firm. Why am I doing this? Why do I want to be in a firm that recognizes my abilities yet denigrates and exploits me and then puts me out on the block like the sacrificial lamb? I really don't know."

Rogers read the memos once again, breathed out heavily and pleaded, "Look, the partners have to see this; if not all of them, at least Dudley Hayes, as managing partner. He's on your side. It's important not to lose this case and your reputation with it."

"Okay, if you think it will help. But we can't change lawyers in the middle of the trial. The jury will wonder what's going on. It could be worse than allowing Jessup to continue. Besides, if I take over and the case is lost, it becomes my fault. So, no, thank you."

Lu stood up and walked to a small refrigerator in a corner of her room. She took out two bottles of soda water and handed one to Rogers with a paper cup. After rolling the cold bottle over her forehead, she opened and drank from it, Seeming somewhat refreshed, she said, "When this trial is over, I'm seriously thinking of resigning from the firm. My mother asked me something that has been running around in my mind for days. 'Can you work for the rest of your career with men who don't trust you?' She's a wise woman, my mother. You would like her. She's independent and can't stand hypocrisy. The answer to her question is 'No.' I can't work under those conditions, Bradley. I'll finish this trial then I'm seriously thinking about leaving Brown, Sykes and Bellham."

"You have to reconsider. When Hayes sees this memo he'll get them to change their minds. Don't be so hasty, I'll arrange to have one of the partners sit in on the trial so that they understand the reality of this situation. I will have to get my partners to understand that this problem is of their own making. Are you sure we can win this case?"

"Read the log. Of course Burn made the right decision. Without the helicopter, there is no speedy evacuation. A launch adds precious time to the equation, because it's slower, which would make a rescue almost useless."

"Will you re-consider? Do it for me? I worked hard to get everyone to accept a woman partner. Don't throw it away. All these years you learned how to be an exceptional trial lawyer and a great all-around counselor; it was all on this firm's time. Maybe you owe it to us to give us another chance."

She did not answer Rogers' question. Then she said: "How you get a partner to observe the trial is up to you." Lu pointed to the memo in Rogers' hands. "Keep that memo away from anyone but a partner. I don't want anyone rummaging around your desk. I'll think about what you just said."

"Have you looked at those notes you told me were made by Dr. Peters, which were the last pages of his medical reports?" Robby Masterson asked Dan.

"No. I've been so wrapped up with our witnesses that I never had a chance. Besides, it's medical. That's Jack Hoffman's concern"

"Well, look at them now. It isn't medical and it looks to be at odds with the deck log. One of those documents has to be wrong."

Dan looked at Robby quizzically and picked up the papers. After reviewing them, he shook his head and said, "You're right. The good doctor made a record of the times and locations of the vessel when he called the Captain and spoke with the other doctors. Compared to the ship's log it looks like the voyage of two different ships." Dan ruffled through a duplicate set of exhibits he had in the office.

"Look here. There's a difference between the doctor's times when he called the bridge and the ship's log when they received his calls. That's odd. They should at least be very close. And look at his notes on landmarks. They are much closer to Plymouth and Culdrose than the ship's log. The log has them much further away. Something's wrong here. I'll recall Dr. Peters to clear this up. This is my fault. I didn't review these records carefully because they were in the medical reports. Luckily, we got to them in time."

ᡐ ᡒ

The next morning, before calling Dr. Stein, the economist, Dan recalled Dr. Peters. The doctor took the stand looking somewhat puzzled. He looked at Lu who offered him no encouragement.

"Dr. Peters, as part of your medical report which is in evidence, there are notes on the back two pages which, for the purposes of this testimony, I will call the addendum notes or memorandum. They refer to times and locations. I ask you to look at them."

Dr. Peters examined the pages, set them on his lap and said, "I've read them."

"Are you able to identify the addendum, for the record, as notes that you made doctor?"

"Yes, they are my notes."

"When did you make them?"

"I made them at the time we were deciding how to treat Mr. Fonseca. They were done just as the events were occurring."

"How did you determine the times you put into the addendum?"

"By my wristwatch."

228

"And doctor, I note that at some places you added landmarks."

"Yes, I entered them so that we would have an idea where we were when I examined the seaman, made the calls to the Captain and consulted with the other doctors."

Dan looked over at Lu's table. She was writing in a fury on a small yellow pad. She was tearing off pages from the pad which she slid across the table to Jessup, who read them and nodded approval with a broad grin.

"And why did you feel you had to do that, doctor?"

Dr. Peters paused, looked up at the ceiling as if the right words for his answer were written high above his head. Finally, he looked at Lu and Jessup and slowly began his answer. "There were three doctors who were volunteers. They were forced into a difficult position. I wanted to make sure that later on, if there would be an investigation or a law suit, it would be clear that they operated only after careful consideration. That it wasn't because they rushed to do it, but because they had little choice in the matter. They were doctors who recognized or felt that they had a professional duty to treat a sick person."

"Wasn't it also because you were concerned about yourself and your personal role in this matter?"

"At the time, it hadn't crossed my mind. Now, of course, it seems as if I was acting in my self-interest."

"Were you aware there is a difference between your times and locations and those on the official ship's log?"

"No. If what you say is true, then this is the first time I am aware of it."

"Doctor, I would like you to compare Plaintiff's Exhibit in Evidence Nine. It is the ship's log."

Dr. Peters read both exhibits twice. He put them down and looked at Dan.

"Dr. Peters, have you compared them?"

"I have."

"From your reading, are they the same?"

"No. The ship's log has the vessel much closer to the ocean and away from Culdrose than I do, and the times are also very different."

With the doctor's answer there was a stir in the courtroom. The Judge struck his gavel. "I want silence here. I don't want any noise during a witness's testimony."

"Before today, were you aware of this difference?"

"No, sir."

"No one ever pointed them out to you?"

"No."

"Thank you doctor, no further questions."

Jessup rose and moved like a race horse out of its paddock. He was holding Lu's notes in his hand and referring to them.

"Dr. Peters, you have never prepared a ship's log before this one?" Jessup asked, almost out of breath.

"No. I never had any reason to."

"Between yourself, doctor, and the officers on the ship's bridge, wouldn't you agree that the officers would be more experienced in preparing a log?"

"The officers on the ship's bridge? Of course."

"Can you say for certain your watch was absolutely synchronized with the same time as that of the bridge?"

"I know my watch was correct. I can't say what the bridge clock was like. I would imagine it was correct and the same as mine. I always check mine regularly with the Purser's clock on the wall above his desk. It's because we pass through a few time zones on our voyage from Europe to New York."

Jessup addressed the Court. "Your honor, I move to strike the last part of the answer as speculative."

"Granted, Mr. Jessup. I instruct you ladies and gentlemen of the jury to disregard the last part of Dr. Peters' testimony. You are not to consider it. Continue Mr. Jessup."

"Doctor, how did you determine the landmarks?"

"I figured out where we were. Some places were familiar to me. I knew them from the many times we have passed them."

"Were you on deck when you saw these landmarks?"

"No I saw them through a window of the ship."

"Were there signs indicating the cities or other important locations?"

"Not that I can remember."

"Supposing you saw a lighthouse and supposing there are three or four lighthouses along the coast on your way out to sea, how could you ever know which light you were looking at?"

"I approximated. But I knew I was very close."

"And the cities you list in your addendum, as Mr. Nikolas calls it, could you be certain which ones you were looking at?"

"I thought I could at the time."

"And it was still dark out, so that it might have been hard to verify landmarks while you were trying to figure out how to deal with Mr. Fonseca, wasn't it?"

"Yes, it was dark. But it was starting to become dawn."

"So doctor, based upon your own testimony, wouldn't you say the observations you put down in the addendum were flawed?"

"I didn't think so at the time. They were the honest observations I made at the time. Now you make it seem I was wrong. It's possible, yes. But not probable that I was wrong; those notes were made to make a clear record of where we were and when we were there. "

"No further questions."

Lu did a good job of casting doubt on the doctor's addendum. The jury now has the job of determining if the doctor or the bridge was correct. I make a low bow to you, Lu. Now let's see what will happen with Captain Burn, Dan thought.

Judge Costello called for an afternoon break. "We reconvene after 2 p.m." he said after a loud strike of his gavel. Dan looked toward Lu, who offered a half smile. Dan, Jack, Charley Becker and Drew Sloan left for Dan's office, where they lunched on sandwiches delivered from a nearby luncheonette. As they went over the morning's testimony, Dan said, "Jack, unless you have some medical testimony to clean up, I'm starting with Captain Burn."

"No. I'm finished and very interested to see how you're going to proceed."

A few minutes before 2 p.m., Dan walked into an almost empty courtroom. Sitting on a bench outside the courtroom was Captain Gregory Burn. As a fact witness, he was required with all other fact witnesses to remain outside the courtroom until called to testify. The only witnesses allowed in the courtroom are experts, who may remain after their testimony to assist counsel during the cross-examination of the defense's experts. As Dan walked into the court room, Lu was at her table, going over notes she had made during trial. She gave Dan a quick look. He thought it was accompanied with a smile. Judge Costello came through the door behind his bench. The Bailiff called out in a booming voice. "All rise."

As Judge Costello took his seat he said, "Please be seated. Is the Plaintiff prepared to continue?"

"We are, your Honor, and we call as our next witness, Captain Gregory Burn."

"I thought we were going to consider the economic expert, Mr. Nikolas."

"We shall, your Honor. But since we had testimony from Dr. Peters about his memorandum, I felt logically we should continue with Captain Burn."

"Alright, go ahead."

When she heard Dan call his next witness, Lu looked up from her notes and focused on Dan with admiration. Jessup seemed puzzled.

"What's up?" Jessup asked Lu, who put a finger to her lips to quiet him. "Just listen and learn something."

The Bailiff went into the hall and returned with Captain Burn. He was dressed in his navy blue company uniform, which at last he had the chance to show off to the jury. They could not have seen him in the hallway, as they never entered the courtroom from that door. The jury entered through another door alongside the jury box, which opens into their deliberating room. When they go to lunch or finish after a day's session, they leave accompanied by a U.S. Marshal, who takes care to insure they have no contact with attorneys, litigants or anyone else. Juries take an elevator, usually free of other occupants, and go to lunch as a group, at the same restaurant under a Marshal's watchful eye. The Marshal takes an oath, at the beginning of the trial, to ensure the jury's segregation during trial.

Before Burn headed for the witness stand he stopped at Jessup's side of the counsel table and whispered to Lu, "Can he really call me?"

"Yes, he can," she answered in a whisper. "And be careful with your answers. Just answer 'yes' or 'no'. No volunteering, please as I have instructed you before." Lu admonished Burn, knowing he would do whatever pleased him anyway.

The Judge called to Captain Burn sternly.

"Will the witness please step up here to take his oath so that we can get on with questioning? We don't want any delays, sir."

Captain Burn took the witness chair after swearing to tell the truth. He sat quietly and puzzled while Dan shuffled through some papers at his desk. Burn took the opportunity during this short delay to look at the jury with a smile, exactly what Dan wanted him to do. He hoped the jury would understand that Burn was ingratiating himself. Dan rose from his seat and walked to the counsel's stand, leaned on two elbows into the flat portion of the dais and said with a wide smile,

"Good afternoon, Captain Burn."

Burn had no choice but to be cordial and turned away from the jury and grudgingly returned the greeting, with a smile that was forced. Before he began to examine his witness, Dan made a request of the Court.

"Judge," he asked, "Permission to treat this witness as hostile as he is a principal witness for the defendant."

"Yes, Mr. Nikolas, granted, Proceed with your examination."

Treating Captain Burn as a hostile witness gives Dan an advantage. He is not bound by the rules of evidence requiring him to frame questions in such a way as to avoid putting answers in a witness's mouth or as it is called, "leading a witness." Now he can treat Burn as if he were cross-examining him, allowing Dan greater latitude as to how he frames his questions.

"Captain Burn, isn't it so that the title 'captain', as I use it today with respect to you and your position aboard the *S.S. American Union*, is not a military rank."

"Yes."

"And isn't it true that the term captain as used by your employer is used for all persons who command any of their ships and, of course, used by you when you are in command of your ship?"

"Yes." Burn was visibly annoyed. The smile he had flashed to the jury moments earlier now transformed into a scowl.

"And Captain, I notice that you are wearing a uniform today. It's not a military uniform, am I not correct?"

Burn sniffed. "Yes."

"It is a uniform that your employer, A.U. Lines, has designed for all its captains that command their ships, is it not?"

"Yes."

"And you have another uniform that you only wear a couple of weeks during the year, that of a Rear Admiral, isn't that so?"

Burn perked up. "Yes, I am a Rear Admiral."

"But you are not regular Navy. You are only a reserve Rear Admiral two weeks out of every year when you go on reserve duty and play sailor."

This son-of-a-bitch is making fun of me. "Yes, I wear my uniform as a reserve officer when I am on reserve duty."

"And you have no reason to wear it any other time of the year, isn't that so?"

"I suppose so. Unless there's a war"

"But there is no war now, right?"

"There is no war."

"And you don't normally wear this uniform, the one you have on today, which is the company's uniform, when you are home on leave from your duties aboard ship and let us say, when you go to the movies or out to dinner with your wife, isn't that so?"

Burn hesitated, but answered in a flat tone. "Yes, that's so."

"So can you please explain to this Court and jury why you are wearing this uniform today?"

Burn sat silent for a moment. He looked at Dan with a controlled anger. *This landsman is questioning my authority and making me look foolish. Had this happened aboard my ship it would have resulted in some nasty consequences for him.* Burn turned toward the jury, this time without any smile and said, "I wanted the jury to be aware of my position. I mean, the importance of my position. About who I am. That when I am in command of my ship, I am the one who makes all the decisions. Wearing my uniform emphasizes my position."

"And whose idea might that be, that you wear a uniform today to court?"

"Both Mr. Jessup and I felt this would be an advantage." Burn pointed to Jessup at the counsel table.

"Would you be so kind as to tell us what you mean by advantage?"

"We wanted the jury to understand that I run the ship; that I am the person in command. The uniform emphasizes that. Like the Judge, his Honor. He wears a robe in the courtroom. Nobody else does. It's a badge of respect and command." Burn looked up to Judge Costello with a smile.

"So Mr. Jessup and you thought you might influence the jury with this phony uniform?" Dan looked at the jury.

Jessup rose from his seat. "Objection, your Honor, as to the characterization of the uniform as being phony." Lu stifled a laugh, putting a hand over her mouth.

"Yes," said the Judge, "Mr. Nikolas, please re-phrase your question if you insist on pursuing that line of questioning."

"Well, let's say that this uniform only has a status within your company. Am I not correct?"

"Yes. When I'm in command it has a status, as you call it."

"But when you are in command you could wear any uniform. You could wear a sweatshirt in the wheelhouse, you would still be the captain because you command the ship, whether in this uniform or not?"

"I have to agree," Burn spat out.

"And if you wore the uniform to dinner with your wife at a restaurant, would it have the same effect that you would like to make on the jury today?" Dan looked at the jury again.

There was no answer from the witness stand. Dan looked at Burn. He knew there would be no answer, but he waited until he was ready for his next question, then he said, "It's alright, Mr. Burn, you needn't answer. I think everyone knows the answer."

Jessup rose to object. "Judge, Mr. Nikolas is answering for the witness."

"Mr. Nikolas, refrain from answering for the witness. Your latitude with a hostile witness does not extend that far."

"I'm sorry, Judge. I do have some more questions for you, Mr. Burn."

Everyone in the courtroom noted that Dan called Burn "mister," because Dan heavily stressed that word.

Jessup quickly rose from his chair. "Judge," he asked, "may I approach the bench?"

"Yes, both sides may step up."

Dan, Jack, Jessup and Lu stood in front of the Judge who had his hand over the microphone so the jury could not hear the whispered conversations at the bench. The court reporter stood nearby to record the proceedings at the bar.

"What is it, Mr. Jessup?" Judge Costello asked.

"I object to Mr. Nikolas addressing Captain Burn as mister."

Lu let out a puff of air. Judge Costello looked at Jessup with a wry smile and said, "What about it, Mr. Nikolas?"

"I believe we have established that captain is not his military rank. And that he is only captain when he is at the helm of his ship, which is not the case today." Then Dan added, "If anyone is at the helm here today, it is only you, Judge."

"Well, Mr. Jessup, I have to agree with Mr. Nikolas. You are, of course, free to use that title when you address your client or refer to him when examining others. Let's get on with the business of this trial and stop wasting time. I don't like these problems. It's like two schoolyard kids bantering with each other."

All the lawyers returned to their tables. Dan continued questioning.

"Now Mr. Burn, I would like you to help the jury understand some definitions of measurements at sea as used by mariners such as yourself. I do that because those of us who don't live on the sea can easily become confused by some of these different terms. Let's get miles, speed and other measurements down right away so that those of us who are landlubbers will be able to follow the testimony as it unfolds. With the Court's permission, I will use the blackboard to set it down for the jury.

"A nautical mile, Mr. Burn. How many feet is that?"

"Six thousand, seventy-six feet."

Dan wrote the number on the board with the words "nautical mile" alongside. "How does that compare with a statute mile or the one we call a land mile?"

"I'm not sure I know exactly. It's over 5,000 feet."

"If I told you 5,280 feet, would you accept it?"

"Yes, yes, that's the number."

Dan wrote that number beneath the first one and the words "land mile" alongside. "So a nautical mile is longer than a land mile by almost 800 feet. That's significant. Wouldn't you agree?"

"I suppose so."

"In fact, a nautical mile is one point one five oh eight miles in relation to a land mile. Am I not correct?"

"Yes, you are."

Dan put 1.1508 on the board. "Good. Now Mr. Burn, let's talk about a knot. That's a measurement of speed on the ocean, is it not?"

"Yes."

What does it equal in terms of land measure?"

"A knot equals one nautical mile per hour."

"So when we say a ship makes 20 knots, she is making more than 20 land miles per hour?"

"Yes."

"Bear with me, Mr. Burn, while I put these measurements on the blackboard. Now we hear the term fathom all the time. Some of us may not know what a fathom equals. Would you please tell us?"

"A fathom is six feet."

"And when you say you put out a 'shot of anchor' what does that mean?"

"It means 90 feet of anchor chain was let out from the ship."

"Good. So now all of us can understand these terms while we talk about them during this trial."

Burn was squirming in his seat. He bristled every time he was addressed as mister and now he was helping this son-of-a-bitch lawyer define the peculiar language of the sea which he had been planning to use to confuse his cross examiner. Had he discussed it with Lu, she would have told him not to waste his time, because Dan was a sailor. But no, Burn had figured that strategy on his own. He didn't need a lawyer to tell him he could confound landlubbers. It happened all the time on his ship when he dined with his passengers, who were always awed and had trouble following him with the peculiar language mariners used.

Now there was a blackboard filled with the comparisons and it would be easy for any juror to follow the testimony. This damned lawyer was screwing up his plans. Besides, he was making him look foolish, calling him "mister" instead of Captain, making fun of his uniform, and making it easy for the jury to understand these nautical terms.

"Mr. Burn, please explain to the Court and jury what a ship's log is and what it contains."

"A ship's log is the history of her navigation. It contains her speed, the weather she encounters and any unusual or significant activities which the officer on watch feels should be noted or recorded in the log. Some logs even note the names of the deck crew on watch. It is signed by the officer on watch. He is the officer in charge of the vessel at that time. It could be me or any other of my officers."

"Let us look at the log for the day in which the deceased, Gaspar Fonseca, had his operation. The ship's log at 6:15 a.m. reads, "AB. That's an able seaman, is it not?"

"Yes."

"'AB Skelley reports AB Fonseca awoke with bad pains in left leg. Called ship's MD. to check out seaman.' Who signed that entry?"

"Looks like my signature."

"But the Chief Mate was on duty, according to Dr. Peters."

"Yes, Chief Mate Farrow. He had the four to eight watch at that time. But I came up later, before the watch was over. I assumed command of the ship and signed the log for the whole watch."

"Isn't that unusual?"

"No. I am the Captain. I can do anything that's legal."

"Look at the notes made by Dr. Peters. He says he was called by the Mate at 5:45 a.m. Do you have any comments on the discrepancy?"

"No. I wasn't on the bridge at the time. But I have to go by the Mate's entry in the log. There's a severe penalty for anyone who makes false entries in a ship's smooth log. I can't imagine why the Mate would make a false entry in any log, rough or smooth. There is no point to it."

"Please explain to the jury what rough logs and smooth logs are."

"A rough log is usually made by an officer on the bridge. It doesn't have to be the one in command. On my ship, it's usually a junior officer. A rough log can be erased or altered. It then becomes the basis for the final preparation of the smooth log, or the official and final ship's log. We cannot alter that smooth log or make improper entries under penalties prescribed by law."

"Were you aware that Dr. Peters made a record of times and places where the *American Union* was during the times he called you to discuss AB Fonseca's physical condition?"

"Yes, I was. I was advised of this yesterday."

"Did you have the opportunity to look at his memo?"

"Yes."

"Are you aware of the differences between the two documents?"

"Yes."

"So, if I understand you, you would place the discrepancy in time and place on Dr. Peters, since it is not an official log?"

"As far as I know, he's not used to making any kind of log. He wouldn't have been under any obligation to prepare a precise log such as an officer must make by law."

"I ask you to compare the ship's log with Dr. Peters' memorandum. Where was the ship at the time recorded on the ship's log when Dr. Peters called the bridge for the first time?"

"She would have been past Plymouth. Heading toward land's End, by the western end of the Channel."

"And according to Dr. Peters' entry, where would the ship have been?"

"Without a chart, I cannot say."

"There's a chart of the English Channel on the easel. Show us."

Burn walked to the easel. "I couldn't say for sure by what I am reading on Dr. Peters' log, but it probably would have been much before the ship would have reached the port of Plymouth."

"Assuming Dr. Peters' memo to be correct, if you needed to make a rescue at that point would it have been feasible?"

"I don't know."

"Can you tell us why you don't know?"

"We might have gotten him to land by launch. But that was not the case here, as you can tell by the official log."

"But I asked you to assume your ship was at the point set forth by Dr. Peters in his memorandum. Couldn't a helicopter have been called in at that stage?"

"I wasn't going to allow a helicopter near my ship, Mister. It is too damned dangerous. There are wires all over the only areas where a pick-up would be made. If the helicopter got caught in those wires it would be a disaster. Imagine! A helicopter crashing onto my ship. Fuel oil igniting and burning all over the place. No sir, Mister, I'm not going to allow that. I'm not taking that chance. Then I can't pull my ship into those little English ports. The piers are too small for my ship. She's over 990 feet long. Then the port's depth is too shallow. My ship draws 31 feet. I'm not grounding my ship in a shallow port. I can't tell you now if there was any other way to get the man off the ship." Burn returned to his witness chair, folding his arms as if to say: "That's my answer, now go prove me wrong."

"At the time of the last call made to you by Dr. Peters, during which you indicated that he and the doctors should proceed with the operation, where were was the *American Union* according to the ship's log?"

"According to the coordinates in the log, we had left the Channel and were past the Scilly Isles entering the Celtic Sea and proceeding into the Atlantic Ocean."

"And according to Dr. Peters, where was the ship?"

"Around Plymouth, or perhaps a little before or around Culdrose."

"Why do you suppose he made a log on the back of his medical record and they are separate from his medical notes?"

"I wouldn't know. I wouldn't have the slightest idea."

"To your knowledge has he ever made such a log before?"

"No. Not that I am aware of."

"Why would you think that he did make one on that day and under the conditions prevailing?"

Burn unfolded his arms, moved to the end of his seat, stuck out his chin in defiance and said, "I have no idea, Counselor."

"Were you aware that Dr. Peters testified here, in this courtroom, that he did it to ensure that he would have a record that would show that all the doctors deliberated carefully before deciding to operate?"

"I am not aware that he testified to that. If he did, that's his testimony. I was told the doctors could operate."

"And that Dr. Peters testified that he told you that Gaspar Fonseca should be evacuated immediately?"

"Yes. I remember having that conversation. And he also told me the doctors could operate if they had to. Knowing we were far from any safe rescue area, in that case I suggested he go on with the operation."

"And were you told that he testified that you were notified of that fact at 6 a.m.?"

"No, but his time is wrong. And again, Counselor, he advised me the doctors on the ship could handle the situation."

"Were you also advised that he also felt his memorandum or log could be used in case of a law suit or investigation?"

"No."

"Do you have any comment on that testimony?"

"He's the doctor. He knew what was possible. I'm the ship's Captain, not a medical man. I would presume he was out to cover himself if a law suit was filed such as the one we have here today."

"Is there anything that happened that might have led you to believe that such a record by Dr. Peters was necessary?"

"No, certainly not."

"Well, Dr. Peters in his record says he called you several times and you wouldn't take any action to get Gaspar Fonseca off the ship. Might that be why he wanted to make a record, when he testified that he made this record with law suits in mind?"

"That's his opinion, not mine."

"At what time did your watch begin?"

"As the Captain, I'm always on watch. That morning I was up on the bridge around 6:45, because I was awakened by Dr. Peters with this emergency. Since I was awake, I felt I should go to the bridge, as I might be needed."

"What time were you first called by Dr. Peters?"

"I don't know. Certainly sometime after the Mate called Dr. Peters. Maybe 6:30."

"You said a moment ago you went to the bridge because, and I quote you. 'I might be needed.' Did you feel that because you wanted to be the one to control the ship's log?"

"A crew member was sick. Dr. Peters led me to believe it was a serious emergency. He wouldn't have awakened me if a seaman only had a cold or a belly-ache. Under those conditions, I felt my place was on the bridge."

"Was it because Dr. Peters felt you might have to make a rescue?"

"I can't remember that. But that surely might have been one of his reasons."

"Could you still have made a rescue when you went up to the bridge? The log says you came up at 6:45."

"We had already left the English Channel. We were on our way into the North Atlantic."

"What was the ship's speed?"

"She was making 32 knots. That's what we always make."

"Did you feel it was difficult to get a man off the ship at the time?"

"I wanted to make sure that the seaman couldn't be helped aboard ship before I called for a rescue. Dr. Peters satisfied me that the doctors who examined the seaman could perform an operation, which was what he needed."

"Have you read Dr. Peters' addendum?"

"Yes, I have."

"You would agree would you not, that he says he told you more than once, in fact three times, that there was no qualified surgeon among the doctors and that they all agreed Gaspar Fonseca should be taken off the ship?"

"He may say that. But my memory of these conversations is that he told me the doctors were competent to perform the operation."

"You are aware that Dr. Peters is not a surgeon?"

"He has told me that more than once, if I remember."

"You are also aware that all three doctors testified that they heard Dr. Peters telling you they would prefer to see Gaspar Fonseca sent to a hospital rather than operate aboard ship?"

"That was not my understanding of the situation. I only spoke with Dr. Peters. I wouldn't know what the other doctors thought other than what Dr. Peters told me. In any event, the ship was out of the area where a rescue was possible without making some very dangerous maneuvers."

"Can you explain to the Court and jury why you preferred one of your seamen to have an operation by four doctors, none of whom was a surgeon, instead of getting him to a proper facility ashore?"

"We were many miles away from the area that was necessary to make a careful rescue free of any danger. Under those conditions, I wouldn't permit a helicopter to approach my ship since it was too dangerous. If the helicopter should fall due to a malfunction and land on my ship it could cause injuries to my passengers and those on deck assisting with the rescue, including the helicopter crew. There are wires and other paraphernalia which I am not permitted to touch as they belong to the Department of the Navy. So they would be in the way of any rescue by air in any event."

"Why didn't you consider a motor launch for a rescue?"

"I would have to slow my ship down or even turn her around and return to the Channel. In a busy waterway like the English Channel, which is probably one of the busiest in the world, that maneuver could be dangerous and imperil my passengers and crew and the ship. Dr. Peters told me the seaman needed attention immediately. Based on his opinion, I felt he had a better chance aboard the ship. I'm not a doctor. I have to depend on what the doctors were telling me. I didn't even know at the time if a motor launch was available. No one ever suggested it to me. In hindsight, I figured that it would not get to us on time anyway."

"No one suggested a helicopter either, isn't that so?"

"True. But it was on everyone's mind, I believe. My ship is not a 35-foot motor boat that you can maneuver at a moment's notice from one side to another or make quick 180-degree turns. No sir, Mr. Nikolas, as Captain of my ship I must be mindful of the lives of my passengers and crew. I have to weigh the security of 2,000 people or more against the security of one person whose physical condition I was satisfied was in the hands of four qualified physicians.

"Then I had to concern myself with getting to New York on schedule as there were tug boats, longshoremen and others waiting for us. If we arrived late, the overtime could be very large." Burn sat back crossed his arms over his chest once again crossed his legs and looked directly at his examiner with contempt.

Dan was thinking that this was a difficult witness, who may have convinced the jury that based upon the location of the ship and his understanding of what the doctors could do, it was too late for anyone to make a safe rescue from the *American Union*. Dan took a deep breath. Should he continue with Burn or end the examination here? If he did, the jury would be left with this last testimony in mind. Dan would try to strike the last blow.

"Mr. Burn, were you aware of the rescue facilities available to you on the day Gaspar Fonseca fell ill?"

"Yes, we keep a list of such information on the bridge, not only for the Channel but other places the ship may regularly sail."

"What was available to you at your location?"

"Helicopters and motor launches, none of which, in my opinion, afforded a safe rescue"

"How fast was the *American Union* moving?"

"We were moving at 32 knots. The company requests I use that speed as the most efficient for fuel consumption and a comfortable passage for my passengers."

"Would you please define a 'following sea' for the Court and jury?"

"That occurs when the sea is at your stern or your back, pushing your ship forward."

"Isn't the effect of a following sea to increase the speed of the ship?"

"It speeds the ship up, yes."

"Please look at your log and tell this Court and jury if you had a following sea at any time on your voyage to New York?"

"Yes."

"If you had made a rescue and were behind in time, based upon the company directive not to exceed 32 knots, you wouldn't have exceeded your authority if you steamed up a few extra knots to make up the lost time since the sea was speeding the ship, am I not correct?"

Burn made no attempt to answer.

"I have no further questions of this witness at this time." Dan finished up with a dismissive swipe of his hand.

"Mr. Jessup?" Judge Costello looked at Steve Jessup. "Have you any questions of this witness."

"Not at the present; we plan to conduct a direct examination of our own, Your Honor." Jessup was looking at a memo from Lu.

"Then Captain Burn, you will make yourself available for further examination. We will adjourn until tomorrow morning at 8:30. Mr. Nikolas how many more witnesses do you have?"

"Two Judge; we will be recalling Professor Stein and our helicopter expert."

"Then I can expect that you will rest your case tomorrow or the day after at the latest?

"Yes, Judge."

"Good, then we will re-convene tomorrow at 8:30," Judge Costello said with a sharp rap of his gavel.

25

UNEXPECTED MEETING
WASHINGTON SQUARE PARK

Dan and Jack Hoffman were reviewing the day's testimony.

"As far as putting a pin into the Captain's ego, we made some points," Dan explained, "but I'm afraid the jury will have a tough problem deliberating about the ship's log. Burn made a strong point about the log being ruled by law and must always be correct under penalty of law. If they accept the ship's log as to her positions, we lose this case because the rule that the Captain's decision is unassailable beats us. And then he has given good reasons for not making a rescue. If we didn't have Doctor Peters' memo, I'm sure the Judge would throw us out of Court if Jessup made a motion to dismiss for failure to prove a *prima facie* case. At least, for us, the jury can consider the doctor's memo. But it's a long shot, since they'll probably accept the ship's log over the doctor's."

Jack said, "I'll be ready for their medical testimony after you finish with Commander Masterson. Your friend Lu told me they are putting on their doctors first and saving Burn for last, so that they can emphasize his testimony with the jury."

"You spoke to Lu?

"Yes, while you were putting your stuff together, she asked me how I felt the trial was going. I told her I didn't know too much about ship's work or ship's logs so I couldn't give her a good opinion. But to tell the truth, Dan, it doesn't take a genius to figure out we're on the ropes."

Betsy Sachs buzzed the conference room. Dan lifted the phone: "There's a man on the phone. Says he wants to talk with you. He says he's a ship's officer."

"I can't speak to him now Betsy. I'm busy with Jack Hoffman."

"He says it's important and he's sailing in three days. He won't be back for another couple of weeks."

"Okay, put him on."

Dan's experience has been that opportunities to speak with seafarers who say they have important information cannot be ignored. A seaman's time ashore is fleeting. He calls from a pay phone on the street or from the office of the ship's agent. If his call isn't taken immediately, the seaman often can't leave a number where he can be reached. For the lawyer, it means interrupting work with a client to take the call. It might be rude but, if the call goes unanswered, the lawyer may never hear from that seaman again. If he does, it may not be for weeks or months later, and it may be too late. The seaman may once have had important information for a trial or a settlement negotiation, which had been long ago resolved.

"Good afternoon, I'm Dan Nikolas. My secretary says you want to talk to me," Dan said in a pleasant voice.

"Yes, sir, I do. I have some information that I'm sure you can use in Gas Fonseca's law suit."

"What's your name?"

"I'd like to save that for when we meet."

"And what is this information you might have for me?"

"Before we go into that, Mr. Nikolas, I want to make it clear I don't do this for money. I was a friend of Gas Fonseca. He was a good shipmate and used to come to my cabin with his books when he was studying for his Third Mate's license. We became friendly. I've been to his house and Mira, that's his wife, Gas and I would go out together. I only just found out he committed suicide. I want to help his wife and little boy."

"So tell me, how can you help?"

"I would rather not discuss that over the phone."

"Can you come to my office?"

"I think it's better we meet somewhere outside your office. Can we do that now?"

"How do I know I'm not wasting my time?'

"I guarantee you can use my information to help you with your case."

"Where can I meet you?"

"Can you meet me at the fountain at Washington Square Park in an hour?"

"I'm wearing a navy blue pinstripe suit and a red tie," Dan explained. "How will I know you?"

"Don't concern yourself with that, Mr. Nikolas. I know who you are. I've often seen you aboard the Big A. talking to one of your clients. Be at the Square in an hour. I'll find you."

"Ok. I'll be there. By the fountain it is."

After he hung up the phone, Dan put on his suit jacket, which was hanging on the back of his chair. He said to Jack Hoffman, "This man says he has some information that will help us. I hope it's not a fool's errand. I have to meet him in Washington Square in an hour."

"Then follow it up," Jack said in an encouraging tone.

Forty minutes later a taxi cab dropped Dan off at the south end of Washington Square Park at the corner by New York University's School of Law. Spring had earlier come to the city and the Park's grass and trees were showing off their shiny green covers. In the Park, across from the law school, chess players enjoying the balmy weather, were hunched silently over several concrete tables with chess boards etched into them. They were moving chess pieces after pondering tactics. The players were surrounded by onlookers, some of whom were anxiously waiting to challenge the victors. There was the smell of cut grass and the branches on the trees were shaking in a soft breeze, their leaves sounding as if someone was turning the pages of a newspaper.

Dan walked north across the Park, passing benches filled with college students enjoying the pleasant weather. He stopped near the Washington Arch, close to the location of the round fountain. He watched traffic moving south along Fifth Avenue and found an empty bench opposite the fountain. He looked around him for a familiar face, but he could see none.

As Dan sat, he took the opportunity to enjoy the spring sun on his face. He turned toward the remaining brownstone mansions on the north side of the Square. They were all that was left of New York's 19th century upper class elite who lived in fine homes once surrounding the entire Square. This was the street which, with its affluent residents, was chronicled by Edith Wharton and Henry James; the street Dan had once aspired to live on when he could accumulate enough money to buy one of these homes. It was too late for him. New York University had purchased every inch of land on Washington Square. And while the Park in the center still belonged to the City of New York, it was surrounded by the school, becoming its default campus.

He scanned the street once more to see if he recognized anyone. No, he saw no one who looked in any way familiar to him. Then, giving up the hope he would see someone he knew, he closed eyes, crossed his arms over his chest, crossed his legs and tilted his face to the sky, enjoying the warmth setting across his face, while he waited for a contact. He recalled the many hours he had spent here years earlier as an undergraduate at the University. He had passed much of his time at this fountain, between the classes he attended in the building he was now facing. It had been his academic home for four years.

In spring, the fountain always came alive after a winter's hibernation. Today, water rose from below the ground, bubbling several feet into the air, making a feathery plume. Its source, the two mile-long Minetta River, had been driven beneath the city's streets over a century ago, where it has remained, hidden beneath the feet of unsuspecting strollers, covered by concrete, tar and grass.

Children now were rushing about, running through the fountain, its waters splashing over them. Across the way another group of children were in a small playground under the watchful eyes of their mothers and nannies. Above their laughter and playful shrieks, Dan could hear two guitarists; their bare feet soaking up the water, tuning their instruments. His thoughts were interrupted by someone standing over him, blocking the sun's warmth.

"Mr. Nikolas. Hello."

Dan opened his eyes and saw a young man standing before him. He was of medium height, about 30, maybe a little older, with straight blonde hair and a broad, friendly smile. He was neatly dressed in civilian clothes - a tan sports jacket and dark slacks that were well pressed. Dan could not remember ever having seen him before. The man had a large manila envelope tucked under his left arm. He immediately extended his right hand when he saw Dan's eyes open.

"I've seen you on the Big A. many times. The seamen have often told me about you. I'm glad you're representing Gas. His family needs all the help they can get. This is a lousy situation. I mean, about Gas's death."

"So what is this important information you have for me?" Dan asked as he beckoned for the man to sit at a spot on the bench beside him. The young man sat down, positioned at an angle so that he could face Dan.

He spoke uninterrupted for several minutes, while Dan listened carefully. When he was finished talking, Dan asked some questions to satisfy himself of the truth of the facts the young man had set forth, and to clarify some points. Dan nodded and smiled with each answer he received. While he looked at this young man, Dan made some quick judgments. Lawyers meet many people, honest clients and witnesses, liars, cheats and con men looking to scam the lawyer or to help a friend with false testimony. Over time most trial lawyers develop an ability to understand if they are being told the truth or being lied to. This young man was telling the truth, Dan was certain of that.

A miniature soccer ball rolled at Dan's feet and a young boy came running after it. Dan picked up the ball and handed it to the youngster with a smile. "Thank you," the boy said in a sing-song voice. Dan resumed the conversation.

"Are you willing to testify to what you just now told me?"

"Yes, sir, I am."

"I can almost guarantee you that it would be the end of your career at sea. But I'm sure you already know that."

"I do. I was planning to leave the sea at the end of this year. I'll leave a few months earlier so that I can help Mira and Ronny. I'm going into business with my brother to help my father in Omaha. He owns a large machine shop and has signed a contract to manufacture farm tools starting next year. When I leave the sea, I can be home with my family and maybe get married, too."

"The case is being tried now. Can you be available for testimony in the next two days?"

"Yes. I will be here on the beach. I'm signed aboard a cargo ship that sails in three days at 8 p.m. from Bush Terminal in Brooklyn."

"In the meantime, I suggest you say nothing to anyone at all about this. If the company finds out, it could be very unpleasant for you."

"I know. You don't have to tell me. I think they already know something about me. I've been getting calls on my answering machine from a guy who sounds like an investigator. I've had experience with that type before, in cases the company needed witnesses. That's why I suggested the park instead of your office,"

"Did Gaspar know about what you told me?"

"Yes. But not everything."

"Do you know why he didn't tell me about you?"

"I can only guess that he didn't want me to get caught in the ringer. I told you, he was a good shipmate. I never told him I was leaving the sea, because my father's contract wasn't a sure thing until last month."

"Here's my number at home. Don't call me at my office, unless it's an emergency. Only call me at home. This is between you and me only. Understand?" Dan handed the young man a business card on which he had written his home number.

"I do, Mr. Nikolas. And I hope I can help."

"I do, too. I'll know better after I do some research," Dan said. "Give me a phone number where I can reach you. You'll have no choice but to come to my office tomorrow morning. I will try to put you on the witness stand tomorrow afternoon. If not, the day after, first thing. You'll have to be prepared for testimony by one of the attorneys in my office, since I'll be busy with another witness and with the trial."

"Oh, by the way, Mr. Nikolas, I forgot to give this envelope to you."

"Based on what you told me I can guess what's in there. I'll need it. Thank you for your help."

Dan extended his hand in a strong handshake. When he returned at his office he went to the conference room where Commander Masterson was working.

"Robby. I just came from talking with the Junior Officer on the bridge of the *American Union*. From my talk with him, I think he'll make a good witness." Dan went over the conversation he had in the park. "He left this with me. Check it out and let me know what you think. I read it in the cab coming back. It has to be compared with some of the exhibits in evidence. Are you ready to testify tomorrow?"

"I'll look at it right away. Yes, I am ready for tomorrow. For tonight, let's you and I and Jack relax and bend an elbow."

26

COMMANDER MASTERSON TESTIFIES
FOLEY SQUARE

Steve Jessup became upset when he saw Commander Robert Masterson walk into the court room. He leaned across the counsel table and whispered to Lu Moore.

"I don't want that guy coming in here in a uniform. Look at all those lousy medals on his chest."

"Don't waste your time. The Judge will allow it," Lu advised.

"What do you mean, Lu? Judge Costello didn't allow Captain Burn to wear a military uniform. Why should he allow that Brit?"

"Do what you think you have to do." Lu responded, shaking her head in disgust. *Dan wouldn't bring a man in uniform here unless he knew he could get away with it. To do otherwise...* her thoughts were interrupted by Jessup.

"I sure am doing what I have to do. And I'm asking the Judge for a conference just like Nikolas did with Captain Burn."

In chambers, Judge Costello asked Jessup to explain the basis of his motion. The Judge glanced at Lu, who maintained a blank face while looking straight ahead.

"Judge," Jessup argued, "you didn't allow Captain Burn to wear a military uniform. Your decision should apply to plaintiff's witnesses as well."

"Let's see, Counselor. Someone call in the witness. What's his name?"

"Commander Robert Masterson, Judge," Dan volunteered.

Masterson was ushered into Judge Costello's chambers. The Judge greeted him with a friendly, "Good morning, Commander."

"Good morning, M'Lord."

Judge Costello smiled. "This is an American court, Commander. You need only address me as Judge, or Your Honor."

"Yes, of course. Excuse me, I was already advised of that by Mr. Nikolas and I apologize for forgetting."

"That's okay. Commander, this uniform you're wearing today, is that the regular Royal Navy issue?"

"It is, your Honor."

"When do you wear it?

"Every day and, of course, while I'm on duty."

"Do you wear it off duty?"

"I do. I wear it to church, when we go out to dinner. The only time I don't wear it is when I putter around in my garden, work in the house or when I visit friends or I'm on vacation. My work is in the nature of emergency. I always have to leave a telephone number where I can be reached. If I get called it saves time if I'm already in my uniform. In my closet I only have three civilian suits and three sports jackets besides all my uniforms, and a formal uniform I wear at events such as weddings, Naval Balls and the like.

"Are there any Navy regulations about your wearing a uniform in a foreign country?"

"None that I'm aware of, your Honor. I've worn my uniform in Canada, France, Holland, Denmark and Germany."

"I'm going to allow Commander Masterson to appear in uniform since he wears it on a regular basis. He differs from Captain Burn who only wears his for two weeks a year. Now, let's get on with the trial. Let's not waste any more time. Is the Commander your witness for today, Mr. Nikolas?'

"He is, Judge."

"What about Professor Stein? Did he do an actuarial for me for an AB?"

"He did, Judge, and he goes on after Commander Robertson."

"I haven't decided whether or not I'll hear evidence on the lost earnings as an Able Seaman. I'll be out on the bench in five minutes. Be ready with your witness, Mr. Nikolas."

"With your permission, Judge," Dan said, "Before we leave, may I ask the Court to have the defendant produce the ship's rough log? If you order it, it will save time. We won't have to issue a subpoena and won't cause a delay in the trial. I am advised that the ship is still in port."

"Are you planning to use it as an exhibit, Mr. Nikolas?"

"Yes, sir, I am."

"Was it listed as one of your exhibits?"

"No, Judge, since it was not anticipated to be used. But facts have arisen since we filed our Exhibits List requiring their use in rebuttal testimony. We ask you to order to be produced in Court in the interests of justice."

"I've given you some leeway, Mr. Nikolas, because we are dealing with a dead seaman. I don't plan on doing any more favors for you. You had better show the Court that new facts require the use of the rough logs. Otherwise I won't permit you to use them."

"I understand, Judge. You have been liberal. I don't believe we will be imposing upon you any further after this."

"I hope not. Mr. Jessup and Miss Moore, have the rough log here this afternoon."

"Yes, Judge. And please note our objection to its introduction into evidence." Jessup said.

"I understand your position, Mr. Jessup. Get it on the record when I return to the courtroom and I'll rule on it subject to Mr. Nikolas's use."

Lu looked at Dan. *Why does he want the rough log? I hope it's not what I think.* "We'll have it here this afternoon, your Honor," Lu said as she turned to Steve Jessup with a look of frustration that she was careful to ensure Dan couldn't see.

When Commander Robert Masterson took the stand, Dan exploited his military history. He had him explain every decoration that covered the left side of his chest. He reviewed his training at the Royal Naval Academy and his service aboard an aircraft carrier, as a helicopter pilot assisting in air-sea rescues in Korea, Malaysia and elsewhere.

"Commander Masterson, what is your present assignment?"

"I have been in command of 771 Naval Air Squadron at the Culdrose Air Base, United Kingdom, for the past year. Culdrose is at a point approximately midway between the city of Plymouth and Land's End." Masterson rose from his witness chair and pointed to the location on the chart of the English Channel that Dan had previously put on an easel.

"The chart you just referred to, Commander, please explain what it is."

"Yes. It's the same chart we use at Culdrose. It's the official Royal Navy Hydrographic Chart that is supposed to be used by all mariners transiting the English Channel. I consult it on a daily basis. I brought this copy with me from England."

"What is the mission of your squadron, Commander?"

"Air-sea and land rescue. I command ten helicopters with 30 pilots, their assistants, medics, office personnel and the maintenance crews that are concerned and engaged with rescue missions off vessels of all types, mostly but not always in the English Channel, We also cover parts of the land territory in Southern England for a radius area of 120 miles from the airbase at Culdrose."

"Who was in command of the 771 Squadron at Culdrose at the time the events involving this lawsuit occurred?"

"Commander Roger Prior-Ames. I assumed command of the facility a year ago."

"And pursuant to my request, did you do an investigation to determine if the rescue procedures prior to your posting at Culdrose differed in any way from the ones you currently use?"

"I did."

"And please tell us what, if anything, you found out."

"We presently follow the same procedures that my predecessor employed. They are the ones that have been established by the Admiralty."

"What system of miles do you use to determine distances?"

"For our flights, we use land or statute miles."

"Commander Masterson, would you, consulting the log of the *American Union*, tell us when the first entry regarding Gaspar Fonseca was made and by whom it was made?"

"The entry was made by the ship's Chief Mate at 6:00 am."

"At that time, where was the ship located with respect to a possible air-sea rescue by your unit?"

"My chaps could have made an easy recovery at that time. The ship was well within the area of a possible safe rescue."

"Now I ask you, did you have the opportunity to read Dr. Peters' memorandum as to the ship's position?

"Yes, I did. You provided me with a copy."

"Consulting Dr. Peters' memorandum only; where was the ship at the same time according to him?"

"Much behind the location set forth in the ship's log. Both positions at that time in its transit had the vessel within the confines of the English Channel."

"Could you have made a safe recovery at that position designated by Dr. Peters?"

"Yes. Absolutely."

"What types of helicopters were being operated by 771 Squadron at Culdrose on the date of the logs you consulted?"

"Mostly helicopters of the Wasp class. There were also some Scout units, which we still have. I prefer the Wasp, as it is faster and more reliable in real emergency situations where distance is involved. It travels at 110 miles per hour. It also has a longer total range of 301 miles from the base at Culdrose. And if necessary, the Wasp can set down on a vessel the size of a Frigate."

"In preparation for your testimony today, what information did you consult?"

"You gave me a copy of the ship's smooth log and the memorandum made by the ship's doctor concerning the *American Union'* location and the times it appeared at certain locations. There were photographs you provided, of the deck of the *American Union*, fore and aft. I personally consulted the nautical charts of the Channel and the weather reports for the day in question. I also personally checked hospital availability for that day. At the base we also keep our own log, which I consulted. Since we were never contacted for rescue, the only matchup I was able to make were those for weather and availability of craft for rescue. I would consider the weather as fairly good for a helicopter rescue at the time. Had the base been called for assistance, either a Wasp or a Scout helicopter was available for a rescue according to log records for that day, which I inspected. I brought a copy of that day's business with me, showing availability.

"I read the transcript of Captain Burn's testimony he gave yesterday. I understand you had the court reporter make one last night, as I was not present in the courtroom to hear it. Before I left the United Kingdom, at your request I checked with the motor launch rescue service as to their ability to affect a rescue based upon the ship's log and Dr. Peters' memorandum."

"What did those matchups reveal?"

"We had for rescue on that day both launches and helicopter craft available, as I have already said."

"Tell us which hospitals you checked with."

"I personally contacted hospitals at the cities of Plymouth, Torquay and Exeter to determine cardio-vascular access for the day the rescue would have been made."

"Why those particular hospitals?"

"They are closest to the rescue area and they are the hospitals regularly used by us in emergency situations such as the one for your seaman aboard the *American Union*."

"We'll get back to the hospitals in a moment. Based upon your reading of the ship's log for that day, what were the chances of your unit having been able to make a rescue?"

"First, let me say that Captain Burn was very clear in his testimony that he could not allow us to hover above his ship to lift your sick chap. So we would have had to use a different procedure to affect an emergency rescue."

"Could you have made a rescue with the conditions that you investigated and existed on that day?"

"Yes, as I have already stated, we definitely could have made a proper rescue."

"Please let us know where the *American Union* was when you could have made the rescue?"

"According to the ship's log, when the Captain was first informed of an emergency the ship was yet inside the Channel. According to Dr. Peters' memorandum, the ship was not only well within the Channel but behind where the ship's log placed her position. Both positions were amenable for a good and uncomplicated rescue at that time. According to the doctor's memorandum, we had a lot more time and were also well placed to do a speedy and timely rescue."

"Reading the doctor's memorandum, when could you have made a rescue attempt based upon her positions?"

"My unit could have made a rescue at any time except for the doctor's last entry, which was made around 8 am and indicates when the doctors were getting ready to operate."

"Why is that?"

"They were now past the Channel and into the North Atlantic. My Wasps only have a total range of 301 miles. From Culdrose to where the ship was located and based upon that last entry, it would have been a flight of 110 miles one way. Coming back to Culdrose is a total of 220 miles. Our helicopter's first preferred stop would normally have been Plymouth, which is 40 miles from Culdrose; that's 260 miles. My check of the hospitals at Plymouth, Torquay and Exeter showed only one hospital could have attended this particular emergency on that day. Plymouth would have been my first choice. But Plymouth was not available. Torquay is past Plymouth, heading northeast. Both Plymouth and Tourquay on the day in question were using every operating theater available and every qualified cardio-vascular surgeon was in an operating room. So our only alternative would have been Exeter, which is 35 miles northeast of Plymouth. They had an operating theater and a surgeon available on that day. That would have made the flight a total of 295 miles, very close to the limit of range of my Wasps.

"I also checked the weather for that morning. The report showed there was a southerly wind blowing in from the north and against my helicopters, at about 16 to 18 knots and gusting to 30, which could have created a dangerous situation for my lads. Not only would they be slowed down by the wind, petrol could become perilously low and a sudden gust could be very sticky. It would have been a risk for my crew I would not have cared to have them take."

"That narrative you gave us, Commander Masterson, was based upon what other, if any, information?"

"It was based on the location of the ship's position in Dr. Peter's memorandum."

"Now I ask if you would look again at the memorandum Dr. Peters prepared on that day."

"I have."

"Taking into consideration the ship's location based on the entry prior to the last one in Dr. Peters' memo just before the shipboard surgery, and your experience with helicopter rescue, do you have an opinion as to whether you could have taken a sailor off the *American Union*?"

"It definitely would have been probable."

"On what do you base your opinion, Commander?"

"According to Dr. Peters' memorandum, the ship was just leaving the Channel. She was less than 50 miles past Culdrose, which is well within our range and an easy and safe flight to Exeter, once we would have collected the seaman."

"But yesterday, Mr. Burn testified that he wouldn't permit a helicopter near his ship. How would you have been able to affect a rescue with your helicopter?"

"The *American Union* is an enormous vessel. She is 990 feet long. If you stood her up vertically on end she would be almost as tall as your Empire State Building. She is 175 feet high from the water line." Masterson shifted in is seat, raising his right hand high above his head.

"Your vessel is as tall as a 17-story apartment house. Her beam or her width is 101 feet. Since I had already determined the wind was heading due south from a northerly direction, I would have requested that the Captain turn his ship sideways with her bow facing England and her stern toward France. If he had done that, her starboard side would be facing north in the direction of the wind."

Masterson strode to his chart and using a ruler to represent a ship, he placed the vessel in the position he had just described.

"That makes an outstanding and wonderful lee."

"Please describe a lee, Commander."

Lu was writing down the cross examination she expected Jessup to pursue. *Dan is something. He didn't put a lee down as one of his earlier definitions on the black board, because he knew I'd figure it out. I would have loved it if he was sitting next to me in Jessup's seat.*

"Yes, Mr. Nikolas. You have a lee when you are protected from the wind. It could be created by a hill, a building, a deep hole in the ground, the side of a ship, anything that affords protection from the strong effects of a wind. We need a lee in this case because when we hover in our helicopter in position to make the rescue, we need protection from this unruly wind or a strong gust that could push us out of our position. It makes for the safest rescue possible under those conditions.

"The *American Union* presents a wonderful lee because of her length and height. The Captain would have put out one or two shots of anchor chain to keep the ship from drifting out of our preferred position. My chaps would fly past the ship. Far away from it, so that Captain Burn would not be concerned about his ship's safety. They would fly on past the bow, the front of the ship, and then make a left turn. Now the helicopter would be on what we call the leeward or port side, relatively safe from any strong winds or gusts which are potentially dangerous for a hovering helicopter. The Wasp would lay off about 200 to 300 yards from the ship. Before my lads would fly to the leeward side, your sailor chap would have been waiting for us in one of the ship's motor launches. We would then hover over the launch, free of any significant wind interference, drop a line, complete with a rescue officer and then winch him up safely in the arms of the medical officer."

"Has your unit performed this type of rescue before?"

"Yes, many, many times. We also regularly practice that procedure. We create lees for our practice sessions with vessels much smaller than the *American Union*. We actually perform this rescue when there are problems on ships that are on fire or have complicated wire or ship's booms that are frozen in awkward positions. On occasion, we get someone like Captain Burn who doesn't want us too near his ship because of perceived safety concerns. Maybe it's a tanker loaded with a volatile fuel and the Captain is worried about a collision or a spark that could set off an explosion. On one occasion I can remember, a tanker had a fire. We couldn't go near the ship and we rescued two badly burned seamen in this way."

"How long would this procedure take?"

"For the ship? Less than three hours. The Channel is at its widest southwest of the Culdrose area. Nevertheless, because there's a lot of traffic in both directions, you don't want to block it completely. So I would have advised the ship to maneuver a little bit out of the shipping lane. She can't go too far out of the lane, since she needs to be in water deep enough to accommodate her draft. Then she has to lower the motor launch. If not three hours, then close to it. I'm including the pickup and the return of the motor launch."

Masterson went to the chart again and using the ruler to represent the ship, moved it across the chart to the area where he wanted the ship to set up for the lee.

"Then the ship would send out its motor launch with your sick seaman 200 or 300 yards or so out past the ship. Once we are advised the launch is in place, we proceed to meet it. I don't want my lads to be in the air waiting for the launch for a long time. Not only is it wasteful of petrol, I don't want my helicopters in the sky longer than necessary, for reasons of safety. Once we lift your man off the launch, we are off to Exeter. The whole trip is less than 150 miles, well within the safe range of my helicopters. The winds are not a factor in this situation. Meanwhile, as we are flying north we notify Exeter by radio that we are on our way and then they begin getting everything ready for emergency surgery. By the time we arrive at the hospital, only the patient should have to be prepared."

"What would a three-hour delay mean with respect to the ship's schedule?"

"She would come in three hours late if the captain maintained his regular speed. But based upon the ship's log, there was a following sea which would have cut that delay a bit. How much, I cannot say."

Jessup stood up to object. "Your Honor, I object. This answer is conjecture."

"I don't think there's a proper objection here, Judge. Mr. Burn has already testified that he had to make 32 knots as a matter of company policy. He also testified there was a following sea which would have speeded up the ship's transit," Dan argued. "All of these situations have to be taken into consideration."

"Yes, I believe you are correct, Mr. Nikolas. Would the court reporter please find that testimony by Captain Burn and read it aloud."

After searching through many feet of paper ribbon for testimony that went through her recording machine, the court reporter located the testimony and read it. The Judge was satisfied and said, "I'll overrule your objection, Mr. Jessup."

Dan continued his questioning of Commander Masterson. "At my request, did you check with the possibility of rescue with a motor launch?"

"Yes, and I was advised the Sea Rescue Patrol was, of course, too far from the ship, based on the ship's log. With respect to Dr. Peters' log, at the early stages they could have reached the ship on time. We have to consider that they are much slower than a helicopter; they also move at 32 knots, as the *American Union* does. The Wasp can fly at 110 miles an hour. Then, the launch only delivers the seaman to a dock. From there he has to be moved by ambulance to the hospital. A helicopter lands on a pad alongside the hospital. It could be risky to use a launch with respect to the time constraints you have advised me we would be facing."

"So, Commander, taking into consideration what you learned from the research you performed with respect to the weather, the establishment of a proper lee, the helicopters available to you and the medical facilities and surgeons available on that date, do you have an opinion as to whether a successful helicopter rescue could have been made of Gaspar Fonseca from the *S.S. American Union* on the day in question?"

"Yes, I do."

"Please tell us, what would your opinion be?"

"A rescue could definitely have been affected."

"Thank you, Commander Masterson. No further questions."

It was Jessup's turn to cross-examine Robby Masterson.

"Commander Masterson, in your analysis as presented in your direct testimony, you relied upon the ship's log and the so-called memorandum prepared by Dr. Peters, isn't that correct?"

"Yes."

"Have you ever prepared a ship's log?"

"I have, while I attended the Royal Naval Academy and while I commanded a naval tug early in my career and while I served as a Junior Officer on several of Her Majesty's vessels. At Culdrose, I often prepare logs concerning our rescues."

"Then you know that a ship's log is prepared with great care and that any unauthorized or false entries are not allowed and can be punished?"

"Yes."

"Between the ship's log or Dr. Peters' memorandum, would you agree that the ship's log is a truer picture of where and how the *American Union* was navigating?"

"Yes, it should be under most conditions."

"So would you also agree that your analysis based on Dr. Peters' memorandum to be incorrect?"

"No. The positions I plotted were based upon Dr. Peters' observations. In that sense, my analyses of the positions were correct, using his notes."

"To make it clear for the record, Commander, based on the entry in the ship's log at the time the doctors began operating, the ship would have been too far away in your opinion for a helicopter rescue?"

"Absolutely."

"How about a rescue by motor launch?"

"At the time you have mentioned, the ship was also too far away for a speedy recovery by a motor launch."

"Between accepting all the times and positions set down in the ship's log and the times and positions set out in the Peters memorandum, you would agree with me that the ship's log is more accurate?"

"Normally I have to say yes, unless, as I have pointed out, some other factors arise to change that basic premise."

"I don't understand your answer. There isn't any testimony presented during this trial that you could rely on to make you believe otherwise, isn't that so?'

"I have to assume that Dr. Peters prepared a log that has a basis of truth."

"Why would you believe that?"

"Because I can't believe the doctor would have prepared a false log under the conditions I have been advised were existent."

"But you must agree that the ship's smooth log is the legal and correct portrayer of its activities?"

"Yes, except if it is shown to be incorrect."

"Then I have no further questions."

Judge Costello asked Dan if he was ready to put Professor Stein back on the witness stand. "I'm going to listen to his testimony about lost earnings relative to an AB, but I would like to hear some testimony about the deceased's ability to pass his officer's test."

Professor Stein testified as to his projections for lost earnings in the future for an AB, which were lower than that of a Third Mate. Jessup made a fast cross examination, attacking Professor Stein's methodology.

When Jessup was finished, Dan stood up. "Your Honor, plaintiff rests its case. Of course, it reserves the right to present rebuttal, if pertinent."

"Any objections, Mr. Jessup?"

"None, Your Honor."

"Then in that case I will withhold my ruling as to whether I will admit the testimony Professor Stein gave this morning. Is the defendant ready to present its defense Mr. Jessup?"

"Yes, it is Your Honor. Before we do that I would like to move the Court for a dismissal of plaintiff's case for failure to prove a *prima facie* case. Plaintiff has failed to show the ship's log is incorrect since as a matter of law it is deemed correct unless proven false, based upon the Presumption of Regularity. Plaintiff has failed to show it was false, as they allege. Therefore, taken with Captain Burn's testimony that the vessel was past a position where a safe rescue could be affected, the plaintiff has failed to prove its case."

"Mr. Nikolas or Mr. Hoffman, I'd like to hear the plaintiff's position."

Dan rose and addressed the court. "Your Honor, first I would like to call attention to a legal position that only a seaman enjoys at law and that we ask you to apply. That is that the Court may not dismiss a seaman's case brought under the Jones Act, which we find at *46 U.S. Code 688*, as long as there is a scintilla, no matter how small, of evidence in his favor. That is a much lower standard, as the Supreme Court has said, 'than the ordinary garden variety of negligence cases.'

"Then the jury should have the opportunity to determine if Dr. Peters' memorandum is correct *vis a vis* the ship's log. And the jury may consider Commander Masterson's testimony that he could have made a safe recovery under the conditions existing in the Channel on that day. For these reasons, the Court should deny defendant's motion."

"I agree, Mr. Nikolas. Defendant's motion is denied. Then we'll hear the defense after lunch."

As they walked out of the courtroom, Dan saw the young officer he had spoken with in the park, sitting on a bench in the hall. He acknowledged him with a slight nod. Captain Burn noticed him, too, and with a puzzled look went over to say hello, and then caught up with Lu and Jessup. He did not make any comment to them about the man to whom he had just said hello.

27

IT'S JESSUP'S SHOW

Before the afternoon session began, Dan walked past the young officer who had been waiting to be called. Dan slipped him a note. It read: "Go home and come back tomorrow morning at 8:30."

The afternoon session began with A.U. Lines' economics expert, who told the jury that the methods Professor Stein used to arrive at economic losses were all wrong. "You should accept my analysis, which shows a much lower figure for economic damages for an AB and an officer," he confidently told the jury.

Dan attacked the expert, who admitted that some of Professor Stein's approach was not necessarily wrong and that it was also widely accepted by a significant school of economists and that it was a matter of preference as to which analysis could be used. When he was finished with this witness, Dan was satisfied that the jury understood Professor Stein's numbers could be used by them to determine damages; that it was a matter of which approach, or school, was the fair one. Captain Burn would be next.

The night before, anticipating Captain Burn's testimony for the next morning, Lu Moore and Steven Jessup sat in one of the conference rooms at Brown, Sykes and Bellham. Over sandwiches and coffee, they were discussing strategy and when they should rest their case.

"The jury should have Burn's testimony once again. See him again, to bolster his position. I would like him to be fresh in their minds," Jessup was advocating. "After the jury hears his testimony tomorrow, I'm sure it will cement their thinking in our favor."

"You're right, Steve. That's good basic strategy during a normal trial. But Nikolas has turned it around so that we are not in a normal situation. The jury has already heard Burn's testimony. You'll be giving Nikolas a second shot at Burn. This is not the usual way a trial unfolds. Dan purposely changed it around by calling Burn as his own witness and then challenging him. So we are faced with this dilemma. I really don't like it and we shouldn't play into his hands. I wouldn't call Burn back."

"I'm sure about this, Lu. We need to put him on again to reinforce our position. The jury likes Burn. You can see it. He's like a father figure. And besides, he has to refute Masterson's testimony. And I have already told the Judge we would call him. What will the jury think?"

"So far, I haven't been able to make out what the jury thinks about our egotistic Captain. How is it that you come to that conclusion?"

"That's what I saw in the jury's faces when he was testifying. Let's do it. We have nothing to lose."

"We can lose the case. But it's your show. If you insist, then go ahead, but think about restricting him to a very limited area."

"Like what?"

"Limit him to the final rescue effort that Commander Masterson testified to. You know, making the lee. I would keep it at that. Stay away from the logs and his conversations with Dr. Peters. It's been settled and everyone admits that it's the ship's logs that are the ones that count, not Dr. Peters'. No sense going over it again and giving Dan another whack at that issue. I've been thinking hard about why he asked for the rough logs. Whatever it is, it can't possibly benefit us. Don't give him another chance to go there and open up the log issue again."

"Okay, what do you suggest we do?'

"You call Burn at his home right now and find out if he is sure he can attack Masterson's rescue attempt based on the lee, without going into the maps or the logs. If you are satisfied he can, then tell him to meet us in front of the courthouse at 7:30 tomorrow morning. We'll need that time to prepare him. If he says he can do it, you and I will write up a set of questions for him tonight based on what he tells you he can testify to. Emphasize that he is absolutely limited to the area of the lee, only."

Lu sat alone in the conference room, finishing her sandwich while she waited for Jessup to return. She drained the last of her coffee and crumpled the empty cardboard container, shoving it into a paper bag. She placed a yellow lined-legal pad in front of her and began writing, detailing the instructions she gave Steve Jessup about Captain Burn's restricted testimony and the reasons why. Then she dated it, looked at the clock on the wall and entered the time, signed it, folded it into fours and left it on the desk in front of her.

From here on in, Steve is on his own. I'm turning over the management of this case to him. He can handle that difficult Captain without my help. He can manage the minefields of the closing statement, selecting the right charges he wants the Judge to instruct the jury with, and any motions that should be made at the appropriate times. I did the best I could. Now I'll just sit back and watch the show.

Jessup returned a few moments later. He was smiling and rubbing his hands together in satisfaction.

"What did Burn say?" Lu inquired.

"He told me he can't wait to get back at the sons-a-bitches," Jessup said with a broad smile. "He told me he will show the jury and that Limey what it's like to command the world's greatest ship."

"Did he understand that his testimony would only cover the rescue and the lee?"

"Yes, yes." Jessup was excited. "We'll let the jury deliberate this case with our testimony on the rescue as the last one on their minds. Great! Couldn't be better."

"Steve, I prepared a memo of our conversation about Burn and our strategy. Sign it in case Burn decides to go off the track." Lu unfolded the paper and slid it in front of Jessup.

Jessup signed his name next to Lu's without reading it, which he should not have done. Lu had put a sentence in the statement indicating her reluctance to put Captain Burn on the stand a second time but since Jessup was lead counsel, she wrote, she gave way to his judgment.

The two lawyers spent the rest of the night preparing questions for Burns. It took a while, not because there were many questions, but because Lu wanted to frame each question and its wording very carefully, to make sure Burn didn't open the door to allow cross examination on the ship's log.

Jack Hoffman had a tougher battle but, as Dan knew he would, he held up with the doctors. On direct examination, the company's expert surgeon testified that it would have been too late to help Gaspar, so a rescue would have been senseless. Jack forced the doctor to admit it wasn't too late, based upon the observations of doctors Peters and Grinstein with respect to the stage Gaspar was at during their examinations. Then he forced the doctor to admit the company's menu for its crew was not conducive to good health and that it was immaterial with respect to the issue of a rescue. Finally, the doctor agreed the ship's hospital was not the best place to try locating and removing a block, especially since none of the four physicians were surgeons and the ship's hospital lacked proper drugs and other necessary equipment.

When the company's psychiatric expert took the stand next morning, he testified that Gaspar was, psychiatrically speaking, a mess even before he lost his leg. Gaspar, he argued, was a loner, morose and depressed; all signposts of a candidate for suicide. Jack attacked him immediately, by getting the doctor to admit that Gaspar showed ambition and a real desire to better his life's conditions. He forced the doctor to admit that the symptoms Gaspar exhibited before his loss were those which most psychologically healthy people exhibited, at some time during their lives.

"Yes," the doctor finally admitted, "Mr. Fonseca's symptoms were reasonably under control and he was able to function up until the loss of his leg. The loss of a leg would have been a significant and traumatic event in anyone's life and could cause the symptoms that led to Mr. Fonseca's suicide, or exacerbate his already pre-existing condition."

28

THE TRIAL CONTINUES
BRANDT VS. BURN

At 8:15 the next morning, Dan's officer witness was waiting at the entrance to the Courthouse. They spoke briefly and quietly in a corner of the entrance. Following Dan's instructions, he went into the building and sat on a bench in the hall outside the courtroom. Captain Gregory Burn had been there several minutes before the young man had arrived. They nodded a perfunctory "hello" to each other. Captain Burn's greeting was mixed with surprise, puzzlement and some anxiety.

Inside the courtroom, spectators gathered for the last days of this hard-fought trial. Dan noted Jerry Keller sitting next to Bradley Rogers. There was a third man sitting with them whom Dan did not know. It was Grady Roul, Rogers' partner. Judge Costello entered the courtroom and everyone rose from their seats. As Judge Costello sat, he asked everyone to do the same.

"Do we have anymore witnesses for the defendant, Mr. Jessup?"

"Yes sir, I would like to call Captain Gregory Burn to the stand."

After the Bailiff called for him, Captain Burn strode into the courtroom and headed straight for the witness stand. He had a smile on his face and was looking at the jurors.

"You are still under oath, Captain," the Judge advised Burn.

"Yes, Your Honor, I remember."

"Captain Burn, did you have the opportunity to read the court reporter's transcript of the testimony Commander Masterson gave in this court?" Jessup began.

"Yes, I did."

"Did you form any opinions solely with respect to rescue attempts Commander Masterson testified he would have made, under the conditions on the day of Gaspar Fonseca's attack?"

"Yes, I did, and I strongly disagree with his description of the rescue using a lee."

"Please tell us why."

"Well, it's easy to tell me to move my ship out of the shipping lane. There's always a lot of other traffic out of the shipping lane, too. The English Channel is a very busy body of water. It's an international waterway. You know, there are private boats and fishermen and commercial vessels coming into the lanes from all directions outside the Channel. Then the Channel is noted for its nasty weather. Squalls come up at any moment without warnings. A small boat like the ship's launch, that he was proposing to use in the rescue, could easily turn over in a storm. If that happens then I lose my crew, the sick man and maybe even my launch. I can't even begin to understand what dangers the helicopter itself would face."

"What was the weather like on that day, Captain Burn?"

I won't do a thing to stop this moron. He's departing from the questions we prepared. Now he's going to open it up. Just as I expected. He's so anxious to show how good he is, he put his foot into the trap, Lu thought as she turned to look at Jerry Keller, who was beaming. He had leaned across Bradley Rogers to make a positive remark to Grady Roul. She could tell, because Keller pointed at Jessup and smiled.

"I can't recall. It's often grey and cloudy. Rains, too, often come up in squalls. Then there's the wind, as the English officer testified to, that was evident on that day. The sea in the Channel can be tricky too."

Here we go, thought Lu.

"If I could check my log I could answer your question better."

Jessup looked a Lu with alarm. She pursed her lips and stared at him with a disapproving look.

"That's okay, Captain you needn't go to the log book. Was there anything else you found in Commander Masterson's testimony which you disagreed with?" It was a poorly worded question that Dan or Jack should have objected to. However, both men remained silent and Lu could guess why.

"I should go to the log if you want to know about the weather for that day. May I please have it?"

"Not for now, Captain, not for now, just answer my last question."

"I really need to consult the log. I can't recall the exact conditions that existed over a year or two ago."

"It's okay, Captain. Just answer my question." Jessup was on the edge of panic.

"Well, Mr. Jessup, Commander Masterson would have no way of knowing whether there was enough time to help my AB, that's for starters. I knew from what the doctors said that they could perform an operation to help him right there on my ship. So why make wasteful and possibly dangerous maneuvers that added to the time needed to help the man, when the man could be helped aboard ship and right away?"

"Thank you, Captain Burn. No more questions."

Dan walked to the lawyer's stand, stood silently for a few seconds, all the while looking straight into Burn's eyes. Burn looked back at Dan, but he was the first to break eye contact, moving his gaze to the jury with a smirk.

"Good afternoon, Mr. Burn," Dan asked in a pleasant tone.

Captain Burn thought not to answer, but then, looking at the jury he knew they were waiting to see how he would respond.

"Good afternoon, good afternoon to you, sir." Burn finally said in a low, grumpy voice.

"I noted that when you were being examined by Mr. Jessup, you wanted to go to the ship's log to clarify a point. I would like to give you the log so that you can answer Mr. Jessup's question with a degree of certainty."

"Yes, if you so wish."

Lee Moore shot a look of disdain at Jessup, shielding it from the jury.

"Let the record show that Mr. Burn is looking at the ship's smooth log already entered into evidence. Now sir, was it raining that day?"

Jessup stood up. "Objection, Your Honor, testimony as to the ship's log is outside the scope of cross-examination. There was no testimony based on the log."

"I'm afraid not, Mr. Jessup. The door was opened on your direct. Captain Burn wanted to refer to the log on three occasions. So now let's hear what he wanted to say," the Judge ruled.

Burn smiled. Now he was going to give those bastard lawyers for Fonseca and the jury a few lessons in seamanship; how to be a proper and cautious captain.

Jessup sat, elbows on the counsel table, his head held up by two hands clasped at his ears. He looked at Lu and thought he detected a faint smile on her lips.

"Well, Mr. Burn, now we both have copies of the log. It wasn't raining at the time you were having conversations with Dr. Peters, according to your log, correct?"

"Yes, that's true, but it did rain that morning."

"At what time?"

"One a.m." Burn ruffled through the log's pages and put a finger on an entry.

"That's more than four hours before Mr. Fonseca began complaining, right?"

"Yes."

"So you must remember now that it wasn't a consideration on that day, with respect to safety at the time of a potential rescue. You would agree, would you not?"

"It isn't in the log, but my testimony was that it was something to always consider, because rain or a squall could come up at any time in the English Channel and there was a strong wind on that day. Even the log shows it."

"So your testimony is that you would not rescue a critically sick man because of the possibility that the weather could change and create a problem?"

Burn did not answer.

"That's all right, Mr. Burn, you needn't answer. I believe we all know the answer. I'm finished with this witness and I would like to call William Brandt to the stand."

Jessup shot up from his seat.

"Objection! Who is William Brandt? He's not on the witness list and if he was, it's too late to call him. He should have been called on plaintiff's direct case. Plaintiff has rested his case. He's a surprise witness." Jessup was waving his hands almost uncontrollably.

"Mr. Nikolas?" Judge Costello asked.

"Of course, Judge. This witness is in rebuttal to Mr. Burn's testimony. Even if Mr. Burn's last testimony was not given here today, we would have presented his testimony in the nature of a rebuttal witness. He will also testify as to Mr. Fonseca's chances of becoming an officer."

"Then go ahead, counselor."

While the Bailiff was calling for Brandt in the hall, Jessup leaned over to Lu. Covering his mouth so no one could hear him, he said: "Lu, who the hell is this guy?"

"I don't know, but I have a hunch." As soon as she heard the word "rebuttal' Lu was already digging deep into her file for the crew list of the *American Union*.

"Aha! Here it is," she said to Jessup as she ran her fingers down the list of officers. "He's William Everett Brandt; Second Mate, Omaha, Nebraska. I think we're in for it Steve. We've been had."

As Brandt walked to the witness chair, Rogers, Keller and Roul were nervously whispering to one another. Captain Burn stared at Brandt as he proceeded down the aisle past him. Brandt ignored the Captain. The young officer stepped up to the witness chair. While he was standing and prepared to take his oath, he placed a large yellow envelope on the seat of the witness chair. The oath administered, he retrieved the envelope, sat in the chair and placed it on his lap, holding it with great care.

Dan began his examination.

"Mr. Brandt, please state your full name, where you reside and your profession."

"My name is William Everett Brandt. My home is Omaha, Nebraska. I hold a Second Mate's license issued by the United States Coast Guard."

"Did you know Able Seaman Gaspar Fonseca?"

"Yes, sir. I did."

"Please tell us how you came to know him."

"We were shipmates on the *S.S. American Union* for over a year and a half. We became good friends during that time."

"How was it that an officer became friendly with an Able Seaman?"

"From time to time, we stood watches together on the bridge; he would handle the wheel. He was a Quartermaster, you know, that's the quartermaster's duty. One day when the watch was over and we both went to get some chow, he showed me a book and he asked me if I had ever seen it. I told him I had and that I studied from it to become an officer. I told him I was once an AB like him and that I had also taken the test to qualify as an officer.

"He asked me some questions and I told him to come to my cabin when we were off watch and I would try to help him. From that time on we would get together about once a week or so, to review the materials for the officer's course."

"You testified that you took that course. Was it the same one Gaspar Fonseca was going to take?"

"I would say yes, except for some very minor changes."

"How many times did you take your exam for Third Mate before you passed it?"

"Just once. And then once more, to upgrade for my Second Mate's license."

"Based upon your knowledge of the course you took, the one Gaspar Fonseca was also taking, and the Coast Guard exam you took, do you have an opinion as to whether Gaspar Fonseca would have passed the Coast Guard test he was scheduled to take?"

Jessup stood up. "Objection. There's no testimony here that this man is an expert on Coast Guard exams."

"Yes, Mr. Jessup. But I will allow it subject to further proof. Let's hear what he has to say. You may answer the question, Mr. Brandt."

"Yes, I am sure he would have easily passed it."

Jessup stood up again. "Objection. It's speculation."

"Yes, Mr. Jessup, I agree. However, as I have already said, I will make a final ruling. For now I am holding it in abeyance until I hear all of this testimony. I have some questions of my own for this witness, Mr. Nikolas."

"Certainly, Judge." Dan returned to the counsel table. Jack Hoffman, who sat beside him, patted him on the forearm.

"Mr. Brandt, was the nature of these meetings you described like tutoring sessions?"

"Not really, Judge. It was more like I would ask him questions and he would answer them. Then he would ask me what I thought he needed to study for the test. There was stuff like navigation and radar that was essential. And I would ask him questions. I wasn't teaching him anything he didn't already know. He had it all down very well. In my opinion, he was a cinch to pass."

"Thank you, Mr. Brandt. You may continue, Mr. Nikolas."

"Where were you employed on the day that Gaspar Fonseca fell ill?"

"Aboard the *S.S. American Union*."

"What was your rating on the ship at that time?"

"Second Mate."

"Would you explain to us what a watch is?"

"It's your duty hours; Four hours on and four hours off. On the voyage, when Gas Fonseca got sick, I worked the four a.m. to eight a.m. watch. Excuse me, I called him Gas. All his friends did. It was his nickname."

"That's fine. You can use that name as you wish. Where were you working that morning?"

"I was on the bridge."

"Who was commanding the ship?"

"John Farrow, the Chief Mate."

"If you know, where was the Captain?'

"In his cabin. I believe he was asleep."

"Objection, speculation," Jessup called out.

"Sustained. Mr. Nikolas, do you care to rephrase the question?"

"How did you know where the Captain was?"

"I was on the bridge when Gas's roommate came up to the bridge to report that he was sick. Mr. Farrow called Dr. Peters right away and I heard him tell the doctor he could find the Captain in his cabin. We always have to know where the Captain is in case of an emergency. When Mr. Farrow called the Captain, I heard him say over the loudspeaker, he was up from his sleep."

"Was an entry made in the log concerning this event?"

"Yes, but not right away."

"Please explain."

"We don't make the ship's log entry on the spot. First we make what we call a rough log. Then we make what we call a smooth log. The smooth log is the final log. That's also called the official log."

"How is each log prepared?"

"The rough log is the first notation of a fact we note on the bridge. It includes the time, the weather, any unusual or important facts that occur during the watch. Some logs include the names of the men on the deck watch. We can always erase the rough log to correct or change it before we put it into the smooth log."

"Who makes the rough log?"

"Usually it's the junior officer on watch. When we are satisfied as to its contents, it's put into the log book and becomes the smooth or official log. This last version can't be changed. If anyone changes it, they can face penalties."

"Who signs the smooth log?"

"Usually it is the senior office on the bridge, the officer in command on that particular watch."

"I show you a copy of the smooth log of the *American Union* for the day that Gaspar Fonseca fell ill. It is Exhibit Three in Evidence and I ask you if you recognize it?"

"I do."

"Whose signature verifies the entries?"

"Captain Burn."

"He wasn't on the bridge as you testified. Do you know why he signed it?"

"He came up later and was on the bridge for the last part of the four to eight watch."

"Where are the smooth and rough logs stored on the *American Union*?"

"On the ship."

"With the court's permission, may we be advised if the ship's rough log has arrived?'

"Yes, Mr. Nikolas, the Marshal advised me that he has it."

"Then, with your permission I would like to mark it as an Exhibit for Identification and I expect to make it an Exhibit in Evidence soon."

"On the morning we are discussing, during the four to eight watch, who prepared the rough log.?"

"I did. I was the junior officer on watch that morning."

"I show you the ship's rough log for the day we are discussing. Do you recognize it?"

"Yes. Some of it is my handwriting. There are other notes not in my handwriting. There are erasures too."

"I note that you have an envelope with you today. Please tell this Judge and jury what is in that envelope."

"It's a copy of the rough log that I made at the time."

"Would you please allow me to look at your copy?"

Brandt took a deep breath and rose from his seat, handing the envelope to Dan while giving Captain Burn an accusatory look.

"As I said, I made an extra copy of the rough log. I made it for myself."

Someone in the back of the court room said "oh" then a wave of chatter spread throughout the room. Judge Costello called for order, rapping his gavel several times. The room became silent.

"Go on with your examination, Counselor," an angry judge ordered Dan, pointing his gavel at the witness.

Dan took out a copy and gave it to Jessup. Then he handed a copy to Judge Costello's clerk and continued with his questioning.

"And why would you have made an extra copy, Mr. Brandt?"

"I heard what was going on, on the Bridge, about Gas. In my opinion at that time, when Mr. Farrow called the Captain, we were in a good position to get him off the ship but the Captain wouldn't do it. Gas was a friend of mine. I was angry about how he was being treated. Then I heard the Captain talking to Mr. Farrow, the Chief Mate. Captain Burn said: "'I can't make a rescue. If I do it brings the ship in late. That blemishes my record. And then the company would have to pay some big overtime for all the services waiting for us at the pier. It could come to a small fortune. I'll be the one to catch hell for it. It would be the first time my ship missed a schedule under my command, other than being forced to do so by weather. Everyone on the ship knows the company is losing money. This extra cost will be very unwelcome. Besides, we have four doctors on the ship that can tend to him.'" Brandt fell silent as he stared at the Captain.

"How did you know it was the Captain speaking to Mr. Farrow?"

"I recognized his voice."

Dan faced the Judge and said: "I would ask that this copy of the rough log be marked as an Exhibit in Evidence. I have already given copies to the defendant. The original is the one for the Court's use. Now, Mr. Brandt, I ask you to compare your rough log with the one that has been filed on the ship."

Brandt looked at the two copies, comparing entry by entry. When he finished he put the pages down his lap and looked at Dan, waiting for a question.

"Are the two copies the same?"

"They are not."

"Now I want you to compare your rough log with the ship's smooth log and tell us if they are or are not the same."

"They are not." There was a soft murmur in the room, which Judge Costello ignored.

"Now I would ask you to carefully compare your copy of the rough log with a memorandum prepared by Dr. Peters between the hours of 5:30 a.m. to 8 a.m. on the same day."

Again Brandt compared entries. He put them down after he was finished and did not wait for Dan to pose a question. "The ship's smooth and rough logs as I compare them are not the same as Dr. Peters' memorandum, Mr. Nikolas."

"Now Mr. Brandt, I would like you to compare your rough log with Dr. Peters' memorandum."

After his comparison, Brandt said: "They are almost the same. There are some differences but they are not significant, in my opinion."

"Why did you wait to bring your copy to my attention?"

"Gas didn't know I made a copy for me. But he knew about the conversation the Captain had with Mr. Farrow. When I told him about it, he got angry. I asked him if he wanted me to contact you and tell you. He said he didn't want me to lose my job and he said no one would believe me, anyway. When I found out he committed suicide, I had to do something to help Mira, his wife and their child. It was the company's fault and they have to pay for it."

"Objection," Jessup called out. "We ask the Court to strike the witnesses last remark."

"Yes, Mr. Jessup. Ladies and gentlemen of the jury, you are not to consider Mr. Brandt's last remark about the company's responsibility. You and you alone are the ones to determine that issue. That is why you are here today."

"No further questions."

"Your Honor, the defendant would like a short recess to prepare cross-examination. As you can imagine, we were not prepared for this surprise witness," Jessup pleaded, while looking very nervous.

"We'll start again at 3 p.m."

29

A LUNCHTIME CONFERENCE
DUANE STREET

Lu walked out of the court house, very angry. She had a few hours to work with Jessup preparing cross-examination. She didn't need all that time; what she needed was time to compose herself; to recover from this last blow Dan had dealt her client. And she was angry at Jessup's failure to rein in Captain Burn. She looked for Captain Burn, but he wasn't around. He had quickly disappeared, shortly after Brandt began testifying. As she walked down the steps of the court house someone grabbed her by her arm. It was Rogers.

"We have to talk and quick." He pointed to Keller, Jessup and Roul, who were at the bottom of the steps. They seemed to be waiting for Lu. Rogers suggested they all go to a small Italian restaurant he knew on Duane Street. It was just a few blocks away from Foley Square. Here they could discuss the latest distressing situation in the quiet of the restaurant.

Once seated Roul said, "You are going to have to do the cross examination this afternoon, Miss Moore and finish up the case. We've decided you have to do it."

"I don't have to do anything. I already told Bradley I was thinking of resigning, Mr. Roul. Now that's what I'm doing. This whole case and its management by your partners, has been a farce."

"You can't resign. You have some professional obligations to our client and to your employers to finish this case," Roul said in a hoarse whisper as he looked around the quiet and dimly lit restaurant to insure himself that no one was listening to this conversation. Lu sensed he was desperate and smiled at him. She waited to respond as a waiter came over to take orders. When he was finished Lu said: "You'll have to explain this obligation to me, Mr. Roul, since it was you and your partners who downgraded me to second position in this trial."

"Miss Moore, you have always been telling us, our client and the partners, that we would win this case because it was the Captain's responsibility to determine safety. That's why you have this obligation. And now you have to make me understand why we can lose this case." Roul lowered his conversation to a whisper as he looked about the restaurant again, this time to make sure he recognized no one he had seen in the courtroom.

"Yes, that's true. I did advise you we would win here. But none of you told me the Captain possibly messed with the logs which, because he so suddenly disappeared, I am inclined to believe to be true. Did any of you know this?"

Jerry Keller looked down at the floor and moved uncomfortably in his seat He pressed his wrists down on the arms of his chair in a gesture that signaled he wished to leave the table.

"Jerry, you knew?" Lu asked with an accusing look. There was no answer as Keller sat back in his chair.

"Damn it, Jerry. Silence is sometimes the best answer. You should have been the one most anxious to settle this case, knowing what you knew about Burn. Instead, you put your company and my law firm against the wall. And then you have the nerve to accuse me of offering Dan Nikolas money without your approval."

The waiter came back to the table. He set water before each diner and a basket of bread. While he was doing this, all conversation stopped. When the waiter left, Rogers and Roul looked at Jerry Keller. Roul said, "Jerry, you had better answer Miss Moore's question about what you know. And you better answer now. We are in a deep ditch and I want to know why we got there."

Keller rubbed at the sweat of his palms. "Honestly, I tell you I didn't know anything about the logs. Burn did tell me he never considered delaying the ship to get the AB off. That he wouldn't have stopped for anything or anyone. I asked him how he was going to show that he made the right decision, because Lucille was saying we couldn't lose. He said he had already taken care of it. But he didn't say how he would do it or even what he did. Now I understand what he meant. If I had known he messed with the log, I would have let you know, Bradley. That's the honest truth."

"Miss Moore, I insist you take over the case," Roul demanded.

"Insist? Mr. Roul, you have no right to insist on anything from me in this case, or anything of Bradley, either. You made your decision to downgrade my role, now you want me to pick up the pieces of your mistakes? No sir, I refuse to do it."

"Then I'm afraid I will have to ask the Bar Association to inquire into your unreasonable professional behavior, based on your refusal to offer your client proper representation." Roul smiled, showing his teeth.

"Yes. I'll go along with that." Keller piped in, sensing a way out of his dilemma.

The waiter returned. He placed salads in front of Lu and Keller and pasta dishes for Rogers, Jessup and Roul.

"Didn't Bradley give you my memo?"

"What memo?" Roul asked, still smiling, teeth bared as if he were ready to devour Lu like a wolf after catching up with a stray hen.

"I didn't have time, Lu," Rogers explained.

"Well then, here it is Mr. Roul," Lu said as she reached into her briefcase. "Read it and then go file your baseless charges against me with the Bar Association. You shouldn't waste your time, however, because I'm going to file charges against you, your partners and Jerry Keller, who also has a license to practice law in New York State. The only innocent one among you is Bradley Rogers. You preferred using an untested hack to defend your client instead of a proven professional. By the way, do all the partners know Steven Jessup is Jerry's nephew?"

"Is that true, Jerry?" Roul asked incredulously, as he picked up Lu's memo. "You know we have a rule that no relatives to partners and employees can be hired by our firm."

Keller mumbled something that no one could understand. After Roul read through Lu's memorandum he scanned the attached notes which Lu had passed over to Jessup during the trial. He licked his lips nervously, bit on the lower one and nervously shoved the memo in front of Jessup and said, "Is this true, Steven?"

"I can explain, Mr. Roul. Either I ran the case or she did. We can't have two bosses. I had to act as I thought best. You gave me the authority. I used it."

"You were told to work closely with Miss Moore. What a mistake we made, Bradley," Roul said as he handed the papers back to Lu.

"Keep them," Lu said in a sarcastic tone. "I have many more copies, gentlemen. One for each member of the committee investigating your behavior and you'll need this one to refer to when you appear before the proceedings I will initiate. And in case that memo doesn't convince you about the incompetent you selected to try this case, then read this one. It's much better."

Lu pulled out the memo she had prepared the night before concerning her reluctance to recall Captain Burn to the stand.

"You can keep this one, too. I have a dozen of them. Unfortunately, Mr. Roul, you and your partners thought they had a pliant and gullible woman you could manipulate, and who maybe could take the fall for the firm. It was your big mistake. The lamb going the slaughter won't be me. You gentlemen can pick him out." Lu looked at Jessup with a smile and a nod.

After reading the memo, Roul shoved the paper into Jessup's face.

"Steven, you signed this? Didn't you have the sense as an attorney to read it before you signed it?"

"No, I didn't read it."

"A lawyer who signs a paper without reading it! Who the hell are we hiring in our firm nowadays, Bradley?"

"I don't know, Grady. I didn't hire him. Perhaps you should find out which one of our partners did."

Roul was shocked. He wiped the corners of his mouth, which were moist, with his napkin. He now turned docile when faced with the latest document.

"That's Jerry Keller's nephew," Lu hissed. "Bradley's right. You'll need to find out which one of your brilliant partners slipped him into the firm, since the Bar Association will want to know as part of the charges I'm filing against you all. They'll probably want to know what the arrangement was between Keller and whoever that partner may be."

Keller moved nervously in his seat. He could not evade the stern gazes of Bradley Rogers and Grady Roul.

Lu laughed. "I've decided not to work on the cross examination or any part of the rest of the trial. Let Steve finish it on his own. After all, he's been doing what he wanted until now, anyway. He should have the privilege to continue with the management of the rest of the trial. But I will sit beside him. That's so the jury doesn't suspect problems. I believe I owe the client and the firm that much."

"I could use your help, Lu," Jessup pleaded.

"I know you could Steve, but no thanks. You're lead counsel now, act like it. Assume all the responsibilities attached to being the head man. Grow up. Be a responsible adult and go in for the final aspects of this case."

Bradley Rogers looked at Lu with admiration. Even after six years of working closely with her, supervising her work, watching her grew into a highly competent attorney, he had no idea she could be so calculating.

"I ask you to reconsider your position, Miss Moore," Roul whimpered.

Lu slid out of her seat, snatched up her brief case and said, "Now, if you gentlemen will excuse me, I must relax and prepare my letter of resignation. And you, Jerry, have a lot of explaining to do to your bosses at the Battery, the partners of my former law firm and the insurance carrier in London, too. And gentlemen, I suggest you hunt Captain Burn down and drag that bastard back to court, by his nose if necessary. If he doesn't show up this afternoon, the jury will most certainly take notice and I can almost guarantee a plaintiff's verdict. And for big money, too.

"When they go out to deliberate, they may send out some written questions. If Judge Costello brings them back into the courtroom to explain his answers, it would be good for them see Burn there. If he is, it just might give them the impression that he is not as guilty as he seems. It's a long shot. If he's not there, well, you figure it out. Twice failing to show up in court; the jury will have some questions about his unexplained absence. I would also strongly suggest you find out which of your partners was stupid enough to find a place for Jerry Keller's incompetent nephew in the firm."

Lu beckoned to Jessup with her finger. In a voice loud enough for everyone to hear she said, "You had better leave now and prepare for cross examination of the Second Mate. You have some work to do in order to comply with your professional obligations to your client."

Bradley Rogers followed her into the street, stopping her before she disappeared into the lunchtime crowd.

"Lu, you have to reconsider. You can't be serious about that Bar Association business."

"I will not finish this trial. As I told you a while back, I will not take the blame for losing this case. About the Bar Association, let your partners stew a while. Of course I'm not bringing anyone up on charges.

"I'm sorry I'll be leaving you without an associate, Bradley. I'm sure Steve's going to be leaving, too, so you are lacking any backup. You can blame your partners for that. Now let me go. I have work to do. You'll have my resignation on your desk after the jury renders its verdict. Of all of this, I am really sorry we couldn't continue our professional relationship. I thank you for giving me the opportunity to grow in our profession"

Lu rose up on her toes, grasped Bradley Rogers by his shoulders and kissed him on his cheek. Rogers put his hand to his face, smiled and watched one of the best young lawyers he had ever known walk out of his professional life.

ๆ ๙

Steve Jessup was back in Court doing cross examination.
"Mr. Brandt, isn't it true that the smooth log is the one that prevails over all others? "

"Yes. That's so."

"You made an extra copy of the rough log because you felt you could work together with Mr. Fonseca to win this law suit and share the money, am I not right?"

"That's nonsense, Counselor. If it were true, I would have given Gas Fonseca's lawyer the rough log a long time ago. I wouldn't have waited until now."

"The reason you waited until the last minute to give it to Fonseca's lawyer was to make a dramatic point. Isn't that so?"

"No. When I learned that Gas was dead I felt I had an obligation to help his family."

"Are there any changes on the rough log that do not appear on the smooth log that we have in evidence?"

"Yes. You can see the erasures. They were not made by me. They were made by someone else. Who it was, I cannot say."

"Do you recognize the writing where the changes were made?"

"I'm not a handwriting expert, but it looks like the Captain's."

"How can you say that?"

"I sailed on the ship for over a year and a half and saw the Captain's signature on logs, orders he issued and other papers many, many times. As I said, I'm not a handwriting expert."

"Objection as to the witnesses identification of the Captain's signature; he is not an expert." Jessup shouted.

Dan rose to his feet and said: "Counsel asked the witness if he recognized the handwriting. I believe he has to live with the answer, your honor."

"Yes, I'll allow the answer to stand."

"Have you ever made a smooth log entry?"

"No."

"Between you, a Second Mate, and the Captain, who is better qualified to determine if an Air-Sea rescue is possible?"

"Under normal circumstances, I would have to say the Captain."

"So you are not qualified to make the decision as to whether or not a rescue could have been made?"

"I didn't say that. You asked who was better qualified, not if I was qualified. My answer is: if I were in command at that time, taking into consideration the location of the ship and the type of emergency that I was facing, I would definitely have immediately ordered a rescue based on the situation prevailing. And I was qualified on that day to make that very important decision."

"Objection, your honor, the answer is speculative."

"I'll allow it, Mr. Jessup. His answer is based upon his being in command of the vessel."

"But you weren't in command, Mr. Brandt, Captain Burn was, isn't that so?'

"Yes. That's true."

"You testified on direct examination that your friend Mr. Fonseca didn't want you to get in trouble by testifying for him."

"Yes, that's so."

"Then why is it you aren't concerned about getting into trouble today?"

"I'm leaving the sea."

Jessup rocked back on his heels trying to show the answer was not so important. It was, however, a futile attempt.

"Please explain, Mr. Brandt."

"My father owns a tool manufacturing company in Omaha. He just got a big contract to manufacture tools for a large supplier. He needs help. So my brother and I decided we would go into the business with him. I was planning to retire from the sea in December, at the end of the year. I'll do it a few months earlier."

"So you have nothing to lose by testifying for the plaintiff today. Isn't that so?"

"I don't know what you mean."

"I think you do. Were you paid for your testimony here today?'

"No. I made it clear to Mr. Nikolas I was not doing this for money but to get things straight. To right a terrible injustice."

"So Mrs. Fonseca is going to pay you if she gets an award?"

"Certainly not."

Jessup knows how to beat a dead horse, Lu thought. Now she made no attempt to hide her displeasure. She sat stony faced and still.

"You can't say with absolute certainty that Mr. Fonseca would have passed the Coast Guard exam for a Third Mate's license, isn't that so?"

"With absolute certainty? No, of course I can't."

At least he got that one right, Lu thought.

"You've looked at the smooth log carefully"

"Yes, I have."

"You are firm in your belief that it does not reveal the actual movement of the vessel."

"Yes, sir," Brandt said as he held up his copy of the smooth log and pointed it at Jessup. "This is a false passage."

"What was that?"

"I said it was a false passage; it is a tracking of the vessel that does not reflect the reality of its movements through the English Channel on that day."

"No more questions."

Dan thought: *A rotten cross by Jessup. I don't see Lu at work here. I wonder what's happening. But they did shoot down my attempt at trying to get a Third Mate's earnings as an economic loss.*

"Before you hear closing arguments by both sides and I charge the jury," Judge Costello said, "I must resolve two motions I held in abeyance. The first one concerns Mr. Fonseca's Coast Guard test for Third Mate. I will not allow the jury to determine whether or not Mr. Fonseca would have passed his Third Mate's license. You are not to consider it under any circumstances. It is speculation and inadmissible for you to consider.

"You are not permitted to consider it, if it should happen that you have arrived at a point in your deliberations where you may have found the defendant liable and where you then have gone on to weighing damages.

"Although I will not allow the jury to determine that Mr. Fonseca would have passed his Third Mate's license, I will allow the jury to consider his economic losses for the past and future earnings of an Able Seaman. You are limited to that alone. Again, I emphasize you may consider it only if you find the defendant negligent and you agree to determine the loss arising from that negligence. Those two matters having been resolved, I now turn over the final arguments to counsel."

30

CLOSING ARGUMENTS

Dan, Jack Hoffman and Steven Jessup now have their only opportunity within the trial to address the jurors directly. The three men will logically martial the facts and the evidence that was elicited during the trial, and try to convince the jury that their view of this case is the correct one.

Part of the presentations must be an exposition of logic; presenting each important and significant fact for the plaintiff or the defendant's case; explaining to the jury how each lawyer sees and understands the facts, and testimonies to convince them to find for their client. The rest, as far as the plaintiff is concerned, is an unabashed plea for compassion. For while an attorney's summation should be limited to a clear presentation of the facts, leading to only one solid conclusion, a decision in his client's favor, sympathy for the plaintiff, especially where he has lost a leg which led to his suicide, is part of what an attorney must bring out to the jury. While the Judge in his charge admonishes the jury that sympathy or pity has no place in their deliberations, in a case such as this one, few jurors can fail to include, if only sub-consciously, some element of compassion in their considerations

Legally, of course, no lawyer can rely on sympathy alone. So Dan begins his attack against his opponent by emphasizing the significant differences in the ship's logs, rough and smooth, and those prepared by Second Mate Brandt. Dan points to the witness chair and exploits Captain Burn's absence, since he has not been seen in the courtroom since he was accused of illegally tampering with the rough and smooth logs.

"Where was Mr. Burn, when the time came to explain the changes in the logs?" Dan asks the jury without answering his question. It requires no answer from his lips. It is a rhetorical question; one the jury, it is hoped by Dan and Jack, will answer negatively and in favor of their case. The jury has been prodded with this question and hopefully it will be discussed in the jury room when they deliberate, secluded and apart from the pressures of Court and Counsel. Dan goes on to review the testimony of Commander Masterson and his statement that a lee could create the security Burn was so careful to raise and hide behind, to avoid Gaspar Fonseca's rescue.

"Thus we have destroyed the defendant's argument, ladies and gentlemen, that any rescue by air was a danger," Dan emphasized. Then he continued: "You, ladies and gentlemen of the jury, are the sole arbiters of the facts presented to you in this case. You and you alone are to determine if a witness is lying or telling the truth. We, the attorneys, can suggest the answers to you, yet only you can decide those issues to the exclusion of everyone else who has participated in this trial."

Dan goes on to review Professor Stein's economic conclusions and admits that there are two possible ways of awarding damages in this case, resulting in which interest rate is applied, that urged by the plaintiff or the one the defendant espouses. In any event that, too, depends upon them as triers of the facts. They alone have to decide how they will determine damages. Dan speaks for over half an hour before giving way to Jack Hoffman. As he finishes, he does so in a whisper, causing every juror to lean forward for a better opportunity to hear him, guaranteeing their attention. As he speaks his voice grows louder.

"Do not lose sight of the fact that Gaspar Fonseca was almost a prisoner on his ship, at the mercy of his superiors. He could not leave his ship to seek the services of a physician of his choice. There are no medical centers to go to in the middle of the ocean. He could not call on a private ambulance to take him to the nearest hospital. He had only to rely on his Captain to do that for him.

That was Mr. Burn's ancient legal duty as a Captain, the Master of his ship, to each of his crew members, As Master of his vessel, he had a duty to my client which he failed to carry out. As a result, Gaspar Fonseca not only lost a leg, he lost his life."

Dan concluded with a short sentence, after pointing to the empty top of his counsel table, "Ladies and gentlemen, we have delivered every promise we have made to you."

Jack Hoffman rose from his chair and approached the jury. With his compact body and closely cropped hair, Jack seems like a bantam rooster ready to attack his opponent. Yet he quickly assumes the role of a friend. He refuses to use the medical terms doctors have affected arising from medicine's centuries-long use of Classical Greek and Latin for the words used to describe humanity's deadly physical conditions, diseases and parts of the body. He brilliantly describes Gaspar Fonseca's condition in simple, everyday language and the operation necessary to treat it in words easy to understand. Then he attacks the company's defense that it would have been too late to rescue the unfortunate Gaspar Fonseca.

"Doctors Peters and Grinstein both noted, after examination, that Mr. Fonseca's leg was still cool. In other words, perhaps no serious infection had yet set in. Dr. Welles, who has had plenty of experience in these matters, says taking this fact into consideration, there was still time for a rescue and the saving of Gaspar Fonseca's leg."

Jack pauses to let his last argument settle in each juror's mind. After re-arranging his notes, which he did not refer to in his presentation, he continues on, attacking the air with an open hand to emphasize his arguments. "And don't allow the defendant's lawyer to confuse you," he says in a voice now raised in indignation. "The issue of what kind of physical condition the late Gaspar Fonseca was in is immaterial to this case. The issue for this jury is simply this: Could his Captain have gotten him off the ship in time to treat the block and save Gaspar Fonseca's leg? And if you should by some wrong reasoning, take Gaspar Fonseca's physical condition into consideration, remember who fed him the foods that contributed to that condition."

Jack waved the ship's menus over his head fanning his face as if he were cooling himself on a warm summer's day. "It was the defendant. It daily fed him the foods that should be eaten only in moderation.

"I want you as jurors to carefully consider Captain Burn's testimony that he was satisfied that the doctors were competent to operate. That statement flies in the face against the overwhelming testimony of four honest physicians who have no motive to lie and who have testified that they were united in their professional belief that the unfortunate Gaspar Fonseca should have been evacuated. They have all admitted that none of them was competent to perform the complicated surgery necessary to help this man. Gaspar Fonseca lost a leg and later his life, because a ship's captain failed and refused to comply with his legal obligations and was only concerned with, and I use his own words, 'getting his ship to New York to avoid overtime charges.'"

Jack then went on to detail, symptom by symptom, Dr. Feinberg's analysis of what drives a person to commit suicide. He set them out on the blackboard and then proceeded to show how Gaspar Fonseca's personality, after the loss of his leg, fitted into each of these categories as a result of his tragic loss. He did this by reading the testimony of his family and the entries in the medical records concerning his psychiatric treatment.

"What happened here was a tragedy that could and should have been avoided by a mere timely call for rescue. Instead, a man with many hopes for his future, whose hopes were not only for himself but for his family as well, had them destroyed on that day in the English Channel. You, the jurors, are not only charged with the task of having to consider much more than the loss of Gaspar Fonseca's leg; you also have to consider the tragic and senseless end of his young life, which resulted from that loss."

It was simply and unashamedly a call for sympathy, concern and pity, and Jack knew it. As far as he was concerned, it had to be done. He stared at the jury silently for a few seconds, sweeping across all of them with his eyes, and then he turned to go back to his place at the counsel table.

Jessup now addresses the jury. He reminds them that the smooth log is deemed the only one to be considered unless they and they alone determine and are convinced otherwise. He reminds the jury that it is up to the plaintiff; no, more than that, it is his legal burden under the law, to show the log to be spurious and tampered with. Fraudulent. They are harsh words which Jessup spits out and enunciates them as if they were some sort of pestilence to be avoided. He also screws his face up in disgust as he pronounces the words.

"You should carefully examine Second Mate Brandt's motives. He holds on to the rough log until the last minute in this case. It's very dramatic, is it not? He sat here and testified that he wanted to help a friend's wife and child. All of Brandt's testimony is purposely designed to draw your attention to the fiction that the Captain changed the logs to back up his position that he was unable to make a safe rescue.

"Who will you believe? A Captain with decades of experience at sea and a spotless reputation, who holds the important rank of a reserve admiral in the U.S. Navy, a position his country has given him after years of service? He commands the world's greatest cruise ship. Will you cast all of that aside to accept the word of a young Second Mate with a mere third of the years of undistinguished experience at sea, to that of his Captain?

"Captain Burn was convinced after talking with Dr. Peters, that the passenger-doctors could rectify this problem by operating on Mr. Fonseca. Under those conditions, why should he have even considered endangering the lives of his passengers and crew and the ship to make a rescue? Logically speaking, it doesn't make sense. And ladies and gentlemen, the Judge will charge you not to allow sympathy or pity to enter into your considerations. My two opponents have already improperly touched your nerves on that issue. I might add that I certainly have compassion for what happened to Gaspar Fonseca. I would not be a human being if I did not express sorrow at the events that caused him to lose his leg and then his life. But you are charged by law with determining, in a dispassionate and unprejudiced manner, whether or not those events were caused by my client's failure to act properly under the circumstances. Think hard and objectively about it.

"I say my client acted properly. The ship's logs speak for themselves. The plaintiff must prove them to be wrong. I believe he has failed to do that. I ask you to believe that too. Because in that concept lies the crux of the plaintiff's case. Keep in mind that the so-called log, or memorandum made by Dr. Peters, was the first one of that type ever made by him. Remember his testimony that he agreed the logs made on the ship's bridge are made by crewmembers who are more expert at preparing them. Dr. Peters couldn't even verify if his watch was synchronized with the clock on the bridge. He checked his time with the Purser. And there is no testimony that the purser's time was the same as that on the bridge. And so you are not permitted to speculate about that.

"Remember, ladies and gentlemen, the Captain of a ship is also called the Master. The reason for that title is that he, and only he, has the last word as to every decision concerning the management of his vessel and the safety of its passengers and crew. He alone, while the ship is at sea, has that power and responsibility. That is basic maritime law. You must be convinced that Captain Burn somehow, under the facts of this case, strayed from this basic principle in order to find him remiss in his duties in this regard."

Jessup went on to cover the suicide as not being causally related to Captain Burn's actions. He covered the methods of determining loss of future earnings.

"But," he cautioned the jury, "You are to go on to consider the issue of damages only in the event you find my client acted improperly. Once you decide that issue in my client's favor, and I am confident that you will, you need not go any further. You have exonerated my client from any wrongdoing so you cannot, by law, contemplate damages.

"Remember, both of my colleagues, Mr. Nikolas and Mr. Hoffman, have the burden of proof. They must prove all the charges they have made. I am certain that you will be as convinced, as I am, that they have failed to meet that very heavy legal burden."

Jessup placed his two hands on the jury box, leaned forward, and thanked the jury for their attention and then took his seat. Taking into consideration all that preceded his actions in this case, his closing was better than adequate.

Judge Costello turned to the jury and said, "I will now charge the jury as to the law and what you may and may not consider in your deliberations."

After over an hour detailing the law and telling the jury they could examine all the exhibits that were entered into evidence, Judge Costello made a point of charging the jury that they could consider Gaspar Fonseca's suicide as one of the damages in this case only if they found that it was directly related to the defendant's failure to save his leg.

And he continued, "You must find that the company, through its employee Captain Burn, was negligent for its failure to properly arrange to treat Gaspar Fonseca's condition before you can go on to consider his suicide as one of the damages in this case. If you do not find the company responsible for the loss of the plaintiff's' leg, then you may not go any further on that claim and must return a verdict for the defendant.

"On the other hand, if you should find the defendant was responsible for the loss of plaintiff's leg then you may go on to consider if the plaintiff's suicide is a further result of that failure. If you so find, then you may continue further to determine damages, if you should find any, based upon the results of your final deliberations."

The Judge ordered the Marshal to escort the jury to their room, where they would deliberate over the rights a dead man might have had, were he still alive. The Marshal was to remain outside the jury room at all times. No juror may leave except to eat as a group or to go home at the end of the day, if they had not yet reached a verdict. At times, a Marshal might hear through the door, shouts and hands banging on a table, punctuating a point that was forcefully made. That is not unusual.

❧ ❧

Dan told the court clerk he was returning to his office, three streets away. He gave her his phone number as he left with Jack Hoffman, Sloan and Becker. On the way out, Lu stopped them. It is not unusual for opposing counsel to wait for jury verdicts together, sometimes pacing back and forth like nervous and expectant parents awaiting the birth of a child.

"Quite a trial," Lu said as she saw Dan and Jack in the lobby of the courthouse.

"What happened in there?' Dan asked

"You know better than to ask me. I can't reveal any conversations I had with my client. It's privileged. C'mon you two, want a drink? I'm buying. Charley and Drew, you come along as my guests too."

It was now between mealtimes at Kreager's. All but a few of the restaurant's bright overhead main lights were turned off and there were only three sets of diners enjoying late lunch meals at tables in a corner of the dimly lit dining room. Uniformed bus boys, in hushed tones, were laying out table settings for dinner patrons expected to arrive in a few hours. Two small cocktail tables at the bar's large and empty lounge area were shoved together to accommodate the five lawyers. Everyone ordered drinks while Dan called his office to let Betsy Sachs know where he was, should the Court call. While Dan was on the phone, Lu opened her briefcase and pulled out a yellow legal pad.

"Okay, everyone," Lu called out while vigorously waving the yellow pad over her head. "How long will the jury be out? And who will they find for and for how much? Who's going to be the first one among this learned group to make an educated guess?"

"They're going home tonight and tomorrow before three in the afternoon they'll find for the plaintiff. Two million dollars" Charley Becker said with a bright grin. "Write it down, Lu." he urged. "Hey, Lu, where's your man Jessup? How come he's not here?"

Lu did not respond but scribbled Charley's guess across the pad. Dan, returning from the telephone at the bar sat down beside Lu. "What's going on?" he asked.

"We're having a sweepstakes on the jury's decision," Lu explained. "How about you, Jack? What have you got to say?" Lu asked in a frantic tone, pointing the pad at him. Dan looked at Lu with a puzzled expression.

"Plaintiff's verdict in four hours. Two and a half million dollars" Jack predicted, setting down his Scotch and soda and laughing out loud. That was followed by a lot of good natured laughing which echoed throughout the almost empty restaurant.

"Where are you, Dan?" Lu urged as she patted him softly on his hand. "Give us your opinion."

"I see a plaintiff's verdict in six hours. Before that they're coming up with at least one question for the Judge. I don't know how much they're going to give Gaspar." There was a round of applause and then more laughter.

"Drew, you're next."

"Plaintiff's verdict in eight hours. Two million. Maybe they go home tonight and give us a verdict tomorrow. I don't know the time. Let's say late afternoon. This way they get lunch on the court."

Charley Becker banged on the table with his fist. "Okay Lu, you're next. It's your turn as if we don't know what you're going to say."

Lu smiled then scribbled her thoughts on the pad. She turned the pad around for Dan to read and pushed it in front of him. He sat silent for a moment.

"C'mon Dan, clue us in on to what Lu's thinking," Charley shouted as he held his glass out toward Lu in a mock salute.

Dan returned Lu's pad, sliding it in her direction.

"Well, Gentlemen, Lu says 'verdict in 8 hours for the plaintiff with a jury question coming out before that.' Then she has a question mark for how much they'll award."

Everyone was quiet. Charley and Drew swallowed more of their drinks in one gulp than they should have. Jack reached across the table, smiled and clutched Lu's hand, folding it in his own. Dan looked at Lu and said, "It must have been some conference you had with the partners and Jerry Keller."

"It was, Dan. It certainly was."

It was quiet at the table and no one asked Lu why she answered the way she did. Then, to break the tension, Charley and Drew told stories about their children, both of whom were toddlers. Then Jack got a few long laughs when he recalled how he laid his trap for Jessup, with the ship's menus.

After a while the bartender came over to the table.

"Mr. Nikolas, there's a call for you. You can take it at the bar."

Dan walked to the end of the long bar and picked up the telephone. He nodded, hung up and returned to the table.

"This party is over, folks. The jury has a question. The Judge wants us at Court right away."

31

THE VERDICT

Although there is much laughter and banter among counsel while waiting for a jury's verdict, it can often be the worst stage of a lawsuit. The lawyer no longer controls his witnesses: offering up objections, planning moves, preparing cross examination and thinking only of the answers witnesses make. The case is now out of his or her control. The trial lawyer no longer exerts any power over the route his case is taking. Waiting for a verdict, the trial lawyer is tormented.

"Did the jury understand that important point?" Or, "Should I have stressed that fact a little stronger?" Or, "That juror in the back row: was she paying attention? Several times I thought she was asleep or at least not paying attention."

The jury is out, Counselor. After carefully preparing your case, you have presented the best picture you could. Whatever happens, you hope that you did your best. And your best and that of your opponent are what are now being considered by the men and women of the jury, as they deliberate in the jury room. Each juror has his or her own interpretation of the exhibits or witnesses statements. Can they all agree on an interpretation which will bring in a verdict for my client? Or will they find for the defense?

When a jury asks questions, lawyers look for clues as to how the deliberation is going. Does the question indicate they are for one litigant or the other and need some clarification to resolve their decision? Does the question indicate they do not understand a point of law and need help?

As the lawyers arrive at the courthouse, the Fonseca family is already waiting for them in the large entry hall. A nervous and puzzled Mira Fonseca asks Dan to explain what was happening.

"The jury has a question, Mira. The Judge will tell us what it's all about. Come inside with us."

Lu saw Rogers with Jessup standing quietly alongside him, his face looking at the ground.

"Where is the rest of the Gestapo?" she asked Bradley Rogers.

"They decided to go back to the office," Rogers responded, with a laugh at the word Gestapo.

"And where is our Captain Burn?"

"We can't find him."

"If the jury hasn't decided anything yet, when they come out and they don't see him for a second time, they may make some unhappy conclusions against our side. You should be prepared for that."

"I know, Lu, but I have no idea where he's gone to. What's your opinion as to what the jury will do?"

"They'll come in for the plaintiff."

"I was afraid you would say that."

Jessup piped in. "I don't understand you. You should be pulling for our side. You're counsel for the defendant."

"I'm a realist, Steve, as you should be."

Judge Costello entered the court room, buttoning his robes, and took his place at the bench. Silently and with folded hands, he waited for the court reporter to set up her machine. When she was finished threading her ribbons of paper through her machine, he told her to note that all the lawyers were present and to enter the exact time as well. After she was finished entering the information, Judge Costello addressed the lawyers:

"Counselors, an hour ago I received a note from the jury. It reads as follows: 'Judge Costello, must we accept as a matter of law that the decision of a ship's captain and the ship's log is always correct regardless of the circumstances?' I have them in the jury room waiting for an answer."

There was a shuffling of feet and nervous laughter from both counsel tables.

"Here's what I'm going to do," Judge Costello advised, "I'm bringing the jury back and telling them that I have already covered this in my charge and that they should review it carefully again, because the answer is already there. If they insist, I'll read that portion of the charge to them again. Anyone have an objection?"

Dan and Jack huddled and after a moment, Jack rose from his seat and said:

"We would ask the Court to read the charge again in the courtroom and at this time. This way, if the jury has any more questions, they can ask them of you immediately. It will save the time of having them come back again for more clarifications."

"How does the defendant feel about that, Mr. Jessup?"

Jessup looked to Lu. "What should we do?"

"You're the boss Steve, you make the decision."

"I'll agree to that, Your Honor." Jessup said, arising from his seat.

"Alright then. Marshal, bring the jury in."

The jurors filed one by one into the jury box, finding their way to their assigned seats. Dan looked at them for a sign, but no one was looking at any of the attorneys. All the jurors were focused on the Judge. Lawyers have a tradition that says if a juror looks away from you after they have arrived at a verdict, they have decided against you.

When they were all seated, Judge Costello began.

"Ladies and gentlemen, the Court has received your question. I have consulted with the lawyers for both parties and they all agree that what I will do is read to you again that portion of my charge that is pertinent to your question. If, after you have heard it, you still have questions, write them down and I will try to immediately clarify the issue for you. Here is how my charge read:

"During the trial, there have been some legal doctrines which, if not controverted, are deemed to be true as a matter of law. It is what the law calls *the presumption of regularity*. It is a legal principle that assumes that once it has been shown that a regular transaction has been properly made; that is to say, it was carried out in normal fashion, as it is supposed to have been done, it is pursuant to law.

"An example of such a doctrine would be if I put a stamp on an envelope and drop it at a post office box, we may presume under law, that if I have witnesses or other proof to that event, it will be delivered to the addressee in the regular course of Post Office business. This is so unless it can be shown, for one provable reason or another, that it was not delivered. In other words, it is not a hard and fast rule and may be rebutted with proof. If it is not rebutted then you may accept it under the doctrine of *presumption of regularity.*

"The party attacking the premise that the presumption does not operate in a particular case, has the burden to show it did not operate under those circumstances. The party must show good and sufficient reasons for that position. It is not enough to just allege the envelope was undelivered. The Party is put to the proof of that allegation. Then you, as the triers of the facts, and only you, in your good judgment, may decide whether this legal doctrine has been put into controversy because of other facts that have been presented to you through witnesses or exhibits or any other facts that may show them to be otherwise.

"The controversy as to its truth or the attack upon the *presumption of regularity* may arise from the testimony of a witness or witnesses to whom you have given greater credence than the legal doctrine itself, or there may be some exhibit or set of exhibits which may also show the particular doctrine to be unsupportable. In such a case you may discard the doctrine entirely if you find that to be so. That is if the burden has been met by the party attacking it. On the other hand, if you are convinced that it has not been effectively attacked, then you may properly apply it as law.

"In this case, certain documents belonging to the ship *S.S. American Union* enjoy the presumptive rule I have just have explained to you. There is both the oral testimony of a witness and those of a documentary nature which purports to attack this rule. Only you may consider and determine whether the presumption has been attacked and not available in this case. I trust that you now have a clear picture of how to apply the doctrine. Madam Forelady, can you return to continue your deliberations?"

"I believe so, Your Honor."

"Then continue with your deliberations. If you don't have a verdict by seven tonight, I will instruct the Marshal to release you. In that case I will expect you back here at nine tomorrow morning so that you may be able to resume your deliberations. Thank you. Without you and your work as jurors, our system of justice could not work. And please remember that when you do go home tonight, you are not to discuss this case with anyone."

After the jury left, Rogers came over to Dan and Jack, and extended his hand.

"Gentlemen, I have to congratulate you on a hard-fought case. However the jury decides, you both have my respect." Rogers turned to look at Lu who was talking to Jessup. "She's leaving the firm," he told Dan "I have no idea what she will be doing next. Whatever it is and wherever she goes, she'll be an asset. No matter how hard I tried to convince her, I couldn't get her to stay."

"She wouldn't talk about it." Dan told Rogers.

Jack said, "You should do everything to keep her in your firm. But from what I see, she's not a cookie-cutter lawyer. She would be at odds with the members of your firm. She's a true independent."

"I also learned a lot about my partners during this case," Rogers said without elaborating.

Part of Jack Hoffman's prediction prevailed over all the others. The jurors were released that night. When they returned the next day, they finished deliberations at one in the afternoon. As all the lawyers had predicted, they found for the estate of Gaspar Fonseca, awarding it sixteen million dollars. Judge Costello dismissed the jurors with his thanks.

When they announced the verdict, Mira said, "oh, my God," sinking into a courtroom bench like a limp towel. After receiving a translation of the verdict from Bobby Fonseca, Mamma Fonseca shouted: "*Madre de dios*" (Mother of God). Jack and Dan hugged each other while Charley and Drew joined in creating a mass of bodies. Jessup sat quietly with a look of dejection. He looked to Lu for solace, but received none.

"An appeal is necessary on several grounds!" Jessup exclaimed. "Sixteen million is excessive and the jury obviously believed the witnesses about the log. I objected to that portion of the Judge's charge when we were preparing them in his chambers."

"Save your breath and the client's money. The award amount wasn't excessive and the charge regarding the log was perfect," Lu advised Jessup.

Rogers agreed. "She's right, Steve." Then he turned to Lu and said, "I'm sorry the whole thing fell apart. And you know, I am sorry you have decided to leave the firm."

Lu and Rogers walked away from Jessup as Lu said, "I'm not upset about it, Bradley. I realized I didn't belong in this firm as a partner. I would have always been an outsider and a constant source of irritation for everyone. I can't remain as an employee. I have more ambition than that. You were the only one at Brown, Sykes and Bellham that understood what it meant to have a qualified woman sitting among you. I thank you for taking me as far as you did and for helping me to understand that I could have made it. Now that I know I could have, it isn't so very important to me anymore. I hope that other women may be considered as partnership material."

"You'll get the best reference from me wherever you decide to go."

"Thank you. I really will miss you."

"So you're finally out of that men's club, Lu?" Dan asked.

"Yep."

"I can always use a first class trial lawyer. Charley and Drew are still learning. You should consider it. We'll be together. I don't have that silly rule in my office that we don't hire family. If family is talented, I want them with me."

Lu laughed. "You're corny. I'll think about both your offers. For now I need some time to deflate."

32

SIX MONTHS LATER

Six months later Dan walked into Lu Moore Nikolas' office. After he gave her a kiss he said, "Are you getting the Shaw case ready for trial?"

"Yes. I think it will take two weeks at trial. Just make sure you get home happy tonight. And I hope you haven't forgotten that Ray is coming over with her new man friend for dinner. What's that you have in your hand, sweetheart?"

"Today's *New York Times.* Have you had a chance to look at it?"

"No, not yet. Why? What did I miss?"

"The Shipping News section says the speed of *S.S. American Union* is no longer a military secret. She can exceed 42 knots."

Lu breathed a nostalgic sigh and then said, "Well, I'd guess that's the end of the Big A."

"I'm afraid you're right. I expect that she'll be laid up and out of service very soon. It's really a shame." Dan shook his head as he folded the newspaper and set it aside.

EPILOGUE

PHILADELPHIA, 2006
ON INTERSTATE I-95

"So Dan, finish the story," Cynthia Marks urged. "Don't leave me hanging. That's not nice. You always do that."

"Yeah, finish up fast, we're almost at the end of this trip. I'm turning off the highway," Bill Marks informed Dan as he turned off the ramp leading into Central Philadelphia.

"Well, Lu and I were married and she became my partner. We were unbeatable for four years, then our professional lives got in the way and we divorced. Lu now heads up the litigation department for one the largest banks in the country. She's a senior partner and very happy there and very good at what she does.

"Steve Jessup was requested to resign from Brown, Sykes and Bellham. They tried to keep the whole affair quiet, but the news of what happened got around. It's hard to keep that stuff quiet. Jessup tried, but wasn't successful at finding any work in a law office. Today, he's a claims manager for a four-ship cargo line. We never did learn which of the partners hired him. But we heard that it was one of the sources of a big fight among the partners, which finally led to a break-up of the firm. The partners at Brown, Sykes and Bellham weren't too anxious to advertise who it was.

"Jerry Keller got fired from A.U. Lines and could never find another job. He started up a newsletter for claims managers and has had some moderate success with it.

Bradley Rogers resigned from his law firm before it broke up. He became a professor of Admiralty and Maritime Law at Columbia Law School. He was very happy there. He eventually retired to Florida. We became good friends. Lu and I would have dinner with him; he was a regular visitor to our home. He often told me that that the biggest disappointment in his career, aside from the breakup of his firm, was watching Lu leave the firm. From time to time, when he was still teaching, he would invite me or Lu to address his students. He banged the drum to get them into the joy of practicing the Law of the Sea. He passed away two years ago at his home at Steamboat Cay.

"Brown, Sykes and Bellham were forced to disband. Aside from the internal strife as a result of what came out about the Fonseca case, they suffered the loss of many unhappy clients. You can't keep secrets from other lawyers and the story of how they handled the A.U. Lines case was all over Wall Street. The partners went their own way. Those who could retire, did. And there was a fight over retirement money, as it seems to have been mishandled with bad investments. The rest looked around for positions for over a year or more before they could get settled. When they did, it was not with the plush offices and perks they had been used to.

"Some years after my divorce, I married Terry Bache, the daughter of a good friend and client. And she's a first-class admiralty lawyer, by the way." Dan turned in his seat to smile at Terry.

"I made a lifetime friend in Jack Hoffman. We worked together on many cases over the years. He taught, too: Federal Trial Procedure at Brooklyn Law School. He trained a whole generation of young lawyers to become malpractice specialists. He lived to happily see two granddaughters and a grandson graduate from medical school."

"And the Big A?" Cynthia asked.

"Ah. The Big A. Four months after her secret speed was revealed in the article published in the *New York Times*, she was laid up forever. And you saw what's left of her a while back."

NOTES BY THE AUTHOR

The *S.S. American Union* is a fictional vessel. However, the ship is modeled on the historic *S.S. United States*, long known around the globe for her impressive size, distinctive silhouette, luxurious interiors and record-breaking speed. Her records as the fastest ship in the world still stand today.

If you should happen to travel along the I-95 corridor around the Philadelphia area, you will see the *S.S. United States* laid up, as she has been for many years, at pier 89. She is berthed east of the highway. Fittingly, she sits at Columbus Boulevard. Her funnels (the world's largest) are no longer the bright red, white and blue that once proudly signaled her many swift passages across the Atlantic. They have receded to a hazy, pastel pink and blue, the victims of decades of the ravages of sun, wind, rain and neglect.

Over the years after she was decommissioned, the *American Union* has been rescued at the last minute from the wrecker who planned to reduce her to scrap; she has been the subject of abortive attempts to re-commission her, and efforts to make her into a museum-hotel similar to the Queen Mary, which is docked permanently at Long Beach, California. Today she sits, purchased from the scrapper, awaiting a viable plan to restore her in a way to make Americans aware of the ship's role as their country's greatest entry in the glorious and lost era of the luxury passenger liner, when the only way to get to Europe was by ship.

I went aboard the *United States* for the last time in 1984 when she was berthed at the Naval Yard at Norfolk, Virginia. She had not sailed for 15 years. I attended an auction held in one of her dining rooms. I bought some silverware, menu covers and other items like the pilot flag and the aluminum birds that flew along the bulkheads of the grand stairway leading to the dining rooms and other social spaces.

Victor Chico, my step-father, sailed on the *American Union,* first as a chef in its kosher galley starting with her first voyage in 1952. When that galley was shut down because it was not profitable, he continued sailing as a sous chef until 1966, when he retired from the sea. From time to time, during the years he sailed aboard her, if there was a call for kosher meals (such as for Passover or other religious holidays), the old kosher galley would come to life again, its kosher status certified by a rabbi after a strict ritual restoration. Then Victor would prepare the appropriate dishes.

I attended that auction in 1984 because I wanted something to remind me of Victor and the ship. During breaks in auction activity, I walked through the ship's alleyways, common rooms and the crew's quarters. I was saddened to see her in such a reduced state. I had always remembered her from the many times I had gone aboard during her glory days and I recalled the food I once ate in the galley with Victor and his sailing companions. They would always fix up a tasty dish for me. Sometimes, I also ate in the First Class dining room with opposing counsel, when the ship was docked and I was there on business.

I had been able to go aboard the *United States* scores of times when she was still sailing. It was a time in America when we were not preoccupied with security. I could go up the gangway to the *United States,* and other cruise ships and freighters for that matter, without having to undergo any security checks whatsoever.

On that day in Norfolk, as I freely wandered throughout the ship, she was barely recognizable to me. I recalled how passengers wearing formal clothing had walked through her passageways and public rooms, happily anticipating their sea voyage. Then, the ship was alive with activity and lights were shining everywhere. On the day of the auction, the ship's only light (aside from the auction areas) came from the bright sun shining through her portholes. Papers were strewn throughout the deck. Crewmember's cabins were bare; all linen and mattresses had been stripped from the bunks. Empty drawers and closets with wire hangers lacking any clothes, made the crew's cabins even more depressing.

Despite the disarray and her unkempt state, I could see she was still staunch and could have begun a new life if properly overhauled. The Big U. was built with extreme care, love and attention. It would take a whole lot of decay to destroy her. I fear that now, more than 35 years after the day I last walked through her, she is swiftly approaching that point.

For all of her grand history and for what she represents to America's ability to build the very best, the *United States* deserves the chance to live on again as a symbol of the type of quality America used to produce and can still churn out when it has to.

North of the *United States*, also on the east side of I-95 along the Delaware River, dozens of U.S. Navy ships also float silently and unused, their blue-slate colors announcing their military ownership. These vessels are in much better condition than the *United States,* as the government regularly maintains them in case of a national emergency. This whole area is an example of the loss of maritime shipping, both military and commercial, that America has experienced in the past decades.

The reader should have noticed the extreme efforts lawyers had to undertake to prepare for a major trial in the days before the computer. In 1968, serious trial preparation required reading and cross-matching the deposed testimony of every witness, every affidavit and every exhibit in order to refute or verify important facts. I can personally attest to the fact that it was a tedious labor.

In the novel, I purposely allowed both Dan and Lu to fail to read, early in the case, Dr. Peters' notes on the ship's trajectory. It was certainly not representative of the way these two accomplished lawyers would have handled their task. But I put it into the story for two reasons: first, I wanted to demonstrate that in the days before the computer, even the best lawyers could slip up on discovering certain important facts because they were overwhelmed with the volume of work they were required to deal with. And then, I wanted readers to understand what could have happened if that important bit of information had not been discovered. Imagine, in this story, if there was no log by Dr. Peters to be compared with the ship's spurious smooth and rough logs to verify the truth of Second Mate Brandt's rough log. It gave the jury the opportunity to overcome the legal doctrine of *presumption of regularity.*

Getting ready for a major trial was, as I have said, a long process. In major cases, lawyers had to review thousands of pages of documents, and digest them for their proper significance. Small law offices were at a disadvantage when matched up against the larger firms, which had the luxury of assigning many more people to this laborious task of trial preparation.

Today, we trial lawyers can't utilize the theatrical spectacle of heaping piles of exhibits on our tables and making a show of dramatically reducing them one by one, fact by fact. In today's modern courtrooms, trial counsel's exhibits are all scanned into a computer and then beamed on to a screen for everyone in the courtroom to see.

Twelve men and women no longer constitute a jury in civil cases in the federal judicial system. Since the 1990s, we use only six jurors with two alternates. If you are being tried for a crime, however, you still have 12 men and women, "tried and true," to judge you. That is a constitutional right that cannot be taken away.

Harry A. Ezratty
Baltimore Maryland
2020

ACKNOWLEDGEMENTS

When authors write about technical matters of which they have little knowledge, they need to consult with experts to make their stories believable.

For medical matters, I consulted with Dr. Frank Laudonio, who has been my friend since before we entered kindergarten. Frank says the doctors who operated were guilty of malpractice and no ethical physician would operate in a situation where they lack expertise. When I told him that four doctors actually operated in a situation mirroring the one in this book (with a failed result), he found it hard to believe. As a result, I had the fictional Dr. Welles ask, more than once on cross-examination, whether he thought the doctors were guilty of malpractice.

For issues of the ship's transit and other issues concerning logs and ship's protocol, I was assisted by Captain Daniel Murphy, a Master Mariner, Harbor Pilot and instructor on ship handling at the Masters, Mates and Pilots school in Maryland.

Using the internet, I gathered vital material as to the types of helicopters available, the differences in their capacities regarding fuel and the distances Gaspar would have had to travel between the cities in England in order to get the treatment he needed. I learned about weather situations. I hope it all meshed together to make a believable story.

Richard Gottesman, my talented stepson, always creates intriguing covers and attractive interior designs for my books.

Finally, nothing I ever write, from a one-page letter to a book, ever goes out until my wife, Barbara Tasch Ezratty, sees it. She edits my work and makes other suggestions which make a letter or a book more readable.

To Barbara, Frank, Dan and Rich: thank you again.

ABOUT THE AUTHOR

Harry A. Ezratty is an attorney who has specialized in Admiralty Law for almost 50 years. He is a graduate of New York University and Brooklyn Law School. After practicing in New York City for ten years, he moved to San Juan, Puerto Rico, where he practiced for thirty-five years, representing shipyards, shipowners, the island's Harbor Pilots, ships' officers and seamen in all types of cases ranging from groundings and collisions to salvage and desertion.

False Passage draws on Mr. Ezratty's many years of experience in maritime law and his frequent appearances before the United States Coast Guard, defending America's mariners.

Mr. Ezratty presently resides in Baltimore, Maryland.

Made in the USA
Middletown, DE
27 October 2020